THE
QUINARY

TRACY SIMMONDS

BALBOA.
PRESS

A DIVISION OF HAY HOUSE

Balboa Press books may be ordered through booksellers or by contacting:

Balboa Press
A Division of Hay House
1663 Liberty Drive
Bloomington, IN 47403
www.balboapress.com.au
1 (877) 407-4847

Print information available on the last page.

ISBN: 978-1-5043-1292-9 (sc)
ISBN: 978-1-5043-1293-6 (e)

Balboa Press rev. date: 05/21/2018

ACKNOWLEDGEMENTS

Tracy would like to thank her amazing family who supported The Quinary; Mark for providing much needed logic to the magic, Emma for the copious cups of tea and encouragement and Sarah for enduring endless discussions about magic.

Addy knew the minute she woke up and opened her eyes, that today things would change. She stayed on her side for a few seconds and looked around her stark room under Rodic's house. The wind shuddered the door and forced dust bunnies to eddy around the cement floor. The hot water tank, the makeshift clothes line and her mattress, all shades of blue in the pre-dawn, made the room even colder than it usually was.

The phone had woken her up. She heard it scream out in the dining room above the floor boards.

She stretched behind her and pulled the chord on the wooden blind. Between the lines heavy mist descended on the countryside. The phone continued to hack into the shrouded silence.

Addy sat up and pulled her stretched cardigan around her slim body. She swung her legs to the edge of the mattress and still sitting, shoved her feet into old school shoes.

The phone continued to ring, its urgency set her nerves on edge. Rodic never received calls this early. It was surely not good news.

She rubbed her palms together to will warmth into them and breathed hard into their cupped shape. She pulled her hair into a messy bun and stood as she pulled her pink blanket with her. It was the only thing she had from her childhood, from her mum. An anxiousness enveloped her.

The blanket's down was soft and thin between her fingers, the edging had long since come off. She folded it neatly across the mattress on the floor.

Addy glanced up, Rodic had finally moved. The floorboards creaked as he shuffled down the passage towards the incessant noise. Addy heard him mumble under his breath, her own name rolled from him. She shook the omniscience away.

"Hello" Rodic's voice, as he answered the phone, was still confused and thick from sleep.

"Verity!"

Addy's heart pounded. She felt the thin mattress hit her knees. Oh shit! What does she want?

"Today?" Rodic was awake now, he did not sound himself. The one-sided conversation continued.

"Yes ma'am. Yes." He murmured.

Addy held her breath. She pulled her blanket towards her. She needed its comfort.

"Yes. She's here"

Fear settled on Addy. She gently rocked herself, hugging her blanket. No, no. This can't be happening.

"W-What do you mean, strange things?" Rodic asked.

Panic gripped her stomach. Addy sat up straighter, waiting for Rodic to impart more information. How does Verity know? How can she possibly know?

"You - are you talking about w-witchcraft?" His voice wavered as the door shuddered.

Addy felt the tell-tale pinpricks of her power run across her arms. She expelled a breath she hadn't realised she was holding. The power was stronger now. How did Verity know? She'll be so mad. Oh shit, what am I going to do?

Rodic's conversation continued above her "well, look here,

Miss. I have kept Addy all these years, just as you asked. I have all the accounts to show you. But I-"

Addy felt like she had been struck. She sucked air into her mouth. Exhale, she silently coached herself.

"Yes. I understand." Rodic shuffled on the boards above her.

"Yes. I'll see you soon" he sounded retracted.

"Addy can't leave Darton." Rodic said.

Hot darts of panic ran up and down her insides. She absently felt for the chip-implant in her left arm. I have got to get away.

"Bye." The finality in Rodic's voice caused her to take in a swift breath. Silence filled the space. Addy cocked her head to hear better. Rodic breathed heavily above the floorboards and then he stomped angrily. Dust sprinkled all across Addy's room.

"Addy, get up. Now!"

Her throat felt constricted. She stood up. I won't go with her. She can't make me. I'm twenty-three years old. Rodic will help me. He must help me. This, this stuff, is not witchcraft….

"Addy!" Rodic did not sound himself, "Get up here."

"Coming Rodic" she called.

The dim interior through the swing doors looked untouched. Rodic's mother had a tendency for shades of brown, when she died Rodic had enshrined the house to her memory. Not a thing had changed. Grey light fought to get through the gap where the brown curtains did not quite meet; a vertical line formed on the opposite wall in their dim beam. The heating in the library droned and rattled in the background. Addy walked slowly, avoiding the spots where the floorboards creaked.

She caught her reflection in the mirror.

Ugh. I look like I've escaped an institution.

Her old Math teacher's words, rang in her head,

"All that olive skin and those intense green eyes, Miss Piper. You are a distraction to any lad in a ten-mile radius,"

So wrong.

She glanced down at herself.

Too large jeans held up with an old school tie. A white

school polo shirt, its now faded green logo reading Darton High School.

Five years since school and I still have no normal clothes. I wonder if Verity even realised that? Some excuse for a mother.

The library door was open, just a crack.

I have to leave. What else can I do? The chip-implant will kill me if Verity doesn't. Rodic is my only chance.

"Rodic?" Addy called. Heavy breathing filled the air. The drone of the extra heating hurled stale energy into the sour room. The furnishings were sparse; a dark desk, two overstuffed brown arm chairs, a steel filing cabinet and a wall of books. He called it the library.

"Rodic?" Addy repeated.

The grey morning barely made a difference as Addy pulled the curtains back. The weak light fell on Rodic's dark yellow curls around his pink bald spot. Sweat beaded and ran, pasting the curls to his head. His shirt bowed over his large hips and revealed his pink flanks, rubbery and bulbous, they roasted in the humid room. Rodic's hands lay large and fleshy beside his head, his nails were deep in their sausage beds. Sweat outlined his form on the desk. Addy pushed the window open and pencilled the sticky remote control, the heat and noise stopped simultaneously.

"Rodic!" The pencil poked deep into his rubbery back, "Rodic!" she shouted.

Phlegm ground in his throat, spittle lined his pink fat lips. He tried to move,

"S-sick" he slurred.

"Rodic wake-up. You're sick" Addy had never seen him like this.

"Burrgh," his sour belch permeated the air.

"Rodic. I can go for help. But you must turn the transmitter off. Where is it?"

Addy had learnt the hard way, that the transmitter would send an electric shock to the micro-chip in her arm if she tried to leave the village. She had spent years testing the perimeters of her freedom.

The wooden desk drawer stuck on its tracks as Addy frantically opened it.

This can work. I can be free. I'll go far away. Where is the bloody transmitter?

"Rodic. You need to help me! Please? Tell me where you keep the transmitter."

Addy grappled at Rodic's shirt collar, it caught his neck and pulled his fleshy jowls. Using both hands she pulled at him. Sweat trickled down her torso, her hair stuck to her neck.

Rodic moved with her, he was weak but it helped. The desperation pooled in her chest.

"Rodic. You need help. Where is the transmitter? I can go for help." The fever gripped him again, his eyes fluttered squeezing moisture down his crow's feet; she watched the drop roll along his jaw and fall into his maroon shirt.

"V-Verity" the noise hissed and rumbled from his chest,

"Yes. She will be here soon. She's no good. Please help me. Please?" Addy heard the pleading in her voice and winced.

The filing cabinet screeched as she pulled and slammed its drawers, "Rodic?"

"Verity," he breathed noisily, "must pay first." His voice was low and rattled from his ribs.

"No. Please?" her throat constricted, "please?" she was across the desk. "She will kill me. You know that." Truth was uncomfortable.

"P-pay," he breathed.

"No. Dammit!" she lurched at him. Her hands stung as they hit the desk. The paper knife skittered towards her hand. Addy grabbed it pointing at Rodic.

His eyes widened, fear and fever glazed them over. The fever had hold of him again,

"Now, now." He rumbled. She kept his stare.

"Please help me?" Addy appealed to him.

5

In the distance an engine hitched a up a gear as it accelerated away.

Rodic stared ahead.

Addy was disappointed in Rodic and fear pooled in her stomach. She bit down hard and stabbed the point of the paper knife into her inner arm. A crimson pool gathered at the indented tip and then ribboned slowly down her arm dripping on the desk. She stared at it, the relief of action, was strangely liberating.

Rodic squeezed his eyes shut and then opened them in disbelief, more sweat drops trickled down his sideburns. Addy clutched the knife between her jaw and her shoulder, pain weaved through her. With her right hand, she pushed the micro-chip out of the hole she made. A lump of chip and blood and tissue plopped onto her arm. Rodic's horror brought him to his feet. Addy flicked the chip and the knife onto the desk.

The gravel crunched under a car's tyres.

As Rodic and Addy watched, the wound sealed.

Rodic swayed on his feet. "Addy?" he murmured.

The power welled inside of her. It swirled around her body, the electric buzz enhanced her senses. She looked at Rodic.

I can kill you. The thought sobered her. She pushed the trickle of energy back down.

"Rodic, I am dialling the emergency number, you need help" she whispered.

She moved swiftly. Two people were walking to the front door. She dialled the emergency number on the phone in the dining room and then left by the kitchen entrance as the doorbell rang inside the brown house.

Addy walked quickly. The large black bird in the Oak tree in the front of the kitchen window hopped down, urging her forward. She hung back, until she was sure it was clear and then ran.

Rodic's house was the last one on the outer perimeter of the village. Large blocks of land meant neighbours were far away. She ran without looking back. She sent a silent hope on the wind that Rodic would be okay, that the emergency services would trace the number somehow.

Mrs Harris whipped her washing in the cold breeze as she moved it to the line. Summer breeze softener filled the air. Mrs H. was tall and stick thin. She nibbled at lumps of bread she kept in her dusty pink house-dress pocket. Her mass of grey frizzy hair stood wild and untamed. She ruled the Oswald household and ran it with military precision. She looked pinched and disapproving in the way she held her face and head but Addy knew her words were warm and her thoughts kind. Especially for the four boys she looked after since their mother passed away.

"Mrs. H" Addy ran up, breathless. She rested her hands on her knees, her quick breath frosted the air.

Mrs. H squinted her eyes as she looked up the road. "Are you okay, Love?" she asked.

Addy nodded, her chest still heaved.

"This way" said Mrs. H as she moved towards the back garden. She left the washing and walked briskly up the slope away from the house, her grey tights sagged into her large men's moccasins. She popped a piece of bread into her wrinkled cheek. Addy followed.

What's going on? Adrenalin still clouded her thinking.

"Mrs. H?" asked Addy.

"No time to explain, Lovey," she walked, head down, but frequently peered over her shoulder, "been waiting for this a long time."

"Waiting for what?" asked Addy.

Mrs. H pulled a dark green Juniper bush aside and gestured with her head.

"Just go." Her face was grave and wrinkled, "Addy. The help you need will come. Trust me."

Addy nodded and stepped into the lane, it snaked out ahead of her, Blue-bells drooped their heads into the scruffy pathway.

Addy looked behind her but Mrs. Harris had already left, her dusty pink house-dress faded behind the Juniper bush as she strode back to the house. Addy brushed the loose hair from her face and took a step. The earth raced beneath her. Another step and the lane ended.

This is weird. Addy swallowed hard.

The portal dumped her in a field. She clutched at her heart and willed it to slow down. Addy bent forward and rested her hands on her knees as she surveyed her location. In the greyness of the day, the green of the grass popped out vividly.

I can do this.

She threw a panicked glance over her shoulder and noticed her breath frost around her. The green fields rolled to her left and right. Behind her, the sun fought the mist to rise.

There's nobody here. Where am I?

As she stepped through the hedgerow, her shirt snagged on a bush. She tugged it loose. She huffed in the frosty air around her and wished she hadn't been so hasty in discarding her stretched cardigan. She crossed the narrow lane.

Addy recognised the village centre with a mixture of relief and panic. She looked behind her in surprise. The walk from Rodic's house usually took an hour to the village centre.

This is too close. Verity will come looking here.

The lights weren't on in the Tall Tale Bookshop, or any of the shops, it was too early for most of Darton Village. Addy turned in the direction of Pickett's Bridge, her feet crunched in the silence. She walked briskly. She looked around again, there was still nobody there. Her breath was loud in the close mist.

"Just get to the Bridge, dear" she heard Mrs. H's advice from moments earlier.

Addy kept moving. In the distance, the train rattled through Darton Station.

Why did mother come back now?

Fred Mills waved as he weaved his neon green bike between

the bins on the opposite side of the road, she nodded in acknowledgement.

Addy wondered how everything can look so normal on the surface, when her heart beat a storm in her chest and anxiety threatened to choke her.

Her mother had left her at Rodic's years ago. Rodic wanted compensation. He was a quiet sombre man. Never cruel. Not like Verity, but not warm either.

A black car passed through the cross road three hundred metres off. Addy had a sense of hollow fear claw at her, it grabbed her heart. Addy knew her mother's cruelty from years before. She had become complacent living at Rodic's.

Addy ducked left, down Archer Lane and moved behind the green grocer's. The engine grunted, a predator in the mist. The stench of rotten vegetables filled the air and her stomach turned.

She stayed parallel to the High Street and kept moving in the direction of the bridge.

I must get away, if I can just get across the bridge.

Addy wiped the hot tears from her cheeks crossly.

The shops ended abruptly and Addy moved back onto the High Street. Her distorted image caught and hooked in the gold reflection of Doctor Mack's Rooms, the same black car growled behind her.

She pulled at her jeans. She was ready to run.

Picketts Bridge was just ahead.

If she gets me, she'll kill me.

Addy glanced back quickly. She knew that her life was in danger.

The memory flashed into her mind. The last time she saw her mother, Verity's silver stiletto latched across her young throat. Verity had screamed in rage and ten-year old Addy didn't know what she wanted.

Addy clenched her jaw, annoyed. She had put all that behind her. Verity had not been part of her life for over ten years. She had learnt to do without a mother. Oh, yes, she had yearned for love, but Addy knew Verity wasn't capable of that. She knew that now. But then, so young, so hopeful.

But why was she here? I can get away. I must.

Addy ran. The bridge clunked beneath her feet. The wind whipped at her nose and eyes. She felt the cold claw at her throat.

The pathway at the end of the bridge drew her in; both trepidation and hope built with each step.

The water beneath her churned loudly. The wooden slats changed to the solid smack of the earth. The car revved behind her. She ran.

I can make it.

The evergreen tree line beside the pathway stretched up over the gradual rise of the land like soldiers at attention, they guarded the way.

Nearly there.

Behind her the black car stopped. There was no return.

The car door slammed. The finality in the thud, shivered Addy's spine. She didn't stop. Just a few steps.

The air pulled and puckered behind her and Addy gasped for breath, unaware of what was there.

No no no.

Leaves withered on the trees and the air thickened. Addy watched in disbelief as the grass shrivelled around her.

Her steps slowed as no breath came to her, the air was too thick to pull into her desperate lungs. Addy clutched at her throat.

Tears sprang in the corner of her eyes.

She held her neck, the vacuum around her complete, she gasped like a fish.

Ahead of her, Verity stepped out behind the last tree. Addy leant far forward willing a breath. She silently pleaded for it, her fingers clawed at the dirt where she fell on her knees.

Her own power crawled inside her, and also wrapped around her. Familiar, but also a prison.

No. No.

Everything moved in slow motion, disbelief replaced dread. Tears ran hot down her cold cheeks.

"Adera" Verity was cold, dismissive. She always used Addy's birth name, no-one else did.

Air came to Addy in a rush. She breathed through her energy, instinct said to keep her secret. She straightened and willed herself to get in control. Her chest expanded as her lungs consumed the cold air in greed.

Her mother looked twenty-five years old.

How is it possible?

Her cream-skin and blonde hair, magazine perfect. Verity was classically beautiful; high cheek bones, a full mouth, large eyes, a straight nose. Her hair was tucked into a neat chignon.

She's sober.

Verity's look, cold as steel, jarred Addy's spine. She slowly walked around Addy. Addy saw her mother's mouth pull in disapproval.

Addy knew Verity would hate her hand-me down jeans and old polo school shirt. She saw Verity cringe at the mass of dark hair which had escaped its pony tail. Her chest still heaved quickly as she fought to control her panic.

Verity's tight black pant-suit had a high collar secured around her slim neck but left nothing to the imagination as it split open from neck to navel. Her stiletto boots completed the liquid ink look; in the cold grey day, the red coat hooked over her index finger, stood out, a blight on the land.

A man approached, the driver of the black car; he ignored Addy. She watched and willed her heart to slow down. He cupped Verity's breast in his hand and bent to nuzzle her neck. Addy saw Verity's jaw twitch, a slight almost imperceptible movement.

She's annoyed.

"Zyklon. Adera" Verity stepped from him as she gestured

in distaste, to Addy with her head. He wore black from head to toe, a thick coat whipped behind him. A pale face with chiselled features and a prominent square jaw sat beneath brows arched unusually high. His jet-black hair created a jagged hairline across his forehead. Dark eyes sucked the energy from the air. He had seldom seen the light of day.

He removed a glove as he inspected Addy. A pale white hand with thick dark nails reached out and touched her. Addy flinched but could not move. The spot between her brows ached as the numbness spread through her. The cold pain invaded her mind. Her own power wrapped tighter around her but did not release. Could not.

"Get in the car" he whispered.

A ddy hissed in a breath.

Power prickled across her arms and into her hands, tightly bound against a board behind her head. Pins and needles ran up and down her arms. Her head hung upside down, blood thumped into her temples; her forearms pushed her head forward, her elbows were above the crown of her head.

Where am I?

Tears squeezed from her eyes and were absorbed by the blindfold. She bit down hard on her bottom lip.

Pain slammed into Addy and fear pooled in her stomach.

"Hello?" her voice was rough, "is anyone there?" she struggled to talk, panic seized her vocal chords. "Anyone?"

The constriction at her throat annoyed her; her feet were tied together above her. Grinding gears whirred in the blackness and Addy felt herself move slowly. A loud click snapped in the dark, she was still upside down but slightly angled now.

A wheel? I'm on a wheel.

The sobs racked her body which knocked her ribs against the hard board. The rope ate into wrists and ankles.

Addy heard the moaning and was surprised that the keening came from her own throat. She spoke into the emptiness, "I must pull myself together."

Addy tugged at her wrists and feet in turn, frustration pulled in her chest. She arched her back and then lifted her neck off the back of her bound arms. "Shit, shit, shit." She hissed.

Pain struck into the soft underside of her throat. She pushed her head back as far as she could go.

"Aaargh! Son of a bitch! Ssshit! Shit! Shit!" A large pin, the irritation at her throat, pierced the soft underside of her jaw and lodged into her skin at the hollow of her throat. Power ran across her body, she knew the wound was already healed.

Her breath came in short gasps as the panic seized her.

"Uugh! Calm down!" she admonished herself, "just frigging calm down!" She breathed deep, soothing breaths, careful to keep her head as far from her chest as she could.

Listen. Just listen.

She focused her thoughts on her senses. Far off in the background there was a scuffling noise, and somewhere, water dripped.

Metallic smell, damp. Blood? No, flesh. What's the tick, tick, tick? So, faint.

She carefully moved her face keeping her chin up to better hear the tick, tick, tick.

Sweat trickled from her body. She was alive with pain.

This is it. This is the end.

She squeezed her eyes shut behind the black blindfold. Silent sobs burned her throat.

No friends, never saw the ocean. Never hugged. Never hugged.

Her nose felt thick from crying.

A familiar power prickled and flared within her, she automatically clamped down on it. She used her will to back it down.

This power is dangerous.

Tick, tick, tick the sound amplified in the stillness. Then it picked up on its gear and ground as the wheel turned another notch. Her head was at twenty to the hour.

Sinew stood out on her neck as Addy strained to hold her head back against the board so that the pin strapped to her throat didn't impale her again.

"Mother? Verity?" she shouted into the stillness.

"Goddammit! Somebody! Mother! Rodic! Anybody?" she shouted over and over again into the darkness.

Finally, she heard running feet slap the floor.

"Don toush! Boss say vely power. Pffff." The voice was foreign and had a sing-song lilt.

"Please help me? Please? I won't hurt you. I have no power. Please?"

"No toush! Tell Boss! No toush!" A second voice enforced and then two sets of feet padded away.

Addy was hysterical. Anxiety raced her heart.

"Nooooo! Pleeease! Come back!"

After three cycles of the wheel and five piercings, pain rode her nerves, sweat and blood ran across her body. Addy was now upright with her head at ten past the hour.

Exhaustion taunted her and she tried to stay awake, "Water? Please" she whispered to nobody. Power still rippled up and down her body, it reminded her that she was alive; she ignored it from habit.

An animal scuffled behind her knee.

"Get away!"

Blood congealed down her throat and chest.

Click, click, click, clack, high heeled shoes stuccoed a rhythm in the dark silence, Addy's senses came to attention.

"Oh, good! I see you're comfy, Adera" trilled Verity, "I want to have a catch-up, mother daughter-like" she laughed.

"You! Remove her blindfold. And you! Get that torch in here." Feet scurried to obey.

The blindfold was roughly removed. It knocked the pin into her throat. Addy soaked in the pain.

When her eyes adjusted, Addy saw the cave was quite large, two torches lit the entrance to the chamber, one was being removed as she watched. In the chamber, from her vantage point, she confirmed that she was indeed pinned to a large wheel. Opposite her was a steel box with latticed iron mesh across the top. Rats yanked at flesh through the lattice. Addy shivered involuntarily.

The fire pit on the left was empty.

"Put the torch on that wall behind her. Now leave us, make sure we are not disturbed" Verity commanded. Two black creatures, the likes of which Addy had never seen, jumped to obey. Addy glimpsed their four arms as they hunched and scuffled away.

What is this place?

Verity wore a black dress and silver stilettos. Her hair framed her cool face and, in her hand, sliding between her long silver tipped fingers was a whip.

"What now? Always so many questions" she caressed the whip as she spoke.

"What do you want?" Addy kept her head close to the board.

"Simpleton! Do you remember the words Adera?"

"What words?" her throat was dry and sore, "I don't understand."

"Oh! You will soon enough" she laughed. The sound rang off the cave walls and reverberated in the room, "you will" she repeated.

She moved the whip over Adera's throat and pushed the pin into her, "This heretic fork is a nice touch, no? What are the words, come, tell me?" Verity's teeth were clenched, Addy recognized the spite in her eyes.

"So, this is almighty power? Look at you! A rat! You should remember by now!" She pushed hard on the fork. Pain burst in Addy's throat, the blood trickled down her neck.

"It is believed" she began to pace, her heels clicked on the cave floor "that you are an incredibly powerful witch. One of the Quinary. Ha!" she stretched her arms wide, "Look at this Marjy! Look at all that power!" she shouted upwards.

She's lost it. What the hell is she talking about? Who is she talking to?

"In your Grimoire, Adera" she pronounced it slowly, "are words, that a Quinarian will chant on their death. To pass power to another" she spoke coldly, deliberately.

"I don't know what you're talking about" the pain seared across Addy's throat.

"Come on! Don't be difficult Adera."

"I don't know what you want! Just tell me?" Addy was confused.

"If you have the power, you would know by now. Others would know. There would be a stream of struggles, you would probably have been dead by now, in fact. Some power-hungry monster would have killed you in its rush. I probably did you a favour," there was a madness in her eye, Addy was wary, "hiding you out in the boondocks. Clever me."

"But you see Adera", she slowly etched the whip across Addy's cheek. The power is mine, I deserve it. It should have been mine!" Her lips were clenched in a cold smile.

"I had it once, not a Quinarian no, but a good amount of power. I want it back, more. Rumour says you can give it to me, if you have it." She stepped back and let the whip unfurl, it sucked in the air and struck across Addy's stomach.

Addy hit her head back against the board, dropped her chin and the fork pierced her skin again. The pain stung across her stomach.

"I am patient Adera. If you are indeed a Quinarian, I will help you get your memory back. Your Grimoire. But I'm not convinced. If you are, you will remember how to give me your magic" she fluffed Addy's cheek with the whip, "Quinarian or not, I'll have what you have".

"W-why?" Addy struggled to breathe, her mouth was dry and her skin burnt from pain.

"I'll rule the world" she whispered, "even Zyklon will bow to me" she laughed maniacally.

Addy caught the mad gleam in her eye.

What is she talking about? She must be drunk.

Nausea pulled at her throat. The power flowed up and down her body, ready to heal her.

I must hide it from Verity. She's definitely been drinking. That's how it used to happen. The beatings. I need to distract her. She can't see the power.

"Have you been drinking?" she whispered.

The whip jerked her body up from the wheel and as she sprang back the fork dug in hard. Blood ran freely down her throat.

"Urgh!"

"How is your memory Adera?"

Addy scrunched her eyes in pain, her flesh knit together around the fork, she would need to move her head and release the wound again. She extended her neck far up and dislodged the fork with a pop. This time the whip caught her thighs and her throat caught the fork again.

"Think!" Verity shouted, "Remember!" The anger lashed across the room.

The whip stung her diagonally across her torso, she breathed through it, sweat ran freely, blood pooled below the wheel. The gears ground as the wheel turned. Addy's head was now at quarter past the hour. Her head rolled onto her chest, the fork pierced the wound. She didn't have the energy to flinch.

"I'll be back! If you have the Quinary's power, you will beg me to take it before the next Sabbat. Beg me!" Verity spat out angrily. The heels clicked away quickly.

Addy passed out.

"Two, one two" giggled the little brunette girl. Her pink dress had tiny little roses across her chest.

"You have to pick the token up" called the blonde girl in the yellow dress.

"Oooh" laughed the brunette, "I forgot".

"Well, I win then, again." Declared the blonde.

"That's alright." Extended the brunette smiling.

"No, it's not. You always do this! Let's float magic balls instead, I dare you. Hopscotch is so boring." The angry child snapped.

"We'll get in trouble, you know we can't do it until we pass our exam" warned the brunette.

"Scaredy-cat. Scaredy-cat." The blonde chanted. Two red fire balls hung in the air above her as she looked smugly at the brunette.

"Oh, don't?" pleaded the pretty brunette.

"Well. Whatcha gonna do? Hey? Scaredy Cat?" she challenged.

The chant stuck in her head as Addy came back to reality, the image wavered and faded away.

"So, tired" she mumbled, "just a small rest." Addy came back to her plight.

"You had power" she spoke to the absent Verity, "but you had power, you want power! Just power, never loved me...." She faded off. Addy's head lolled onto her chest and the fork dug in deep. She jerked awake, the pain numb and bone deep now.

A furnace was coaxed to life somewhere down the corridor, the drumming urgency of its consumption loud in the cavernous hollow.

The geometric pattern wavered and moved in her vision, Addy blinked hard. "Hallucinating" she whispered through cracked lips, "pretty" the image became three dimensions and then merged in on itself. The triangular pieces wavered and blurred and then suddenly flipped over and became vibrant again. They were beautiful, hypnotizing, calling to Addy. Love came from the image, she basked in it.

"Must. Stop. Dreaming." She tried to relieve the pain in her shoulders and moved gently. The fork scraped against the tender spots on her throat, "The Quinary" she whispered then loudly, "What?"

I am totally delusional! Tripping out.

But, the words reverberated around Addy's mind and settled comfortably in her. A knowing grew inside.

The Quinary.

She felt the tingle across her skin as her energy soothed her, familiar, like a blanket.

"I am bad. I killed the bird," she heaved as the tears burned her eyes. "Go away!" She spoke to the energy harshly, "Go away! You never helped me".

She was five years old when she found a sparrow fallen from the nest. The bird's wing was broken. Instinct pulled her to help and as she had gone to mend it's wing, Verity had screamed at her.

"Don't ever use that evil power here! Ever!" In fright she had lost concentration, too much power had killed the bird. She killed a living creature. She had never forgotten. It's too large beak and bulgy eyes were limp in her small hands as it lay dead.

The emotional effort brought her back again, her head banged against the board and the fork cut in deep.

I will never use it again!

She had vowed. Her pain was deep and real. She had tucked the power away. Until recently. The energy could not be put to sleep; she tried, but it kept coming back. Each time it was stronger than before.

The geometric patterns soothed her. Power hummed in her ears. Addy distantly heard the flutter of bird wings interrupted by the blazing furnace and two little girls playing on the docks.

Her eyes sprang open, she hissed a breath into her painful body. Zyklon's cool touch at the column of her neck felt like a painful needle slowly driving into her. She was now at quarter to the hour on the wheel.

"Oh, little Addy! Poor, little Addy." He whispered.

Dressed all in white he shimmered in the dark cave, "so much potential, I feel the power. I can taste it" he licked her cheek, "so wasted on you".

Nausea collected at the back of her throat. She felt the sweat trickle between her breasts. Zyklon stood back casually and hooked his hands in his back pockets. His shirt was partially unbuttoned and a silver triangle rested on his smooth chest, an eye blinked in its flat surface.

"Come to me" he whispered, "remember the words so that I can relieve your burden, come on" he coaxed in sickly dulcet tones.

"Piss off" she whispered surprised.

His eyes flashed red in the dark cave, "Your memory will return. Tomorrow is the new moon, we'll have a ritual" he giggled like a boy.

Noises down the corridor caught his attention, "Aah, the show must go on" he wrung his hands together and smiled at Addy.

"Come in, just over here" he indicated to a spot right in Addy's line of sight. A large black four-armed creature brought in a chair, another effortlessly carried a sack over its shoulder. He dropped it on the seat and pulled the bag down roughly.

In the chair, wide eyed but unseeing, sat Mrs. Harris. Addy inhaled swiftly, the jerk of her head pushed the fork deep into her jaw, it pierced through the bottom of her tongue.

Mrs. H's pink house dress was creased and ruffled more than usual, her grey hair, wild. Addy saw her sad grey tights pooled into her men's moccasins.

Addy's eyes welled up. Deep in her core she felt power unfurl.

"Let her go, Zyklon. Your issue is with me," she spoke around the fork.

"Oh! Goody! You're the hero type! How charming. This will be so much more fun!" he sang.

"Vigilate." He murmured.

Mrs. Harris jerked back to reality. The fear on her face was real and raw. Addy felt warmth invade her heart. Zyklon walked around her three times, he chanted under his breath as he whirled his arms in large circles. He ignored Mrs. Harris who rocked in fear. Red bands of light settled over Mrs. H., it snaked up her body until it unfurled beneath her chin and tilted it up.

Mrs. Harris rocked harder, she held herself, and started to wail.

"Stop Zyklon." The energy in her voice surprised Addy.

Zyklon stopped, looked at Addy and whispered towards Mrs. Harris, "Give it to me, Brownie".

Mrs. Harris stammered, the red bands tightened at Zyklon's hand-wave. Addy felt anger claw at her, the power within her pushed her senses high.

"No! Mrs. Harris, don't listen, please?" she begged.

Mrs. Harris glanced Addy's way. Addy saw her neck constricted, her grey face sagged in dejection, she whispered, "Sorry, my Lady" then in Latin she whispered, "et dimittam te fortitudinem meam".

"I concede my power to you" Addy translated in her mind, she did not question how she knew that.

"No. No!" screamed Addy.

Zyklon held Mrs. Harris's head up and coaxed the power from her. A bright golden orb, like a tiny galaxy orbited on itself in mid-air above Mrs. Harris. Zyklon leaned in to inhale the orb. Addy blasted involuntary, uncontrolled power from her tied hands. It knocked Zyklon over. He immediately shielded himself and sent a cold blue whip of anger back at her. The power bit into her for a micro second and then her own shield settled on her, such that it trapped his whip of pain against her.

"Ha ha ha!" he laughed, "such a rookie error, no control! I should just watch, you will kill yourself!"

Addy realized the error she had made. Now he was sure she had power.

Addy willed her power away and forced it to drain along with Zyklon's chord of pain. The pain burned her skin. Mrs. H lay still on the floor.

The wheel turned; ten to the hour was her angle, directly in line with his face. He raised a hand and swept the hair from

Addy's face and then let his hand slowly trace down her. He caught her eye as he leant forward, "Mine to play with now" he spoke right into her mouth.

Addy heard Verity's heels but kept Zyklon's stare.

"It's all win-win for me" he puffed in her face.

"What's this?" Verity's voice was shrill. For a split-second Addy thought that Verity would help her; then the cold stare and the taunt in her words from before replayed in her mind, "I'll have your power, no matter what..."

Zyklon held his palm out toward Verity. She immediately stopped speaking but her anger sparked in her eye.

"There's been word," she said formally, "they're moving" she had her palms together and her jaw firm. She stared at Addy intently.

Zyklon pushed his forehead up against Addy's and ignored Verity, Addy felt the angry energy roll off of her. Addy tried to pull back, Zyklon raised his fingers and set them on the open fork wounds, his cold bone-numbing power trickled into her. Addy chattered from the cold pain.

Suddenly, he flicked his white collar up against his neck, stepped away and walked out of the cave. Verity hung back a moment and then whispered, "It's mine Adera! The power is mine!" She swept out dramatically after Zyklon.

Addy swallowed hard.

How long can this go on?

"Mrs. Harris! Mrs. Harris! Wake up, please? He's gone, it's Addy, wake up!" Addy pleaded to the still figure, "Mrs. H., they're going to come and get you, pleeease" she urged.

Addy heard a scuffle. Her power arced to her attention. A man appeared at the cave entrance dressed in black, he had a black mask through which berry brown eyes peered. He had broad shoulders and a strong jaw. He moved gracefully, silently. A warrior. Addy stared intently, frostily at the man.

Finger to mouth he indicated silence, "I am here to help" he beckoned her to be calm, his palms up. Addy waited a moment, felt no threat.

"Help her please?" she indicated with her head. The fork twisted in her wound. He stepped towards Mrs. Harris.

"A Brownie." He assessed with conviction.

"Mrs. Harris, my ol..." Addy quickly changed tack, "Mrs. Harris, please help her?"

He knelt down and put his thumb between her brows.

"Overloaded. She will be fine. She needs time to recover."

He moved towards Addy, where she hung on the hour. He held up an oval water skin, Addy caught his eye warily.

"I'm here to help" he said.

Addy held his gaze, she felt deep in her core that he was trustworthy, she nodded fractionally.

What more can anyone do? If it's poison it may speed my demise.

She saw him swallow hard. His eyes darted to the entrance. Who is he?

Her eyes felt swollen; sweat and blood layered her face, neck and torso, layer upon layer, it congealed and then peeled away from her through its own weight. She felt the thickness drop off every now and then.

His eyes flashed in anger as he followed the scabbed blood drop from her.

She opened her mouth and he poured water in. Addy closed her eyes as the cool liquid slid down her dry throat, it roared an impassioned thirst to life. He held it up again and she drank long and hard, much of it washed down her blood-soaked front.

"Slowly" he whispered, "there will be more later." She saw him glance at the entrance.

"The guard changes in an hour, they will check on you before that. I will be back, just after they've been"

"No. Don't leave me, please?"

He looked away.

His eyes showed his sorrow, "I need the time that it takes for the guard to change to untie you and for you to recover; we'll have about twenty minutes. This chamber is in deep, and its complex to get out," he pulled a brown bag from inside his shirt and unwrapped it, "this is Elven bread, just a bit will satiate you for a long time, it will bring more energy." He broke a piece off and put it in Addy's mouth.

It melted away. Sweet and warm. She immediately felt her body respond.

Oh. That's good.

His eyes were sad and concerned, "It will all be better soon" he held up more water.

Addy drank again, "They'll be back soon" he said. She could hear that he didn't want to leave her.

He strode over to Mrs. Harris, sat her up against the cave wall and with a thumb at each of her temples, he closed his eyes. He stumbled back a little and then moments later Mrs. Harris's eyes fluttered open.

Addy was intrigued. For years she had never met anyone else with power, and now half of Darton Village was coming out.

Mrs. H. panicked and tried to scramble backwards up the wall.

"Mrs. H, he's here to help you" she whispered, "listen to him".

"You're a Brownie!" he stated. She stared at him, her rat impression became starker as he stared back at her. Finally, she nodded, too shocked to speak.

"Go home now. Tell Glock what has happened" he said. She nodded as she struggled to stand against the wall.

Mrs. H looked across at Addy, blinked hard in thanks and then clicked her fingers. The crack was loud in the chamber and Mrs. H disappeared right in front of Addy's eyes.

"Where is she?" The panic was real. Addy had no other friends.

"She's a Brownie. She's gone home. I'll be back!" He moved silently out of the cave without further explanation.

What the hell? What is a Brownie? Where is she? Why isn't any of this making any sense?

Within seconds of his retreat, two guards marched into the cave. They barely glanced at Addy but looked for the fallen victim they were obviously instructed to collect. Then they checked Addy's ties, and left. Addy heard flutters in the outside chamber but then all was quiet.

The wheel turned. She felt slightly revived, the burn in her throat was gone.

I wonder if he will come back.

The wheel continued to turn. Addy heard the cave's drones, drips and ticks echo in the chamber. Pain ran up and down her body and power lapped across her, it taunted her to engage with it. The torches spat and hissed in rhythm to her wounds which opened and closed under her jaw. The dull ache was constant.

Upside down again.

Blood ran down her throat Addy felt it trickle to the back of her neck, it snailed over her face and into her nose. The metallic taste coated the back of her mouth. She forced air through her nostrils which sprayed blood up into the air and across her own face. Her eyes bulged from pressure and stung where the blood dried on her lashes and flaked into her eyes. She drifted in and out of tortuous sleep.

The squish of blood and sweat where her forearms chafed her ears and hair, woke her.

He's not coming back, why would he? I'm nobody. Nothing.

Her vision wavered behind her eyelids and a beautiful face gazed at her. Addy felt the love radiate from the woman,

"I love you my little Addy, come home, sweet girl. Please keep strong. The Quinary will help" she whispered in Addy's vision.

Addy let the dream wash over her. She imagined the caress on her face. She slept for two-wheel rotations.

When her eyes fluttered open, the stranger's knees were at her face.

"You're back or am I seeing things again?" she whispered hoarsely.

"Ssh" he spoke from above her.

"U hum" Addy responded.

No energy. Can't think.

"Keep still" he knelt down in line with Addy's vision, "I have to tighten the fork before I can loosen it" he fiddled with the strap at her throat. Blood thick and sticky hampered his task, Addy felt him tug and squeezed her eyes shut. He swore under his breath.

Addy felt the fork come free. She blinked and moved her neck all the way down so that her chin touched her chest. Tears pooled in her eyes. Her chin was sticky on her chest.

"Just hang in there, okay?" he advised.

"Ha ha. So funny" she retorted drily.

His mask moved in a smile, "Sorry. I'll untie your hands first" he tugged and cut at ropes, "the blood will rush to your extremities, you will get pins and needles" he was curt.

"I've had those for days" she replied

His hands faltered, "Sorry," he said.

"It was just a few turns of the wheel" she whispered, eyes closed.

A sudden tug and her hands were free; Addy brought them down in front of her, the movement was both painful and yet an instant relief. She rubbed her upper arms.

"Here, let me," he grabbed each arm in turn and rubbed gently. Addy had not been touched by many people, often by Verity when she was younger but not without violence. The sensation was strange to her and she pulled back.

"I'm okay. Can you get my feet?"

He nodded, "push back into the board and then stabilize yourself by holding onto me" he instructed from above.

Addy followed instructions, her legs crumpled in on her. The stranger caught her before she hit the ground.

She struggled to sit, overwhelmed by the pain and relief, tears streamed down her bloodied face.

"Just rest a moment, have water and bread"

Addy drank deeply, the stranger stared on.

"Sorry" he said simply again.

"Not your fault" she stood up slowly and stumbled.

"Easy" he whispered.

"Got to go" she said with urgency.

"You have a minute. Get the feeling back in your limbs" he encouraged.

Addy moved her arms and legs slowly.

"I know the passages. I'll go ahead. I'll call out to you. Like a bird." He made a soulful noise in the back of his throat, "only you will hear it. It means the passage is clear and you can enter." He stared intently, gauging her movements.

"To get out, you go left from here, then, at the fork, take a right. Be careful, a furnace-room is occupied on the right at that point. You still with me?" he cocked his head to the side.

"Left out, right at the fork. Room on right. Got it," she summarized hoarsely. Addy stretched her limbs slowly. Pins and needles invaded.

"Good. After the furnace room, the passage becomes dark. It goes for a long time. It winds back and forth on itself. There are four corridors that break off to the right. Stay on the main passage. It becomes narrow and winds downwards. Keep going. Do not break off the passage. Still following?" he asked.

"Aha" Addy nodded, "keep on passage pass four corridors". She squatted slowly to get her blood moving. Pain exploded everywhere.

"When the passage drops down, it will start to smell damp, it will get uneven and rough underfoot. I have a torch" he passed it to Addy "do not use it unless it is an emergency. When you step into the water, feel to the left. Stone steps, hardly noticeable. They start narrow and get wider. There are a few hundred steps. Will you manage?" he asked.

Addy nodded.

"Keep winding up the stairwell. When you find the window on the landing, behind you will be three doors, take the right door, I will wait outside, listen for my call before you open the door".

He grabbed her shoulder. She winced. "Sorry" he grimaced.

"When you get outside, run. Fast. Get away from here. Do not stop. Run" there was an urgency to his voice.

Addy nodded, "Let's go; what is your name?" her throat was raw.

He stared at her a moment. "Aquilae" he murmured, "wait for my call".

Aquilae stepped into the passage.

Addy flattened herself against the dark wall and waited. Seconds ticked by, she heard the bird-call and stepped into the passage. Adrenalin surged through Addy, the pain momentarily forgotten.

Left.

Her bare feet were silent on the cold floor. Torches flared and sputtered as she passed and light danced on the cave walls, it shone on streaks of stalactites. Addy heard scuffling around her, "delusional" she chided herself.

I'm so weak. Everything's sore. I must get out. My breath is so loud!

She stopped at the fork, waited for the call. The ventilation was cooler from the left, warm on the right. The furnace drew oxygen noisily, it drummed in the hollow space.

Everything so stiff. Pain, so much pain. Just keep going.

She leaned against the rough wall and swallowed hard.

She finally heard the bird noise.

Right fork, she mentally ticked off. Her heart beat loudly.

I'm sending frigging alarms out. I've got to get out.

The entrance to the furnace room was well lit, from the right wall Addy could see the roaring fire, the strange cave-creatures shoveled coal from a chute into the fire. The beings were pitch black, leathery and had two pairs of arms. One set shoveled and the other swept up simultaneously. Their eyes were shiny black like beetles. No nose, just a slit, horizontal in the centre of their face and each breath made a soft 'puc' noise.

My God, what are they?

Addy stood a moment, waited for them to turn their back to the entrance and then quickly dashed across. She took a second to calm herself.

The bird call came from further away.

Shit, I took too long to cross the furnace room.

Addy looked ahead. Her power warmed her.

Yeah, long dark passage, four corridors, keep going.

She walked quickly her bare feet silent. She heard her own breathing heavy in the dark space. After the first corridor the passage plunged into pitch darkness. Water ran to her left. Addy felt for the wall, rough and cold to the touch. She took one step at time with her hand firm against the wall surface.

Keep going, three more corridors.

The bird call was a comfort but far ahead.

On my way.

The wall was rough under her palm. Her feet had pins and needles which burst into pain at every step. The going slow. Where the second corridor opened, a channel of air sucked at Addy. It threw her off balance.

Oh shit! What the hell is that?

The pull of the air distorted her face and skin. She felt it wrinkle and dip as the air current tugged hard.

Ugh! Fuck!

She clung to the main passage wall, then went down on hands and knees to crawl across to the other side. Spider webs tautened across her face close to where the wall met the floor.

Ugh, she shivered as she brushed it away. "Anything else?" she whispered into the blackness.

Once across, Addy relaxed a second.

Keep going. You can do this. You must get out. Must.

Something brushed against her, she stood up.

Ugh, creatures of the night.

The passage narrowed and started to decline.

Right on cue. All good.

A holler came from above, "Find her!" Zyklon's anger reverberated across the caves. Addy felt the fear smash into her. She ran.

With her hand, firmly on the cave wall, she kept going. Muscles constricted and pain shot through her. When she reached the final corridor on her right, her hand suspended in mid-air something grabbed it and pulled her in.

"Ugh! Let me go!" she kicked and punched and swung out. Addy thrust the torch at it. The thing was soft and pulled at her. Addy ducked onto her hands and knees and fumbled to switch the torch on, "this is an emergency" she whispered, "goddammit, switch on" she cursed just as the torch created light.

"Oh my God," she whispered, "what the hell are you?" she breathed heavily. In her torchlight a large pale worm wiggled away. She kept the beam on it for a few more moments until it she was sure it was gone. She checked where she was headed and switched the torch off.

Where the hell am I? Shit! Which way?

The noise above her was frantic. A siren was activated.

I must get out.

She walked blindly. Her heart raced, she felt her pulse beneath her jaw.

Oh my God. Where am I? Aquilae? Please?

A panic rose up in Addy. She grabbed her blood encrusted throat.

I'm going to die here.

The splash of water brought her to her knees.

Thank-you. Thank-you. Find the steps, find the goddamn steps.

Her hands slid on the torch and she dropped it in the water. Shit!

Addy leaned into the water. Something slimy moved between her palms.

"You have the torch" she whispered.

She walked arms outstretched to the wall, the blackness complete. Addy closed her eyes, there was no difference but it felt more comforting than not seeing anything.

Steps must be here. Come on. Where are you?

She felt around, the water was at her knees. The floor was rough but covered in a slimy layer. She frantically moved her hands in wider circles as she edged forward.

Please. Please. Where are you?

Water swirled around her, icy cold. It smelled damp.

Addy felt a small smooth in-step in the stone wall. She leaned forward and felt another step, much higher up.

Got it.

The relief flooded into her. Her eyes stung with unshed tears.

She pushed her toes into the first step, the second was much higher.

Shit. I'm so weak.

She pushed her fingers out, grabbed the cold stone and slowly, painfully pulled up her weight until she rested on her elbows. A door banged up ahead.

Shit! Where is the call? I haven't heard the call.

Addy scuffled on her elbows and heaved her tired body up onto the step. She curled up in a ball and waited.

Feet running. Water running. Where are you? Aquilae?

Addy slumped her head back against the wall, in the darkness a shiny glint caught her eye. She shuffled on her backside and reached for the shiny ring embedded in the concrete step diagonally above her. Her hands felt around silently. The next step was to the right of the ring. Far off in the distance she heard the call. Her heart thumped with relief.

Addy jumped forward and just caught the step with the tip of her toe. She felt the whoosh of the air as she stabilized on the step.

Fuck! Too close!

She teetered for a second and then moved forward on the ledge. Feet drummed down the passage. She scrambled up the step and sent silent thanks that the pathway upwards had started. She ran blindly, the only sound was her feet as they slapped on the cold steps.

Up, up, around. How many more?

Her breath labored. Water splashed below her. She clambered up, exhausted, up, up around.

Light came through and eventually she saw the window on the landing. The sudden brightness made Addy squint.

Right, take the right door!

Addy pushed the handle down, her hands slipped and it 'clacked' loudly in the small stairwell. Her heart dropped.

"Up!" shouted someone below, "move".

Addy used both hands, heaved the handle down and the heavy door opened slowly.

She squeezed her backside into the door opening first, then let it spring closed behind her.

Outside, the rain pelted down.

Addy ran. The freedom of movement heady. Her body battle scarred, complied with her command. She ran.

Rain hit her face and bounced off in large drops, it obscured the dusk. Thunder rolled overhead and the line of trees that Addy charged towards swayed in the wind.

She threw herself under a large pine, the branches bowed low and creaked and groaned around her, "It's okay" she soothed, "It will go over" she told herself, as she breathed hard.

"Move!" she heard Zyklon's command over the wind. Black cave-creatures cloned from the furnace room, marched out in untold numbers like ants. Addy felt the earth vibrate with their movement. She scrambled on her hands and knees further into the trees. She cursed as she slipped on the needles. The tree line was narrow but extended far out to her left. She looked down her front where blood washed across her dripping body.

An eagle swooped down and landed gracefully in front of her. Addy noticed the colour of his outer eye - a golden yellow, surrounding a large black pupil that bore into her. His beak, closest to his face was also golden and then it dipped down sharply and turned grey. The rest of him shimmered black, atop golden feet that dug firmly into the forest pine cover. Addy felt strangely calm being close to such a majestic wild creature.

"I have had a hell of a day. I am sure you come in peace?" She held her palm up, as she heaved in gulps of air.

It stared at Addy intently, wings folded but slightly arced on his back.

"You also looking for shelter?" she asked breathlessly, "just stay here, you'll be safe. It's me they're after." She kept moving cautiously towards the back row of trees furthest away from the cave exit.

"About a three hundred metre dash" she reckoned, "and then more trees, further away. Or.... I stay in this line and run along to the left? What do you reckon?" she asked the bird, her voice lost in the torrents of rain above. He looked at her and then out towards the sodden fields as though contemplating her question.

I'm not in good shape.

Addy took a deep breath. Her heart hammered in her chest. She fisted her hands into her solar plexus as she stayed the hunger and nerves,

"Well, I'm going to run for it" she spoke against the storm.

At the first step, the bird swooped its wings at her. Its wingspan took command of the space, Addy dropped to the soft floor.

"Shoo!" she shouted. She cocked her head, to her left in the distance, she heard the command shouted against the thunder, "Bring her alive!"

Addy did not wait another second, she found her legs, and tried again to escape the sparse forest cover. The bird leapt at her, she ducked and then rolled in the undergrowth. As she looked up into the clearing, cave-creatures swarmed the space she would have been in.

"You are frigging mad!" she said to the bird, "but you just saved my life. And now I have finally lost my mind…" she tapered off. The hunger spasmed her abdomen.

Movement felt better. Addy stayed in the centre of the narrow tree band and walked as fast as she could manage. She peered frequently into the night from beneath the pines. Her ankles and wrists were raw from the ropes but she felt her power continuously lap at them.

The eagle hopped and flew alongside her. She murmured soothing noises occasionally, more to comfort herself. The earthy dampness clung in her nostrils and soothed her, she let her power sing gently around her, the sheer effort to reign it in too much for her tired body.

She stumbled over a root and rested where she fell. The bird was relentless,

"Go away, leave me alone! I will wait here. Go home. Where is Mrs. Eagle?" she muttered eyes closed.

"Ouch! That hurt!" said Addy.

The bird hopped up close to her face, Addy opened her eyes, the stern eye of the beautiful majestic eagle spoke to her conscious, "you're right, I will probably die if I stay here" her voice was rough and it hurt to talk, she rolled over with great effort and found her feet.

The tree cover became sparse and the moon would have long been out, but rain pelted in large drops, and jumped the pine needles on the floor, the large splats hit Addy on the head and shoulders and still they walked. The trees ran to a narrow point and then open fields rolled out in front of her.

Where Addy would have curled into a ball and slept, the bird urged her forward,

"Do you know where to go? I don't hear anyone anymore. I think it's okay, you're bossy."

Her feet were in auto motion, step by step by step. Her spirits flagged and her need to sleep almost overrode but for a troublesome bird that nudged and fluttered and dodged at her so that she kept on the move. At one point, she regurgitated the visions during her torture, Addy could have sworn she heard the bird talk to her, "Nearly there, Addy. You can do it. Come on".

"Can't" she whispered but kept walking anyway, "Can't".

Rain hit down hard and they were surrounded by open fields and lightning. The bird flew up ahead, stopped and waited. Flew and waited, continuously. His stubbornness compelled her forward. She hoped Aquilae had found shelter.

Many hours of near comatose movement later, the bird took flight over a fence. Lights beckoned from the nearby farm house. Addy took stock, it was beautiful and she felt welcome.

The large house had two stories. The lights around the house and in the windows soothed Addy.

I'll just wait for the storm to pass… gone before daylight.

Sheets of rain rolled across the flashing green fields. In the intermittent light, Addy saw dark clouds to the west, a promise of more rain.

I need to stop. I can't. Just can't.

Her body screamed with hunger as it gripped her abdomen in spasms. The shed was just inside the fence, far enough from the house.

Nobody will notice if I shelter there.

Her jeans hung from her slim form and her blood dripped from her shirt.

The fence was flimsy, she stepped on the bottom wire and took the top with her right hand as she ducked through. The electric pulse hit her mid stride, her body convulsed, she whipped in the air and then rolled down the hill.

She grappled urgently at tufts of grass but her body rolled and rolled. It finally stopped in a heaving mess of mud and hair. Her hand tingled, her leg throbbed in pain and the smell of burnt flesh invaded her nostrils. Addy lay still a moment.

Fuck.

She pulled herself up onto her knees, the rain pelted the back of her head and ran rivulets across her face and down her nose.

I must get to the shed. Safe. I'll leave first thing. Far away. Just get to the shed.

Driven by survival she pulled her feet underneath her. She winced as the pain seared up her leg into her abdomen. She tried to stand on one leg.

I'll hop to the shed.

Her lungs woofed as the fall winded her. She cleared the mud from her eyes and smeared blood across her cheek. In the angry lightning, Addy watched the blood ooze out of her hand and she stared, dazed. She remembered when Verity had left red welts in the same spot.

I will be free. I am free.

The deep sobs took her by surprise. Her body shook and hiccupped. She pushed and turned onto her stomach and put her arms out in front of her. The bird ran its beak down her arm, softly, in sympathy. Slowly Addy crawled through the thick mud as rain pelted her back.

When she reached the shed the rain stopped abruptly, now only a gentle rumble far above her. She rolled further in. Up in the rafters the black eagle winked at her.

"Thanks" she whispered at him.

The storm spent itself. When dawn rolled through, it found Addy, a lump of encrusted mud, still on the shed floor.

The roller door rumbled on its tracks and then squealed on its spindle. Addy struggled to open her eyes. Mud cracked along her face as she came fully awake. Her hair, heavy swung against her cheek. She scrambled on the floor and dirt dug into her finger nails.

Oh no! The wheel. I am not going back on the wheel!

Where the hell am I?

Fatigue still sat in her and she struggled to see in the weak haze of the sun, "the furnace" she whispered in confusion. She scrambled back in panic, her body protested, and took her breath away.

Two shadows moved towards her, she could not find her breath, "No, no!" Her voice came out as a wail.

The power surged from beneath her, she pulled at it instinctively, it felt comforting as it welled and flowed to her command. The shadows approached. In the haze of her power, from far away, Addy heard, "Don't pull so much power! We are not here to harm you! You are not in danger. I repeat, you are not in danger."

So, good. It feels so good.

The female voice was panicked but Addy was beyond reasonable thought, all senses abandoned her and she acted on primal instinct.

The power pooled into her body and surged through her energy channels. Every cell was energized, the energy surged and churned inside of her. She felt it in her core and let it embrace her.

She tilted her body into the power and let it caress her, somewhere in the deep recesses of her mind she saw a man, kind with gentle grey eyes under busy eyebrows, "Balance" he whispered, from far away.

Oh no! What am I doing? No!

"Get out!" her voice barely audible, "Get out! Run" Addy shouted, the power radiated away from her. The energy waves spiraled outwards.

The beams shook, Addy saw the woman create a shield; her and a man crouched behind it; the energy panned out and

Addy saw it shatter the back of the shed. Tiny pieces took to the air and moved out into the farm. The power swelled from her.

Fuck! I'm out of control!

The devastation radiated from her palms and fingers, from her body, from every part of her. She was simultaneously fascinated and appalled.

"No!" The word dragged from her as fear pulled at her tendons; brought her to her knees. The primal cry reverberated around the shattered shed.

The power stopped as quickly as it came, the tap switched off. She looked on in horror as the two strangers tentatively stepped forward. Her knees buckled beneath her. The smell of dust tugged at her as she curled into a small ball.

She welcomed the blackness.

4

When Addy opened her eyes, the sun filtered through the curtains as they gently danced in the breeze. Her hand stroked the fitted sheet beneath her; she loved the texture between her fingers.

So, soft.

She rolled onto her side and winced as pain sliced through her. She brushed her cheek on the pillow case, 'so nice' she whispered.

As she struggled to sit up, her memory returned.

"Oh no! What did I do?" Her mouth was dry and her voice rough.

Addy pulled back the sheets to swing her legs from the bed. The thin yellow haze caught her eye. The thinnest bubble surrounded her. She poked at it. The buzz was definitely magic.

I am a prisoner, again!

The door opened.

"Oh! You're awake! Just stay in bed. I have something for you" the woman smiled stiffly. She was pretty. Creamy blonde hair framed her face and her blue eyes looked at Addy nervously. She put a tray down beside the bed, "don't worry about the bubble now. I will remove it in a minute. I was worried that you would panic again" she continued, "I'm Rachel. Have this, it will help relieve the pain. You look like you have been through a bit" she placed a creamy frothy drink in a tall glass, next to the bed.

Addy shook her head, her stomach growled loudly.

"Drink up. If I wanted to hurt you, don't you think I would have done it while you were asleep?" Rachel reasoned.

Addy took the glass warily and then sipped at the drink. Without a blink, she drank the glass down. It tasted sweet and smelled of cardamom. Almost immediately, she started to feel better.

"You should rest now. We can catch up later. Dane is making lunch" Rachel picked up the tray, "You came in a pretty bad shape and you wield a lot of power, stranger, but rest and we will visit later. I sense no ill intent from you" she said coolly as she left the room.

Addy sank back against the pillows and closed her eyes. She put her hand out to the magic bubble and felt it buzz lightly against her skin. She peeked at it again, she used her other vision, it was like an intricate spider web of magic threads.

Her mind replayed the energy release that had taken place in the shed. She rubbed her forehead and felt anxiety flutter at her ribs.

The room was beautiful. Cream walls and curtains and light brown carpets. An old white dresser stood against the wall to her left beautifully adorned with a pink water jug and little pots filled with darker pink pot-pourri. A large magnolia was framed on the wall and near the open French-window, was a pale carpet collecting shadows as the curtain moved in the breeze.

She stroked the comforter. The smooth soft beauty of the room settled on her as she drifted back to sleep.

"You awake?" The man's voice was cautious and vaguely familiar.

Addy sat upright and pulled the covers right up to her shoulders.

"You must eat something now. It will help you get your

strength back!" he explained with a smile. He rested the tray on the side table.

"I'm Dane"

Addy stared at him warily, she eyed the soup and bread that he had put next to her bed. His voice was warm.

"Go ahead" he stated, "you must be starved" he nodded towards the food.

Addy didn't take a second to consider the offer. She pulled the bowl onto her lap and attacked the food. The warm liquid soothed her throat. Her stomach convulsed. She closed her eyes as the too large mouthfuls dribbled onto her chin.

She felt the frenzy but could not stop. The soup was warm and tasty. She had not eaten in a week. She continued to slurp in the silence until there was nothing left.

When she was done, and her senses returned, Dane was seated on the end of the bed, mouth wide open in amazement and shock,

"Well, I. I. Uh" he fought for words, his voice choked up.

"You've probably wondered where you are?" He found neutral ground. Addy continued to stare at him in silence, he wore jeans and a grey T-shirt with the word Fly emblazoned across it. He wore his dark hair, short with a longer front. His face was strong, his nose straight with a square jaw which had feint stubble across it. Addy was most intrigued by his eyes.

Somehow familiar. Warm and comforting. Good to look at.

"So. Rachel's parents own this farm. They've gone travelling and she's looking after it. I arrived in the summer, I came to look for work or even just a meal or two" he looked out of the window, "I help Rachel manage the farm hands and do other odd jobs. I get a room and food. And that is pretty much it." he held his palms up. "Not much happens around here. Until... well, until you arrived. Are you feeling any better?"

"Thank-you" Addy's voice was raspy, she reached for the water on the tray and drank it down in one swoop, "What's the damage?" she asked a little stronger.

"The bubble's gone, come and look from the window" he looked uncomfortable.

Addy pushed the covers aside and moved her legs over the edge of the bed. She curled her toes into the plush carpet savoring the feel and then slowly stood up. She steadied herself against the bed.

What have I done. I could have killed these people.

"Easy now. We can do this tomorrow. There is no rush" he stood up coming to help her.

"No!" Addy shook her head, "I'm okay. I must see," she walked slowly around the bed and towards the French windows. She pulled them open slowly.

"Ugh"

Dane followed her gaze.

"You probably shouldn't be out of bed. You've been through a lot!"

Only half the shed stood. The red roof lay sprawled across the fields. Splintered wood pocked the yard. Feeding bags and trestle tables, wire and equipment lay everywhere. Beyond the shed, the fields were ripped up. Large mounds of soil ripped open and bare of crops. Through her tears, Addy saw a makeshift tarpaulin was rigged at the end of the wounded shed; a few goats wandered around curiously.

"Oh no!" she whispered, "so bad."

"Nobody was hurt. That's what's important" Dane tried to comfort her.

Addy wiped madly at her face as she tried to stop the tears. Pure luck!

"Tell her I will work to pay it back. I can work" she stared into the devastation, "I'll fix it" she rambled on.

"Come now. We can talk more when you've rested" he took her arm gently and lead her back to bed. Addy felt the touch. Warmth flooded her.

"I'm Addy"

"Hello Addy" he smiled, "we can fix it. Don't worry. Get

better first" he soothed as he gently pushed her back on the bed and covered her. Addy blinked rapidly to stop the tears,

"Thank-you Dane" she whispered, "I am so sorry, please tell her".

Two days later Addy got the all clear from Dane and ventured into the yard.

"Why don't you use your power to clean it up?" Rachel walked in hours later, her blonde hair caught in a perfect pony tail. Her blue jeans skimmed her slim form and her red collared shirt was perfectly tailored.

Addy released the wood she had gathered onto the wheel barrow and then dusted her hands over it, she turned to Rachel. Rachel's apple shampoo was fresh in the dusty yard.

"I, uh. No. I made the mess with power, didn't I?"

"It will be quicker" Rachel's eyebrow rose in question.

"Maybe, this is my punishment?"

"Nonsense. Come, I will help you. We can be done in just a few moments" Rachel offered.

"No!" Addy's voice was sharp "I can't. Just leave me, I'll do it this way" she started to collect more wood splinters at her feet.

"Addy. You can wield your magic at will. Can't you?" Rachel approached her.

"I'll do it like this. Thanks for the offer" Addy was short and kept working.

Just go away.

"If you can't control the amount of power that you have at your disposal, we're all in imminent danger. You could kill someone. Tell me that you can command your own power?" Rachel demanded in anger.

"Rachel, there is a lot to do." Addy walked away fast the guilt rose through her.

Just go away. Please?

The physical labour kept her mind and body from wandering to Verity. Addy picked up debris, carted rubbish, swept and carried as the afternoon wore on. The warmth moved out of the day and the cool air rushed in. Her limbs were still sensitive.

"Hey! Take it easy, Addy" Dane called from the corner of the shed, "you're still recovering!"

"I am much better, thanks!"

"You look better!"

"Yeah. Rachel had extra clothes around. She has been more than generous given that I practically… well, she has been generous" Addy shrugged.

Addy recalled the shower she had that morning and smiled. The water had soothed her soul as it cleansed her body. Warm water, shampoo and soap. She smiled at the memory of her first proper shower.

"Well, you looked pretty beat up when we found you. Nobody expects you to put in a full day's work yet" Dane approached.

"I've come to get you for dinner" he stated, as he stepped in next to her, "Rachel has gone out. Not that it matters, most nights she eats in her workshop. She likes to practice her craft" he said companionably.

"How long do you think it will take to fix the shed?" She was cautious, conversation wasn't natural for her.

"In a rush?" Dane's eyebrows raised up surprised.

"Well, I don't like to outstay my welcome" she smiled.

"Nonsense! But, honestly. I don't know. We will start putting the structures back together tomorrow, most of the debris is cleared up now. Thanks to you"

"Yeah! Right. Thanks to me" she added bitterly.

"What is that amazing smell?" She sniffed the air and savoured the smell.

"We can wash up here" Dane indicated an outside sink with soap and water, "then we'll just eat in the kitchen, if that's okay by you?"

Addy nodded, tears threatened again.

What is with me?

"What is it?" Dane was clearly concerned.

"Thanks" she whispered, the lump in her throat prevented her from talking.

Dane smiled and directed her into the kitchen.

Shortly afterwards, she excused herself and had an early night. Her body still needed a lot of sleep.

The wheel grated on its turn, Addy winced and waited for the pain to follow but instead the clocks and watches flew at her. The noise changed from the grrrr of the wheel to the mad tick of a thousand clocks.

Tick, tick, tick. It started slowly and built to a crescendo, tick tick tick and it went on and on. Flames wound around the moving clocks and created geometric patterns, a voice from far away called to her, "Addy, Addy, can you hear me, child?" It was kind and soothed her, "You must listen Addy. The Quinary needs you. You must find us! Addy! Must find us! Addy? Addy?" The voice echoed across a glossy chess board.

Addy sat upright, drenched in sweat.

Just a nightmare. Again.

She breathed in deeply, felt the smooth night gown on her skin and rested her head back on the pillow. Dawn had created a slither of light on the horizon.

The knock startled Addy.

"Thought I felt the stir of power in here" Rachel smiled fresh in the doorway.

"All okay?" she was chirpy.

"Y-yes. Thanks. I will be there in a minute" Addy offered.

"No rush." Rachel walked in and sat on the bed, "I can feel your magic, Addy" she said softly. "it's like a brooding force. You must release it." She took Addy's hand, "you are dangerous to yourself and us if you don't channel it away" she continued, "do you know how to do that?"

Addy took her hand back, agitated, "I'm fine. I'll be downstairs in ten minutes. There is a lot to do today" she was short as she swung out of bed on the opposite side of Rachel.

Addy stood under the shower and marveled at the luxury of

it. She closed her eyes and felt the guilt of Rachel's words, you are dangerous to us.

If I use magic I will destroy you. If I don't use magic, it will eventually destroy you anyway. I must finish the shed and be gone. I won't hurt you.

Addy walked into the kitchen satisfied that she had a goal. Dane came in laden with wood.

"It's fresher and fresher out there every day. Winter's definitely knocking!" He put the wood into the open fire place. "Morning Addy. How are you feeling today?" He smiled over his shoulder.

"Fine. Thanks" she smiled.

"Step away" Rachel waved her hands shooing them back. Then she threw the back of her hand down towards the wood and with a whoosh, the fire was roaring.

She looked directly at Addy.

Breakfast was quiet.

Addy found the work therapeutic. Every plank of wood; measure, hold, drill, screw. Measure, hold, drill, screw. The physical movement eased away her achy muscles.

If only there was an easy cure for nightmares and visions.

Addy shook herself.

The visions are so real. I am there, I can taste the air, hear the noise, feel the pain. What can it be? What's going on?

She felt her energy rise inside of her.

Go away!

"A little more to the left. There we go" Dane guided her.

The smell of her shampoo preceded her. Rachel walked into the shed fresh as a Spring Day in white jeans, pink shirt, white heels. Her blonde hair was freshly washed and dried and hung shapely around her face and down her back. She smiled and waved at them as she approached.

"Wow! You guys are working like demons! This is coming together so quickly! Let me do my bit" she added and waved her arms. The remaining slats shot up to attention and neatly slotted themselves into their designated spots like a pack of cards in line. She looked poignantly at Addy. "I hope that helps! I am off, I will be home late, I suspect" she turned on her heel and left. Apples streamed on the air.

"It isn't as easy as she makes it out" Dane consoled, "she needed us to have done a fair bit of it so that she could reference the grid but now that it is done, she can probably finish it tomorrow. So, don't worry, we had to do the first part the old-fashioned way" he smiled.

"I'm not worried. Work never scared me"

"And magic?" he asked softly.

Addy shrugged, "It's never been welcome".

Dane looked at her quizzically, "Really? That is strange. Most people don't have magic here. Those that do usually stick together" he bent to pick up tools.

"What do you mean?" Addy was intrigued.

"I mean," he looked uncomfortable, "Your mother or father must have had magic? They would surely have taught you about your craft?" He looked at her pointedly and continued to load tools into the carrier beside him. A muscle twitched in his jaw as he held her gaze with intent.

Addy shrugged and got up to help tidy away. They worked in silence.

She felt Dane's eyes on her, the warmth of it caught her breath.

What is this? I can't afford to get distracted. I must work out what Verity wants. Why is she looking for me? Addy shook the thoughts from her mind.

"Do you have magic Dane?" she asked softly as they walked to the house.

"Don't we all have some magic Addy?"

"I mean"

"I know what you mean. I am not a wizard" he offered.

"And what do you mean, 'most people don't have magic here'" she pushed on, "where are you from?"

49

"There are other worlds, beyond this one. Magic is all around us there" he said softly.

"Where's there?" She asked. "And you know of magic. How?" She continued.

"There's magic in my family" is all he offered.

Dane smiled. "Come on. It's cold," he took off at a sprint.

Addy's heart thumped.

Careful Addy. She cautioned herself.

"Come on. I challenge you to a game of Rummie" he offered, after dinner.

"Rummie?"

"Yeah, you know, Rummie?"

"No. I don't think I have even heard of it"

"Let me show you"

In the third round, Addy won. She beat Dane fair and square.

"I won! I won!" she sang. Addy realized deep down that she had never had this much fun in her life. Her heart felt a little lighter and even her power just hummed gently around her, not predatory or waiting to leap.

Rachel walked in.

"What's happened?" She asked.

"I beat Dane at Rummie."

"High Five! Come on. One-more round! I'm in," challenged Rachel.

"Mm maybe I should quit while I'm ahead" Addy giggled,

"Ah, not confident you can do it again" Dane quipped back.

"You are both in trouble," smiled Rachel.

The banter went backwards and forwards, light and friendly, Addy wallowed in it.

"I've missed female company! I am glad you're here Addy" stated Rachel with a smile.

Addy smiled but felt a little unsettled at the comment. Rachel hadn't mentioned her magic once this evening.

What are you up to?

"Have to go to bed." She yawned loudly again, "so tired!"

"Hey Addy. I've been thinking" Rachel smiled sweetly at her,

"I would love to show you some simple magic. You know, to protect yourself" she offered seriously, then continued more light-heartedly, "It would be so much fun! We can."

"That's my cue." Dane stood up, "Night ladies. See you bright and early." He walked out of the kitchen.

"Good night" Rachel waved dismissively not looking away from Addy's face.

"Night Dane" Addy felt a warmth deep in her chest just looking at him.

"We could have so much fun, Addy, and it will help you. I am only trying to help you" she looked sweetly at Addy.

A sudden change closed in around Addy's heart. Her instincts were telling her to back away. The power prickled along her torso.

"Thanks Rachel. I know you're trying to help. It's a lot for me to think about."

"Well don't dismiss it" Rachel stood up and stuffed the playing cards into their box, "think on it, we can chat some more tomorrow" she stated stiffly.

Addy looked at her for a moment unease flooded her senses. She shifted uneasily.

"Good night. Sleep well Rachel"

As Addy left the kitchen, Dane came in from the front door.

"Oh! Thought you were already upstairs." Addy walked up the stairs next to Dane.

"I just brought more wood up for tomorrow. I keep meaning to fill the store inside but the days are still so warm that it seems strange" he slowed as he came to his bedroom,

"Addy, listen to yourself. Inside. You'll know what to do." He patted her shoulder, the warmth seeped into her. She liked the feeling.

Imagine the possibilities? I could protect us. Help people. Ugh! Who am I kidding? This is pure evil. Death.

Addy brushed the escaped strands of hair from her face in annoyance.

Why am I even entertaining these ideas? I can't use this magic. I am what you should protect against. Why would she even suggest it? I have to go. I have to fix this mess and leave.

Her sleep was troubled. Vivid visions of places Addy had never been flashed through the night. She awoke tired.

Rachel expected her early. They were going to sort out herbs today.

The smell of lavender, thyme and rosemary wafted from the shed. Addy loved the smell, it triggered a comfort deep in her.

Who is Celia?

Addy recalled the dream she had. She had dreamt of Celia, whom she spent a considerable amount of time with. She silently yearned for dreamless nights.

"Oh good! You're here. Grab a scoop on the table" Rachel was already busy. She looked frequently to the entrance, distracted. "Scoop each pile of dried herbs into the labelled jars on the back of the table, there's a help."

Addy waved to Dane as he entered the shed on the other side of the screen that separated the herbs and plants from the animal fodder and tack in the shed. He nodded at her in acknowledgement, both his hands were occupied as he carried animal fodder.

"Ah, light duties today," he joked.

Tyres scrunched in the gravel and Rachel, Dane and Addy looked across the shed to the entrance.

Addy dropped the scoop, shock and magic claimed her body as she saw Verity and Zyklon walk into the shed.

Oh my god, oh my god! I must get out.

She twisted on her hands and knees in a panic. Rachel frowned at her but was also on her hands and knees, as they peered out at the visitors.

"Oi," commanded Verity, "where is the owner of this establishment?" she barked as she glanced around in distaste.

"I'll handle this" Zyklon interrupted. Verity's jaw stiffened, she turned her head away from Zyklon, redness crept up her throat.

Addy swallowed hard.

Oh shit!

Zyklon twisted his hand in the air and Dane fell to his knees, the horse fodder fell in a heap at his feet.

"Speak! Filth, where is the owner?"

Dane looked straight ahead and remained silent. Addy breathed deeply.

Go. Just go.

She silently pleaded for her energy to deplete.

Zyklon smiled coldly and then, palm down, sent more power into Dane. Addy felt the pull of it.

Dane writhed on his knees, sweat broke out over his body. Addy swallowed hard.

I must do something.

She saw Zyklon's red bands of magic surrounded Dane's body; Addy knew the cold pain that it sent through you. She felt the cold creep along her own neck and throat where Zyklon had touched her. Addy tried to move, her limbs were frozen.

Dane's jaw clenched, anger shone in his eyes.

"Ugh! What do you want?" Dane forced out between stiff lips. Verity examined her nails, bored.

"We're looking for someone" Zyklon replied in his sickly dulcet tone, "young witch, dark hair, in her early twentiesss?" He let the word sizzle from his mouth as he looked around the shed. He kept the power pumping into Dane.

Addy thought he had seen her. His gaze rested on her and she felt his eyes bore into her. She wanted to distract him from hurting Dane but Rachel came from behind her and put a hand over her mouth,

"I have a plan. Stay down" she hissed.

Addy shook her head furiously but Rachel had already popped up and sashayed over to Zyklon. Addy saw her nervously run her palms down her jeans. Addy's eyes filled with unshed tears.

These people were going to get killed. Why are they hiding me?

"Good day, good day!" shouted Rachel unnaturally "how may I help you?" She asked not even glancing at Dane.

Zyklon ignored her for a moment as he stared deeply into Dane's face,

"There's magic here?" He asked.

"Just me" Rachel smiled, "what is it you're after?"

"We need to talk" Verity offered, "in comfort" she looked around in disapproval and then turned and walked towards the house. Zyklon waved a hand and Dane shot through the air. The screen that divided the room broke as he tumbled to the floor. Zyklon walked towards the two women without a backward glance.

Addy flew from her hiding point, "Dane! Dane! Oh my god! Are you hurt?" Addy sobbed, "Please say something. Dane?" She poured over him, scared to hurt him further. Her power licked across her body, it wanted release. "Dane?" She kept an eye on the entrance.

Dane held a hand up, "It's like he steals a little of your essence" he murmured, 'the pain is intense.'

"I should have done something" she cried, "I am useless. I am so sorry."

"Sssh. It's okay. I will be okay. He is powerful. I just need a second" Dane was disorientated.

"I'm going to train with Rachel. I can't let this happen again" Addy stated firmly, "I won't let this happen again!"

G ravel turned to grass and still Addy walked.

Anger and energy pumped up and down her body. There was a comfort in the knowledge that she had no physical boundary on her. The sun was low and the shadow that danced beside her was long, wind gently swished around her and beautiful, golden light emanated from the fields to her left. Dark brooding ever-greens rustled diagonally in front of her and she peered into the depths of their hushed conversation, briefly recalling the night she escaped Zyklon and the caves.

The tiredness and pain whispered across her body and she instinctively turned back to the light as she rubbed her cold upper arms for warmth.

If I leave, they will leave Rachel and Dane alone. Verity wants my power. It's me they're after. She will keep coming. They'll be safe if I leave.

She clutched her head and shouted loudly, "what must I do?"

In her visions, she had a lot of magic. Love and support flowed towards her when she used her power.

But to have the love and support I must learn to use it. Why is this so hard? Why did he hurt Dane? I should have helped. I could have done something. But, imagine if I killed Dane or Rachel? Imagine that. I couldn't live with that. How could I?

A noise came from the ever-greens. Addy glanced sharply towards the trees, trees that just weeks ago had saved her. The pine floor swirled in mist, thick and unnatural, light filtered through hazy green murky forms in its depth.

What's going on?

The magic flared across her body. Her hairs stood on end. Her senses peaked. In the mist a shape formed, transparent and without substance but definitely Zyklon. She watched, his wavering form, it was arrogant and cold.

Addy ran towards the house, she heard his sickly laughter on the breeze around her.

He will always chase me, someone will always be in danger. How can I live without an attempt to use the power I have, to protect us? How can I?

***

"I think she sees us, Glock," the voice was excited.

"Don't be daft, Ferris old goat, we've been doing this for weeks and you say the same thing every time" the voice belonging to Glock pointed out warmly.

"But, she is using her ether now, something could have changed, her channels are opening. Perhaps, perhaps we can connect?" Ferris said with hushed expectation.

"You'll scare the ether right out of her. She doesn't know of us yet. Aquilae hasn't broached the subject," explained Glock.

"I know! It's just so frustrating! The poor child, no guidance, no love! How terrible Glock, how awful! When can we bring her home? Marjy is getting more disillusioned by the day!"

"My friend, I know. Aquilae says the young witch wants to train her"

"Is that a good idea? Addy is quite powerful. We don't even know the extent of it" Ferris pointed out.

"Mm I know. I know. I don't know what to say to you. She

needs to keep using power, she will be more open to us and we can help to bring her here" Glock rationed.

"But what of Zyklon? He'll use her no? He will target her; he'll taunt her or take her power"

"I don't know, she doesn't use it much"

"Who are you?" Addy sat up and interrupted the conversation in her head.

Silence filled the room.

"Ugh! I wonder if insanity's hereditary?" she asked aloud.

The door rattled.

Addy sat up.

"Are you only working half day?" Dane teased from the other side of the door.

Addy smiled and rolled out of bed. She yanked the door open,

"I'm training today," she announced, "I decided that if Rachel's offer still stands, I'm going to be trained"

Dane just stared at her. The little muscle at the back of his jaw jerked involuntarily.

"Addy" he shook his head as he searched for words, "Addy, perhaps you can wait for an experienced trainer? Rachel has no experience and your circumstances are different"

"How? Why?"

"Most witches, especially those with a lot of power are trained from a young age, your magic hasn't been used, or not much. I just feel, that you should have an experienced coach" Dane stated.

"And you know someone like that? I thought you would be pleased" she didn't mean to be short.

"Addy, I am glad that you have decided to embrace your gift but I just feel you should wait for an experienced person to help you"

"And what? Sit around waiting for Zyklon to kill us? I've thought about this, I think it's the right thing to do"

"Addy, we should talk. I have some things I need to tell you"

"Let me shower" Addy closed the door on Dane.

I am so tired.

"I'll be down in ten" she said through the closed door.

***

Rachel's coffee aroma hung in the air.

"Morning" Addy mumbled sullenly.

"Coffee?" Rachel offered.

Addy shook her head, "No thanks" she said.

"I don't know how you cope without caffeine" she smiled, "Dane says you have decided to be trained. I am pleased"

"If your offer is still open. I think it may be beneficial that I learn. If you'd rather not. That's fine too. I don't want to put you under any pressure, I know you're busy and"

"Oh nonsense! Why wouldn't I want to train you? It will be fun!"

"If you're sure?" Addy felt anxious.

"No time like the present. I will take my coffee in my workshop. I have to do a few small things and then you can pop over and we can start. Say half an hour?"

Rachel sounded distracted.

Addy nodded, "Thanks, see you then"

Addy helped herself to oats from the stove and ate in silence, she wondered what Dane wanted to tell her.

Cold wind rushed in as the door opened.

"It's getting colder every day" Dane rubbed his hands together blowing on them for warmth, "Ah, just the person I was looking for" he smiled.

"Well, you'll have to be quick, I'm off to see Rachel for Witch Training" she threw out.

"Oh Addy, I wish you would reconsider, but I can see your mind is made up" he smiled kindly. "There is so much magical history and so much you should learn about your power"

"How is that helpful?" Addy snapped

"So that you know who you are. Where you came from. How our world, I mean your world works" he listed patiently.

"I already know. Look what good that's done me." Addy was bitter. She felt the words form in her mouth and head and felt helpless to control them. She had never had this freedom to speak her mind.

"There are other things too. The fact that Rachel will make you take a binding oath as her apprentice. Do you know what that entails? Do you? I want you to be trained, honestly, but think about what you're doing" Dane was losing patience slowly.

"I trust Rachel" Addy spat out and immediately felt her skin prickle.

"Don't" Dane leant in close on the counter top. "Don't. Trust nobody with your magic Addy." Dane whispered "There's a legend…"

"Are you coming Addy?" Rachel called from the kitchen door.

"Yes. I'll be right there" Addy got up without losing eye contact with Dane.

Rachel closed the door and Addy moved around the counter.

"What are you talking about?" Addy was intrigued.

"I'll tell you later, in the meanwhile. Promise, Addy, that you will not commit to anything. Please?" He was insistent and Addy felt his concern.

"Okay, I won't commit to anything. But I am going to train now".

Rachel's workshop was dark and grey. A large stone fireplace dominated the room. Wood stacked high to the right infused a subtle smell of pine through the space. Directly in front of Addy a three-seater lounge and two one seaters surrounded a stone coffee table. Cabinets and shelves surrounded the other walls and housed bottles and potions and dried insects. Large flat stones bubbled in a red liquid, in a tall cylindrical jar, on the stainless-steel work top. They exuded a softly popping noise in the background. A large cauldron rested on the bench top and an athame took pride of place on the far end of the bench, it's pitch black handle stood menacingly from its ebony block.

The only window in the room had a red blind pulled down over it, which blocked the beautiful yellow warmth from outside. The fire, together with the torches on the wall, created a dim light which wavered uncertainly in the room. Addy had a sudden flashback to the cave Verity and Zyklon held her in. The pain seared in her throat where the heretic fork pierced her for days.

The doorway was an arch, also rimmed in red; the only colour amidst the shades of grey. A shiver ran down her spine, her power whispered across her body, making her hairs stand on end.

"Come in" called Rachel as she put a well-thumbed book into a drawer.

She turned and smiled, it didn't reach her eyes, "Welcome to my space, Addy" she spoke with forced enthusiasm and Addy sensed a change in her.

"Is this a good time? No rush on my part..." Addy tried to back out.

"Yes of course" Rachel ran her hands down Addy's upper arms. She shook her head, then flicked her blond hair away from her face.

"Let's begin" she gestured to the lounge, "come and be comfy" she moved to the three-seater.

"Most of us, The Magics" Rachel didn't look Addy in the eye, "have simply been born with the ability to use the energy available in the universe. Some who have magic, may have a lot, others, limited ability to tap into their energy sources. Does that make sense Addy?"

"So, you're saying there are various strengths of magic? Right?" Addy checked

"Yes. For example, someone can be a strong witch with an affinity for say, water, this enables them to tap into the power of water to enhance their own magical strength, it enables them to physically manipulate water and it enables them to call on a full water-based storm to do their will" Rachel looked at Addy then, "but an average witch these days, can hardly call the rain. At most, the witches I know, can simply cause a small current in their tea cup" she finished haughtily as she rolled her eyes.

"Are there a lot of us?" Addy asked, intrigued. She had never had the ability to talk about power with Verity or Rodic. She had never been similar to anyone she had ever met.

"Us? You mean witches?"

Addy nodded.

"I wouldn't say, a lot. I have heard rumors about other places, not here on earth,"

"That is just so far out there! Other places in the Universe?" Addy was incredulous.

"Yes; where magic is accepted as part of normal activities. Some say powerful witches and wizards can still connect to other worlds. I haven't seen that happen. But here, in our world, there are a few witches. The ones I know and hear about usually only have an affinity for one element. They often work in groups so that they can strengthen their power through the circle" Rachel stared into the small fire.

"Do all witches and wizards have an affinity with an element?" Addy asked

"I have not met any that don't. We find power, solace, peace in our element." Rachel was contemplative.

"And, "Addy was fascinated, "does your element dictate what you can do?"

"Mmmm. It is open to debate. If you're a witch you are born with the ability to use energy. If you hone your skills you can improve your strength, and the stronger you are, the more your affinity with your element comes into play. So, if two witches, an earth witch and a fire witch, say, were both trained and became powerful, the argument is – who is more powerful? Is it the Fire Witch because of the way the element can manifest its energy with the witch? Or is it the Earth witch?" Rachel looked at Addy, eyebrows raised.

"For most witches though, their element is simply the first energy that comes to their call and the one they find easier to use. But, we can use the energy of all. In fact, literature will tell you to call on all the elements before you do spell work"

"Can you have an affinity with more than one element?" Addy was hungry for knowledge now.

"No. Well, there are legends about a group of people who have an affinity with all the elements and in fact, they speak of a fifth element too. But, just legends...." Rachel shrugged.

"So?" Addy asked, "You mentioned that you only get stronger by practicing and honing your skills. What about me? I have not used my magic, ever" the question had weighed on Addy's mind. She suddenly felt apprehensive about the answer.

"The answer is, I don't know" Rachel was honest, "I haven't ever heard of a situation like yours where you have suppressed your magic for so many years. I would have thought that it would just simply fade away without use," Rachel crossed her legs.

"I had a friend in kindergarten and her family shunned the idea that she had magic, they refused to let her be trained. She lives in the village over, south. She has an amazing garden but cannot use any of the energy available to her. Just dwindled away. Stupid I say" Rachel was getting restless again.

Addy had one more question, which burnt deep in her mind, "Rachel, can you give or take power from another witch?"

Rachel smiled, the vacant stare deepening on her face, she turned to Addy and in a doll-like trance answered, "you need to be powerful to exchange power from one witch to another. The witch giving the power must do so by surrendering it to the receiving witch."

Rachel shook herself and then jumped up.

"The first thing we need to establish is the power stream you have an affinity with. Come" she walked towards the workbench.

Addy's heart hammered.

I'm not ready for this. What if my magic in its evilness, consumes me, tips me over? It's taken over before. Verity said years ago, that's what happened if you used the evil forces. What if it took over and made me do evil things? What if I hurt Rachel? I could lose control. I might never have control! Oh shit! I can't do this!

Addy's head thumped in time to her racing heart.

I must stall her. I'm not ready! Oh no! What if I killed her? What about Zyklon? What happens if I don't do this?

The confusion and worry spun around and around in her head.

"Rachel? Perhaps, perhaps…" started Addy.

'Mm? What is it Addy?"

"Before we delve into the fieldwork as such, perhaps I should learn more about the elements? Or perhaps, more about the rules of magic?" Addy hoped to stall the practical work.

"Rules?" Rachel's brows jumped up surprised.

"There is only one rule Addy" hands on hips she stated matter of fact.

"You mean the Harm None" Addy offered.

"That is outdated thinking! Hang with me, girlfriend! I'll teach you. The only rule is Let the Magic Serve you." Rachel turned on her heel and marched towards the far wall. Addy's heart sank.

This is not the rule!

Somewhere deep inside of her, Addy knew the rule, "Harm None" she whispered to herself.

Rachel held her hands to the wall on the far side of the work-bench. She whispered an incantation under her breath and then with a loud 'click', the door opened. Soft light sprinkled around her hands and then faded as she moved.

"Come. When you're a newbie, it's better to train outside" she stepped through and glanced briefly over her shoulder to make sure Addy followed.

Outside it was cool and crisp, Addy's skin tingled with magic.

Rachel's amber dress swished around as she walked ahead, her heels clicked on the white pavers. The pavers lead through a pristine garden; perfectly cubed hedges intercepted large squares of either black or white pebbles. The path itself was dead straight and ended in two steps up to a dais from which large columns rose to a framed, open canopy.

Addy noted the dais had unlit torches every metre of its perimeter. An alter dominated the space. Rachel walked until she stepped down on the other side of the dais and came to the edge of the mountain that Addy had seen in a distance.

"Oh wow!" Addy was astounded, "how does this work?"

"Very old magic, my parents bought the farm for this spot. Just a few steps, yet miles from home. It's a portal established in the space. My father, when he is home, spends all his free time looking for the lost journal of the previous owner. Rumour says it holds all secrets of this place" she smiled disbelievingly.

"Can you feel the magic here Addy?" Rachel twirled around.

"Yes. Lots of magic" Addy felt the energy around her. The mountain, the air, the earth, she felt alive!

Rachel walked to the edge of the cliff and held her hands out, palms parallel to the ground. She closed her eyes. A hush fell over the space, no bird, no rustle, no wind, complete and utter silence hung over them.

Addy heard the wind rustle.

It rustled and swooshed towards them. The energy was a web of illuminated threads. It ran up the mountain like nets being cast out.

Millions of tiny fairy lights, thought Addy.

Rachel looked spectacular! Her hair, like thick cream caressed her face and rose fluttering from her shoulders. Her amber dress a beacon of light against the purple haze of the far away cliffs. Her face, eyes closed was illuminated by the energy she was calling.

And it came. Strong and steady and Addy heard it speak to her and she felt its pull. It rose from the bottom of the mountain, seeped from the air, hovered above the earth. It all pulled together around Rachel's feet and then it waited for her command.

Addy swayed as the forces caressed her, she let it flicker over her and waited hesitantly, as the energy did, for Rachel's instruction. Then the change came.

The trees cried out and the mountain shuddered. Rachel's face went from peaceful illumination to a determined scowl. Blackness swelled from her and the energy swirled and rose. The crisp purple air turned dark, the winds whipped and snapped at them as they stood at her mercy. Rachel challenged the energy and strained into the fury she unfolded. The evergreens bowed and dipped and birds took cover. Rachel's eyes were open now, glazed over with intensity. Her arms waved about without thought and she laughed maniacally into the gale.

Addy sensed the anger.

The energy is unwilling. That can't be right. What do I know?

"Rach?" she shouted into the wind.

"Rachel! You're at the end of the cliff. Stop!" Her concern was real.

Rachel's senses returned, she calmed her hand movements, the intensity dissipated. The gale turned back to a harmless breeze. Finally, Rachel turned to Addy.

"It's exhilarating! The angrier it gets the more energy it generates. I love it!" she shouted.

"How do you do it?" Addy wasn't sure she wanted to know.

"The anger?" Rachel questioned surprised, but did not wait to be corrected, "as you command the energy you pump it with your own anger, pain, darkness, jealousy. Anything you have. We all have dark in us. I use the magic to serve my purpose. The dark feeds it. It's powerful." She lamented.

Addy walked towards Rachel, "No. I meant, how do you pull the energy to you?"

"Oh. Easy. My affinity is with air. The energy in the air will attract to me and my own energy. The proportion that I can control will be equally matched to that which comes to my bidding."

"That was a lot of energy." Addy was wary.

Rachel smiled, pleased she had noticed.

"Sure was, you should see me with fire." Addy just smiled, trying to appreciate the information.

"So, can you draw more energy than you can control?" Addy asked.

"It can happen. But it usually only does when you have been suppressing the energy. When you arrived on the farm, you looked in pretty bad shape" Rachel looked away, "You probably hadn't used power in a long time. What you dispelled was done in survivor mode. It's like your magic has a protective streak built into it. The minute you feel threatened it activates."

"If I call magic, I can only get what I can control, is that right?" This was really important for Addy. The idea that she could not call it if she could not control it really appealed to her.

"Something like that. When I started training as a teen witch, I could only call a small wispy breeze, and you saw what I can do now. So, I assume, that as you grow stronger, you increase what you control".

They turned back to the dais and Addy's heart dropped.

Displayed on the solid wall as you face the dais with the cliffs at your back was a range of weaponry and other devices. Addy looked closer; ball and chain, swords, daggers, ancient athames, a cross bow, scythe, katana, halberd, heretic fork.

How the hell do I know this? This is not good energy. It vibration is low. Base.

Addy frowned.

Rachel had continued walking, oblivious to Addy's discomfort. She stopped now, and Addy sensed again the familiar energy Rachel pulled. This time it was only a moderate flow.

Not much fire energy.

Addy stored the information for herself.

Rachel gathered the energy to her as she had before, then

like a conductor, parted her palms quickly, the torches around the dais lit up simultaneously, a large orange flame curling on itself in the alter.

"What is this?" Addy gestured to the wall.

"Do you like it?" Again, Rachel didn't wait for an answer, "I found them in the attic. They intrigued me. I thought I'd display it here. I think it's part of the house's history"

Addy shuddered. It seemed out of place to her where the mountain energy was warm and comforting, but she didn't say anything.

Rachel walked through the dais clicking on the cold tiles. "We'll test you tomorrow Addy. Did you feel an affinity with air or fire?"

"I felt something. The energy, I think"

"Good. Perhaps you have an air affinity." She continued walking back to the workshop door, Addy followed in silence.

Later as Addy lay recounting the day, at the moment that you drift from wake to sleep, she heard Glock and Ferris bantering in the periphery of her mind.

"Do you think Glock, that she'll feel it?"

"Well, we do. Can't see why she wouldn't."

"Do you remember the first time? What was it like?"

"Ah Ferris! I can't find the words. It's like the universe is in perfect harmony, singing joyously and then, you're in it. You know it. It knows you!"

"Yes." Thought Addy, "It's exactly like that." She smiled and snuggled deeper into her warm sheets.

The blazing red tattoos on a familiar figure sirened out in Addy's dreams. A woman chanted against the howling winds.

"Igarrro, shintato, anviglati"

The woman shouted over and over, chanting and swaying, her arms outstretched. The veins stood out on her throat. Her black cloak whipped around, the symbols on her arms and the back of her hands pulsated dark and deadly as they stood out, burning into Addy's memory. The symbols cast red reflections on the whipped, churned up water.

The froth, turned into wolverines which clung onto the waves before being whipped away on the gale force wind. The chant went on and on,

> "Igarro, shintato, anvilgati,
> Igarro, shintato, anvilgati,
> Igarro, shintato, anvilgati"

The words were forced out of her hoarse throat, faster and faster. Over and over in Addy's mind, the words echoed as the woman screeched them into the wind.

A large circular flatness formed on the ocean surface, the wind died suddenly and in the black mirror of the dark sea, a pale eerie reflection bobbed and wavered, laughing hysterically...

Verity stared straight at her. Addy sat up, sweat poured off her, bad energy lingered in the room.

T hick grey clouds hung low in the sky. Addy was tired, the chanting and hysterical laughter prevented her from drifting back to sleep.

I'd rather be in bed, in the warm house. I don't want to be tested!

Rachel was insistent, "There's no time to spare. The moon is at its best phase now. New witches need the extra power."

Addy was too tired to question her.

Where is Dane anyway? He's avoiding me! Stubborn man!

Rachel worked in silence and slowly weaved a web of energy in a dome around them. A training net. Addy felt comfortable that Rachel had thought of it.

The cliffs were obscured with cloud and the energy from the previous day seemed to brood expectantly. Down below the brooding mass, Addy still felt the low vibration from the weaponry and torture instruments, it beat slowly, out of sync with the mountains and the sky. Addy glanced back, ensuring that the malevolent energy remained on the wall.

Rachel wore jeans and a grey shirt today. No spectacular drama against the purple haze. Just practical.

No show today.

Rachel stood with bent knees and gathered energy to her.

She then moved the energy over-head and slowly weaved the threads through one another. Addy had never seen power used like this. She saw the net build slowly. It was much like the bubble she woke under when she first arrived.

When Addy glazed her eyes over she could see the magic strands, orange threads intertwined above them.

"That should do it" Rachel straightened up and stretched, "we probably won't need it, but rather safe than sorry" Rachel said acidly.

"Sorry again" Addy said softly, "the shed's nearly back to normal".

"Never mind that. Let's do this" Rachel brushed off.

Evil child! Killer! Addy's memory was strong, Verity practically brainwashed her into thinking this was evil.

"Rachel. I don't think I-"Addy started.

"Nonsense" Rachel held her palm out towards Addy, "Remember how helpless you were when poor Dane was writhing in pain? Remember that Addy?" Rachel stared into her eyes. "Of course, you can do this." Rachel was firm and dismissive of Addy's concerns.

"Now, we'll start really small. My training started like this. Most witches do. I have four candles around us. I want you to concentrate on the energy around. Visualize the wicks taking flame and burning. Use the energy around you. You may only light one for now, one is good."

Addy closed her eyes and let her senses out, feeling for energy on the air. Immediately she felt it. It was always there, had been for as long as she could remember, she had just never engaged it with purpose. Her senses shivered, she sensed the power but was hesitant to pull it in.

"When you sense the energy Addy, gather it. Command it" Rachel advised softly not to break Addy's concentration, "the hard part is sensing the energy, take your time" she continued reassuringly.

Addy frowned.

I always sense the energy. It's not hard. Commanding it is the hard part. I know! I'll ask it! I'll ask the energy!

She smiled to herself.

Of course, don't tell! Ask!

"Come on Addy, quit fooling around, concentrate, I know you can light at least *a* candle today." Rachel was bored, Addy sensed it in her dismissive tone.

The energy swished around Addy, caressed her. It brushed around and around her, flowed through her. Addy thought of Mrs. Harris's cat, Count Pushkin, he would purr and writhe between Addy's legs, "that's what the energy does" she smiled happiness bubbling into her torso.

"Come on Count" she whispered, "let's do this!"

Addy pulled the energy into her, it was effervescent and alive and warm it flowed through her energy centre, lighting her up. She raised her arms in a dance of joy and in her mind, she chanted,

It is my wish,
If you may,
Let us together,
Light these candles today!

Addy twirled around happily, brushing in and out of the magic strands, she knew without opening her eyes that the candles were lit, she felt the energy spark around her and laughed spontaneously.

"What? How did you do that?" Rachel was lost for words, "Addy? Have you done this before? Were you lying?" Rachel's words were snappy and accusatory.

No joy.

Addy thought again of Verity.

"No. I haven't" she looked around her, subduing her happiness. All the candles were lit, all the torches on the dais were lit, the fire was roaring in the altar. Addy still sensed the energy lingering around her. She checked with her magic view that the net was still in place.

"It must be a stroke of luck. Well, fire is your affinity then! Not many of you around" Rachel was dismissive, "I Should have started with the other elements, to build up to your crescendo. Now, it may be that your proud moment in magic is already behind you. Don't be disheartened Addy" Rachel advised.

Addy felt the power whisper across her, she let herself be embraced, enfolded. The first time in her life Addy felt alive with power in her, through her, around her.

Just like the voice, Glock, the universe is in me, I am in the universe.

"Come Addy, concentrate on the energy around us, call a breeze" Rachel threw out the challenge, "you need to use strands of magic to start the movement, then if you have an elemental affinity for air, the energy from the air will combine with your magic strands and you can get the element and the energy therein to do your bidding, if you have no air affinity, you should still be able to move the air immediately around us, like a quick whoosh" Rachel's instructions were delivered in a no-nonsense voice. "Can you see the magic strands?" She asked.

"Yes"

"Okay, good start! Just bid them move" Rachel's arms were folded, she tapped the fingers of her right hand on her arm in a frustrated gesture, "it's your will and your power at the test now. As you hone your skills you may be stronger but just get a small puff of air around us."

Addy instinctively bowed to the mountains, smiling to herself. Rachel had walked over to the wall of evil weapons, Addy turned her back on the ominous hum emanating from that side. She raised her arms up above her head in a salute, immediately the power rushed towards her. She heard Rachel gasp in shock.

The energy filled Addy as before, this time it was fresh and playful. It swirled around her, a soft peppermint mist of magic strands. She pulled in more, not yet sure how much was needed for a puff of wind. Addy noted that this was not the playful stream she had dealt with before, it was distinctively different, introverted and cool but still wanting to dance and perform. The grey sky provided a spectacular stage.

"Ooh cool elegance" she whispered. The magic strands glowed as they twirled in the rich mountain air, "a charmer" Addy giggled, totally absorbed in the dance.

I am in the universe, and it's in me.

Addy lifted her face into the energy and then a deep, instinctive thought unfurled as the energy swelled around her, Addy took a deep breath, air she thought, in me, I am in it.

Addy gently inhaled the energy charged air, closing her eyes, letting the power infuse her, she felt it build from below her feet, through her body, the air travelled inside of her, up and up towards her head and then gently, smiling, Addy pursed her lips and slowly exhaled.

Her breath fanned out and curled on itself pulling energy around with it. The breeze that flowed from Addy was light and it pirouetted with graceful purpose on the mountain top. It eddied around and swirled the grass in its playful tango. Addy gracefully looped her wrists in swirling movements and the breeze performed, it swished around Rachel, lifting her hair and then raced across the mountain, red poppies and white camomiles bowed their heads in the dance of happiness as fairy lights twinkled and glowed. Addy laughed, happy and for a moment carefree. The power sang through her veins, racing through her body.

I'm letting it get to my head! No! I must not get used to this, it will lure me to its power and I will hurt someone!

Addy immediately shut down the power. The strands lost their energy and the light breeze disappeared as fast as it had come.

The grey sky remained sullen and full, dark pockets of cloud slowly curling around the enlarging mass of churning grey.

"Never mind, it looks like rain, we better get back. Enough for today. You're probably exhausted." Rachel turned towards the dais and started walking quickly, she said nothing and once back in the workshop, she let Addy out and locked herself in her grey cave.

"Dane?" Addy called out as she entered the kitchen. It was cold, no fire or heat welcomed her. "Dane? You here?" Addy called out into the empty living room. Silence hung around her. Addy ran up the stairs and knocked on Dane's door, "Dane? Dane?" She pushed the door open but again stillness hung in the air.

Addy lit a fire in living room, put a lasagna in the oven for their dinner and when the silence became overwhelming, ran a hot bath.

So much has changed, just weeks ago, I only had silence for company, now I miss conversation!

She sank back into the luxurious water and let her mind linger on the joy of the energy she felt earlier.

***

Not far away, in the intricate Fellana Cave System, Verity sat alone in a circular room. The amber liquid in her glass alive with the hues from the fire. Her pale hand massaged her throat. She pulled her mouth down in distaste, the skin there, soft again. She'll have to see Ehruh. She needed to be young, taut.

"Take the child from your sister. Wait for her power. When it comes, I'll have her" she recalled the deal with Ehruh. "And, in return I'll take care of you. You will always be beautiful as in your prime" he had gently caressed her cheek.

But Adera had no power. Oh, something was there, but not what Ehruh wanted. No. The old Demon wanted *The Power*. Quinary power.

Fool. If Adera had that power, I wouldn't need you and your

damn elix*ir*. She shuddered recalling the price she paid for her looks.

Verity moved restlessly, filling her glass. She tinkered the ice; thinking.

It had all seemed simple at the time. She would help Zyklon to release his partner, Grindal from prison on Thear; in turn Zyklon would look for the all-powerful Quinarian child.

It surely could not be Adera? She had no power. She would have blasted us away after the torture she endured. No, it's definitely not Adera.

If it wasn't for Marjory; I would never be in this mess now. I would still have my power, I would still be beautiful; youthful. It's all Marjory's fault.

And Zyklon, "The three of us V; the power of three, we'll progress in unity, we'll rule the Earth" she mimicked, clicking her tongue.

"More fool. If we find the child; I can take all the power. I can rule the worlds, Thear and Earth and anything in between" she shouted at the fire.

What the hell am I going to tell him? Not only does she not have the power but she's also escaped!

The thick door muffled the knock. She barely heard it.

"Go away" who would disturb her this time of the night? Unless, they found Adera or the power child? Her breath quickened.

She yanked the door open.

Colonel Geffroi's daughter.

"Rachel?" She pumped warmth into her tone, sensing this was a calculated visit.

"Verity. I have news" Verity pulled the door wider, peeked up and down the passage and then quickly closed it behind Rachel.

"Did anyone see you come in here?"

Rachel shook her head.

Verity poured her a drink while Rachel stood in the centre of the room, silently arguing with herself.

"Here, you go. Please have a seat" Verity sat in her winged back arm chair.

***

"Addy, Addy! Wake up! Goddammit, you sleep like the dead! Addy?"

She heard the urgency.

"Dane? What?"

"Addy! Wake up!"

"Just give me a sec. I only just fell asleep! What do you want? Where have you been? Are you okay?" The questions reeled into her mind as her senses awoke.

"Listen Addy, listen carefully" Dane was serious, he gripped her upper arms and then sat beside her earnestly.

"What is it?"

"Geez, I don't even know where to start." He pulled his hands through his hair."

"I should have told you this a while ago but you know?" He looked at her, "I didn't know if you were the right person! You didn't use your power. And you were so messed up and you were lost. You were so hurt Addy." The emotion choked at him, "I just wanted you to feel what normal was before it got all crazy again. Please understand?"

"Dane. What do you need to tell me?" Addy's heart beat low in her chest, the anxiety slowly building.

Dane jumped up and paced, wringing his hands, "Addy, I have been sent here to bring you back. I am on a mission for the Quinary."

"The Quinary" Addy repeated the word now familiar to her. "The Quinary?"

"Yes! The Quinary!"

"Dane you're not making any sense"

"Okay. Let me try another tact." He spoke to himself, "What do you know of the Quinary?"

"Nothing. I have heard the word, that's all"

"Where did you hear it?"

"Never-mind"

"This is going to sound bizarre. Just hear me out." He started pacing wildly.

"There is another planet, called Thear. On it, there exists a Council called the Quinary." Dane stopped pacing and crouched beside the bed,

"The Quinary is made up of five individuals, pure of heart. One is the keeper of time, one looks after the earth, one guards the lakes and seas, and one the skies and the last Quinarian, Addy, well, it's a long story which we don't have time for, but the fifth Quinarian has been missing since the beginning of time"

"What? Dane? I think you're insane!"

Dane rested his hands on her shoulders he looked at her deeply,

"Addy. The family who were supposed to receive the fifth Quinarian power, is your family. But things happened, big things. And, well, in a nutshell, the power was enhanced and then shot out of the galaxy"

"Dane. Have you hit your head?"

Dane shook his head, exasperated.

"Addy-"

"Have you been drinking? Or other drugs?"

"No. Addy? Listen to me"

"Dane. How can what you say be possible? I live on Earth. What other planets are you going on about?"

I can't even believe I am having this conversation.

"Since the beginning of time, there has been hope that the essence would return to Thear and find its destiny. When it didn't, Addy, it put pressure on the family. Your mother is a twin."

"What? Are you saying that my m-mother, Verity is a twin?"

"Addy. Your mother Marjory's twin is Verity"

Addy leaped from her seat on the bed, "What? How do you

know this? Dane?" Addy felt as though she had just been knifed, "Tell me."

"What are you saying? Dane?" The confusion built in her mind. Dane wasn't explaining quick enough.

"Addy you're not focusing on the important thing here"

"What is that? I just found out that the cruelest person in the world who until now I had thought to be my mother is not, and you think I am missing a main focus?" Addy was snappy.

"Addy, you have the power of the fifth Quinarian!"

"Does that mean my real mother has died?" Addy started breathing deeply to obtain control.

"No Addy. Your mother, Marjory is well and alive."

"Dane are you sure you're okay?"

Dane's eyes were dark and imploring and Addy knew that he spoke what he believed.

Addy's eyes welled up, the lump in her throat constricting her voice, "Where is she? Why did she leave me? How is that even possible?" Addy's voice was just a whisper.

"Verity had some power, she was born to magic after all, but Marjory had greater power. Marjory fell in love and well, long story short, you were born."

"Oh my God!" Addy whispered.

"MOS, Ehruh, the Celestials; most seers declared that you were born to receive the Quinary power. Verity was jealous" Dane went quiet for a moment, thinking.

"Verity was consumed with jealousy. She killed Ivan, your grand-dad, and as insurance, she stole you from Marjory and ran away. She had her power stripped from her. The Quinary Council can do that. It is locked away in a secret location." Dane looked out of the window anxiously.

"Verity paid for an illegal portal to Earth. We never saw her again. But, we have been looking for power surges here. Hoping, to find the fifth Quinarian. Verity knows you have power, but she doesn't think you're the Quinarian."

Tears pooled in Addy's eyes and streamed down her cold cheeks.

"Come here Addy" Dane wrapped her in his arms and rested his chin on her head, gently swaying her.

Addy felt warm and comforted. She wallowed in the human touch.

She felt so small. So, vulnerable. She felt Dane swallow hard.

"Addy, we have to leave. Now. You are in danger" Dane barely whispered the words.

"No. No" Addy was firm, shaking her head as she pulled away from Dane, "I have to learn more, how to protect us, how to defend us. Dane, I have only just started"

"Addy, you need to be trained by a master. Other Quinarians. We need to get you through the portal"

"Dane. What if I'm not the Quinarian. What if you're mistaken? How do you know all this stuff?"

"I told you I work for the Quinary. I am from Thear. I can communicate with the guys there. Believe me Addy."

"It's a lot to take in. What about Rachel. She can help me?"

"Addy, we're not sure which side Rachel is on"

"That's bizarre! This isn't a war!"

Dane gripped her wrist, "Addy, do not underestimate this. People have been killed trying to get at your power. Do you understand the gravity of this?"

His tone had gone cold, hard. Addy shivered.

"Verity in her ignorance has actually protected you by convincing you not to use it. Other magical beings can feel when you dissipate vast amounts of power. It ripples through us Addy."

"You?" She asked, "you have power too?"

"Not the same kind. It's another long story, not for this time around."

"Dane, how long have you known?" Addy needed to know, "About me, and Verity?"

Dane looked sheepish.

"What? Tell me." She insisted.

"I was sent to get the Quinarian. I expected to come home with a young warrior, skilled in their art. Ready to take their place" he looked uncomfortable.

"Ferris insisted you were the Quinarian. I didn't believe him. I watched you. You never used power. I looked around. I've searched for months now" he rubbed the back of his neck.

"That's how you ended up here. Rachel has power?" Addy guessed.

He nodded.

"Your magic is flowing again. I can feel it even as I stand here. Your memory will return, the ether's memory. You have a living Grimoire in your DNA, you will know exactly what to do in regard to magic. Just trust it. But now, Addy, we need to get you out of here. We must talk to the Thearians, they will make a plan to get you there, home."

"And, and my mother?" Addy asked

"On Thear. We need to get to Thear" Dane answered.

"Thear? Another planet?"

Dane nodded.

"How?" Addy could hardly believe she was having this conversation.

"A few ways. Most folk with magic can use a portal. They transfer you magically into another place. Some people have the skill to create a portal. If we contact the Quinary they can guide us to where a portal may already be and we can simply use that."

Addy felt overwhelmed. Hope sparked in her. She paced a few steps away.

"Dane, I want to talk to Rachel. Warn her. Let her know what is going on"

"Addy…"

"No, listen. She may be conflicted but we owe her the courtesy of letting her know. She won't hurt us Dane. She would have done that already!"

"Dammit Addy! This was not in the plan!"

"She helped me! I have never owned clothes. I have never

slept in a real bed! Dane, I owe her the courtesy of at least saying goodbye. And, more, I have to think on what you have told me. It sounds like a mad story! I need until tomorrow."

"Addy, tomorrow is the new moon. Verity and Zyklon. They need your power to strengthen themselves. We have been watching them. Something isn't right! You need to be careful!"

"We can talk at breakfast. I just need to see Rachel" Addy was adamant.

"Fine." He ran his hands through his hair again. Addy saw that he was really tired.

"Thanks Dane" she turned him to the door, "get some sleep, you look terrible!"

The door frame was cold against her shoulder, the dawn's thin arrival crept along the horizon,

A real mum!

The tears welled in her eyes as the emotion swelled through her chest.

I wish I had known. All those nights of sleeping in the corner of the living room of Verity's apartment, strangers coming and going, trying to make myself invisible. Wishing, always wishing that she would just comfort me. Keep me warm.

Addy's thoughts flicked through moments where she would have sacrificed anything for the simple touch of her mother. She brushed her loose strands from her face.

But you are real.

The crisp morning air settled on her as she stood watching the sunrise.

You missed my first day of school, and my last. And when I got the prize for English.

Addy's tears flowed freely down her face.

You missed telling me about growing up and I missed hugs and someone to have my back. I missed coming home to you and wanting to make you proud. I missed you.

What do you look like? I wonder if you smell like a mum? I hope you like gardening. And making pancakes?

Addy smiled wiping the tears with the heel of her hand.

"I hope you don't hate me. I have magic" the whisper misted the air as Addy wiped the last of her tears and walked towards the bed, perching on the edge.

I have magic. Lots of magic.

What do I do? Dane's surely gone completely nuts. A mum, in another dimension? A Quinarian? What do I believe? Think Addy!

She admonished herself.

Verity has taken so much from me. Enough now.

Addy curled into a small ball pulling the warm comforter over her, as the sun rose higher in the sky, Addy thought of her mum, her real mum and smiled in her sleep, "I will find you" she whispered in slumber.

7

Years of wear and weather smoothed the cobblestones between the kitchen door and Rachel's workshop. The cold afternoon reflected from each stone; more shades of grey.

"Hello?" The house and shed were quiet, the cold wind eddied around Addy's feet, the weak sun not yet reaching the courtyard.

The red archway marking Rachel's domain stood stark in contrast to the day. She knocked loudly, "Rach?" The door inched open, "Rachel?" Addy pushed through, "Ra... Dane?"

"Oh my god, Dane?" Addy rushed over, "Dane"

"Addy don't" Dane warned.

Addy stopped, holding her sobs in, "What happened?"

Dane, naked, had his back to the wall, black pedestals extending out of the wall held his hands, palm up to the ceiling, seemingly without any constraint. His neck clamped against the wall was tilted up that his chin pointed upwards. His feet, hip distance apart appeared to be free.

"Dane. What's going on?"

"I am tied with magic. Rachel is working with Zyklon. You must leave immediately. Please go now?" Dane was clipped and to the point.

"No! Let me untie you"

"Addy! No. Leave at once"

"Ssh Dane. I need to concentrate" Addy refocused her vision and then as the shock of what she saw rolled through her, she fell to her knees.

A murky green energy field orbited Dane's head, keeping it in a specific place so that a strong red beam, powering from the ceiling entered his head between his eyebrows. Pulsing beams travelled invisible paths from the ceiling into Dane's palms which were held in place by two separate murky green orbits. His feet were clamped to the floor by the same green orbits and a figure of eight power torch, kept circling his ankles.

"Dane..." Addy choked back a sob, the deep orange band of power around Dane's chest tightened as Addy watched. He winced as he drew in a sharp breath.

"Where is the energy source?" She felt helpless, cold chills running up her arms, she wished the window covered in the red blind was open so that air could wake her up.

"I think it's the panel in the ceiling, but Addy, I can sort this out, please go, run." Dane was frustrated and pleading with her.

Addy studied the energy surrounding Dane, it hummed with a low base, "just like the torture wall outside" she muttered. The individual strands of energy were familiar but tainted somehow, Addy watched them move from the ceiling into Dane and out again, "It's your own energy being used to charge the panels in the ceiling, floor and wall. It circulates your own energy back on you!"

"Thanks." Dane spoke up to the ceiling, "useful information" he quipped sarcastically.

"It is! Your energy is being cycled through these black panels which charges it with, well with something not good"

Addy moved closer to Dane, "Will you stop looking at me?" He was curt.

"Not you, energy..." Addy concentrated, "how do I pull your energy from you? Create a vacuum?" She spoke to herself.

"Addy, for Skenka's sake! Give it up! Please go, now!" Dane pleaded to the ceiling frustrated.

"How could Rachel?" Addy's eyes filled with tears.

Sweat glistened over Dane's body, pain twitched his muscles, his thighs barely holding his weight. Sweat rolled down his brow.

"Dane, I am so scared. Every time I use magic, something bad happens. What if? What if?" Addy could not finish the sentence.

"Dane, I have never…" her eyes brimmed with tears.

"Ssh! If you insist on trying to help, just do it, now!" He realized she was not going to walk away,

The fatigue was evident in Dane's voice. Addy breathed deeply, her eyes darted around the room looking for help in any form. A scrying bowl sat on the bench, its liquid thick and dark and deadly still, Addy's eyes jumped to the athame block, the athame was missing.

The click of the outer door was like a gunshot to Addy's nerves. Goosebumps ran down her spine.

"Oh! We have a visitor." Verity's voice was high pitched, "I knew you would come. *So,* predictable" she trilled. "What do you think of our new decoration?" She waved at Dane, "fine specimen isn't he?" Verity walked over to Dane, heels clicking on the hard floor, and ran her hand down his chest, tapering her caress to one long dark purple fingernail that lingered on Dane's exposed genitals.

Rage rolled in the pit of Addy's stomach.

Rachel held her palms to the fire, ignoring Verity's solo act.

"Rachel? What's going on?" Addy's voice sounded scared, even to her own ears.

Verity's energy surged through Dane and recycled a stronger current back into him. His sinewy muscles tautened and buckled in pain as his legs gave way beneath him.

Rachel's smile was ominous, "Don't play stupid Addy, we all know you need to give your power to your mother" she nodded to Verity, "it's long overdue. Dane, as beautiful as he is to behold" she flickered her eyes over Dane's body 'is simply bait!"

"Rachel?" Addy whined, "we were all friends. What happened?"

"Ah Addy! Opportunity came knocking! You are my ticket out of this hell hole!"

"Rach? Please. Please, help Dane? I know you are a good person, please do the right thing?"

"Please do the right thing" Verity snickered in a nasal voice, "you were always such a goody goody, such an irritating child!"

Addy would previously had winced at Verity's harsh words, "Please let him go! I'm here now!"

"Ha ha ha" Verity laughed coldly, "just like your mother, always the sacrificial lamb" Verity sneered as she walked towards Addy.

"Where is my mother?" Addy challenged

"Oh! You're remembering things! Interesting." Verity stopped just out of Addy's reach. Addy saw the set jaw and the steel glint in her eye,

"It's not too late. Verity" she emphasized the name, "you can still help. Where is she?" Addy's heart raced wildly, the torches flickered across Verity's face. Addy felt the anger and bitterness roll off of her.

Thunder rolled in the distance, Dane's forehead pointed straight up to the ceiling and red power flowed into his head, his knees were on the floor and his hands pinned to the black pedestals above his head now.

"Fool! It's wasted on you. You have no confidence, you will never be strong enough to command it! I am meant for bigger things." Verity stabbed herself in her chest repeatedly, "I am the one. Me." Anger flustered her, "You" she sneered, "are nothing."

Verity turned towards the fire, visibly struggling with her anger.

"Why?" Addy whispered.

"Do not question me girl." Verity seethed, "you have not

tasted power as I have! You do not know its promise." She turned to Rachel, spittle gathered in the corners of her mouth.

"Add more power," she commanded.

"No" Addy's heart hammered, her hands waved automatically, an old memory triggered.

Addy felt the shield she created, it slammed up as a barrier between Rachel and Verity and her and Dane. In her peripheral vision, she saw Dane fall against the wall, released from his hold of magic. Rachel's power pushed against the shield and Addy felt the air whoosh around but the barrier stood firm.

Rachel's surprise was evident as she turned to pull more power, the room grew quiet. Zyklon's image wavered above the scrying bowl, as though he was sitting at the table, steepling his fingers. His pale hologram face held a smirk of amusement, his dead black eyes, like shiny beetles shone across the miles.

"Well, well. An interesting turn of events! Using a lick of power Addy! I can taste it" he bit into his tongue and in Zyklon's image of black hair and white face, red blood ran from his mouth, "I like it"

Addy shuddered, fear creeping into her limbs, "you've become an interesting distraction" his black eyes ran down her body as he licked the blood from his lips, "I'm looking forward to another taste" he laughed eerily. "You will wait for me" he was smug and assured in his tone, "you know why?" He leant forward in the image, "because I control your mother" he smiled, his skew lip sneering up on the right, "you want to meet mummy, don't you Addy?" He sat back, "play nice now," he kissed his two fingers and held his hand up to Addy.

Addy felt the emotion seeping into her, anger and fear pooled in her abdomen, she started to shake. Dane's eyes moved where he lay half clamped to the wall, warning her to keep still.

Zyklon wavered and turned on the bench top, "Rachel" he spoke in his quiet sickly tone, "I'm coming for a visit darling. Be a good girl and be kind to Addy. She's our special guest" he spoke like a petulant child, glimpsing back to Addy, "and recall how you can show me your allegiance?" Rachel nodded, eager to please, "there's my girl" he purred in approval.

Before Addy could fully comprehend what was happening, Rachel pulled a beam of power, Addy felt the air quiver, Zyklon smiled gleefully, she directed it quick as a whip to Dane.

"Ah" Dane's body bucked and writhed in the air, on his abdomen a long red line appeared and as the power dissipated, the line opened, muscle and sinew peeked through before blood rushed in and down the side of Dane's body. He slumped down.

"No!" Addy's scream was primal, she pulled the power available to her and they all came. The gentle and the energized, the helix and the matriarch, they all came instantly, Addy rushed to Dane's side covering the wound with her hand, "help me, help me!" she sobbed.

In a blink, Addy instinctively transported her and Dane to the cliff edge, sun struggled to break through the dark clouds, Zyklon's cackle reverberated in the air. She held Dane rocking him like a baby. "No, no, no" she wailed, the wind whipped the noise away.

A voice, her own, yet rational, spoke calmly, "put your hand on the wound, sense it" Addy obeyed, she wiped at the tears, smearing blood across her face. She closed her eyes and let her energy feel its way through Dane. She sensed the severed membranes, sniffed at her tears, "I don't know what to do. I'm so sorry." She sobbed, Addy saw Dane's hand move slightly over hers, keeping her hand in place. She let her energy flow into Dane, she felt the pain sear through her body but kept her energy pouring into him.

"Please be okay" she sobbed, "Please"

"Ssh, I'm okay" his voice was hoarse and low.

"Dane" Addy rested her forehead on his, "I don't know how to help you"

"It's okay. We don't have much time, I can help myself, just give me a hand" he panted in pain

"Okay, tell me what to do. Keep still. You're still bleeding a bit".

"Bossy" he smiled, "Addy. Remember in the cave?" He licked his lips, they were dry and cracked. Addy nodded confused.

"How do you know about that?"

"Aquilae" Addy nodded remembering the stranger who helped her escape.

"You know Aquilae?" she prompted.

"I am Aquilae" Dane said. Addy gasped.

She looked into Dane's eyes, "I knew you were familiar" she smiled, "Never got to thank you" she whispered.

"More" he whispered

"There's more?" Dane nodded

"I am an eagle. Shape shift" he was struggling.

"What?"

"Help me. Turn me on my side" he winced

Addy moved him onto his side.

"Addy" Dane spoke towards the ground, "I need to shift. I will heal faster that way" he paused struggling for breath, "when I have shifted, catch the energy highway. You will know how" he smiled, "trust yourself. Go to Fengray Village. Find Grit. He will help you get to Thear. Find Glock"

"Dane?" Addy sobbed, "will I see you again?"

"Of course, count on it! Must be my irresistible charm, right?" he smiled.

"Yeah right! Can I help you?" she asked.

"Just be careful" he closed his eyes.

Addy saw Dane transform in front of her. She felt the slight ripple in the air and a beautiful eagle, the same one that accompanied her through the forest all those weeks ago, stared at her, "Wow" she smiled. The eagle bowed its head.

The sun broke through the clouds, Aquilae nudged her leg.

"I'm going" she whispered, "I'm just trying to remember how"

"A tree at three" she mumbled, "Oh, my. I am losing my mind." Aquilae pecked her leg.

"All right." Addy walked to the cliff edge and climbed the two metres down to the beautiful old tree. "This better work. What's the bloody time?"

Addy's magic vision shifted into place and a golden highway shimmered in the air and dipped down just next to the tree. She smiled amazed.

"You coming?" A man in a tall hat and coat tails saluted her, "yes, yes. How?" She asked, "Step on lass, be open" he suggested.

Addy looked up to the cliff edge, Aquilae took to the skies. As Addy stepped on the golden highway she heard the eagle's cry follow her on the breeze.

Her heart contracted.

8

"First time?" The man in the tall hat spoke in a low comforting voice. He had a strong British accent. He stood next to a silver post that floated vertically above the highway.

"Yes" she smiled shyly, blood stiffening her face.

"I'm the Highwayman" he offered

"I'm Addy. How does this work, the energy highway? How does it know where I want to go? Where are the other people? Who can catch it?" Addy got carried away.

"It's magic, lass" he leant down low, conspirationally, "we used to be a lot busier. But folk now, don't believe anymore. They forgot, I think, how to use their power." He became contemplative as he rocked on his heels, his hands caught behind his back. "We're always here. You've just got to be at the right place at the right time to hop on. You say where you want to go. Then leave it to the universe to get you there. Just pure magic." He beamed with light.

"We've never had an incident on my time. Incident free I am. I don't count that time when them lads were playing silly buggers." He smiled reminiscing, "thought they could bleeding shape-shift right here on me patch of highway. Rascals" he smiled fondly.

"What happened?" Addy needed the distraction; Dane's parting left her raw.

"Well, the highway, you will know from your studies," he lifted his eyebrow at her, "is powered by energy. Some say directly from the Celestials, energy moves you through the atmosphere, the ether is thick and powerful on the highway" he was proud and radiant, "shape-shifting is a quick magic at the instant you change" his hands twirled over each other, "or so I am told, anyway. The magic burst is enhanced on the highway, due to the power around. The boys shifted with such a force that it blew their feathers clean off of them." he laughed out loud, "they moved from boys to eagle and hawk and back to boys, the feathers flew all around them. No clothes to change back into. Naked as the day they were born. Ha! Never got to their game, they had to wait for the round back to their homes. Funny that was." He stared into the warm horizon. "Yes. Yes, well. It won't do to day dream now. Will it?" His eyebrows wiggled under his tall hat. "Say where you're headed, out loud, lass. I haven't had such a good chat in many years. As I said, not many folks on here these days."

"I am going to see Grit" Addy spoke aloud. The light changed ever so subtly and Addy felt the sinking feeling in her belly when you go down a steep hill rather quickly. The outside world came into her peripheral vision, buildings materialized, people could be seen about. Addy looked down and realized that she looked as though she were floating, even though she felt a solid floor beneath her feet. "Oh my!" she exclaimed as the energy dipped.

The kitchen was warm and cozy. The pale lemon walls provided a soft glow and the faded tablecloth's whole lemon and olives hinted of happy, lemonade summers that Addy always yearned for. The mismatched chairs scattered around the table, behind which a bookcase squeezed in just out of reach. Jamie Oliver and Hugh Furnley-Whittingstall propped each other up next to a raft of romance novels.

An old basket on the kitchen top held potatoes and onions,

someone was halfway through selecting them. In the window-sill a lone daisy craned its stem to peek its simple white blossoms to the top of a chipped, clear glass vase. An agar stood to the right and a round dog bed, bone decorated, waited beside it for its furry master.

Addy looked out of the kitchen window, a small garden showcased purple sage, the dainty hands of Thyme and further down, the vertical backdrop of Rosemary, basking in the afternoon glow.

Heavy steps thumped on wooden floors above her, people spoke loudly, "I'll be back by dinner time mum!"

"Be careful, dear!"

The kitchen door swung open, adrenalin pooled in Addy's stomach, "How can she explain?"

"What the....?"

The man was young, he had a curly mop of copper curls above a pleasant face. His eyes flashed steel blue, the stubble dark red on his strong jaw. He was tall, at least six foot five, Addy guessed and his dark blue t-shirt spanned across his chest as he grabbed the broomstick from behind the door, holding Addy against the cold stainless-steel fridge.

Addy pleaded palms up, afraid, "please don't hurt me? I can explain!" Her heart fluttered in panic as she felt her magic swirl across her brow.

She realized her appearance would raise questions, blood splattered clothes, knotted, ratty hair, smears across her face.

"Please? Just a minute?" She pleaded, the broom handle's pressure was digging into her clavicles.

The door swung open again.

"Stay back mum!" the man snapped.

"What?" She was tall and yet, petite. Her strawberry blond hair sat in a messy bun atop her head, reading glasses swayed on a beaded chain above the curve of her chest. Her mouth, full was the focal point of her beautiful face and Addy had the fleeting thought that she must have elven blood in her. Fine sun lines said the garden was hers. Linen trousers and a pale pink shirt that read, "I drink wine, naked" made Addy instantly like her.

"Gavin! It's just a girl! What are you doing?" She smacked his shoulder.

"I can't feel or see anything bad here!" She took the broomstick from his hand.

"Mum! She could be…"

"What? Scared witless? In absolute panic? Do you see an evil creature of the dark?" She snapped at him.

"I apologise for my son. He is overprotective and a little melodramatic. Not without reason" she smiled, stowing the broomstick.

"Who are you? Why are you in our kitchen? Speak" he clipped

Addy's heart reeled, how do I even start explaining this?

"Dane, sent me. Aquilae? He said to find Grit?" She cut to the chase.

"Where is he? How is he?" His face transformed from a scowl to genuine concern.

"Mind your manners, Gavin" his mum intervened, "come and sit down, dear. I'll get us tea. It looks like you could use a cuppa. I know I surely could" she waved to the chairs.

"Do you mind if I freshen up first?" Fatigue was quickly replacing adrenalin, Addy felt the tiredness seeping in.

"Of course, dear! Out the door on the left" she tilted her head, frowning. "You look familiar".

"I'll show you" Gavin took her arm firmly.

He pushed the bathroom door open and then stood back folding his arms.

"I wouldn't have come if had intended running".

He tilted his head to one side in a half shrug. Addy closed the door on him.

"I would take a broomstick to you too" she told her reflection. Dane's blood had turned dark brown on her face, her clothes were blotched in crimson stains and her sticky hands had started to flake and scab with Dane's life essence.

She ran the basin full with warm water and immersed her face rubbing vigorously. After several long moments, Addy changed the water and repeated the process. The water formed rivulets off her face, wetting her shirt.

What am I doing here? What am I to tell them?

Addy unrolled the toilet paper mopping her hands and face. Can't soil the towels.

Large tiles covered the floor and walls, a shower enclosure sat behind her and a hand basin and toilet were the only utilities in the room. A French vanilla candle on the cistern emanated its smell without being lit. Addy opened the tiny waste basket and filled it with soggy paper towel. The door rattled.

"Coming" her nerves were springing to the fore again. She pulled her hands through her hair and retied it with an elastic band she took from Rachel. The thought instantly brought pain and anguish back.

Traitor.

She glanced at the sliding window above the toilet.

I could just run now. No. Dane needs help. My mother needs help. I need to get to Thear. If it really exists.

Addy took a deep breath, steadied her nerves and opened the door. She followed Gavin to the kitchen in silence.

"Ah! There we go! Have a seat dear, here's a lovely cuppa tea. My name is Meg. This bodyguard here, is my son, Gavin. His friends call him Grit" Meg confided thumbing at Grit who looked like storm clouds were gathering in his eyes. She offloaded three steaming mugs of tea.

"And you too dear" she spoke to Grit, "I am sure you have time for a quick cuppa" she pulled a chair out for Grit who lowered his tall frame gracefully down.

"I think I even have a few biscuits here" she rummaged in a tin and shook a few biscuits out, "ginger" she said sitting down with the plate.

"You can start" Grit gestured with his head.

Addy cupped her hands around the mug, behind Grit a lone butterfly hovered over the rosemary in Meg's garden.

"I don't even know where to start" her voice came from far away.

"Your name?" Grit prompted, Meg tapped his arm calmingly.

"Yes" she nodded. "My name is Addy"

Meg inhaled sharply and spilled tea over table. "Oh Merlin!" Meg stood up grabbing a yellow cloth from the end of the sink, mopping her tea. She stopped, stared at Addy.

"Addy!" She scooted over to Addy's side of the table, throwing the cloth onto the table. Her hands were warm and soft as she cupped Addy's cheeks.

"Addy" she whispered tears welling in her eyes.

"Mum?" Grit was concerned and clearly as confused as Addy felt.

"It's Addy" she whimpered, not making any more sense.

"Mum. Can you let Addy finish?" He asked.

"Yes of course" she sniffed returning to her seat. Addy glanced at Meg who smiled warmly.

"Dane, Aquilae" Addy smiled, "he came to help me escape from…." she faltered, "from…" Addy thought hard, Dane had been watching over her for a long time she realized.

"If Dane sent you, you will need to be more upfront than this" Grit wasn't won over yet.

Addy nodded, flashing him a look of annoyance. "My life is a tad complicated" she snapped, "I don't know if you even are Grit." She hissed back.

"True" he conceded, "I am" he stated. He considered a moment and then confided, "Gavin is my given name. It's derived from Gawain, meaning 'white hawk'" he let the information hang in the air a moment. Addy smiled, she envisioned the beautiful black eagle and the majestic white hawk soaring through the skies. She nodded to him in appreciation.

"Dane came to save me from Zyklon" she sipped her tea.

Meg visibly paled, putting her hand to her throat, "and, and my- Verity. He got hurt" her eyes welled as she recalled her helplessness and how Dane had almost died. "I couldn't move him like that" Grit sat forward,

"Where is he now?"

She sniffed, "he said he would heal better if he shifted. He said to find you, that you would open the portal"

"I told him he was friggin mad." Grit jumped up pulling his hands through his hair.

"Who are you Addy?" He was frustrated, "why would Dane risk his life for you? Do you know who he is?"

"Gav." Meg warned him.

"I am" Addy thought a moment, who am I? Her left, inner wrist seared in pain. Addy glanced down. A tattoo appeared first in golden lights and then it settled in beautiful ink. Four loops interlinked one another and then a fifth golden circle intersected them all. A beautiful Celtic knot.

Warmth invaded Addy.

"I have to see the Quinary" she whispered. Meg's tears streamed down her face. Grit leant on the back of the chair staring at her.

"Why?" He was clipped and disbelieving. "Did Dane feed you this?"

"He wants me to go to Thear, see the Quinary. At first I didn't believe him" she realized the truth dawning on her.

"And now? You've had an epiphany. And yet, my best friend and the k-, "he stopped himself, "Dane is missing and fatally hurt, and you suddenly want out? he started pacing, a muscle in his jaw pulsing wildly.

Meg jumped up, furrows on her brow. She pulled out a recipe book on the far back of the bookcase. She rifled through the pages as Grit and Addy looked on in silence. She held up her index finger, "Just a sec" she shuffled more paper around and came back to the table with an old photo.

"Lorna, Marjory and me" she handed the picture to Grit, he stared at it for a few moments and threw it down on the table.

"Lorna is Dane's mum. Marjory is yours Addy and then me" she explained.

Addy nodded focusing on the old picture. She looked like Marjory. Emotion welled in Addy's heart. Did she recognize that face? Was that the face in her visions and dreams?

Meg's voice explained in the background of Addy's reeling emotion, "we were best of friends, us three. Always together. Then Verity killed Ivan. For power. She killed Ivan" Meg was visibly reliving the shock. "She kidnapped Addy." Meg looked at Addy, tears welling in her eyes, "Marjory fell to pieces" Meg's voice was soft with emotion.

"Thatcher, my husband, got commissioned to the Earth portal. I haven't seen them since."

"Ivan?" Addy asked.

"Your granddad" Meg said.

Anger seared through Addy. She rubbed her forehead. "So, Marjory is definitely my mother? Not Verity?" Addy questioned.

"Oh my! You didn't know Marjory's is your mother?" Meg asked horrified.

"Dane told me" Addy dropped her head.

"So where exactly is *Dane*? Why are you here?" Grit cut to the chase.

"Dane is healing. Something about a Sky Dancer, Daria? He said to come here so that you can help me open a portal to Thear. See my mum and get trained by a master" she explained simply.

"How did Dane get hurt?"

"We were both living with another witch. She was our friend, we thought. She offered to help me with my magic. You see," she looked from one to the other, "I didn't know it was normal to have power. I have hidden it all my life. She said she could train me. Turns out, she's working for Zyklon."

"Ah! And Zyklon is in need of power right now" he finished.

Addy nodded.

"Who knows you're here dear?" Meg asked clearing cups away.

"The Highwayman."

"You want me to believe that?" Grit was outraged.

"Gav, honey."

Grit and Meg looked at one another, she nodded, squeezing his shoulder.

"Word on the ground has it that Zyklon's kidnapping magic folk and even those non-magic folks who have magic lineage" Grit confided, "He's up to something. I was on the way to a meeting when you arrived."

"Can you help me open a portal?" Addy asked the question on her mind.

"This is not something we do lightly" he looked at his mum, "in fact if you have any power it will be better used here, fighting Zyklon and his forces."

"Gav" Meg appealed to him.

"Jesus! Mum? You know nothing of her."

"Gavin. I know Marjory. I know here." Meg tapped her heart.

Grit grabbed his left shoulder with his right hand, massaging the tension there.

"I will need a circle. Standard process. I can only do it later. I have a meeting that I am already late for" he stood up, kissed his mum on the head and slammed the front door as he left.

"He'll be home later, love" Meg said glancing at the clock. She took more potatoes from the basket and stood to move the basket away.

"It's all a bit overwhelming" she spoke over her shoulder, "I'll send my cousin, Nessa, a text. We will need her to hold the circle with us tonight. Thatcher; that's Gav's dad, and I will help of course."

9

Dusk inspired an indigo sky. Addy felt the cold wind whip around her. She pulled Meg's jacked tighter, pulled the front door closed and looked up the hill. The narrow, cobbled path inclined steadily; a stone house rose prominently on the right, it's red roof and chimney welcoming. A bright yellow door on her left had lazy vines flank each side; it's bright autumn foliage sprouted beneath the white rimmed second storey windows. A sign to the right of the window read Snowey Place. A baby cried inside.

She walked quickly, tomato, toast, fried onions drifted on the air. The day settled into its night. The lane grew steeper and then curved sharply left as it grew wider. A convenient store's green window glowed from across the street. A tired woman on autopilot to her car, laden with groceries. Addy headed further along the hill top.

Some shops had already closed, their darkness an abscess in the mouth of lights. Those that were still open had their owners shuffling about, cleaning and closing. She passed the hairdressers, the bakery, le Boutique, The Best Pies in Town. She stopped at the cross road.

That can't be.

Green and orange etched glass arched above the large

wooden door announcing Murphy's Pub, Est. 1867. Dark window squares revealed that Murphy was a busy man. At the table closest to the street, Rachel sat opposite Grit. She flicked her blonde hair behind her ear.

The anger and power hit her simultaneously.

Oh shit!

Addy gasped for a breath. She saw the slice open in Dane's side and the red rivulet gather and stream in his wound, the wound caused by Rachel's power. Without thought she moved through the pub.

Rachel reacted first. Her eyes widened and she moved instinctively towards the window further away from Addy.

"Now Addy. Just take it easy" Rachel's palms were up warding Addy away. Panic etched a tiny muscle on her face that pulsed furiously.

"Wow. What's going on?" Grit's confusion evident in his furrowed brow, "you know each other?"

"Oh yes. We know one another, don't we Rachel?" Addy was cold angry now, "maybe, I should fill you in, Gavin" Addy's eyes narrowed as she started at Rachel. Power ran up and down her body.

"Rachel here, is the reason Dane is injured" Addy's eyes never left Rachel's but she felt the change settle on Grit.

"What? No" he grabbed the back of his head, "That's rubbish Addy. Rachel?" He stood up, "We need to talk. Away from here."

Outside the wind had picked up. Grit walked around the back of the pub. A few cars were parked in the lot but otherwise it was quiet. Grey shadows lurked between the cars and the trees in the back.

"Addy. You saw the situation" Rachel appealed, "Zyklon would have killed me. I had to react. You know how they are?" Rachel pouted as she peaked from behind her cream blond hair, "And besides, I knew that Dane would be okay. I knew you were with him. It was just a little cut" she lowered her chin and lifted her eyes at Addy and then at Grit, "Come on Ad, you think I would really hurt him on purpose?"

"What's going on here?" Grit folded his arms, confusion rolling from him, "Rachel. You said you could help us".

"I can. Honestly. Addy misinterpreted what happened."

"Addy. Rachel is offering to help our cause. She's powerful. Even our strongest witches can't protect us, we need her power. What are you saying?"

Addy saw the desperation in his eyes. He needed her to fight against Zyklon. He needed to believe that he had a chance. She reminded herself silently that this was Dane's best friend.

Addy knew Verity's anger. She knew Zyklon's cruelty. What if Rachel's right? Maybe she really didn't have another choice? Her power tingled along her torso, her senses were warring with her. The anger lessened.

"Ah, I see you have better control now" Rachel sneered.

Grit frowned. He looked at Rachel as if seeing her for the first time.

"Why didn't you refuse?" He tilted his head towards Rachel, "why didn't you just say no?" He challenged.

Rachel sensed the turn.

She threw a power wave across at Grit. Addy shielded them. Instinct driving her. She pulled for power. Rachel paled. Grit stared at her.

"You'll kill us all" Rachel whispered coldly.

"The game starts in ten. We'll see you there, Frog" the voice was close by and approaching them.

A trash can flew through the air. Addy waved her hand and halted it. It fell with a huge racquet. Rachel ran into the High Street and disappeared from sight.

Addy struggled to pull her power back. The tar road hit her knees. Breathe.

"You okay?" Grit was breathing heavily beside her. She nodded. "Come" he pulled her to follow him.

They raced back to Meg's place in silence.

"What happened?" Meg continued setting the table, the door slammed behind Addy.

"Rachel is working for Zyklon" Addy's voice was flat, soft.

Meg stilled, "Gav?"

He nodded.

Meg sat down silently. The clock marched the time.

Addy felt the fear damn in on her. Crushing her chest. I may never see Dane again. My mum? Rachel's probably talking to Verity right now. Why did he wait? Why? Why? Why? The vast emptiness, there all her life, kept at bay now threatened to invade her. The anger, the desolation, it all struggled for release.

Her voice sound strange in her own ears, "If you had only just opened the portal" they both looked at her, "you say that you're working for the cause. What cause? The same one that needs me on Thear? That cause? Because, from where I am, you've done nothing to help."

"Addy" Meg cautioned.

"No Meg. I came for help. I've had none. Hostility, questioning, nothing else. But Rachel, she prances in and says she can help. Did you question her too? It looks to me that your loyalties are under question" she looked directly at Grit. Addy heard the words, wished as they streamed from her mouth, as she saw Meg's face, that she could pull them back. The emotion released from Addy. The air around her ears shuddered. She needed air.

The garden was small. Addy stood beneath the window, the light from the kitchen didn't quite reach here. Meg stood beside Grit's chair, pulling his head to her. Just love, a mother's love. Addy felt the warm tears crawl down her cheeks. She turned her back and leaned against the windowsill.

The silence hung for a moment. And then Addy heard the conversation.

"She's right mum, nobody else knows him as Aquilae. That message was for me"

"Ssh. It's okay" Meg soothed.

"Who is she? Why is he risking his life for her? She has so much power." He rested his elbows on the table. "We could use that. But, if Dane thinks she needs to be on Thear; I'll open it".

***

The wooden steps descending into the underground part of Murphy's pub were smooth from years of wear, each step had a warm yellow glow light at its base which illuminated the pathway. Each step also brought the rising smell of alcohol. Years of beer spills and wine ferment permeated the air. The steps wound down and to the right and opened up into a large space. Wooden tables and chairs were scattered about, many people were in the pub. A fire was lit in the large hearth. The walls were dark brown, and carried flags, trophies, photos and pictures of beer. The bar itself had a long smooth wooden finish which ran at a right angle; one end had bar stools so that patrons could perch and enjoy their drinks, the other end had standing patrons. Large copper vats provided a dramatic backdrop to the bar, with pipes running up and across the ceiling making the area industrial and homely at the same time.

A game showed on a large screen television tucked all the way in to the pub on the right. On the other end music played over the buzz of chatting people. A door on the left of the bar swung open and a waitress marched out, smile in place and four plates expertly balanced on her forearms.

Meg, Addy and Grit had arrived with a large crowd, they milled in the open space, waiting for the reason for their presence to be spelled out. Addy kept turning around, amazed at her surrounds. She still hadn't eaten, Meg was just about to dish up when they were summoned to the underground pub.

"Oh, there's Melanie, she's the cat lady, dear" explained Meg, turning around "where's Thatcher?"

Meg was clearly distracted, she kept looking around.

"Gav, love, where's dad? Matty said they let everyone know to come, can you see him?" Meg glanced around in anticipation, a frown marring her brow.

A man in a brown robe pushed past them and stood under a column of brick with his right hand in the air, "Attention! Your attention please?" he called in a big booming voice.

"Guys! Listen up!" The room went quiet, people shuffled closer to the brown robed man.

Addy saw the perspiration on his brow and lip. "This evening a terrible thing has happened," the pub went even quieter, "Zyklon" Addy almost felt the collective intake of breath, "Zyklon invaded our town. He has taken several of our kind" the noise level started to pick up, and people started haggling the man, "What do you mean? Who has he taken? When? Where's my son? Have you seen Robin?" He held up his arm for silence, this time it was instant, "He has eight people with him but we suspect that he is this minute, invading our homes, looking for more. He is after power." All hell broke loose, people spoke over each other. Addy saw out of the corner of her eye that Meg had gone pale, she was lowering herself into a stool. Addy rushed over, "Meg?" She looked at Addy but didn't seem to focus,

"They have Thatcher. I knew it" she whispered.

The brown robed man continued speaking, the crowds quietened to hear what he had to say, "They have taken the most powerful of our circle. We, Mary and I, agreed the safest thing to do was to bring you here," the crowds started shouting again, "stop! Let me finish and then we can think about our action plan." He looked pained, sweat stains shadowed his arm pits and ran down his face, "we have a list of the people we know are missing." He looked at Meg and then immediately looked down at the paper in his hand, clearly uncomfortable.

Gavin sat down hard next to his mother, she folded herself into his chest, they held each other as Addy sat alongside feeling their pain.

"Thatcher, Elizabeth Coatiel, Molly Lamper" the brown robed man continued, "Penny Ringtin" he caught the eye of the impacted family each time he called a name, the room continued to subdue and bristle, "Murphy Rowly" Murphy's wife sobbed, audibly, "Bundy White and Mabel Penrose" he lowered his paper.

"And Stanley Brown's nephew, visiting from New York!" shouted a large round man as he tripped down the stairs, "Just took him minutes ago." His face was red and his large moustache twitched on his lip, "Stan's on his way." He jerked his chin down and clenched his neck muscles, "Only Merlin can help us now!"

"Too true' whispered the robed man.

Addy looked around the pub, people were ashen and somber from shock. Everyone was impacted.

Oh no! Thatcher was supposed to help hold the circle so she could get to Thear.

Families huddled together shocked and angry. Addy noted the general sense of helplessness. Overhead thunder clapped loudly and immediately after rain pelted down, the sound travelled around, insulating the pub. Addy walked between families looking for the rest room.

"He's so powerful! What can we do?" Murphy's family muttered as she passed.

"What the hell am I going to tell Margo?" lamented Stanley Brown, red in the face as he pulled hard on his pint.

"Where are they now?" Grit stood next to the speaker.

"Heading here" he whispered. Silence hung like mist.

"We must detract them." Grit stood up. "Stan, Dave. We must detract them. They cannot come here. We'll lead them out of town. They will pick up on the power. We must move now." The three guys were already running up the stairs.

Grit turned around and addressed the crowd.

"Stay inside. Stay quiet." They ran up the stairs. The village's hope sitting on them.

10

Thunder clapped over-head. Everyone jumped. The rain continued to pelt down.

Children sensing the need, hushed their play in front of the hearth.

I should have gone with them.

Addy counted the minutes as they slowly crawled by. They all felt it. The presence was dark and cold but it stayed on the periphery. The pub was protected.

Addy sat down beside Meg who was still silent and shaken.

The football game carried on in the background, the glowing green grass back-dropping the silent players in their slow game.

Time crawled. Meg seemed to have lost herself in the flames. Numb.

How do I comfort her? I don't know what to do. What do I do?

Addy tried to recall being comforted. Dane had comforted her.

Addy thought about the three guys who were trying to distract Zyklon. She focused on Grit. Where was he. Her mind whirled and a fog cleared.

Addy saw. Five kilometres down the road, Grit shifted. The

white hawk swooped up high, the earth tilted on his periphery, the rain pelted at his wings and back. She sensed Zyklon.

She focused on Grit. She felt when Grit saw Zyklon. He stood on the oval, conjuring the storm, lightning flashed green strobe lights around him. She felt Grit looking still,

Where are the others? Where is Rachel?

He circled again, the rain heavy on his wings.

There! Addy zoned on his energy, she could track his movements.

Rachel's blonde hair stood out in the night sky. She was on a balcony across the road from Murphy's.

Oh no.

Rachel chanted, her eyes closed. Grit picked up on Rachel's energy, he felt the energy whirl around her.

What are you doing? She was strong.

He's going to try and pull her away. Addy's heart sank. Rachel was powerful.

The pub was suspended in angst. Addy sat helpless, awkward. Waiting. She delinked from the energy outside, looking at the people in the pub, what could she do?

A boy. Three years old. His cheeks still full of baby, his dark eyes filled with wonder, pulled his Tonka truck along his mum's foot. He tilted his head and pursed his lips trucking with his arm extended.

Addy felt the energy at the same time the boy flew through the air. He looked as though he were pinned to the underground wall. His baby arms and legs squirming.

"Mama Mama!" he cried.

"No!" Addy chased him.

"Mama?" he called again.

"Must be quiet" someone warned.

Addy felt the energy. It was dark. She had to do something. The boy would be drained.

She stood extending her arm to the wall. Feeling her energy draw into her. She focused on the energy behind the wall. She pushed into with her power. Palm up, she felt the energy push the air. The boy dropped into his mother's arms.

Their cover had been blown.

"Out! Get out!" she shouted.

The crowd moved as one storming for the entrance. Meg moved in a daze. Addy grabbed a young girl and moved her up the stairs, her mum struggling with twins behind her.

Grit appeared on the high street. Drenched, heaving. The pub imploded. Dust and rubble rose into the air.

"Addy! Move them up. Up on the hill. Zyklon and Rachel are down in the valley. I will stop them coming up. Just be quick" he instructed, "take mum". He turned and disappeared in the night.

Addy directed people up the hill.

"Keep moving up. You will be safe. Do not go home. No, keep moving" she kept moving along, helping families. Her energy moved up and down her body.

A wiry old man passed her, "Thanks for bloody nothing" he hissed.

The rain continued. They moved slowly. Silence settled around them.

What have I done. Every time I use this power. Every time. I can't even help Grit, I would probably kill us all. The muscles in her back strained as she lifted a child; she checked on Meg who also held a boy and walked stoically.

The energy rolled around Addy. She struggled to clamp her power down. Biting her lip. Just keep on moving. Take them to safety.

On top of the hill a man called Dheeta opened the old stone church door.

"It's dry" he announced. They moved in, exhausted.

Families spread out in the old pews. Children asleep instantly. Adults just sitting, recovering.

"I'm Dana Lamper" her clear blue eyes were watery, "They took Molly she's my twin" she smiled lowering her head fractionally,

"I know you'll help us through this. I can feel it. You know?" She looked into Addy's eye, "Just tell me where and when. I know we'll get her back" she spoke with hope. She squeezed Addy's arm, the momentary warmth comforting. Addy smiled and nodded as anxiety trickled into her chest, she had to find solitude.

Why were they looking to her? She was dangerous. She had to leave.

Addy must have dozed. The back of the wooden pew dug into her temple; as she opened her eyes Stan was opening the church door. The sun dazzled behind him.

Dave walked up the steps. Everyone sat up. No Grit.

No. No. No.

"No!" Meg's voice was a whisper, "Where's Gavin?"

Addy touched her arm. "He has my whole family" tears glistened in the corners of Meg's eyes, "you've got to go for help" Meg grabbed her hand, "please Addy. Go now. Go get help, we can't do this alone" she looked around the church. They looked on, hopeful.

"How?" She asked softly. "I don't know how to get there" Meg looked at the crowd and then back at Addy.

"Ask the Highwayman" Meg suggested.

Addy heard the mutterings and then someone spoke out, "Fischer Penrose" the tall man stood up, he was well built and good looking, dark hair, firm jaw and dark eyes, "They have Mabel. We've not heard of anyone, ever" he emphasized the word, "ever using the Energy Highway. Isn't that just a myth?" He asked amongst a lot of agreed nodding.

"I've used it once" Addy conceded. People looked poignantly at each other, "I caught it to get here, to find Grit" she had everyone's undivided attention, "It was easy enough. It is definitely real" she confirmed.

"The story says," interrupted Dave Ringtin, "that the highway will come to magic folk and will take them where they need to be. I am magic, but I have never seen the Highway" he confessed.

"I'm with you, mate" Stan was still flushed.

"There isn't another option" Meg stated looking at the crowd, "does anyone have a better idea?"

"Why her? How do we trust her?"

"The Quinary are looking for her" Meg stated. The gasps were audible.

Addy felt the energy pool in her stomach.

"And look here" Meg lifted her wrist. The Quinary rings glowed on the inside.

The crowed rumbled among each other.

Dave Ringtin spoke again, "What about, you come with us to rescue them?"

"Dave, we don't have enough power to take them on. You saw what happened last night. That was our strongest" Meg was angry now.

"Meg. We didn't have her with us. We heard the story. She has power. Loads of it. If she is the Quinary, if it's all real why can't she come with us?" Dave was appealing to the crowd. Desperate.

Addy spoke quietly.

"In the cave, there are several chambers" quiet descended in the room. The wind whistled through the church, "in one of them" Addy caught every person's eye in turn, "in one of them are creatures. Black as the ace of spades, largest eyes you'll ever see. Valves for noses that suck and cup and grasp at the air" Addy felt the fear rise in the room, "two sets of arms and legs" she continued as people sat forward intrigued in disbelief but waiting for more, "there are thousands and thousands of them" Addy whispered as she recalled the black army swarming the fields outside the cave, "we need to avoid them. Avoid those chambers. And, the prisoners" she swallowed hard remembering Mrs. H. Families leant in now, clutching at throats and swallowing in fear. Addy saw it flare in their eyes, "they're in a trance. When we get them, they won't know us. They won't react at all." Addy wanted to them to know the cold hard facts of their mission, "I don't know how to get them out of the trance. But I know that

111

when we do there is confusion, panic. It's best to just lead them in that state. Who are healers here? You should prepare for that, for when we bring them home" two women clutched hands biting their lips, concern radiating from them. "I give you the facts as I know them" Addy continued, "When I was there, I saw a few large chambers and several long passages that were dark, very, dark. You can't use torchers unless it is an emergency. It will attract attention. The passage that leads downwards, against your instincts. That's the one that leads out. It goes into a wet pool" Addy stopped and looked around, feeling the mood in the room.

"It sounds so dangerous" Dawn lamented,

"It is" Addy responded directly, "It's dangerous, there are strange creatures, dark passages, blazing hot furnaces, then there is Zyklon. And, and Verity" she stated. Silence hung in the air, amplified by the whistling in the church.

"I'm not swallowing this crap! You want us to hop on a mystical highway, hopefully end up in Zyklon's evil den, crawling with make-believe creatures in the hope we're able to rescue prisoners for whom we don't exactly know a location and then how do we all get back here? This is bull shit!" The man paced angrily.

"You're right Stan." Addy stood up too, "you're dead right! And you forgot something too" she looked directly at him, and then at each of them in turn, "we only have until the new moon to get it done"

"Or what?" He challenged

"Zyklon will instruct them to release their power to him. He will suck it from them. They will die. Be clear, everyone" Addy was earnest in her tone, heart thumping madly, "be clear, that this is extremely dangerous. You may not get back from this" her voice rang in her own ears. She sat down.

***

"We have Fischer Penrose, Dave Ringtin, Dana Lamper, John Kemp who is Bundy White's partner and then me" stated Stan.

"And me" the man in the brown robe from earlier stepped forward. Mary visibly paled.

"You don't have to do this" Stan advised,

"I do, and I am" he stated.

"Grindal killed Mary's husband nine years ago" whispered Meg, "Dheeta is a Druid" he has been helping Mary to run the pub for the last few years" she offered.

"Whose Grindal?" Addy whispered back. Meg's eyebrows shot up in disbelief,

"Zyklon's partner" she whispered, Addy nodded.

"Okay! Addy? What next?" Stan asked, "We have torches, ropes, knives, whatever we could find, what next?"

Addy stepped forward, "Just a reminder that we are to avoid Zyklon. We are only looking to release prisoners. We cannot go up against Zyklon. Clear?" The Rescue party nodded agreement and stood up ready for action.

"Let me think" Addy muttered, "What is the time?"

"Twenty to nine" offered Dawn.

The party started hugging and patting their goodbyes.

"Under a tree at three" muttered Addy, "you will know the words when you need them" she heard Dane shout at her. How she missed him.

"Three, six, nine" she whispered eyes closed, "tree, sticks, line" Stan and Dave rhymed.

Addy opened her eyes, "How do you know?" She asked

"Kids rhyme" Said Stan, dubious.

"We need a line" Addy said aloud.

Two boys offered up their string.

"I'll hold one end Meg, you hold the other" suggested Mary looking apprehensive.

Addy felt the emotion increase in the room.

Oh shit, what am I doing?

Her heart was thudding. She was in over her head.

"You come back to me! Do you hear me Dheeta?" Mary urged as Addy eavesdropped. Dheeta responded by pulling her head down and kissing her, she brushed the tears from her cheek, "Just come back" she smiled.

Everyone lined up beneath the line Meg and Mary held. Addy's heart thumped.

What if this doesn't work? She thought again. I am such an idiot!

"On three" she whispered, throat hoarse,

"One, two, three" she counted,

"Under a line at nine, under a line at nine, under a line at nine" everyone chanted, and then "So mote it be"

Addy glanced at Meg, expecting to be scolded. The anticipation suspended everyone and then the air shimmered and from above them, a golden glow lit up and straight out of the ceiling a carpet of golden light unfolded before them.

"Oh my."

"Gosh"

"Oh! It's true."

Onlookers and rescue party folk looked at each other and then at the highway with awe and wonder.

"Step up! Step on up!" the Highwayman encouraged, "Busy night tonight" he smiled gleefully.

The church disappeared below them as onlookers waved in disbelief amidst their tears and heartache.

"We want to go to Zyklon" Addy advised the Highwayman.

"Ah! It's a matter of what we need lass. Not so much what we want!"

"What do you mean? The last time you said that I just had to say the word out loud and I could get there." Addy was starting to have a prickly feeling across her chest.

"Yes, I did! You could get there! You're right! If the Highway thinks it's what you need".

"Well, we all need to rescue prisoners of Zyklon" interrupted Stan.

"And you will get what you need" he smiled eerily.

"Say the words aloud. Each of you" he advised.

Everyone, including Addy muttered, "Zyklon's prisoners" in an instant the highway dipped, Addy saw Dave's head descend, then Dheeta, she was next, she felt her tummy dip and sink and then she was on hard ground.

"Dave?" She whispered loudly, "Dheeta?" Addy waited a moment for a response, then, "Fischer, Dave, Dana? Anyone? Dammit!" she called.

No sound.

11

When the shimmery haze of the highway cleared, Addy was alone.

"No! No! No! No! Ugh!" The ground hit her knees and power prickled across her chest, rising as it moved down her arms.

"Why? Why?" She shouted digging her hands into the soft sand.

Addy looked up across a still lake, glass reflected the dark sky, the edges closest to her showing the tall firs that loomed up behind her. The view was familiar and an uneasy feeling stole across Addy.

"Where the hell am I? She shouted in anger. The power rippled strongly across her body.

"Go away. Take it all away. I can't help anyone. I can't do it. Just leave!" She shouted her voice hoarse as her strained vocal chords went on and on, "Go away! I don't want power! I hate this gift! I hurt and, and kill! Just go away!" She screamed at the power inside of her, battling with her rising urgency.

Hot tears blurred her vision and power crackled and stung across her body. The soft sand caked around her knees, and as she rose up her arms felt heavy. She looked to the lake and felt the power overwhelm her. She poured it into the water.

Euphoria stole across her and relief and adrenalin flooded into her system. The blue electricity ran from her fingers into the water. A tap of relief poured from her.

Like lightning the power forked beneath the surface and the lake lit up rust brown, immediately the blackness Addy recalled from her vision appeared, the darkness drew a curtain across the view and the moss green below the surface lit up, Verity's image bobbed and smiled at her.

"Igarro, shintato anviglati"

The image taunted and again,

"Igarro, shintato, anviglati"

Verity's image became focused. Addy saw her throat veins elevated, distorting the clear water, it rippled and rolled towards Addy,

"Igarro, shintato, anviglati"

The wind whistled the trees behind her, the water churned around Verity's image.

Fear flooded her body. Her throat constricted painfully. She stood as the image began to laugh. "Oh no" whispered Addy, "Oh no! What have I done?" the hysteria got whipped away by the wind but echoed through the forest for a moment.

As quickly as it came up the wind disappeared. The lake became still and Verity winked to Addy, "Welcome to Thear, Adera. And, thank-you" she whispered and the blackness from the lake escaped, laughter lingered a moment.

The sun returned, Addy was numb. She held her head, nausea climbed quickly and Addy spilled her insides beside the lake as dread and pain and anguish pummeled her from inside.

She found a flat rock. Tears, thick and heavy soaked her face. Addy curled into a tight ball and welcomed the blackness.

Hours later, the jagged edges of the rock pierced into her skull, waking her. She moved and squinted, her limbs ached from where she had lay still in the fetal position.

I wonder how long have I been here? So this is Thear.

The thoughts penetrated her numbness, she saw the light filtering through the pines.

Heaviness began to build in her chest again. She sat up. What have I done?

Pain and general uncomfortableness gradually became her reality.

"Remorse" the word reverberated in the air. The first syllable annunciated clearly, "Re morse".

Addy looked around.

"Sh sh sh ame" the sound was dragged out again. Addy stood, wary now.

"Stu pid it y" the voice laughed as it pronounced the word slowly.

Addy was bewildered. She whipped around. "Who's there?"

"That is an interesting question."

Her heart pounded. "Where are you?"

"Here and there."

"I can't see you anywhere" she said.

"Not too perspicacious."

"Ugh"

The air pixelated seeming to gather and pull apart simultaneously, a large tree wavered above the rock. Silver plumes rustled and moved above a beautiful glistening trunk.

Addy's eyes widened in awe. Oh my.

The tree suddenly transformed. A sleek, black, large cat stretched lithely. "Oh" she made little murmurings in wonder. The beautiful creature with silver whiskers and large green eyes stared at her as it reached forward, claws extended, it stretched its graceful body from front to back. As the stretch rippled across the muscular frame, the cat changed into a person. Beautiful beyond words. Addy's breath caught in her throat. She stared intently, the face in front of her glowed silver with white light streaming from its eyes. Its body moved from being male to being female freely, ethereally.

"What are you?" Addy barely whispered, "Who?" She said again in awe.

"Not a who"

"Why?"

"That's better"

"How"

"Even better. Thanks" the image settled on a male form. It smiled at Addy.

"You're not making any sense" she was still wary

"That is not my purpose"

"What is your purpose?"

"As I choose"

"And, your choice?"

"Choice of?"

"Ugh" Addy was getting frustrated

"Ah. Purpose, Quinarian. Purpose." He said in a soft whisper that seemed to come from all around her. Her body ached, her head was throbbing and her patience wearing thin.

"If you'll excuse me, I have had a terrible day. I'll be on my way now."

"Yes. Indeed. Terrible." He pronounced the word rolling his r's. "Likely to cause terror. Accurate summation" he nodded.

Addy frowned.

"Twenty-eight years Verity's power has been trapped in this lake. Odious." He traced a hand down his own body, "it's not Odious, interesting having form" he traced his contours, slowly, changing to female half way through. The process was distracting and spellbinding.

"How do you know Verity? Who are you? Where am I? What are you?"

119

"Ethereal, perpetual, whole, you, me" he or rather she whispered.

"Ugh" Addy felt like she was talking to a three-year old.

"We are five or we are eight but we are all one" it said on the breeze and right before Addy's eyes, the person started to fade.

"Wait."

"Celestial" she whispered on the air and disappeared.

"Oh, come on! Nooooo!"

"I have sentenced Zyklon's prisoners to death as well as their rescuers. What the hell? Verity's power is back! I have effectively doomed them" she whispered to herself. The breath whooshed from her and she held her stomach as nausea threatened again. Energy drained from her as shame and guilt swelled in its place.

Sobs caught in her throat and tears trickled hot paths of anger and pain down her face. Addy dropped her head into her hands, dark strands sticking to her wet face, "How can I keep you alive?" She asked the absent Rescue Party hopelessly "two evil, powerful killers" fresh tears swept her breath away, "make that three" she whispered and doubled over in agony.

Shadows had shifted when Addy's numbness became conspicuous. "How do I get out?" She was hoarse and cold. A forest of fir trees surrounded the lake as if on guard, in every direction the dark soldiers lined up equidistant from one another. The squad on the other side of the lake cast their shadow tips at Addy's feet. The trees rustled in their ranks, discordant birds shouted at one another. Addy rose from the rock and the sun caught her face, warming her.

She stood on the flat rock and took stock of her surrounds. Trees and water. Great!

The water shimmered silver as it snaked through the trees "I'll have to go up" she spoke into the stillness.

Pine needles crunched softly underfoot as Addy walked among the tall pines. She felt a presence.

Not a good one.

"You smell of pine" she spoke aloud. "No lower branches on any of you" she observed, "that is not helpful" she touched the rough tall trunks peering at the tops several metres up, "oh well," she sighed exaggeratedly. Talking broke the stillness and enabled her to ignore the weight of the guilt in her chest.

With her magic vision, Addy saw the energy surround her. She pulled her arms wide and welcomed the energy in; power sprang across her body, twitching and sparking, Addy's vision shifted and she was clear on her immediate need.

I wish I might
I wish I may
Elevate myself above the trees today

Addy's feet immediately left the floor, the thrill of the movement stole across her. She stretched arms wide and crossed her ankles as she ascended up and up. The branches swayed and creaked as she passed them, leaving the ground behind.

Delicate fir tops danced in the sun, a carpet of dark green spread out against the cloudless sky. Addy saw the lake glint on the horizon to the west and turned slowly, feeling the warm air tug at her clothes and hair.

"So, beautiful" she whispered, the trees spread out in a sickle from the lake and then green rolling hills undulated to the horizon. Majestically an eagle surveyed its domain, swaying and circling. Her heart contracted.

I wish Dane was here. He'd know what to do.

"I'll follow the lake" she decided, descending gently.

Addy landed on a branch hanging over the lake, leaning into the trunk she looked over the water, planning her path. Lazy orange dragon flies skimmed across the surface.

"Hey there" the voice was loud and unexpected, Addy jolted in shock, her feet slipped from the rough branch and she fell into the shallow ice-cold water below.

"Huh," she took a deep involuntary intake of air as the ice-cold water shocked her.

"What are you doing in the tree?" Shouted the stranger. He leant forward and extended his hand to assist her.

Addy ignored his hand and stood up angrily,

"Why did you shout at me?" She asked crossly, "You made me lose my balance!"

"Me? You were way out of your depth already. If I wasn't here you would probably have been stuck in the tree for the rest of the day. Why were you up there, anyway?" He asked with arrogance.

Addy was angry at this stranger. She stomped her wet feet. Realized she was still in the lake and then kicked the water angrily. A jet of water washed from her onto the stranger standing on the bank of the lake.

He stood unbelieving for just a moment. Water running down his face and clothes. Then leapt forward,

"You ungrateful little..." he started. Addy sprang out of the way but he was faster than her and they collided and both fell into the water. He looked at her and Addy returned the stare.

Addy heard the peals of laughter and was shocked when she realized they were coming from her.

They both laughed loud and long. After much splashing, they walked onto the banks and started wringing their clothes out.

"My name is" he hesitated a moment then proceeded, "Andrew" he extended his hand.

"Hello Andrew. I am Addy" Addy reached for his hand automatically.

Their eyes met and Addy felt she knew him. Something was familiar. His hair was dark and short, the front flopping onto his forehead, just above his dark eyes. His features were rugged and handsome. He was much taller than her and had a broad chest. He wore a loose light brown shirt over dark brown trousers and boots. He smelled of horses and polish.

He laughed loudly.

"You are most charming. I am so pleased to meet you. My brother asked me to come and get you" he offered.

"Who is your brother?" Addy asked.

"Why are you here, Addy?" He gestured widely, "you do know this lake is home to an evil power? Trapped here, they say until a powerful witch releases it," he glanced around in disbelief.

Addy felt the dark presence she had earlier. Andrew looked around suddenly, "Whose there?" He asked aloud.

Addy glanced around. There wasn't anything around them. She started moving towards the flat rock she had occupied earlier, it was slightly raised and afforded a view down the lake. Andrew followed behind.

"Do you live close by?" Addy's voice was just a whisper

"No" he whispered with a chuckle.

"What's so funny? And why are you whispering?" She whispered back.

"Why are you whispering?" He smiled but Addy saw him glancing around.

"Do you think someone is following us" Addy asked

"Not sure" he kept a look out over the lake and into the forest, "this forest and lake are steeped in history and legend. You must have heard the stories too? Never know what to believe and what is pure story. But something about this place is a little…. uneasy?"

Andrew stuck his fingers into his mouth and whistled once.

"What are you doing?" She turned on him sharply.

"Apologies. I should have warned you. I am calling my horse," he pointed to the fir trees. A tall pitch-black stallion walked from the trees, owning his space. He was beautiful, a long main whisked in the breeze and his tailed swished, almost bored as he strutted towards Andrew. Andrew patted his neck as he approached. "There's a boy" he muttered. Addy looked on in awe,

"He's beautiful" she murmured.

"He is and he knows it" he laughed, "Addy let me introduce you to Henry. He is actually my brother's. Needed a run."

The horse bowed its head low and whinnied in the back of its throat, "How do you do, Henry," Addy smiled as the horse hoofed the ground in front of her. Addy tentatively put a hand out to the horse's neck. As she touched him, Henry bowed down low again.

"Well. He's never done that. He must feel a great connection to you," Andrew laughed.

A loud noise like paper tearing had Andrew, Henry and Addy snap to attention, "Brownie?" Asked Andrew. Addy just frowned at him.

Like someone switched a light on, Mrs. Harris, whom Addy hadn't see since Zyklon's cave, materialized out of thin air right in front of them.

"Mrs. H!" Addy shouted enthusiastically, "What are you doing here? How did you do that?"

Mrs. H smiled her wrinkled face lighting up, "M'Lady" she bowed,

"Mrs. H! It's me, Addy. Remember from Rodic's?" She looked at her old neighbour, confused at her reaction,

"She's a Brownie" Andrew tried to explain,

"What?"

"You know? A Brownie" he repeated.

"No. I don't know" she was irritated, "I have heard this term before" she remembered Dane calling Mrs. H a Brownie in the cave too

"Where have you been?" He looked surprised at Addy. "They live in the Woods here and have the amazing knack of being able to transport themselves magically to distances a few hundred kilometres away." Andrew looked at Addy as though she were a different species, "They can only stay there briefly but this is sufficient to deliver messages or communicate during times of great strife. They are relied on during wars and therefore carry a great deal of secret intelligence." Andrew looked from Addy to Mrs. H. "This makes them suspicious of people, generally. Now days, they work in and around the Tower and Quinary because it was where they feel most trusted and can trust most" he summed up looking at Addy strangely.

"Hmm mm" Mrs. H cleared her throat, "this message is from Glockenstein" she nodded her wrinkled face pulling to a point at her mouth, "With Verity's power returned to her, she has kidnapped Marjory, her sister, your mother" she paused and looked at Addy who had visibly paled, "Glock says to make your way to the Time Tower where you can consider next steps".

Addy noted that Andrew had walked a few steps into the forest and was peering through the trees.

"Oh my! What have I done? No" Addy heard the whooshing rush through her ears, the guilt and remorse at her actions physically impacting her.

"Mrs. H. Where is the Time Tower? How far away am I? Where am I?" She walked towards Mrs. H in the hope of having answers, "do you know the way back?"

Addy felt physically beaten, "Mrs. Harris, I have so many questions, where is my mother? How do you know that she has been kidnapped? She is meant to be on Thear"

"M'Lady" she bowed again,

"Mrs. H! Stop calling me that! I'm Addy! Do you remember? Did Zyklon take your memory?" Addy's heart was racing, "Are you okay?"

"M'Lady! I am fine. Thanks to you. I am a Brownie as the P..." Andrew interrupted her

"Addy, we have to go! Now"

"What? Where?"

He jumped up onto Henry, "Come along, quick! The Brownie will relocate! Move!"

Addy put her foot into the stirrup and held her hand to Andrew, behind her howls and grunts were moving closer quickly.

"What is that?" She asked as he pulled her up behind him

"Later! Henry move!" he shouted.

Addy wound her arms around Andrew as the horse sprinted away, Addy noted Mrs. H disappear with a loud 'clack'.

The grunts and snorts got louder and louder.

Henry reared on his hind legs, his hoofs hitting in the ground.

The vibrations jolted Addy's insides, winding her. She clutched her arms tighter around Andrew, "Move!" her throat screeched with adrenalin.

Creatures poured from the forest; shredded garments flapped in the wind, their footsteps clanging from their weapons. Their eyes were vacant; animal, human, hybrids, dead and alive came from the dark forest.

Fear pummeled into Addy, she pushed up against Andrew, "What are they?"

"Don't let them touch you! Just hold on!" he shouted above the keening and roars.

Henry was at full sprint, the ground thundered beneath them, several creatures, tattered and soulless flew inches from his flank.

Addy willed Henry on, she made herself small, curling into Andrew's back. What are you? She thought and then loudly, "We can't outrun them."

"Just hold up! I have a plan!" he shouted.

On her left Addy saw the sockets of its eyes, gaping holes. Rags floated behind it and the creature leant forward, a long-gnarled finger inching at Addy's leg. Its skeletal insides stood stark white against the grey and wind whistled through its body, needling into Addy's ears. The air turned cold.

Addy's power flickered across her body, "How can I help?" She called cold and afraid.

"No! Just hold on" Andrew comforted as he focused on Henry and getting away.

Henry turned to the right coming up at the point of the

fir trees, the haggard creature was seconds off the move and Henry charged through the narrow firs. The incline was steep and the scent of pine followed the thudding hooves. As he crested, lines and lines of soldiers, glinting in the late sun welcomed them.

Surprise knocked through Addy, she closed her eyes a moment willing her power to calm, "Do you know them?" she asked.

"Friendly" he gasped, "doing a few drills" he shouted above the thudding hoofs.

"Charge!" he shouted as they ducked through the ranks.

Henry did not stop until he ran through the last of the ranks. When it was finally safe, Henry slowed, his breath pushed the pine needles away beneath them. At the first ranks, Addy heart the battle rage.

She looked back. Concern sank in on her.

"They will be fine, Addy" Andrew comforted, "they're trained for the unexpected." He patted her thigh in comfort.

"We must not stop! Henry, mate, we have to keep going," Andrew patted his neck and they charged on.

Countryside rolled past them, green and yellow hues rose and fell. Panic subsided in Addy and she relaxed her grip, "What were they?"

"Dark creatures brought to life by magic. They serve no good purpose. They act on command only. They are just numbers, there is no thought in them, no will of their own" Andrew explained.

Addy fell silent, the weight of the day heavy in her heart.

Hours passed, only Henry's hoofs beating a pattern on the earth. Addy moved in her position behind Andrew. Dull aches bunched her joints and muscles, "Can we rest a moment?" She broke the hypnotic silence.

"Yes. Up ahead" he pointed further down the dip where a small stream glinted in welcome.

"There you go boy. Well run! Have a drink and a graze," Andrew patted Henry fondly.

"I'm afraid I don't have any nourishment for us. I hadn't planned on having a grand adventure today" he smiled.

"I'm surprised" she teased in her sadness, "I thought all country lads spent their days saving damsels in distress"

His eyes glinted mischievously, "Ah, I sense that you would probably have saved yourself" he conceded, then more soberly, "who are you Addy? What were you doing in the dark woods?"

Addy moved uncomfortably, stepping away, "I, ugh," pain seared through her head, the ground hit hard on her knees. Addy held her head, feeling the pressure at her temples,

Grrr, tick, tick, tick.

She knew that sound, the image sharpened. A cage covered the cave wall. A young girl, about eight years old looked directly at her. Her heart shaped face scrunched against her clasped hands under her cheek. She lay on her side, eyes vacant. Beside her, Grit stood shackled against the wall, bleeding from a gash on his head, his shirt was off and his welts blazed across his abdomen, his eyes too were unseeing staring at Addy.

"No" she whispered, "No!"

"Wha ha ha" Verity's voice reverberated around the cave, "so nice of Adera to get aunt's power back! Wasn't it Marjy?" she mocked.

Addy saw then, her older likeness strapped to the wheel. Blood trickled from her mouth and down her neck where Addy knew a fork bit in.

Verity trickled her riding crop over Marjory's face, "Not so strong now hey Sister?" She giggled, "I hope you're around for the reunion? I told you Ternion will come" she whispered.

Addy's head throbbed. She felt the vision slipping from her, her power crackled across her body, she willed the power to Marjory in her image,

"Ah, a visitor? Wha ha ha ha!" Verity's laughter echoed away as the vision faded.

"There, there! Just take it easy" Andrew eased her back into a sitting position, "have some water, easy does it" he crooned, "It's been a tough day" he handed her his canteen.

12

Tears trickled down her face, Addy was exhausted and sobs built deep in her soul. She wept and wept.

Andrew sat beside her rubbing her back concerned. Henry returned and nuzzled at her arm where she rested them on her knees holding her head.

"I'm okay Henry. Thank-you" she wiped the tears from her eyes with the back of her hands, "will you take me to the Quinary?" Her voice was breathy and soft, apologetic.

Andrew smiled and holding his hand out, "your wish is our command".

Henry kept a steady pace and the Tower gates rose on the horizon as the moon lifted over the hills.

"Addy, you'll be safe here" Andrew helped her down, "I must be away. I need to check on the soldiers. Keep walking down this lane, it will take you into the Tower", "I think" he whispered to himself, "our future king has his work cut out" he smiled.

Before Addy could respond, Andrew leant forward and softly ruffled her hair.

"I'll see you around" he called as Henry carried them around the wall. Addy couldn't quite make out what Andrew was on about.

***

"Razzy, you've had too much to drink; you can't even walk in a straight line" someone giggled,

"I am fine; of course, I can walk in a straight line…"

"It's a good thing there are no stray Ogres in town anymore, I would feel unsafe with your level of consumption"

"Ha, I would protect you, I would walk right up to that Ogre and I would tweak his ears just like this" he held his arms out and rubbed his thumb and index finger of both hands together demonstrating just how he would fix that imaginary Ogre when and if he came across it.

It was at this instant that both the strangers noticed Addy at the gate.

Addy stepped forward and towards the hill. They took a few steps back.

"Hello, I'm Addy. I - Can you direct me to the Tower?" she awkwardly tried to set them at ease.

They both just stared at her. She took the opportunity to take in the picture. He was tall and broad shouldered. His blonde hair spiked up and then swung down low on his forehead just above his blue eyes. His skin was smooth and pale and she noticed that his ears were quite large for his features and formed a point on the top.

She looked at his companion. She was shorter than he was and she was beautifully built. Curvy yet elegant. She had a pixy face, pretty with large eyes, her golden hair was held back by a beautiful comb and she also had pointy ears.

The male had light brown three quarter pants on with an emerald green shirt that had a large collar. He had sandals on that looked as though they were made of twine and leather. Her simple blue dress had a round neck, quite low and the skirt skimmed down her hips.

They continued to look at her. She was about to ask for directions again when a big noise thundered really loudly, just one crack. Brownie, she thought now. What initially looked like a large brown paper bag appeared from nowhere. She gasped, noting her aching head…

The brown bag, not Mrs. H this time, turned slowly, in a haughty dry voice announced,

"His Lordship, Glock of The Quinary is expecting the girl, Addy. She is to be escorted by Rasem Lochlear and Pelany Jones to his Lordship's home immediately!"

"I am really tired, please be so kind as to show me the way, I won't keep you any longer…"

"My Lady, I am Rasem Lochlear, known as Razzy – I will escort you to his Lordship as requested, it is a great honor to serve his Lordship."

"And I am Pelany Jones, I will accompany Razzy on this short trip, it is an honor to be requested at the home of a Quinarian, you must be terribly important to have been summoned. I am so sorry I thought you were just a wanton…."

"Pelany, hush! Let's go" said Razzy, almost shoving Pelany out of the way…

Addy starting walking and then realized that she had no idea where she was,

"Could you please just tell me where I am….?"

"You are expected. Where are you from?" Razzy asked excitedly

"I am from *Earth*" Addy said almost questioningly – as though she wasn't sure whether they needed that detail, she was unaccustomed to mentioning her planetary origins in her greetings.

"Wow, wait till the lads hear this."

"Let's go" said Pelany starting to walk briskly towards the lights.

Addy shrugged and fell into step with Pelany. They walked a few moments in silence and then Razzy had a realization,

"Lady Addy, are you *The Fifth Quinarian*?"

"Please don't call me Lady" Addy avoided the question… her head hurt really badly.

"No, La…, I mean Addy, it's just that we have heard of Earth. The Quinary - do you know of it? The name of the assembly of the five ancients who hold the ruling powers of balance? Obviously, I am mistaken" he gave when he saw Addy's lack of enthusiasm. "You would know if you were the lost Quinary. I just thought that maybe…. Don't worry, Lord Glock will explain why you are here. Let's speed up, it isn't much further. I just heard down at the museum that there was a chance…" he broke off awkwardly.

Addy was left to her own thoughts; they walked for a time. Her head was pounding, she was hungry. They were steadily heading up hill; the bushes were getting closer and closer to the pathway so that everyone was now in single file. Her companions chatted between themselves but didn't ask her any more questions. She was about to ask for a rest when the pathway widened again, the moon was hanging low by this time and as the land flattened out she looked ahead and saw an enormous tower.

The view was a fairy-tale. Turrets rose up on the corners of the pentagonal building. Each turret a different colour, elegant and regal in shape. The turrets were connected by long tubes which dipped and weaved through one another. Addy momentarily thought she was at a water theme park. The tubes were completely enclosed. Just in front of each of the five tall turrets were large cubes suspended in the air, glowing and pulsing. Wide roads swept around the outside of the tubes and these were surrounded by walls. The walls looked strong they were made of large grey stones. Gargoyles, sprites, insects and creatures of dreams decorated the outside walls. Addy felt them watching her. The place looked magnificent. Bright flags on the gates to the entrance flapped loudly in the breeze.

Addy and her companions stood in awe looking at the turrets and the tubes. The road leading into the castle swept in from the left. The large gates stood firmly closed. The trio ran down onto the road and followed it up to the gates. As they approached, the gates creaked open. They continued walking

133

along the road, the gates closed behind them and the road continued on. Addy wondered what she was getting in to.

The gravel crunched beneath them as Addy followed Razzy and Pelany up the drive. She kept turning her head to look at the turrets and the cubes. She felt them beckon to her and when she looked at them they turned greyish blue and pulsed a little quicker. She shook her head to dispel the silliness that had come over her.

The door to the first turret opened widely and Addy felt herself grasped in a bear hug, before she could even peak inside.

"Welcome Addy, welcome child" the deep booming voice of the hugger rang in her ears. She peered under his arm at her travel companions, trying to get their attention,

"Raz... Pel?" She tried,

"Oh, how ill-mannered of me, my emotions take over completely when you come into play... I am so excited to see you, let me look..." he let her go so abruptly that she nearly fell over again. He held her up and then looked dismayed,

"Oh, no, you are injured? Did the travel upset you? Come inside, sit down, have a drink, where's Pearl?" he rushed on while staring at her. He started pulling her towards the house then suddenly everyone glanced up and looked over at the far tower that was now pulsing madly and throwing off colours like a lighthouse....

"Oh my, your tower has never glowed like that...." The hugger nostalgically whispered.

Addy was overawed by the scene in front of her but her head hurt really badly and she needed a drink.

"Excuse me?" She whispered then more strongly as the tiredness washed over her, "Please?"

A motherly figure appeared in the grand doorway at that moment. Clicking and fussing she came down the few stairs, glanced briefly at the pulsing light beams and then said,

"How rude, Glock, the poor child has travelled miles and miles, she is tired and hungry. Why are you keeping her out here in the cold air? And the pair of you?" Turning to Razzy and Pelany,

"You better come in for a warm drink… this way dear…" she steered Addy through the doors into a beautiful entrance hall.

If the tower was large and imposing on the outside, it was homely and warm and cozy on the inside. She was steered through the hall way into a living area where a large fire roared in the fireplace dominating the room. Portraits hung from prominent places around the room smiling down on the company. Addy was pushed into a plush velvet seat that was so large, she briefly wondered if they had an obesity issue on Thear. Pelany and Razzy sat on a two-seater shyly across from her and Glock, paced up and down the worn rug excitedly without actually doing anything at all.

"I'll just put some more light on the situation" the woman called Pearl spoke. She pulled a crystal from a basket set into the wall, inserted it into a slot and gave it a half turn towards her. Light glowed from it, lightening the room immediately.

"Do sit down Glocky; you exhaust me to look at you. The children are sound asleep, as they should be this time of night…. Now, I will get you all warm drink while Glocky here answers your questions, or explains what has happened. He seems to be the only one who really knows at this moment. Oh, and I am sorry for my manners, it has been an exciting night indeed. I am Pearl", she waddled away smiling as the other four stared after her.

Glock cleared his throat,

'U-hum, where to start?' he paused thinking,

"Lord Glock?" Interrupted Razzy,

Glock looked confused for a moment, as though he had forgotten there was anyone else in the room, "Yes, lad?"

"Is Addy from the other world?"

Before anyone could answer the doors swung open from kitchen and Pearl came back in laden with drinks for everyone and heaps and heaps of pancakes, dripping in syrup. She put the pancakes down on the small table to the left of Addy and then offered a tray of steaming drinks all around.

Addy took the large mug in both her hands. The drink was glowing. Briefly Addy considered putting the drink down and legging it out of the house but the smell of the drink was sweet and inviting and she felt herself compelled to sip at it.

Smooth, comfort coated her throat and she almost felt her headache melt away as the liquid filled her. Razzy and Pelany were tucking into the pancakes with gusto.

Pearl just smiled and then sitting down, picked up her knitting needles. They clicked and clacked in the quiet room for a moment and then Glock started talking again, this time it felt as though his voice was coming from a great distance. She smelt the sweet drink, heard the fire crackle and hiss and the click, click, click, click of Pearl's needles.

"Addy is from Earth" Glock continued,

"Not, well…." He jumped around trying to find a good starting point. "When the Ethers shook the world, the day they exploded, another dimension was formed – Earth… We literally live in parallel worlds…" there was a silence filled only by the click click, of Pearl's needles… Addy's attention waned, she felt herself nodding off.

She sat up with effort, catching the end of the explanation,

"You are right, that is what legend says…. But enough for tonight. Addy is tired, she must rest. You two can stay the night, separately, mind you, we will catch up in the morning, and there is much to do."

Razz and Pel looked disappointed. Addy was so relaxed. Her eyes were heavy and tired. She snuggled down a little deeper into the couch; it smelt of chocolate….

Glock was really tall – taller than Dane who was six foot five inches and the tallest person she had met until now. He was broad shouldered, with grey hair that was tied roughly with twine at the base of his neck. He had large eyes that looked blue and then quickly went really dark brown. He had about him a timeliness that made you think he may have been much older than his first impression. The strangest thing about Glock, Addy thought, was that he, like the rest of the people in the room, appeared to be in dress up. He had a heavily brocaded gold jacket on; it had fine green woven threads in a paisley pattern, he wore this over an open necked jaded green shirt, a faded golden waist coast and a fawn coloured three quarter pants which were tucked into brown leather boots. He had a gold pocket watch attached to his waist coat. He took the watch out frequently and the dials lit and glowed importantly. When Addy glanced at it she was struck by how unfamiliar it looked.

Pearl wore a dress the same jaded green as Glock's shirt. The dress was long and skimmed over her figure. She was average height and although she would be considered motherly in stature it came across more because of her attentive nature than her size. She had a beautiful face. Her hair was dark and had rich gold highlights; it was tied in a beautiful knot at the base of her head. Her eyes were soft and kindly and when she rested them on Addy, she felt as though her soul was being soothed. Her smile was ready and large and Addy sensed that she laughed often and heartily.

Addy drifted off into a peaceful sleep.

The next day Glock was caught up. Addy waited impatiently around Pearl's kitchen table, the Brownies were chopping rhubarb and talking quietly among themselves at the workbenches. Addy had a warm drink that she was sipping on, hoping to unwind. Visions of her mother, Grit and the young girl kept flashing in her mind. She willed her breath deep into her so that she could relax. Eyes closed she noted her surrounds, something gently bubbling on the stove, the soft murmur of voices around her. Pel and Razz teasing one another gently, Pearl chopped something on a wooden board.

A violent and intense pain swept across her chest. She jumped up clutching her breast, staggering across the kitchen.

"Ugh" the pain was intense. Waves of heat passed in and through her. Pearl got to her first, shouting,

"Razzy get Glock immediately. Pel, we need you and the Brownies – put your palms up link your hands palm to palm against mine, quickly" shouted Pearl

Pearl, the Brownies and Pel formed a circle around Addy. The instant the circle was complete the pain evaporated. It went as fast as it had come. She grabbed a chair and sank straight into it. Pearl insisted they keep the circle until Glock had arrived.

Glock rushed in followed by Razzy and a man in a dark green jacket.

"Addy, how are you feeling?" Glock pulled at her eye lids and felt her forehead,

"Glock, if you please?" Enquired the man in the dark green jacket. Glock stepped aside and granted permission for the man to look at Addy,

He bent down low over her and stared intently into her eyes. Addy felt a disturbance within her. It was not painful or intrusive, rather curious and questioning. She instinctively wanted to block the feeling. He smelt of pipe tobacco, sweet almost. His eyes glowed a clear striking turquoise. She felt as though light was entering her mind. As he continued to peer and she continued to feel the tug at her mind, she suddenly felt she needed her space back. She blinked and the man smiled,

"That took a while; you should shield your mind quicker." He turned to Glock,

"Her powers simmer at the surface; we will need to explore how to unleash it without hurting her. We don't even know what they are or her strength yet. We must start immediately Glockenstein" he nodded at Glock and then turned back to Addy,

"Forgive my manners. I am Ferris. I am a Wizard entrusted to assist the Quinary. I am also chief advisor to Mum" he bowed and then smiled at Addy; his smile lit his whole face up. The smile was quick and his eyes twinkled. She felt at ease and immediately trusting of this man. He had a blonde-grey beard; short and trim. His face was square and strong. His striking eyes shone from beneath bushy eyebrows. A wizard! She felt suddenly she was living her own mythical tale. The thought made her giggle. She could not explain this to everyone staring at her intently since she was keenly aware that she was the only one in the room wearing jeans and a blood-stained t-shirt and really did not have the majority rule so to speak. Ferris started stuffing tobacco into his pipe which he conjured up from somewhere Addy did not see.

"I am Addy" she said simply

"Oh, I know my child. I know. The Quinarian…" He carried on filling his pipe distractedly. Addy had the feeling that he really did know. And perhaps much more than her name…

"Come Addy. We must talk. Glock, where can we go?" Ferris questioned

As they left the room she heard Glock say to Pearl,

"Good, quick thinking Love. The Quinary Circle will protect her until she can do it herself" he kissed her forehead.

Addy followed Glock and Ferris out of the kitchen. They went down the hall and into a room, best described as a personal library. It was not big but, comforting. Books lined the walls floor to ceiling. The smell of old pages and leather and tobacco were somehow familiar to Addy even though she had no recollection of every having smelled any of these things together. There was a large dark wood desk in the far end of the room but immediately in front of the fire place were two large lounge chairs and a single arm chair. Not Rodic's library. No this was warm and welcoming. The rug in the centre was once rich in colour – burgundy, gold and green but was now faded and homely. Ferris took the single seat and left the two lounges for Glock and Addy to sit on. As they sat down, a fire sprang into flame in the fireplace.

"Verity is a is a powerful sorceress. We suspect she knows that you are on Thear. This will enrage her. She will try to find

139

you again and again. She probably tried to get into your mind earlier. The Quinary Ring put her off. She will get better at this. Addy, we need to start lessons and training immediately. You must be able to protect yourself, the ki-"

"Dane. Dane" Glock interrupted.

Ferris looked at Glock in confusion, "Oh yeah, that," he rolled his eyes.

"You must unleash the powers inside of you." He continued, "we don't know how this must happen. We do not know what you are capable of. We can only go on what we know of the others in the Quinary. You were all bound by the same Ether yet you all have different abilities." Ferris's voice faded and there was hung silence.

"Addy, we have sent people to scourge through all the libraries, ancient collections, and wizardry and potion books, anything we can find. This may provide an insight into what Verity thinks you can do. If she thinks you can do it – it may work to our advantage to know what that is" Glock explained,

"In the meanwhile, you must learn to shield your mind and your emotions. We will teach you of the Quinary. There is one other thing…" Glock looked unsure for an instant. He glanced at Ferris and then continued,

"We need the whole Quinary to defeat Verity and Zyklon. We don't know how strong they are, or how strong she has become. The greatest strength we have with all of the Quinary and the forces that support the Quinary is the wholeness of us." Glock hesitated, Ferris stood up and started pacing behind the couch Addy was sitting on, he continued,

"The Quinary is Glock, Celia, Nebulus, Roz and you. Glock looks after time, Celia minds the earth, the ground, and the planets so to speak, Nebulus looks after the skies, Roz after the waters and you… when your Ether was plucked, the world was in chaos. The Celestials shouted 'Vitali' – we are not completely sure. Do you know of a gift, an ability that we can work with?"

Ferris stopped and looked directly at Addy. She shrugged but he did not wait for an answer,

"We need the whole Quinary as I said before. Celia, Glock and you have understood the danger we face, maybe felt that danger?" He peered at Addy,

"Nebulus and Roz still need convincing. We think, Addy that we; Glock and I, should train you as best we can, then we must prepare for a journey."

Silence descended in the room. Addy thought about what she had learnt.

These were the voices in my head. How?

She stared into the fire, it hissed and crackled. The enormity of the problems facing her bore down on her, weighing at her. She kept looking at the fire. In the glowing embers, she saw balls of fire shooting out from a mountain. She felt the heat of the burning around her. She sensed the danger... She shook her head to dispel the images.

"What is it Addy?" asked Glock

"It's nothing. I must still be tired. That's all"

A booming voice angrily shouted,

"Nothing is SOME THING. You must tell us what you see, what you feel. How you feel. You must let us into your world. If there is pain, we must know. If there is anger we must know if there is happiness we must know. Is that clear?"

Addy jumped up and looked around the room. Nobody had shouted yet she felt that Ferris had spoken into her mind,

"Did you do that?" She asked him

He nodded. And much more softly said,

"Addy, you are young and your ether has been free for almost a million years, untethered to human DNA. To awaken it and to understand and live it you must keep us up to date with everything in your mind. You saw something in the fire. You dispel it as nothing. It could be a vision. It could be a sign. It could even be a communication.... Maybe it was your living memory waking up; do you understand that you are now an open book? You need to trust us to guide your ethereal light back to its purpose. If darkness gets you first, chaos will reign…."

"I saw balls of fire being thrown from a mountain top" she felt suddenly tired. The room was in a dark orange glow. Glock and Ferris both stood up.

Ferris handed her a book. The pages were empty as she flicked her thumb over the top. She looked up questioningly

"It has been a full day Addy. You are exposed to new things and people. It will take some getting used to everything, I imagine. Record what you see, feel, remember in that book. Like a diary. Let us join the others for dinner now. We will start our training tomorrow" Glock said kindly and started for the dining hall.

'Glock, Ferris' Addy stopped them, "what about my mother?"

They looked to each other.

"My mother, Marjory? Is she on Earth?"

Ferris looked at Glock and then nodded.

"Verity has other prisoners too. When can we help them? Zyklon and probably Verity, thanks to me, will take their power on the New Moon. I think?"

They looked at each other, "Addy we're thinking through a plan, for the greater good" Ferris explained and then they walked out.

13

"Igarrro, shintato, anviglati" Verity shouted over and over, chanting. The now familiar large circular flatness formed on the ocean surface, the winds died suddenly and in the black mirror of the dark sea, a pale eerie reflection bobbed and wavered, laughing hysterically...

Addy sat up with a hissing in-drawn breath! She ran down the stairwell, rushing into the kitchen.

"Good morning, Glock, Ferris, we must talk immediately."

They both stared at her for a moment and then quickly followed her back to the library room in the house. She retold her awful nightmare. Glock and Ferris stood for a long moment in silence. Thinking and not speaking openly to her. Glock went to the corner of the room and incanted something under his breath. A drawer popped open and silently offered its contents. Glock reached into the drawer and lifted an enormous book.

Leather bound and strapped, it held intrigue. He carried it over to the desk and deposited it in a pile of dust. He started explaining,

"My great-grandfather's memory, if I interpret it correctly, thinks there may be an answer to your vision in this book, Addy" he opened the book "I have never seen this book, it poses a rather unique challenge for me" he had turned the front cover when the book took on a life of its own. The pages ran backwards and forwards. Dust hit up into the room making Addy cough. She covered her nose and mouth and stepped backwards. The book stopped moving on its own.

"Interesting," said Ferris, "Move forward again Addy"

Addy stepped forward. The book frantically spun on its spine. Addy knew instinctively to put her hand over the book. She held it steady mid-air just over the book. The book calmed down, found a page it seemed to be looking for and then settled on the open page. The three moved forward at the same time.

Symbols lit up red and angry on the page – light dazzled from the book and hit the ceiling.

Addy's heart was pounding so fast, her breath caught in her throat. "These are exactly like the tattoos in my vision."

"Keep your hand over the book" Ferris was distracted, studying the symbols on the ceiling.

Glock leant forward and started reading. Addy could not understand the words. It was not in English.

"I am slow to read like this. I must access many life memories ago to understand the script. We must find a protection spell, Addy you can't stand like that all through this chapter. It will take me hours." Glock frowned, "I know. Find Razzy. He will understand this."

Addy was about to move when both men shouted simultaneously, "Don't move!" She froze.

Ferris must have called Razzy by some other means. He appeared in the doorway, huffing from exertion.

"What's wrong?" He asked innocently

"Come closer Raz, look at this script. Can you translate?" Ferris almost barked at Razzy

Razzy leant over the book. His eyes lit up, he instantly recognized the script.

"Yes, I can understand. Do you want me to do it now? I can just sit with the book for a few hours and write my translation?" He asked

"No. We need you to read and do it now. We must put the book away as soon as we can. Addy is protecting us as she stands there…" Ferris explained.

Razzy glanced at Addy and smiled. She smiled back.

Her arm was already too heavy for her. She felt the aches run down her shoulder and back.

Addy's mind began to wonder as she stood guarding the book.

She felt the wind on her face and heard Verity shouting, "Igarro, shintato, anvilgati" The ocean roared behind her, the chanting louder and louder, "Igarro, shintato, anvilgati" it droned on and on.

Wind howled above the monotone, "Igarro, shintato, anvilgati", the ocean evened out. The tattoos glowed angrily. On the wall, on the sea, on the wall, on the sea.

"No Verity!" Addy's voice reverberated over the ocean, echoing and mocking and rattled around the room simultaneously.

Verity was angry but a smirk adorned her face. Her eyes glowed red and she stared from her vision directly at Addy. Addy felt she had won a battle. She was so tired.

The room was normal. The symbols that previously glowed bright red on the ceiling were gone. Addy knew they were safe now. She didn't know how she knew. She just did. She put her arm down and sank to the floor in a pile.

Glock and Ferris helped her up while Razzy finished the translation.

"What happened?" She asked exhausted.

"You connected with Verity. She is searching for you. She did not know that she had found you, unfortunately now she does. You interrupted a ceremony of some kind. Evil no doubt. Why don't you get a drink with Razzy and we will read over the interpretation? Find us when you are ready to continue." Suggested Glock

Addy followed Razzy out of the library. He was quiet and subdued. Unusual for him.

The sunshine felt good on her skin. The grass tickled her ankles where the socks and jeans left a gap. She stared out at the rolling hills and city beyond. Silence was comforting.

"It's not good, is it? The translation…" she asked tentatively.

Razzy cast his eyes to the ground. He continued to pick at the grass seeds for a few moments, then with a deep sigh he rolled onto his side and leaning on his elbow looked at Addy, slowly he answered,

"Addy, the translations are cryptic. They are a collection of previous generations Quinary memories. "He hesitated as he tried to find the words to explain.

"You know how we may have a thought that may seem significant at the time but we cannot understand what it means or why we have that feeling? Well when members of the Quinary have these thoughts they sometimes don't understand if it is a memory from their ancestry or if it is a vision of the future. It is sometimes clear but other times they aren't sure. Well these translations are a collection of such thoughts that the ancient Quinarians had which they did not understand. It is not from only one Quinarian. The exact translation I was asked to look at belongs to Nebulus's great grandfather" Razzy went quiet for a moment.

Addy tried to comprehend what this meant.

"Razzy what did the translation say?"

"The translation was one paragraph. There may be others that I need to look at to make more sense of what I read. Also, there is the problem of Nebulus's kind." he looked at Addy imploring her with his eyes not to ask him this.

"Nebulus's kind? What do you mean? Why are you being so vague? If I am to help you and Thear, I need answers," Addy jumped up, agitated.

Razzy was on his feet and he took both Addy's hands into his.

"Addy, I simply work at the museum in Nedsy. It is an honor for me to be here and to have met and become your friend. But you must understand that I am bound in service to Glock. He

146

has a plan for your training and I am worried to mess things up…. This is important. It's like national security. Do you understand?"

Addy nodded. "You better come with me to get that drink then. I need to find Glock and Ferris and get some answers before my head explodes."

Razzy stood up and opened his arms wide. Addy instinctively stepped in for the hug.

Little things, she thought smiling.

Pelany crested the hill; Addy saw her step falter and the pain in her eyes, just seconds before she recovered. With a fake smile, she waved cheerily.

"Hi! Pearl said to call you for lunch" she smiled.

One more thing to fix.

"Everything all right?" Razzy asked

Pel nodded without catching their eye. She turned and they followed in silence.

Addy wished she could somehow make Pel understand that she only thought of Razzy as a friend and was no threat to her. No. the only person she wanted was flying over a cliff edge in another world. How she missed him.

Lunch was a quiet affair. Addy left as soon as she could to find Ferris and Glock. They were still in the library pouring over the book and making notes furiously.

She entered hesitantly, hovering in the doorway. Without even glancing up Ferris said,

"Come in Addy. Come and look here"

She leant over the book they were looking at. Glock pointed to the symbols on the page.

"Are these the symbols in your dream Addy?"

The crescent shapes mocked her senses.

She nodded and he continued,

"Have you seen them before your dream this morning?"

She shook her head.

"No. I had never seen them before…" before she could finish

the sentence, her mind had strong vision. She must have visibly flinched;

"What is it Addy? Tell us?"

Addy held her head and squeezed her eyes shut,

"I see them in my head now. Like a memory. But it's not my memory. It's so vague. Just flashes. They aren't glowing red. They don't look so angry. They are just tattoos, on a girl. A young girl. There are two of them – girls. They are laughing, they are friends or close. I can't hear what they are saying… that's all" she opened her eyes.

"What does this mean?"

"It's your living memory Addy. It is slowly being activated. Seeing those symbols must have helped. Your Ether history is being activated. We will start putting the memories together. It will be the first we have from the fifth Quinary. This is your history Addy," Glock said excitedly.

"What about the translation?" She asked

"Ah yes. The translation" said Ferris

"Come and sit down my dear" Ferris indicated to the lounge chair as he moved along to join her. Glock closed the book and returned it to its resting place. He slowly joined them and only when all were seated did Ferris continue,

"Neb's great grandad," Ferris paused and chuckled fondly, "Nimbus, he was something else! The translation Razz did was one of Nimbus's memories. Unfortunately, we do not know if Nimbus had a memory or a vision. This is the drawback of having a living memory Addy. Sometimes you will know and sometimes it's all guesswork." he smiled and rested his hands on his wooden staff, "That's why you write them down. So that others can help solve the pieces. Nimbus like Neb now, viewed the world in a different way and this makes interpreting some of his memories more difficult."

Ferris paused then looked at Glock,

"Do you have the translation Glocky?" He asked. Glock straightened the paper he was holding and started reading

"A pact was sealed with blood.
But five are not alone.
Ternion will come.
And only Kivnon can deliver us from despair".

Power prickled across Addy. "Do you know what it means?" She asked softly.

"We can only surmise what it means. We need to take it before the whole Quinary. Our joint collective memory may be prompted to shed more light on this. It may also be Nimbus's vision of something unrelated to any of our histories. Does it make you feel or think anything Addy?" Glock asked.

Addy shook her head, "No. It means nothing to me."

Ferris stood up.

"Verity looks evil. Different to normal" she whispered, "how can we save my friends from her? Her and Zyklon?" Addy spoke softly.

"Patience, my dear" Ferris held her shoulder momentarily, Addy was getting used to the warm gestures.

Later in the day, Addy followed Razzy to Glock's workshop. The room was large and round; the transparent floor was suspended over an enormous pocket watch. The walls all around the watch flickered with lights. Addy noticed the earth just above 3 o' clock, it was all lit up with tiny sparkling lights, and she saw the jiggered line dividing the world into day and night. Above 9 'clock was a similar map yet there were small differences. At five o clock, there were amazing images of supernovas moving and changing across the screen. The large arms of the clock in the floor moved across a notch and the star images at 5 o clock changed. There were other screens that flickered and moved continuously.

There's too much for one peek.

The miniature cubes similar to those hanging around the estate, were suspended in one five-minute zone.

Definitely for later exploring.

The timeline appeared to be continuously changing across the ceiling of the pocket watch, in the opposite direction. The inner floor of the watch was a pentagon, the edges ending in triangles with glowing orbs. Each orb had a different colour, it pulsed gently.

Men and women and, Addy was sure, even a few animals were working at intervals around the clock, either watching the screens or on their hands and knees touching the floor.

Razzy and Addy stepped into the room at 1 'o clock, Glock came over arms extended,

"Welcome, my dear, welcome! Don't step into the zone yet, it's not ready." He lead them along the outer rim of the clock and then pushed a button on a panel somewhere close to 4 o clock and a door slid open. They followed Glock into the small room, dominated by a large window or screen – Addy wasn't sure. It looked like a window but the images on it did not look like the scenery she had seen that morning.

"This is my space. We can talk here. Addy, how are you feeling now? How is your head?" Glock enquired.

"I feel fine. I don't have a headache anymore. But...?" Before Addy could continue, Glock held up his hands,

"Let me first bring you up to speed dear, then you can ask as many questions as you want" Glock said with some finality to his voice.

"Our planet, Thear is old. Much older than Earth. Many angry forces and Celestial beings have been at war for many billions of years. Ethers, which are like large invisible bands of strength and power, hold planets and stars and suns in place." Glock got really animated and jumped up drawing on the glass wall," Ethers have other special properties and if you are lucky enough to be born with ethereal power, you are considered magical."

Glock's hands moved rapidly, drawing arrows in green and red and black. "Long, long ago, about four and half billion years ago during the Split Wars, strong forces in the universe had a notion that they could control all of the ether and thus have ultimate power in the universe. They rallied a large following but the Celestial beings chose to keep the balance in the universe. A large battle followed, nobody conquered the other, but the ethers were tampered with signficantly," he faced them, eyebrows twitching excitedly.

I need to follow this.

"The world as we know it rumbled and rolled, there was darkness and chaos in our world. When the sun did shine she burnt the surface of our planet, seas rose and deserts spread." the picture he painted was bleak, "There weren't many Celestials left but they came together and to restore balance they plucked five strings from the Ether holding us in place in the universe and plaited that ether into the DNA of five Thearians that are pledged to eternity to maintain balance." Glock's eyes glazed over, the colour of dark chocolate. He looked old and tired for a moment.

"Five Thearians: representing life through earth, water and air and then time and balance. These five forces require one another to work." Glock's voice went quiet for a moment, he reached for a glass of water.

"Addy, in my DNA I have the fourth strand of Ether interwoven. I am known as Father Time. The first second and third strands are interwoven into my dearest friends who live here on Thear. You are the fifth force of the Quinary. You have the last strand of ether intertwined in your DNA. When the Celestials plucked the Ether Strands they underestimated the damage that had already been done to the ether at that time. In their attempt to restore balance, they effectively created a phenomenon so magnificent that it has no name in our universe. This process created Earth. Unfortunately, when the bang happened, the fifth force was plucked from our world and flung onto Earth. The big bang itself restored balance and we only had to restore local imbalances and put our world right.

We have managed with only four forces for the last four billion years. Ah, before you ask, I am not four billion years old. The ether enables us to have a living memory of the last 4 and half billion years through my father and his fathers before him, so functionally I am much older than what you are accustomed to – having lived about Eight Hundred years now – but my living memory goes back to the day the ether was put into our DNA. And so does yours".

"How do you know that the ether is in my DNA? There are seven billion people on the planet Earth. My magic is evil, I have no living memory. I really think you have the wrong person" Addy had the sinking feeling that they had made a huge mistake... "I can't even meditate, I forget what I had for lunch yesterday, and I don't even know my parents..."

"Addy, we know you are the one with the Ether in your DNA because we have been tracking the ether for years. It's a strand of the force of nature. The force of the universe. It emits a pulse, an energy."

Glock's eyes were now a deep blue colour and he gazed, expectantly upon Addy...

"I don't even know where to start...." Addy was confused, she jumped up and started pacing,

"Glock, if I have the Ether DNA, it is useless to me. I can't do anything. Do you know that people are waiting for me to assist them back on Earth? My real mother is on Earth, friends relying on me, I, I" Addy faltered, she could not quite formulate an argument supporting her life on Earth.

"Addy, we deliberated on this. We know. But I must show you something." Glock jumped up, Razzy and Addy followed him out.

He went back into the clock room and quickly walked along the outer edge of the clock's perimeter until they got to about 10 'o clock.

At the spot a creature, light blue and wearing a lab coat stood. He had two fat sausages in the shape of fleshy hair locks hanging down the side of his face. His large eyes took up most of his face and his nose was on his forehead. He had a big friendly smile.

"Larkin, My Lady" he bowed low.

"Just Addy" she whispered in amazement.

"Larkin, bring up the Cramfloor View, focus on the earth hot spots" Glock turned and started pushing buttons and tapping on the panels,

"Cramfloor is the halfway mark between Thear and Earth – our combined abilities have enabled us to zone in to both planets from this angle." The screen changed rapidly and split down the centre, one side was the earth and the other was Thear, they looked similar but Earth was a bigger planet. The view focused in and then zoomed again; it kept zooming up closer and closer to earth.

Snow sheets drove across the tundra. Addy shivered as she envisaged the cold and dreaded conditions. Almost immediately the view changed, forest after forest were being mowed down. Large machines crunched at the trees like a computer game. The view switched, rain and wind pummeled a city centre, people ran for cover, water ruthlessly bearing down on all. The sun beat down on the dry parched land cracking the earth open and yet another view showed masses and masses of pollution swirling in the ocean. Animals caught and dying in its wake.

Cities and towns continued to beat at their own pace. Addy watched, fixated at the destruction and horror she saw before her.

"The biomass on earth is being depleted faster than it can restore itself" Glock spoke as he continued to punch buttons and touch screens, "that is what humanity is doing to themselves" he stated flatly, "but this" he touched and zoomed the screen in, "this is Verity and Zyklon and their doing" he jabbed at a grey mass moving over the earth, zooming in close.

"What is that?" asked Addy,

"It will cause storms, hurricanes, tornadoes, the energy

released will cause fires of mass devastation, and it will destroy crops and throw lakes and seas in turmoil. It will spread like wildfire…. neither of us will survive." The screen went blank. Addy turned to Glock,

"Is this why I am here? Bundles of bad energy in the middle of nowhere?"

"Yes, Addy. These bundles of energy cannot be controlled by any of our forces in isolation. We need the Quinary to restore balance. These forces have been in motion for many years already. We have attempted several times to get rid of them…. We have also tried to help parts of Earth that have been lost during the Dark Forces experimentation. Tsunamis, cyclones, recent events on earth…. We need your help to stop them. We need you to balance the Quinary. Will you help us?"

The room went quiet. The ticking and whizzing and buzzing all faded to nothing. Every breath was held. The room appeared suspended in time.

Addy had a sudden vision of mass devastation sweep through her head. Storms of such magnitude that she gasped for breath,

I don't think I can. Her inner voice whispered.

"Ye-yes, I will do what I can" the whole room erupted in applause. Glock seemed to visibly inhale. Everyone smiled. The room started to spin whiz and pop as before. Under her breath she whispered,

"Glock, I don't know what it is that I can do. I have friends there. Dane…"

"Ssh. All will be fine, child".

14

Addy liked the library. The overstuffed cushions propped her up as she contemplated what to do. The fire warmed her, she trailed her finger over the faded carpet's pattern.

So much happening. Oh, Dane, Grit! Hang in there. Mum? Please hang in there. She silently pleaded.

I wonder if I can contact Meg?

The door opened, Addy scrambled to a sitting position.

"Addy, we need to put you on the Ether-reader. It measures the strength of your ether. We need to do some tests so that we can establish your power" Ferris moved into the room reaching for his pipe, "Bloody new rules, been smoking me herbs for hundreds of years" he muttered under his breath toying with the tobacco. His large bushy eyebrows jumped up and down in frustration.

Nerves ran through Addy. "What if I'm not strong enough to assist? What if my power is useless? Nobody else should rely on me. I haven't come through once yet"

"Natural stuff this. Nothing harmful in here. Bloody grow it me self," he muttered as he trailed back out, distracted. Addy followed the Wizard.

They entered a translucent purple cube. Ferris waved his arm and then showed her to exit first.

The room was large and pentagonal in shape. Each tier of the room had a large symbol on the floor. The floor was smooth like marble and each symbol was dark and suspended beneath the smooth floor. The area above the symbol had a perfect circle in the ceiling – the late afternoon sky could be seen through the five holes. To the one end of the room just at the entrance of the cube was a separate symbol, the actual pentagon shape itself. A half circle shield ran up the back of the wall embracing the symbol on the floor. The most amazing thing about the room was that when you looked to the right, across the five floor symbols the room seemed to go on forever. Smooth marble floors leading from the archway to another to another and so on. The place was intriguing and also made Addy feel energized and excited.

Ferris seemed to vocalize her thoughts,

"This place is ancient and magical Addy. We do not try to comprehend how it works or how it came to be. We only use it like The Quinary remembers."

Glock was standing in front of the wall to the left of where they entered the hall. He was whispering and holding his palms up to the wall. Addy moved closer to Glock, she noticed the previously white wall was slowly changing colour. Almost as though the wall was blushing the pale pink crept up from the bottom and when it reached Glock's hands the wall parted and a long cylinder swung into place soundlessly. Glock stepped aside and looked to Addy,

"Come on Addy. Step into the cylinder. You will experience a lovely sensation. It will feel like the air is hugging you gently and then your ether will be read. The strength of your ether will be indicated by the amount of sunshine that is captured on the inside rails of the cylinder. The higher the rays reach the stronger your ether. We all have our ethers read from time to time you can see the standard markings on the tubes" he indicated the markings.

"What are the markings on the other side?" Asked Addy

"Many folks with power come here to be tested. Most people that have magic have an ether reading." Glock was patient as he explained, "It is a special gift that they can tap into the external ether in the universe when they require power. If they are powerful sorcerers then theoretically they should have unlimited power from the external ethers" it made sense so far, "so, to answer the questions, it's for magical folk that come for readings. We encourage this so that we can assist in developing their powers for good. See that mark over there? Well, that's Ferris's last reading. He is the most powerful sorcerer we have on Thear. If you follow the marking across you will notice that his power is on par with The Quinarians. The Quinarians can only use the power they have inside of them," this didn't sound right to Addy recalling the mountains outside of Rachel's workshop. Glock continued "We suspect that that when the five of us are together we will have five times the amount of power available to us at that moment. The downside is that we expect we will only have this power available to us when we are physically together. We hope to utilize this to conquer the dark forces. Unfortunately, this is all surmised at the moment. We will only know when we gather at the next Quinary. Step in when you are ready, Addy. Do you have any questions?" Glock asked.

"What if I have no power?" She asked.

Glock and Ferris both smiled indulgently at her.

"You have power, Addy. That is how we managed to find you – this is just a reading. We suspect that you will have the same ethereal power as The Quinary. We have documented visions that unknown powerful forces will attempt to take this power from us and we have made it a habit to monitor everyone's reading so that we can be sure we are safe." Explained Glock

Addy took a deep breath. She stepped into the cylinder.

"When I close the door, take a deep breath. Just relax. Ancient magic will do the rest."

She turned to face Ferris and Glock and then smiled. She nodded to Glock. The door closed and she took a deep breath.

The air immediately became quite thick and just like Glock explained, she felt she was being hugged. Glock smiled and nodded. She saw the yellow rays running up the sides of the cylinder. It reminded her of an old mercury temperature thermometer. The colour rose steadily on both sides of the metre. She saw Glock and Ferris look poignantly at each other. She felt relief that there was a reading but she felt by their exchanged glances there was something not right. The metres continued to rise and as they did the captured sunlight changed from yellow to orange, to green to blue and continued to move through the colour spectrum. The light that was given off shone brilliantly in the hall, it bedazzled everything. The floors that were so smooth reflected the colours onto the walls and the walls bounced the colour onto the carved stalactites. There was colour everywhere. The colours continue to rise she could not see the end of metre so she continued to look around her. She saw Glock and Ferris talk animatedly. They both stared at the cylinder's monitors. The colour rose and rose. Addy suddenly shut her eyes; the colour had turned into a blinding white light. It felt like an enormous star had suddenly exploded right in the cylinder. The glare was overwhelming. She felt the power of the light through her closed eyes. She heard Ferris shout that she must keep her eyes closed. She crouched down on the floor of the cylinder covering her eyes. A long way off in the distance she heard a small popping noise. It started to rumble and come closer and closer. She heard the thunder, a loud clapping sound. It made her jump. Suddenly the door was open and Glock was dragging her out of the cylinder. He quickly closed the door. The noise quietened down and Addy blinked a few times to adjust her eyes to the room that now appeared dark in comparison to brilliant white of just a moment before.

"Are you hurt Addy?" Ferris asked concerned

"No, no, I am fine. What happened? Did a storm come over?" Asked Addy

"We can talk in the library, Addy. Let's go." Ferris nodded to Glock. Glock moved to stand to the left of the cylinder. He placed his hand back on the wall and the cylinder moved back into it. When the cylinder was put away, they started moving towards the cube when out of the corner of her eye; Addy noticed coloured lights down the hallway in the distant arches.

"Oh, look," she pointed, "How lovely!"

Ferris and Glock both stopped and turned to where she was pointing. At a run both men went towards the far arches, stopping short of entering the second archway. Addy caught up.

"What is it?" She asked

"I haven't seen it before" Glock whispered

The lights looked like solid round cylinders. They popped up and became really bright then just as it started to fade away, another light of equal intensity popped up in another place. From where the they stood they could not see what was generating the light or what it was highlighting.

"Can we get closer?" Asked Addy, "It looks like its highlighting markings or symbols on that wall"

Both men put out a restraining arm at the same time

"No" they simultaneously said

"Sorry, Addy. Let me explain. This is the Archway of Reality. You need to be completely at ease with yourself. Balanced. This room will show you memories, visions, situations unique to you. Situations that can challenge even us Ancient Quinarians and make them doubt themselves. It is not the room we wish you to look into at this time of your training." Explained Ferris

"It is most intriguing" said Glock, "We must send word to Celia, Roz and Neb immediately"

They turned from the Archway of Reality, more questions springing to mind for Addy. They started to move back towards the first Archway. A light suddenly shone from above. Ferris stopped and Addy nearly knocked into him. The yellow beam shone through one ceiling opening of the pentagon and lit the floor up, it shone with a gathering intensity and then just when it became almost unbearable to look at the light stopped. When her eyes adjusted, Addy noted that the symbols underneath the floor were glowing. The colour changed continuously but what became even more significant was that the symbols beneath the floor that were glowing most certainly matched the symbols that Addy had seen tattooed on Verity.

The symbols continued to glow and change colour. The three visitors stood in a long silence before Glock said,

"Let us return to the library. We need to convene."

***

On Earth, in the Ferrana Caves Verity paced her chamber. Her reflection caught in the mirror. She felt her power – it was good to have it back. She waved her arm agitating the flames. The swell of power was blissful. But not enough. She wasn't at full strength. She needed more.

But now, I can take it. No more waiting!

"Yes" she hissed in satisfaction as she headed down the corridor.

The prisoners sat on benches in rows in the chamber. They weren't restrained; no need, Zyklon commanded their cerebral cortexes, ordering them to stay. Mind manipulation, he always liked that.

Verity touched each prisoner on their third eye; searching for the energy field that was most trying to resist the charm.

"Ah! Should have guessed it would be you Marj" Verity knew they heard her. They knew they were imprisoned, knew they were unrestrained, knew that on the New Moon, they would have all their power drained and would probably die. They knew

160

all of this but could not move themselves from the situation. His charm was strong.

Verity caught the tear falling down her sister's cheek. Her sister was strong. Stronger than her. Zyklon must have been harvesting power in the last few years to have overcome her. She filed the thought for later.

"This will only hurt a bit. In fact, I'll be doing you a favour, Sis." She crouched down in front of Marjory, sweeping the hair back from Marjory's face, "you will have a little less power, less resistance to the charm on your mind" she smiled insincerely.

Marjory stared vacantly ahead. She felt the tears trickle down her face. Tears for the pain and cruelty her daughter must have endured. If only her mind would engage her own thoughts. What had Zyklon done? Her head thumped. Verity looked spectacular. How had she managed to stay so youthful without power? She couldn't be at full strength. She needed a full lunar cycle for that.

It was just days since the last New Moon; thankfully a long wait until the next one. Someone would come. Verity needed the New Moon to drain all of them completely. But Marjory knew that she could harvest free power now, without a new moon. It wouldn't kill her, just weaken her. Someone will come. She knew it.

Why is Verity doing this? Where has all that cruelty come from? How did she get so involved in the dark stuff? Ugh! Get a grip Marjory!

Her mind picked at the same questions she had pondered for years.

Dad always thought she was just experimenting. "She's a good girl inside Marj. She won't venture far. She's made from the same stuff as us." He was convinced, even when Verity held a knife to his throat, urging Marjory to concede her power; even then he thought she would see the light; "Come on Ver – you wouldn't hurt yer old dad? Let's just settle in and talk about this?"

Verity stood, bored of the waiting. Her arms cast long shadows on all the walls of the chamber as she summoned her power to her. Marjory felt it whoosh up against them. Not like her power. Different.

Verity pulled back Marjory's head, yanking her hair down so that her neck was exposed, her mouth up to the ceiling.

Stop. Stand up. Marjory urged her limbs. Nothing. Zyklon's command rendered her totally spineless, totally useless, not even a facial expression could be made. But a full working mind.

Inches from her mouth, Verity started chanting," Voco potestas terræ. Et potestas maria iubes? Ted obtestor per ventis? Audi ignis Quod in potestate mea sit, et annuntiaturus est?"

Marjory heard her;

I call the earth,
I command the seas,
I implore the winds!
Listen fire!
The power within is mine!
I declare it so!

She felt the energy moving inside of her. Rising. Her mind could not resist. She was a puppet. This would not kill her. Not until the new moon. Until then they would just harvest her free energy. The more her body made, they more they could harvest. Until the New Moon. Then, the source of the energy would be extracted from her. Then she would die.

Verity became more animated. The hundreds of arms shadowed in the cave embracing them all in their dark depths, "I declare it so!" she repeated in English.

"I declare it so." She breathed above Marjory's upturned mouth and inhaled the energy that curled there, rising from Marjory's core.

The energy infused into Verity, she lit up for a moment, the movement fanning her hair in its momentum.

"Yesss!" she breathed deeply, eyes closed, reveling in the high it brought.

***

The library was warm, Addy sat down gratefully, Glock followed. Ferris pulled his pipe from somewhere in his tunic and as he rubbed his beard, the pipe lit up, cherry tobacco wafted on the air, curling and twirling mesmerizing.

He puffed and puffed causing large plumes of smoke to escape the end of the pipe. The fire leapt shouting for attention, and the room felt more comfortable and warmer instantly.

Glock and Addy sat down on either end of the three-seater lounge and just waited quietly. Time seemed to slow for a moment. The fire crackled and popped and the smoke swirled around the room. It lingered lazily before dissipating into nothing.

Glock started talking as he rested his elbows on his knees staring into the flames, "Great power comes with great responsibility" the fire crackled, each lost in their thoughts, listening for Glock's words, "My great-grandad met a Celestial at the Lakes of Catherine many, many years ago. My grand-dad was weary from travel; the Celestial was a welcome distraction. They talk cryptically and often don't make sense. They each spoke of their lives, how they spent their time, where they found value." Glock paused for a moment, thinking

"The Celestial told his version of the Ether Split, the Big Bang. My grandad dismissed the story at the time because it did not make any sense. The Celestial spoke of bleak desolate years, people were on the verge of starvation, fighting and corruption ruled the land. There was no reason, no emotion other than hatred." Glock paused letting the words sink in slowly as he recalled them, "He told of the heavens rumbling as the Celestials convened. Dark forces threatened to overturn this world. The Celestials agreed to weave Ethereal Power into living beings from Thear to assist in protecting, not only this planet but the balance of things in the universe. He told how they worked and struggled to pluck the right strings for the right beings. He sat on the riverbank and told my grandad about eight Ethereal Forces…" Glock let the news sink in

Ferris sat forward, his eyebrows knitting up and down. He puffed furiously on his pipe,

"Go on, Glock" he barked. Addy looked from one to the other, not sure what the significance of this story was.

"The Celestials story was that four ethers had been plucked and woven into beings that had pledged allegiance to working for the causes of good. Whilst working on the fifth element, as we know, the Ether's were forced apart and with a loud bang, Earth was formed. The fifth force, as we know was taken from us at this time. All our living memories recall being advised by the Celestial Council that the force of five will maintain balance. The Celestial on the riverbank told my grandad, that during the turmoil of the aftermath, dark Celestials managed to pluck three more strings from the Ether." He stopped again, pulling the information to him, "They were woven into three beings with more power than we have and intent: opposite. He did not say where they reside or who they are. But the fifth force was the most powerful ethereal force, it was plucked at the moment of the Big Bang, the power it holds is unchartered. My grandad and the Celestial had shared much mead by this time; my granddad recalled the story but dismissed it as the ramblings of a drunk Celestial."

"But Five was not alone, Ternion will come" recalled Addy

"Ternion is three" stated Ferris

"The ethereal whole is made of eight?" Addy asked

Glock jumped up and started pacing backwards and forwards.

"It's all coming together now" he stated.

We are five or we are eight but we are all one. Addy recalled the Celestial at the Lake.

Glock turned to Addy dramatically,

"Addy, your inner power was off the charts in that reading. You have more power than the whole Quinary. You have not pledged allegiance to do *Good*. You are being sought after by the Ternion, if they harness your power, they will destroy the universe as we know it."

"But I… You think… I might be the third force with Verity and Zyklon?" Addy started to protest

Ferris spoke directly into her head,

"Hush, Addy. We need to help you properly unleash it. Your heart will lead you to the right conclusion, I know it" he smiled warmly at her

You don't know what I've done Ferris. I am already evil, already lost to you. I am a killer.

Her heart constricted.

Glock broke the moment, "We must send word to The Quinary immediately. Then we will start your training Addy"

"Devlin, can you organize comms? We need to alert Roz, Celia and Neb. Be brief and to the point. Also send a Brownie to the King, he needs to know what is going on. Jordy? Where are you? Ah" Glock was efficient as he spoke into the open space, communicating with his Lab. "Jordy, we need to train Addy. Can you set up a training field for this afternoon?"

"Sure thing" the dwarf responded.

Several hours later, the message for the Quinarians was ready.

Glock stood at the edge of the lake, arms outstretched. Silence filled the space around them. The piercing noise sliced into Addy, it reminded her when Rodic's television used to be off station. Addy glanced over and realized that Glock was making the noise. Addy also realized that she understood what he was saying.

"Messenger of the Lakes, please assist us?" he called out.

Glock repeated the request twice. Then waited. The grey waters were smooth as a mirror, not a ripple, not a current. There was no noise. The bulrushes lopped their heads low, nearly touching the water. They looked on expectantly.

Noiselessly ripples appeared on the surface of the water. They fanned out and lapped on the edge of the banks. The lake surface broke to reveal the most beautiful face.

The woman's skin was pale and perfect; her lips were full and her eyes large and aquamarine in colour. Her hair hung perfectly over her right shoulder; it was bright green and just skimmed her naked breasts. She twisted her lower body so that she was in a sitting position. Her tail glistened in the morning sun, translucent aquamarine. Her eyes were the same colour and appeared to search into her soul. She made a sound that Addy understood as a greeting,

"Eeeek, eeek ek" she said, then switched to English,

"Greeting Land lovers" she breathlessly whispered. Addy noticed that Razzy was practically swooning. Her voice was like a lover's whisper. Soft and breathy. You felt like she was talking to each one individually.

"Greetings Myra! How are you?" Glock asked.

"Well! Glock." She whispered on the breeze.

"Let me introduce you, this is Razzy, Pelany and Addy. You have met Ferris before" Glock pointed at each in turn,

Myra studied each person and inclined her head. When she got to Addy, she clasped her hands together, the shells around her wrist tinkled. With her palms together she propelled her hands forward; Addy felt the puff of wind on her face, like a soft embrace.

"It is an acknowledgement of your status Addy, it is like an embrace" explained Glock.

Addy felt embarrassed and unsure of how to accept this. Thankfully, Glock continued.

"Myra, how is Roz?" He continued with the formality.

"She is well, Glock. She is busy. How can I be of service today?" She tinkled.

Razzy had to sit down. Pelany was getting more and more agitated with Razzy. Glock continued,

"Myra, important information needs to be communicated to Roz as soon as possible. We have prepared it in the usual way. It should be easy for you to carry, if it is your will to assist us?" he enquired.

"Of course, Glock. I am willing to assist." Glock waded into the lake and handed Myra a locket. It was a beautiful shell on a thin thread of fabric that appeared to shimmer against her skin.

"The information is contained therein" explained Ferris at Addy's side "Only Roz will be able to open it".

Myra looked at each in turn, almost causing Rasem to pass out. Addy realized that Razzy's reaction was due to Myra's ability to speak into your head, just like Ferris did with her,

"Welcome, little one. Do good," was the soft whisper in her head, she instinctively responded.

"Thank-you Myra, I hope to" she thought back and almost fell over when she heard, faintly,

"You're welcome, follow your heart".

Addy must have audibly reacted. Everyone stared at her. She blushingly explained,

"I heard her, in my head".

"She spoke to us all Addy" explained Glock.

"I mean, I spoke back to her and she answered me" stammered Addy excitedly.

Glock and Ferris smiled at each other.

"That is good Addy. Our first tool to work with" said Ferris.

"Come" said Glock, "we still have two more to deliver and then training," he started walking up the banks of the lake. Everyone followed.

"What is the matter with you?" hissed Pelany at Razzy, "You were acting like a love-struck puppy".

"I was not!" Razzy hissed back, red in the face.

"Pelany, it is an ancient ability that the Mermaids have perfected. They can make any male swoon at their fins. Some believe that they enchant males that are confused or have not taken a mate yet. Others believe the Mermaids hypnotize them so that they can't remember the details of the encounter. Each way, it is commonly thought that it is a security tactic. A little outdated now, I think." Glock stated." I should ask Roz when I see her next" he trailed off.

They walked for a few minutes climbing the banks of the lake. Moving back towards the Towers. Glock ducked into a side path in the dense shrubs and everyone had to get into single file. They walked like this for a few minutes.

Addy felt easy, the birds were twittering and playing in the trees around them. When the path opened into a clearing, everyone filed out into the opening. There in the opening was a magnificent old tree. Large and proud and tall.

"This is MB Ficus" announced Glock.

Addy looked around but could not see anyone.

"Where?" She asked Razzy.

"The tree" he whispered.

"What?" She asked.

"The tree." He whispered again.

Addy looked at the Tree. It was a beautiful tree. Its plumage formed a half circle from one side all around the top of the main trunk and over the other side. A striking olive green with greyish green highlights, magnificent to behold. The trunk twisted, forming large grooves from every aspect. The branches twisted manically. The roots stood above the ground forming a vein structure around the base of the trunk.

Glock strode up to the tree and followed the twisted trunk until he was almost out of sight. He beckoned to the others to follow. They followed him into the trunk, the twisting almost enclosing them inside the tree. Glock put his hand on a knot, about shoulder height to himself. The tree shivered. Everyone waited. The area was warm and smelt earthy. The silence filled the cavity. Still Glock stood with his palm to the knot of the tree trunk.

From deep inside the earth Addy heard the rustlings of the tree. She closed her eyes. It was communicating. She felt the tinniest vibrations travelling in the roots around her. Before the tree actually spoke, Addy knew what it was communicating. A deep gravelly voice spoke slowly,

"G-l-o-c-k-e-n-s-t-e-i-n." there was a long pause then, "w-e-l-c-o-m-e" said Ficus

"Thank-you, Ficus! How are you?" Asked Glock

"M-m-m-m" pause "T-r-o-u-b-l-e i-n- E-a-s-t" Ficus slowly rattled out, "N-e-w v-i-s-i-t-o-r?"

Addy put her hands on the root reaching to her knees and bent down. She still had her eyes closed. She could feel the vibrations from Ficus much quicker now. She heard him in *tree language,*

"Not many of your kind understand me. You have travelled far. Your vibrations are strong. Who are you?" Asked Ficus.

Addy formed the response in her head and let her hands communicate the message back.

"I am Addy. I am the fifth Quinarian. I have not learnt my powers yet. I am in training with Ferris and Glock."

Addy heard Ferris say to Glock,

"She can speak Tree. That is an ancient language. Ask her to ask Ficus if we can send a message to Celia?"

"Addy, yesss. Your sap is young, but vibrant. Why do you wake Ficus? Can you stop the trouble in the East?"

"I hope to help. That is why I am here. I wish to send a message to Celia. Will you allow us to do this?

The leaves rustled and she felt the rumblings deep in the veins of the majestic tree. She sensed rather than heard that he was in pain.

"What is the matter? Why do you shiver in pain?"

"When a tree nation dies, I feel the loss. The network conveys the feelings" he shivered again.

Addy felt the loss. Tears sprang to her eyes. She could feel the pain of the tree. She had visions of forests being annihilated. Whole areas burnt. She could feel the pain as machines crushed through the trees and as other areas died of thirst and malnourishment in the baking hot sun, she felt the silent vibrations, felt their need.

"Ficus, I can only try to help. I cannot make promises. But I need to send Celia a message. Can you do this?"

"Yesss Addy. I will send the message. All help is needed" said Ficus. He sounded old and tired. Very tired.

She opened her eyes and looked from Ferris to Glock.

"He says he will send the message. What now?"

Glock pulled a small vial out of his jacket pocket.

"This vial contains a drop of tree sap. We have embedded the message into the sap. If we drop it onto his bark it will be absorbed and sent along the network. Celia will get the message quickly."

Addy took the vial. She rubbed the tree root and communicated,

"Ficus. We have embedded the message to Celia in this sap. Can I drop it onto you – will you send it on the network?"

"Scratch some of the bark off, where you touch. I will send your message."

Addy took her nail and gently scratched the bark. She felt his rustling,

"Does that hurt?" she asked

"No, it tickles. It feels good."

Addy smiled. When the bark had been removed on the small patch, she dropped the contents of the vial into the open area. She felt Ficus's change in attitude,

"What is it Ficus?" she asked

"The message is important. Evil forces are already on the planet. Also on the parallel. Celestials have told me; these forces

have caused havoc on Earth. Good luck Addy. Follow your heart"
said Ficus

Addy knelt down and kissed the area she had cleared.
Instantly the opening lit up and then bark grew over it. She
gently rubbed the spot and then whispered in her head,

"Thank-you Ficus." Peace for you and your folk. I will do
what I can."

Addy stood up then and started walking away.

The others followed at a distance. Finally, she slowed down
and allowed them to catch up with her.

"Addy, you obviously have a gift of languages" stated Ferris

Addy nodded. She still had tears in her eyes from feeling
Ficus's pain.

"Are you all right child?" Ferris was concerned.

"Oh Ferris, he was in so much pain! I felt it. It was so sad, we
must help them!"

"We will try to help" his voice was a whisper.

They walked for a long time then Glock caught up.

"I think the key is emotion"

Ferris's eyebrows shot up. He considered this statement for
a moment,

"You may be right! We will try" he said excitedly.

"What is emotion the key to?" asked Addy. Pel and Razzy
were holding back. She smiled when she saw them holding
hands. Desperately trying to not let anyone see.

"Your power" said Glock, "When you felt friendship, you
connected with Myra. When you felt compassion, you connected
with Ficus. You uncovered new abilities this morning. How to
speak Mer and Tree, how to communicate telepathically, and you
healed Ficus. We did not teach you this. You unlocked the power
to enable this by your emotion. Speak to me, telepathically" he
instructed.

Addy thought for a second and then conveyed the message
directly at Glock's forehead,

"Where is our next stop?" she asked.

Glock grabbed his head and screwed up his eyes in pain,

"Wooow, Addy you don't have to scream my head off," he said.

Everyone started to laugh. The seriousness of the previous moments just dissipating into joy.

"Sorry" she whispered into his head.

"Accepted" he said aloud. Addy smiled.

Friends.

They walked for a few more minutes, coming out in sight of the Towers. Next to the stables on the left of the third tower a pathway led out towards the trees. They followed it, stopping a few metres from the trees. On the side, furthest from the Towers was a significant drop. The cliffs dropped vertically into dark crevices below. Addy caught her breath and moved closer to the trees. Glock stepped onto a lip on the cliff. Everyone went silent. He raised his hands to his mouth and belted out a whistle; loud and clear over the cliffs. It echoed for a few moments. She focused on the skies, not quite knowing what to expect anymore. A large shape appeared from below them. It slowly rose.

Addy felt her insides warm. Joy circulated, molten rich.

The shape came up to eye level and then gracefully settled in front of them. It stood majestically in front of Addy, snorting and huffing. Ears just outside of its little horns; prettily placed on top of the scaly head. Such a long graceful neck! The lithe body shimmered in green armor. Scales of emeralds flashed in the sunshine. Leather wings were tucked neatly at its side. Addy was in awe. The dragon was sitting like a graceful kitten, just looking down it's snout at the party on the cliff.

"Nova!" greeted Glock, "How are you?"

The dragon snorted, a brief flame rushed from its mouth and nostrils. The cliff face turned black with soot.

"Greetings Glock! I am well. My Father said to send good

wishes if I saw you. Who are your companions?" She nodded her graceful neck towards Addy and company.

Glock introduced each one and then turned to Addy to explain,

"Nova is on a sabbatical. She has been through her schooling and is going to be apprenticed to her father, Neb." Glock was clearly excited to see Nova. He could hardly stop himself patting her neck. Addy tried to recover from the fact that she had in one day met a mermaid, spoken to a tree and now was standing next to a dragon, in the company of a wizard, sprites and Father Time.

Must be dreaming. Their world was so far from Earth. From Dane. From her mum. Grit, Meg suffering without her family. So far away.

When pleasantries were exchanged, Glock turned to the serious matter that called them to the cliff edge in the first instance. He explained to Nova who Addy was, the news of the Quinary interpretation from the old book and also about the problem of the three evil Quinarians. He explained about Addy's power which made her embarrassed. Nova agreed to take the message back to her Father without delay. Addy was keen to know if she was able to communicate with this majestic creature as she had done with the Mermaid and Tree. She formed the thought in her head, and then gently pushed it towards the Dragon;

"Thank-you for helping us Nova" she gently pushed.

The dragon turned and stared at Addy. She immediately received the thought in her head,

"You're welcome Addy. I have a feeling we'll see much more of one another." Before Addy could respond, Nova neatly dropped off the cliff edge. She disappeared for a moment and then made a majestic turn in front of them,

"Farewell, Addy of Earth! See you soon" she shouted.

Glock turned back towards the trees, "Now we wait".

Addy grabbed his arm, "Glock, how long? We don't have

time! My mum, all those prisoners of Zyklon? Is there nothing we can do now?" Frustration edged her voice.

"Yes, we train now! We ready you, now" Ferris came from behind linking his arm in hers, "first lesson starts right now" he was firm.

15

"First lesson. Meditation. You calm the mind. Centre yourself. Find your inner peace" Ferris stood on the grassy bank of the lake.

"Glock will guide us" he pointed at Glock whose eyebrows sprouted on his brow in pure surprise.

"Yes. Yes. Of course. Good idea. Let me see?" Glock's poignant glance at Ferris made Addy smile, Glock sat down heavily on the grass gesturing for them to join him.

Yeah, right. A carefully thought out plan!

"Close your eyes" he crossed his legs and rested his hands palms up on his knees, "be comfortable" the richness of his voice soothed. Addy saw Ferris follow instructions without hesitation. She did the same.

"Take a deep breath" he breathed in, "long and deep. Steady. Chase it through to your core. All the way to the base of your spine where your first chakra is. Your energy centre." In the silence Addy opened one eye. Both men were peaceful, breathing in evenly. She quickly closed her eyes.

Right, breathe.

"Deep breath. Feel the energy moving now. Release your breath steadily. Slowly" he breathed out. "Again" Addy heard them both inhale deeply. She followed. Relaxation folded over her body.

"Meditation will centre you" he breathed in again, "you need to this daily, twice a day" he breathed in noisily, "and release. Bring your breath to normal" he was silent for a moment, then from a great distance, "wholeness. Complete. One. You. Me. All. We are all one" he continued in a soft monotone, "meditation enhances awareness. When we are aware, present, we free energy tied to the past. Breath in" he breathed soothingly, "we free energy tied to the future. Breath out. We surrender to freedom. Surrender. It enables wholeness of being. Just surrender to now" Glock's voice was soothing. Addy felt herself slip into a peaceful rhythm.

"Surrender" he remained silent a moment. "It will show you the universe. Spirit. Energy. Whatever name you call it" his voice lulled in the rhythm of her breath. "There is only now. Only awareness. Accept now" a long silence followed. Addy felt the wind whisper across her neck, in the distance crickets stirred.

I'm hearing crickets. Amusement diverted her attention. With great effort, Addy concentrated, Glock was still talking, "Wholeness. Presence. It's outside of time; the construct of our making".

Oh boy. Addy shifted quietly trying to ease the stiffness in her lower back. Concentrate!

"When you see the energy. The universe. Feel it. Feel the energy inside of you".

I can do that. The energy flickered across her torso, familiar now.

"The same energy that's in me" he continued, "in all of us, in all things. The same energy that binds us as one. Makes us complete. Makes us whole" he breathed in again, "that's the magic" his voice was hushed, "the essence of us. Our oneness"

Addy felt that gravity of his words. She opened her eyes. Ferris stared straight at her. A small smile twitched across his mouth.

He pointed at the trees and then put his index finger over his mouth showing silence.

Addy followed as he unfolded himself and they tip toed away from the deeply meditating Glock.

When they were a distance away Ferris slowed down. Autumn leaves crinkled under their feet. He stopped and waited for Addy's attention, "You will need to practice meditation. Every day. It will be something you look forward to. It brings peace. Keeps one centred" he stared deeply into her eyes, "it is hard to focus when you first start, but soon enough you will feel the pull of yourself, your inner self. It's where all the answers are Addy. Inside of yourself. Just slow down enough to listen." The gravity of Ferris' speech settled over Addy. She nodded. "I will try". He continued to stare into her for one more moment, then cupped her shoulder warmly.

"Come. Today I have asked Larkin to help – he and I will start you off. We will look at your defense tactics and perhaps start developing those. Neb specializes in communications and transport and Celia or Roz will look at your healing powers and try to hone those skills. Glock is also our resident historian, between him and I, we will bring you up to speed with politics and communications in the region. Then we have Val, the best Seer in our realm, she will teach you to cast out in different situations and if you have the sight, she will help you. Neb or I will teach you Morphology, or as he prefers to call it, dynamic reconfiguration. "There are various ways to defend yourself physically" explained Larkin, appearing from mid-air, "the first is simply to block any power or force thrown at you. You do this by creating a quick shield. It simply stops the energy from getting to you, it does not dissipate it or destroy it, just blocks it. The second defense is to reciprocate the force with your own. The downside to this is that you cannot always tell the force that you need to block so as to counter balance that force. These are the two most commonly used forms of defense. Once you can protect yourself, then you can also protect others. The third we will look into another day," finished Larkin.

Larkin walked part way down the field with Ferris and Addy on his heels. He suddenly stopped and seemed to turn an invisible knob in midair. Addy squinted to see if there was an ether web in the area, but she could not see anything. A seam opened up in the middle of the fresh air, like a poster of an empty football pitch, being ripped apart. Larkin stepped through the door and Ferris indicated for Addy to follow him. Addy was constantly amazed in this world. She stepped into the open 'seam'.

They were in a forest. Tall trees were everywhere, in parts they were dense and in other areas scattered about. Before Addy could ask about where they were or what they were going to do, both Ferris and Larkin had disappeared. Addy was looking intently at the area they should have stepped through when she heard, in her head, *be careful Addy, remember to defend ONLY, see you on the other side.*

What? Addy asked, but got no response.

Suddenly bright neon light made its way towards her, Addy instinctively looked for a tree to hide behind and then remembered that she needed to shield herself.

She pulled at her power to shield up, the neon light broke into thousands of smaller lights as it impacted on her shield. Addy knew she needed to get to the other side. She ran from tree to tree looking all around her. Two light blue lights were coming her way from opposite directions. Addy shielded both throwing up barriers with power, they were more forceful and she felt slightly rocked by the impact against the barrier. She kept moving between the trees, there were lights everywhere now. Green and red and yellow and more of the light blue ones. Addy tried to judge the impact of the force by the colour of the lights, she knew that the light blue ones were more powerful than the neon and yellow ones, she did not know the force of the other colours. She held up her hands to send a counter balance force to the light blues but nothing happened. Addy realized she did not know how to send a force, only how to create a shield.

"Think Addy" she spoke to herself.

It suddenly became clear that she need to transfer the energy available to her in the right volume to the lights, she pulled power and physically bowled them at the lights. The power was obviously too strong, the lights shattering and continuing on behind the impact zone. Making little craters in the earth.

"Too much Addy" she whispered to herself.

Addy had created a shield bubble around her but could not move the shield to enable her to get to the other side. She was adamant that she would get this right.

Lights were bouncing off the shield, she felt the impact of a few of them as it jiggled the shield around.

I need to capture a light and send it back to the same colour that way I'll match the force.

Addy pulled at her ether, a shabby power net appeared, she flung it at a small red light. She captured the light, before it hit her shield and then felt the energy, gently with her power she felt the make-up and the structure of the power and then flung it back at an approaching red light. The lights clashed and disappeared without any impact or repercussion. Addy did this with a green light and the same thing happened. As soon as she understood the magical make-up of the energy heading her way she was able to respond like for like. Addy realized as she captured and flung lights that she needed to look at the make-up of the force approaching her.

The lights starting coming faster. Addy looked at the pink light motoring its way towards her, she saw the magical structure, felt the energy on her magic fingers and then sent off an opposing force, it hit the pink light square on and disappeared. Addy did the same to four other lights but then realized she was still in her shield, stationery. She released the shield and ran forward, buzzing energy to the lights. She got into a pattern, assess, release, assess, release. The ability came faster and quicker and she realized that she could do it intuitively. Addy noticed the lights were buzzing even faster, she ran as fast as she could. She shielded two lights, assessed and buzzed several more. She kept running faster and faster; the lights were whirring at her now. Suddenly she heard a chirping. Addy stopped and looked for the source of the noise.

She kept neutralizing the lights with her power all the while looking for the noise. At the base of a tall evergreen she saw movement. Addy was momentarily distracted and almost had a few lights hit her, she ducked and neutralized while, scampering towards the noise. A tiny bird, hardly any feathers was scuffling around in the undergrowth of the forest. The mother was beside herself in the branch just above Addy, and was screeching as the baby peeped. The lights hit the tree all around the mother. Addy neutralized a few more and then instinctively cast a shield around the base of the tree. She zapped a few more lights and then brought herself into her own shield. She recalled the little sparrow she had killed by accident. Her heart beat in her throat.

I must get this baby to its nest without touching it. The mum must not reject this poor little thing. Addy thought for a moment, the lights were rocking her shield. She sent of a frenzy of neutralizers and then carefully put the baby inside a shield bubble and lifted it up towards the mother. She carefully moved it up and up until the baby was just above the nest and then gently released the bird. The shield was starting to show signs of wear and Addy let out a barrage of neutralizing power, waited for the mother to reconcile with the baby and then left a shield hanging around the nest. She walked a few steps and then while holding off the lights she ran as fast she could. She headed for a clearing, turning and neutralizing continuously.

Addy finally stumbled into the clearing and the lights all stopped.

Addy looked around her, feeling for a power source tentatively.

A tree shook and the large knot in its bough opened up. Addy took it to mean that she should enter, which she did.

She was back on the field near the lake.

When Addy saw Ferris and Larkin playing chess, she was quite relieved.

"Thanks for the warning, guys" she said calmly. Sweat trickled down her back and her heart raced. She collapsed on the grass next to them.

"Addy. You did well. You learn quickly" said Ferris, not looking up.

"You have exhausted many students" laughed Larkin.

"What do you mean?" Asked Addy

"We recruited senior students to send off light powers at varying speeds – like a war game, they were running out of energy trying to keep up with you" he smiled.

The sky lit up with sheets of lightning. Addy scrambled to her feet.

"Is this part of the lesson?"

"No! Shield!" Ferris shouted.

The attack was relentless, power bolt after power bolt aimed directly at them.

"Ternion!" shouted Ferris

"No. Just Verity" Addy shouted back trying to shield and block as she had just learnt, "I can feel it".

"She wants the same as you do," Ferris moved his arms in wide circular motions, moving energy back through the bolts."

Addy frowned shaking her head, "I don't think so!"

"Yes! She wants you to get your Grimoire!" Ferris was moving towards the source of the bolts.

"Why?"

"It has the words to transfer your power."

"Glock is on his way" Larkin was out of breath and clearly struggling.

"How do you know?" Addy stepped in front of him pulling her shield over them both.

Larkin smiled his thanks.

"Glock was your next lesson; communications" said Larkin.

"I feel like I am back in high school" Addy rolled her eyes and blew a strand of hair from her face.

Glock suddenly appeared, startling Addy.

"Form a 'V-shape behind me" he instructed.

Addy and Ferris moved into position all the while shooting power up against bolts of power.

"On my count, release" he crouched down low, his arms hanging loose, behind him with his palms forward.

"One, two, three! Release" he pulled their power into alignment and sent a barrier charged with power at the source of the power bolts. A thunderous clap and sheet lightning lit up the afternoon sky. Then quiet.

"We are fine now" he whispered.

"How is she penetrating our barriers?" Ferris asked sitting on the floor.

"She's involved in dark stuff, my old friend. Dark, dark stuff" he murmured looking into the distance.

"Ugh! We have to stop her! Ferris, Glock? We must help them on Earth. They don't stand a chance! Why are we wasting so much time with shit? I've had enough," the anger swirled in her limbs as she stomped off.

16

I should turn back.

She stopped a moment looking from where she'd come, "oh! Further than I thought" she murmured. The natural clearing dipped down low, trees scattered the landscape, thickening to her left.

Her head needed clearing. She needed ten minutes alone.

So much going on. Why aren't they doing anything to help my mother? And Grit?

"Oh hello, dear! I am so pleased you've found me" Addy was startled at the voice. The woman was old, she came from behind the tree, Addy's magic ran up and down her spine, prickling awareness had her on high alert. The old lady looked familiar.

Where have I seen her?

The dusk put her in shades of grey, a messy bun tied behind a lined and sagging face, a black pinafore showed her as square and small, supported by a walking stick.

"Are you lost?" Addy's tone was cautious, her magic arcing across her torso, she absently rubbed at it, willing it to calm down.

"Yes. I've been looking for Betsy. She sometimes wanders off but never for this long" she started shuffling towards Addy.

"I didn't realize how far I'd come. I'm so tired" she yawned to emphasize her point, "so tired. Will you walk me home dear?"

Addy looked behind her, they'd be wondering where she was soon,

"It won't be long. I'm not far from here" her gnarled, arthritic finger pointed towards the thickening forest "I'd really like the company" she pulled her mouth down, furrowing her lines further.

"I guess I can spare a few moments" Addy heard herself say as she stepped towards the woman.

"Thank-you, dear" she muttered and started walking alongside Addy. Addy felt that something wasn't right. Silent footsteps accompanied by the rustling dress in the otherwise still forest put her nerves on edge,

"How much further? My friends will be looking for me soon"

The old woman looked at Addy, her eyes flashed once and she twirled around her walking stick, the magic strands curled around her and the air frizzled and popped. The woman transformed. Her smooth beautiful complexion shone in a strong elegant face, her eyes were dark now and her messy bun had changed to familiar long loose curls. Her confidence oozed from her. Her curvaceous form arched over stiletto heels. She was clad in black leather from head to toe. Rachel!

"Don't you loooooove magic" she giggled conversationally, simultaneously she lifted her palm and pushed a long red beam of power right into Addy, pinning her to the tree.

"Addy. Shield" Faasi murmured into her head, shivering uncontrollably.

"I can't" she pushed back, "I'm not trained. I will hurt us all!"

"She is evil" the tree relayed back.

"She's been led astray".

The power was strong. The continuous voltage of her ether drove into Addy.

"I'm Inap now" her palm pushed the ether a little harder, "Verity sends love" she giggled again. "Inap... suits me? No?"

"Do you feel this power?" Addy asked the tree telepathically. She clenched her jaw and felt the sweat bead across her face.

"No. Just your pain" word came back into her head.

Addy tried to pull it in. Her power and her pain. The effort was draining her.

"You know" she pulled out from her dry throat, "you won't be rewarded" she tried to let Rachel see reason.

Her face dropped into a pout, "You're just jealous. She's giving me a spot in her cabinet. When she rules, you know?" She boasted, "because I do her little favors" she smiled absently, a mysterious smile lingering on her lips. Addy could see her eyes that Rachel had indeed been turned to something else. Inap.

Inap stepped forward toward Addy, her stilettos digging slightly into the dirt. The pain intensified, Addy struggled to bring her power under control, the effort pulled at her energy. Inap stabbed at her. Addy felt the athame enter her skin. The energy in it was dark and burnt into her flesh. It wrenched through skin it pierced and popped as it found its way.

"Ugh" Addy tried to move her right arm to stop the searing pain in the left shoulder but Inap was pushing energy from both her palms now. The tree rustled behind her uncomfortably. She felt her power flare instinctively but managed to hold it close, like an aura, not inside anymore but not far away.

"Rachel!"

"No! Inap! I am now Inap!"

"Inap!"

"No talking" Inap ran her hands over Addy's pinned body, resting on her breasts. She leaned in inches from Addy's mouth, her eyes once blue, now dark, focused on her mouth.

Addy felt the power surge again.

Inap's eyes widened. She felt it. She leant over and yanked the athame out of Addy's shoulder letting it fall to the earth. With her free hand, she grabbed a vial from her pocket and captured the blood flowing freely from Addy's wound. She peered cautiously at Addy, "Verity will be so pleased" she looked slightly mad as she pulled her other palm up and slowly closed the cap on the vial. Without the power, Addy sank to the base of the tree, holding her left shoulder.

"You have no appreciation for the craft" Inap stated.

"I. I" Addy tried to get out. A loud crack jerked her attention up. Glock, Celia and Ferris came lurching at her. Inap turned behind a tree, another crack and she disappeared.

"Why didn't you shield?" Ferris scowled at her,

"You could have been killed," Celia interjected,

"Why are you even out here alone?" Glock demanded

"Back off boys," she's hurt! Faasi says she wouldn't use her ether power" Celia was already leaning over Addy, touching the wound,

"We need leaves. What have I got here?" She mumbled looking around her. Some plants pushed their way to the surface of the earth.

"That will do! Marshmallow root" Ferris moved to get the plant Celia pointed at. Celia started rolling up the leaves "You will heal quickly anyway, but I need to check there isn't poison in you"

Addy nodded as Celia was already scanning her shoulder. Celia put her hand to Addy's wound and she felt instant relief. Celia nodded and then starting pushing tiny bits of leaf and spittle into the wound,

"Ouch! That hurts!"

"Don't be daft! You just endured Verity's puppet stream an ether torch into you for ages. This is nothing" she continued spitting and wiping with leaves. "That's better" she declared and stood up. "Let's go".

Ferris and Glock looked tired and concerned, "What? I am fine." Addy wasn't in the mood for this.

"You didn't even try. No protection?" Ferris's jaw was firm.

"I haven't" Addy sighed, "I can't! I will kill us all! I don't know what to do with it. There is so much power. Until I know, it's safer this way" she spoke sullenly, "besides, isn't it my right? I can decide when its used and when it isn't?"

"No!" they all barked at her,

"You have to protect yourself," Glock explained, "you have bigger responsibilities now Addy".

Ferris was stern, the muscle just above his beard on his jaw pulsed angrily. He turned away, Addy felt the disappointment shoot through her body, the hurt was worse than what Inap delivered. Addy was suddenly angry,

"I never asked for this!" Ferris stopped walking, frozen. He waited for her to continue, "And what's the big deal anyway? I'm okay. Everyone's okay," she wiped at her forehead, the dull pain slowly beating her down.

"Did you feel your ether power warn you?" Glock asked tiredly.

"I felt it" she spoke truthfully, "I always feel it. It's there every moment of every day. It never goes away. It's always prickling, struggling to free itself. The power, the visions, they're my whole life. I don't know how to use it. What it means" Addy felt exhausted, her energy spiraling down her quickly, "every time I use it something goes wrong. Every single time. When I decide not to use it, it's also the wrong thing! I will never win, will I?"

"Addy..." Glock stepped towards her.

"No! Leave me" she felt her final energy wane.

The air rippled and pulsed and immediately Addy was in the corridor leading to her room. Ugh! Why do they do that? Everyone's so bloody nice all the time!

"Get some rest dear" Celia advised. "We'll talk later".

I will not slam the door. I am not a petty teen.

The anger and frustration pumped through her nerves, into her hands, itching to hit out at something.

Hours later, with no appetite, Addy found herself in the library.

Ferris sat staring into the fire silently. The warm fire glowing on his forehead and cheeks.

Addy folded herself into the leather. The black embers in the fire's base, pulled at something primal within her.

"Do you know why Verity took the blood?" The space in her chest felt crowded again.

"I have these long hours been thinking on it" he did not look at Addy, "do you?"

"I think" she paused hoping she was wrong, "it connects us" tears welled in her eyes. She brushed them away angrily.

"I think you are wise beyond your years" his voice was grave.

"But it need not be a bad thing, Addy" he turned towards her, the leather squeaking beneath him.

"If she makes the connection, it can work both ways. As much as she can connect with you, you can also connect with her" Ferris stroked his jaw, "we need to be smart about this. The magic is not new but using blood for the connection; we have not done that" he turned back to the fire, "Glock may know".

"Ferris?"

"Mm?" Ferris was completely invested in his thinking,

"My mum?"

"Mm?"

"Why didn't she have Quinary power?"

He looked at Addy then. His eyes were kind and warm and she felt his protection.

"Your and obviously your mum's ancestor had been chosen to receive the power but it got scattered before it got bestowed into the DNA. Our ancestors knew she was meant for it but it just disappeared" he leant forward resting his elbows on his knees looking at the fire again, "she is powerful, your mum, very powerful. But the Quinary power never came for her" he warmed his palms deep in thought.

"Can she protect herself from Verity?" Her voice was small, scared.

"Addy" he rested his palm on her hands resting on her curled-up knees, "there is a plan; it must be hard for you to see this but we have to ready you. The plan for you is bigger than returning to Earth now. Please trust me? There is a plan" he squeezed her hand.

Years of touch deprivation had caused Addy to create barriers around her. Having Ferris gently push at them warmed her. She nodded, a stray strand of hair swinging to cup her face.

"The timing is an issue Ferris. Glock says the battle is in a seven days. The new moon is in six days" she felt the panic return to her throat, clutching at her.

"Ssh. Calm down" Ferris moved closer to her pulling her into his chest, "there there. Trust me Addy. There is a plan. I will not leave Marjy out on a limb" Addy nodded, he was so warm. So, comforting.

This must be what a dad feels like.

Addy struggled through her morning meditation. She couldn't wait to get out in the fresh air.

The day was grey, the sun struggled to have a presence. The path wound from the back of the tower and gently inclined for a few moments. Addy stopped where it evened out and leant against a tree. She watched her whispy breath on the cold air. The pentagonal tower castle sprawled below her, she noted she was behind the tower that represented herself in the Quinary. "Feel free to explore the grounds" Glock's voice rang in her ears, "but don't leave the parameters of the castle again".

The exertion of the brisk walk calmed Addy. The rhythm of her step and the stillness of the landscape brought with it a welcome escape. The path descended, little alcoves of leaves and shrubs ran off like small veins from the main artery. Her boots knocked on the sandy floor, accentuated the downward momentum.

The path split; one path turned sharply to the right and the other dwindled steeply down. "Interesting" she muttered "where do you go?" She wondered aloud. The path to the right twisted out of sight around the hilltop, the path directly in front was slightly more overgrown. Ferns enclosed the way; a lazy butterfly rode the Colocasia leaf down on the left. Addy bent down peering into the undergrowth. "What's that? Tiny lights?" She shuffled and ducked down the path, peering ahead, intrigued. A kaleidoscope of colour caught in a raindrop. Addy felt compelled to look.

Addy immediately knew the woman she'd never met. A deep pull instantly connected them. The hazy curtain, opaque and raindrop laden, hung between them. Her long naturally streaked bob framed her face. Addy recognized her own features; large eyes, full mouth, straight nose. She was bound tightly to a large iron-grey door. Nails the size of chisels held chains across her slim body. Her hands were shackled above her head, nailed to the door, mirroring her feet.

She lifted her head, sensing something. She looked concerned. Her eyes eventually found Addy. Addy saw her features change. Soften. Tears welled in her eyes. Addy felt the ferns brushing up and down her arm, comforting, mothering her. Tears trickled down her mum's face and Addy wiped at her own cheeks.

She stepped forward. The woman frowned, shaking her head, not approving. Addy's power prickled across her arms and torso.

My mum. My real mum.

Her heart beat against her ribs.

"No, no, no. Addy go back" her mum cried.

"Sweet girl," she caught her breath as emotion heaved her chest, "it's a trap! Go back" her voice cracked, "Go back my Addy! Don't come through the portal! It's a trap!" she cried.

Addy felt warmth gather and grow in her chest. She stepped through the veil. The portal distorted space, Addy felt the hazy flutter, she knew she had been transported. "Mum?" She whispered, emotion deepening her voice.

"Isn't this sssssssweet?" Verity strode out from the right, "family meeting at the prison" she sing-songed, "ha ha!"

"Verity! Leave her out of this," Marjory insisted. Verity ignored her.

Verity's white hair streamed down her back. Her midnight blue dress hugged her curvaceous figure. Heaving breasts were on display and on her left shoulder two crescent moons glowed in bright fiery red. Red light rimmed her pupils.

Verity held her slim arm up dangling a hollow bracelet filled with Addy's blood as she moved her wrist. Addy felt the pull from deep within her. Verity's red finger tips jiggled gracefully,

"You're nearly there, Adera! Nearly at full power" she reflected as deep red lips sneered in her pale face. Red light beams shot from her eyes into the bracelet, "Nearly time to give me my gift back" she gleamed. "In the meantime, you can help me" she moved her arms elaborately. "This prison" she grimaced, "has my...." she paused in thought, "my partner" she smiled, "and you will release him" she walked over to Marjory, "wont she Sis?"

Marjory shook her head, dejected, "She can't Verity, I told you. Only the whole Quinary can release him."

"Oh! But Marj, don't you know? She," Verity thumbed at Addy, "she's got power, oh so much power! So much more than all the Quinary combined, isn't that right, Adera? She's growing it for her dear aunty Ver. A little thank-you for all those good years. Ha ha ha" Verity laughed folding her arms as she leaned in towards Marjory against the iron door. Suddenly Verity tensed and jerked around,

"Ritsa! You filthy worm! Where are you?" She spat out, "show yourself, now!"

A rat moved from below the door, falling on the next step with a soft 'phlat'. As it fell, it transformed. A thin man of medium height with oily dirty blonde hair stretched up. His crooked back and broad shoulders made him look like a python about to strike. He held his hands behind his back. His large jaw ended in an overbite, as if he still were in rat form. His face was badly scarred, pocked by disease.

"Welcome mistress" he spoke in a sleaze.

"Shut up! Monster!"

Ritsa dropped his head to his chest, his eye twitching, uncontrollably as he peered to the side.

"Did you prepare as I said?" Verity was short and angry at him.

He nodded. Verity strode towards Addy.

"On my word, you will engage your power" she pointed to the sky above the iron door, "where the crescents meet."

Addy looked at her mum who was shaking her head, tears trickling down her face slowly. She looked at her surrounds, the whole prison was on a platform in the middle of the sea. Black water churned around them, the movement heavy and disturbed.

Verity waved her arms, torches blazed alight along the platform encircling the iron doors, like dominoes, they lit in turn and knocked on to the fortress walls. Wind whistled through the doors, they rattled ominously.

"Yes!" Verity hissed, lifting her chin to the wind as her arms rose in the air, "Yes! Finally!" She smiled malevolently. Verity started chanting. Addy knew the words, they had been the same when she released Verity's power, "Igarro, shintato, anvilgati" the wind grew stronger, icy cold shards sitting on its edge, "igarro shintato, anviglati" her tattoos glowed, their crescents illuminated in red, bouncing off the black ocean.

Addy felt the cold seep into her, the wind stung her eyes, her power sparked through her hands. She looked from Verity to her mum. Marjory was looking at her, "run" she mouthed, "run".

Addy felt the warmth melt in her core, it pained against the ice-cold wind.

"Shintato, anviglati, igarro, shintato" Verity continued, eyes glowing red. Her neck strained as she chanted. She held one hand up to towards the fortress, the other she pointed at Addy, "on my word" she hissed.

A single, strong beam of light appeared above the fortress, culminating in a red crescent. Seconds later a second beam came from the opposite side. The two red crescents shone above them. Verity smiled.

"Illuminet cornu meum" she shouted. The red beam extended from her palm. It reached the two crescents pivoting above and the third crescent extended from it.

Addy felt the dread invade her. She saw the pyramid of red slowly, taunting as it moved above the fortress.

"Adera!" Verity shouted, "Now!"

Addy looked at Verity, "No" she shook her head. From the walls of the fortress a dome of light became visible, blue and green, it rose from the walls in broad bands, their hollow ends forming rings, intertwined, four rings. Addy saw the same symbol as that which now lived on her wrist. She glanced down and saw the golden glow.

"Don't," Verity spat, "disobey me" she spoke through her teeth. "Now," she hissed.

"No!" Addy shouted. She looked at Marjory, care and warmth swelling in her chest, "Go to hell Verity."

Verity drove fire into her body. Cold, numbing fire. Addy buckled to the ground.

"Stop! Stop! Please Verity?" Marjory shouted.

Addy's ether licked across her, she bit down hard trying to control it. The numb pain invaded her left shoulder, slowly moving across her body.

"You will" Verity spoke slowly, struggling to control her temper, "obey me. Insolent child." Verity's face distorted, she shot another bolt of energy at Addy.

Addy sprawled down, the icy wind biting at her face.

"Wha ha ha ha" Verity laughed, "very well. Let's do it your way then" she grinned knowingly, "I'd hate to kill you before you have developed my power fully"

She lowered her arm and immediately pointed at Marjory, two red hot beams of power struck Marjory. Her body buckled forward, thrashing against the chains,

"Ugh," Marjory struggled.

"No," Addy's pain was raw, "no".

She sprang to her feet. The power snapped at her command, Addy gathered it, anger broiling.

"Adera! There's a girl! Now use it to strengthen the crescents" Verity was emphatic.

Addy's hatred sprang to the fore, "I will kill you Verity" she hissed.

"Oh! Let go of it" Verity hissed, "before you can say 'hello mama' I will have her killed" she gestured to Marjory.

"You want that?" She sneered, "do you?"

Addy felt the fight leave her, dread flooded in, and pooled in her abdomen.

"Don't do it Addy" Marjory pleaded, "don't listen to her" she cried, "Addy shield yourself. Go. Please?" She pleaded with Addy, her face contorted in pain.

"Verity, let her go" Addy commanded, "let her go and I will help you" she looked at Marjory, warmth circling her heart.

"Fool" Verity laughed, "You're not in a good place to bargain" she ground her teeth and pushed electric bolts into Marjory.

"Stop!" Addy commanded, "If you hurt her, I will kill us all. Stop" Addy was angry.

"Only when you power the crescents" she hissed, "Do it now"

Marjory's head lolled to the side, blood trickled from her nose. Addy saw the pulse beating in her neck. Love and tenderness overwhelmed her.

We need a chance.

She raised her hands and palms up pushed the ether energy from her into the crescent pyramid. The blue green structure rose and expanded, Addy felt its resistance. "These are my friend's bonds" she thought fleetingly.

"Oh yes" Verity crooned, "look at that" she whispered as the bracelet on her arm lit up, "so much power and still to grow! Ha ha!" Verity taunted.

Addy's power fed the crescents. They flared and dimmed alive with Addy's ether and then, suddenly, the blue green structure shattered. Hundreds of lights burning a moment and then dying. Embers drifting and then fading. The stillness hung on the air and then the iron gate clattered and swung open, slowly.

Addy fell to her knees.

What have I done?

Grindal sauntered down the steps dressed in a dinner jacket, he adjusted his cuff link. Three red crescents glowed on the back of his neck, the same as those on Verity's inner shoulder. His face was long and square and his dark hair stuck out at angles. He walked towards Addy, stopping close enough that she could feel his stony cold ether. He stared at her imprinting her face in his memory. "I will have your power" he whispered so that nobody else could hear, "soon" he trailed his finger along Addy's cheek, the cold trickled behind.

Grindal walked away. Verity's heels stuccoed against the dark as she ran towards him. Zyklon appeared on the curve of the wall, they marched away without looking back. Ritsa moved from the shadows, "Ternion will be" his gravelly voice confirmed.

Addy moved quickly, running to Marjory, "m-mum?" She whispered. Addy touched Marjory's face, her eyelids flickered open.

"Addy. Duck" she shouted. It all went black.

Addy shivered uncontrollably. The fire could not warm her. She turned her head and found Ferris hovering concerned at her side. The guilt and pain of what she had done sliced through her.

What have I done? How can I fix this? They will cast me aside, for sure when they know what I've done.

Ferris put his hand on her back, to cover her with a blanket. Addy visibly flinched from his touch. This did not deter him.

"Hush, child. Have this" he handed her a tall drink.

Addy looked the other way. I don't deserve his kindness. Tears glistened from the corners of her eyes. She needed to fix this problem she had created.

Addy geared herself for the rejection. She took a deep breath, her sobs catching in her throat.

She turned towards Ferris.

He sat beside her, his kind eyes inviting her to lighten her load,

"I will leave shortly," she started, Ferris frowned at her.

"Where to, lass?

"No. Ferris, I-uh" Addy looked at her hands feeling the tears roll down her nose and drop into her hands. She raised her head and looked into Ferris's eyes,

"I have done a bad thing. I, I" she looked up again, bracing herself for the hate and rejection that she would surely see in Ferris's eyes.

He covered her wet fingers,

"Addy, Verity is a manipulative and skilled player. We know Grindal is released. We are only sorry we did not realise what their game plan was. We are so sorry for putting you in danger. My dear child, it pains me that you were exposed to those awful people" Ferris bundled Addy up under his chin.

"What? What?" Addy tried to extract herself from Ferris's comforting arms,

"You know what I did and you aren't angry?"

"Why would I be angry?"

"I have put the worlds one step closer to destruction! I…"

"Sssh, Addy. You are not at fault. We knew that Grindal's prison required a significant power to release him. We should have realized that you had that power before he did. We have underestimated them. It won't happen again! Now drink this. You have been hurt."

The waterfall glittered in the moonlight, it's gentle roar back-setting the crickets and night owls. Lights shimmered and moved across the opposite embankment and a different ethereal light infused across the water and lit the banks up with a hazy pink glow. Addy's feet moved without thought, she was drawn to this place.

There were people in and around the waterfall. On second glance, she wasn't entirely sure they were people. They glistened silvery-opaque and appeared and then immediately disappeared into their surrounds, their outlines changing and becoming at one with the water and then just as suddenly standing out in stark contrast. They were beautiful people, happiness shone from their beings and vibrated the air surrounding them. She approached breathless and awe-struck.

A woman stood from the lake, water glistened down her body, she was naked and spectacular; breath-taking to behold.

She looked at Addy approaching and nodded her consent. Addy stopped where the waterfall streamed from the sheer cliff, she put her hand out to cup water into it and then slowly took a sip of water. The small sip slipped down her insides, cooling her and quenching her thirst. It was the purest, sweetest water she had ever tasted. When she had sated her thirst, she moved to a flat rock on the waters-edge. She sat down cross-legged and watched in awe. The woman who had stood from the lake came to sit beside her.

She spoke softly, gently, such that Addy wasn't immediately sure that she had spoken.

"We hoped you would join us, Addy" she turned large liquid eyes on Addy and then her stare deepened. Her eyes became pure black for a moment. She blinked hard and the liquid blue reappeared. Addy jumped from the rock.

"Who are you? What are you?" She asked suspiciously.

The woman smiled and patted the rock.

"Be seated, child. We mean you no harm. We are Celestials. Where you are from, we are called Angels" she imparted softly.

Addy recalled Glock saying that Celestials often talk so mystically that you weren't sure if they were talking about the past, present or future. Addy geared herself.

"Do you know what will happen? In this war? Oh, I beg your pardon – I am Addy, what is your name?" She finished sheepishly.

"It has most poetically been said before, but I repeat, what's in a name?" She smiled. "I am called Arga, when I am summoned, but, I am who I need to be. You, have not yet become what you need to be. You fight with your own heart. I see many paths for you, Addy. Each one is different and each one can change, join me in the water" she beckoned.

Addy realized that she suddenly had an overwhelming need to swim.

I guess if you're a bunch of Angels you've pretty much seen it all before?

She slipped out of her clothes and joined Arga in the water. It was heavenly. Addy ducked into the water and swam a few metres letting the cool, soothing streams clear her mind and caress her body. She surfaced smiling. The Angels had started to retreat, she could see their shimmering essence leaving.

"Hey, you didn't answer my questions" she called.

"Someone special this way comes, young one. I will help you. Ternion – Verity, Zyklon and Grindal" she said looking deeply into Addy with her black eyes, "but they need your eyes to see the way. You will need all of the Quinary to help Kivnon! Strength" she whispered and disappeared.

Addy sat in the middle of the lake staring at the space Arga had been a second before.

"Well, you must surely be a Water-Nymph! Addy, it is so good to see you again," drawled a familiar voice.

Warmth and joy invaded Addy, she went to stand and realized she had no clothes on.

"Dane? Dane. Oh gosh, Dane!" Addy repeated his name.

"What are you doing here? How are you? Where have you been? Are you okay?"

"I came for a mid-night swim to clear my head" and indeed he was undressing behind the rock.

"When did you get here? How did you know where I was? How are you?" Addy had so many questions.

The longing to be held and to share her troubles nearly overwhelmed her. Addy looked for an escape route but heard the splash as Dane dived into the water and swam the length of the lake towards her.

"Come on!" he shouted as he past her, "I'll beat you to the waterfall."

Addy wished that he would take her in his arms. She had missed him. But obviously he didn't see her like that.

Addy, competitive by nature, struck out in a fast-competent crawl across the lake. She arrived just a second after Dane. He pulled her in under the waterfall.

"It's so beautiful here." He laughed as he held his face up to the flowing water. Addy smiled and lifted her face to the streams above her. A tinkle accompanied by a tiny little spark caught her eye. "What's that?" She pointed to the tiny light flickering above the water.

Dane smiled, "It's a fairy messenger. Or that is what my mother used to tell us when we were wee high to a grasshopper! If you catch one, you will receive all the good luck that they carry! Come on," Dane charged through the water leaping around after the tiny light. Addy followed him, her heart beating erratically.

Oh, I have missed him.

They ducked and played and swam and splashed after the fairy messenger. Then Dane turned to her. She saw the longing in his eyes. She knew he was pleased to see her. The joy bubbled in her chest.

"Oh yes," he said smiling, he had a naughty glint in his eye, Addy tried to dive out of the way but he caught her around the waist. Suddenly the mood changed. Addy saw desire smoulder in Dane's eyes. He caught his breath. Addy felt his strong arm pull her from the water towards him. Her heart stood still. He moulded her to him, she was aware of him, electricity ran the length of her body. Tiny rivulets ran down his rugged face, dripping from him. Addy instinctively moved in towards him, her lips parted.

"Dane" she said and the same time that he whispered her name.

The kiss started soft and sensuous and then turned deep and passionate. Addy lifted her hands to bury them in his hair. Hunger for him like she had never known consumed her; she arched into him, eyes closed in hedonistic desire. He lifted his lips briefly to whisper her name again, "Oh Addy! So much to tell you..." he whispered between kisses.

Addy felt safe. The comfort enfolded her, she just wanted a little more time, right here in his arms."Ssh." She closed her eyes as she leant against his chest.

In the distance she heard her name.

"Addy! Addy?" Ferris called for her.

She pulled herself from Dane's embrace.

"Oh no. I must go," she said and rushed to get her clothes on.

"Addy!" called Dane, "I need to tell you something."

She ran away from the lake, clothes clinging to her wet skin, hair dripping down her back, shoes clutched to her breast, "What am I doing" she spoke loudly to herself, trying to calm her heart beating, "I'm here Ferris," she called waving at the old man waiting at the end of the tree line.

"There you are! You can't be wondering off alone at this time of night! Have you no sense?" Ferris started at her, "come along, before the whole tower is worried sick about you. What were you thinking?" His concern was evident.

"I am sorry Ferris! I never meant to cause alarm. The Celestials were swimming in the lake, I felt compelled to see…" she broke off when she saw the look on Ferris's face.

"Celestials?" He raised his eyebrow; "Glock is on his way, save the story for when he arrives" he suggested gently.

Addy sat next to the fire back in the library. Ferris paced back and forth, puffing furiously on his long pipe. She pulled her journal out to capture the Celestial's encounter and the swim with Dane. Her mind drifted dreamily.

Glock finally appeared looking pretty harassed.

"What did they say? What did I miss?" He tried to put his arm through his coat, which happened to be inside out on that particular side. It resulted in Glock turning around and around like a dog trying to catch its own tail.

Smiling, Addy relayed the Celestials message, carefully leaving out the part where she met Dane in the lake.

"Mm. Ternion is the triplets, I suspected as much! But they

need your eyes to see the way; I wonder what that means?" Ferris contemplated.

They paced backward and forward. Both thinking about the message that Addy brought.

"What do you think Kivnon is?"

"You will need all of the Quinary to help Kivnon," repeated Ferris, "Aristotle used to always go on and on about Kivnon. What was it about? Give me a moment" he said in thought.

"Ah yes, I recall! Aris used to say that to be non-Kivnonic was the determination of the presentness of being - 'there as such', so Kivnon is..." everyone leaned in towards Ferris, "Change" he stated.

"Change?" Questioned Addy, "what do you mean, *change?*"

"Kivnon is change," stated Glock.

"Oh boy," said Addy stifling a yawn, "that is so weird!"

"It has been a busy night, get some sleep Addy" said Ferris in his fatherly voice.

Exhausted, Addy stumbled to her room. She lay down and touched her lips and recalled Dane's kiss. He never did answer any of her questions. She hoped to see him soon. Addy fell asleep with a smile on her face.

The central chambers of the Tower Castle hummed with activity, chefs and cleaners, groomsmen and guards poured through the space. Everyone had a task and was focused. Addy was frustrated, half the morning had been spent in training. She sat in her favourite leather couch in the library reflecting;

"The secret to awakening your potential is inside of you Addy" Glock's eyebrows zig zagged up and down as he spoke, "the Quinary's main purpose is and will remain, to keep balance" he paced the office one arm resting behind him as the other gestured to his words, "But Addy" he stopped and suddenly time itself breathed in, "What is balance?" His words dropped like lead in the room, "is it between good and bad, light and darkness, power and no power? Is it?" He repeated staring intently at Addy.

"I'll tell you. It's a constant change, tweaking around commons themes" he offered, "are you following me" Ferris cleared his throat,

"Uh-mm. Do you mind?"

"Of course not" the affection between the friends was obvious,

"If you were extremely hot, Addy" Ferris explained, "sweltering in Celia's tropics, laboring in the midday sun, you'd want to be cool, not so?"

Addy nodded, "yes"

"But you wouldn't want the freezing cold. Would you?" He asked.

"No-o" Addy frowned.

"So, you see, somewhere between ice cold and sweltering hot is the balance you want. If you moved from one to the other you would be uncomfortable, so little changes to get you back in balance" he raised his eyes in silent question.

"Okay" Addy tried to connect her thoughts, "what constant tweaking are we as the Quinary trying to do?" She asked.

"Excellent." Glock slapped his hands together, "great question, he smiled, "individually, we live to adjust imbalances in our specialty. For example," he pointed animatedly at Addy, "Neb. He looks after our skies, he represents the fire element and he understands and teaches the concept of limits" that's his purpose. His skills are honed to that. Now, Roz. She is the water element, she looks after our seas and rivers and lakes. Her job is underpinned by the concept of flow. Addy, we have, each of us, a unique gift that we use to balance an element; fire, water, earth, air and the corresponding life concepts of time, limits, flow and wholeness" Glock was fired up.

"And as a whole? As the Quinary?" Addy was tired.

Glock and Ferris exchanged a glance, "we don't know".

"We are physically more resilient, tougher, but we are not sure. That is the truth of it, my dear" Glock sighed.

"And Glock. My element? The life concept that my element

is based on? What is it? What is left?" Addy stood, "how do I know?"

"Addy, you need to meditate on it. Think on it. Write it down." Ferris suggested.

The door opened, "Lord Glock?" Larkin interrupted. Glock looked at Addy,

"Go. Time waits for no man" she laughed.

"Cheeky" he smiled.

"There you are, beautiful girl" Pearl interrupted her thoughts, "You're reading 'Magic for Beginners'?" Pearl stated looking at the unopened book in Addy's lap,

"Ugh. Trying to. Why we can't just pop onto Earth and save my mum and friends?"

"Don't fret. A plan is in the making. We have to go through this. And here is your lovely dress for this evening" Pearl announced.

"Do I really have to go Pearl" Addy pulled her mouth down in distaste, "I have nothing to contribute"

"Of course, you do. And besides you will finally get to meet the Prince."

"Oh. I really can't be bothered. He's probably a fuddy-duddy." Addy was petulant.

"Addy. The Earth Walkers Association are coming too. They've never visited us before. It's important."

"Earth Walkers?"

"Yes. I understand that a few people, from Earth have always known about our connection. Thear's and Earth's. Mystics, Shamans, some Clan Elders. Ternion are already active, we've got to plan, pull together. It won't be so bad" she patted Addy's cheek, "here's your dress dear. I'd better go and help those Brownies," she smiled, the concern for Addy radiating from her.

"I'll be fine, thanks, Pearl" Addy smiled.

The passage was cooler than the library, Addy held the dress over her left forearm as she headed towards the kitchen. The room was busy. Brownies chopped and sliced with efficiency.

People Addy had never seen moved around with purpose. Dane's face popped into the window behind the Brownies, he held his index finger to his lips indicating silence and then showed her to come outside.

Addy lay the dress over a kitchen stool and ran to the door. Dane grabbed her hand,

"Sssh, come with me" he whispered smiling.

"What are you doing here? How did you know where to come? What do you do anyway? Don't you work?" She laughed.

"Ssssh" he laughed running into the garden behind the third tower.

"I wanted to see you" he pulled her into his chest. Addy giggled

"You're crazy!"

"Hmmm. I think you're right" he whispered. "I need to tell you something" he smiled.

"Sssh" she put her fingers to his lips, "someone's coming."

"Guards" he looked behind them.

"They're everywhere! The Royal family are coming for a meeting tonight" Addy realized what she had said, "Ooh. Sorry. You are not supposed to know that" she frowned.

"Never mind. This way" he pulled Addy into the courtyard, "Addy, I..."

"Dane, they're following us" Addy laughed, "what is it?"

"Addy, I have to run. I will chat to you later. Please do not be mad at me! Okay? Let me explain to you later. Chat soon?" he enquired.

Addy nodded. Dane leant in and softly touched his lips to hers. He sped away quickly.

Two guards came from the other entrance of the courtyard.

"Pardon us, My Lady" they both bowed. Addy smiled and calmly walked away as her heart contracted with emotion.

The dark blue folds of her dress skimmed her curves and sashayed around her legs, "I'm not so thin and gaunt" she observed, "but this hair? It took so long to do it. What a waste of time," she scowled at her reflection. The French twist felt proper and chic.

Ugh, let the show begin.

"Maybe I'll see Dane later on" she smiled lighting her face up.

"Oh! Look at you! Lovely, simply gorgeous," Pearl fussed, "Well, the Prince won't know what bowled him over. You heard he broke his engagement to Lady Fi? Anyway, he will be fixated with you" she smiled, "he's eligible, Addy." Pearl teased.

"No thanks! I have enough problems on my hands" Addy smiled.

"Come, come" Ferris knocked his staff on the floor, "enough gabber" he scolded in jest. Addy noted that he looked very handsome in his formal dress. The green jacket was replaced by a navy coat with thick embroidered scrolls across its edge.

They walked around to the main entrance of the Towers, into the Grand Hall. People milled around, the air was vibrant with expectation.

"We'd better stay close by" laughed Ferris, "won't do to have half the eligible bachelors distracting you."

"Too right" Glock agreed, nodding his head at a distinguished looking couple, "Never can remember their names, bloody Goloves" he muttered under his breath, all the while smiling.

Pearl tutted, "Ingsang and Lingson" she whispered. "Addy the Crowne Prince will be here too" she winked in conspiration.

"But you are the guest of honor" she smiled.

18

Addy met so many people; her head started to spin. She tried to remember all their names as the courtesies ran thick and fast. She recalled The Duke of Estanvar, because he was young for what Addy thought a duke should look like and he made a comment about claiming her before Prince Thomas. She liked Lord and Lady Trawathin, because they were so down to earth and kind, they made Addy feel at ease.

She met a tall, striking man. He had no hair; his face had defined features. A long aquiline nose and dark warm eyes. He had a dark, coffee complexion and he wore a bright orange light weight garment. Addy thought it looked like a beach robe. He introduced himself to Addy over a glass of fruity punch.

"Koeaia." he said.

"Koooie?"

"My name". He laughed a full belly laugh. It reverberated through the building. She did not feel intimidated. She liked this man.

"My name is Koeaia. It means Earth Mate. I am committed to Mother Earth – Celia" he shared.

Addy smiled shyly and said,

"Sorry. I didn't mean to be rude. My name is Addy" she said. "I don't really know what it means."

"Balance." Said Koeaia "many meanings, depends on the origin" his voice was rich and warm. She felt protected and safe. He gave off an energy that pulled you in.

"Aah, Addy. Meet my dear friend, Tyeh" exclaimed Koeaia.

He stepped forward and pushed his forehead against a short, bearded man. The bearded man's forehead was large and his eyes were close together, his flat nose flared as he breathed. Steel blue eyes stared from his reddish-brown hair, including a full beard and moustache. Addy stared at the little steel aglets on the end of his moustache and the large, matching one on his beard.

He wore a leather tunic, big black boots into which dark brown leggings were tucked. He was a large girthed man. When Koeaia stepped back from his embrace, he announced, while holding onto the man's elbows,

"Addy, this is Tyeh. He is the man to have on your side in any battle. A master engineer and a bloody good friend, if there was ever one to be had," he stepped aside to let Addy into the circle. Then said,

"Tyeh Braveslayer; Addy" he introduced.

Addy felt small. She wasn't quite sure how to greet this overwhelming person.

"Pleased to meet you" she said softly extending her hand.

"Well said for the both of us," said Tyeh and then ignoring her hand he looked into her eyes and then smiled,

"You'll do, I reckon," he announced, "Now where did you say the ales were kept?" He laughed.

"How was your trip?" Asked Koeaia of Tyeh

"Some trouble. Nothing we could not handle mind you. But not normal. Let us talk tomorrow on this. I need another pint," he wiped the foam from his beard and marched off to find another ale.

A loud trumpet called attention.

"Please be upstanding" the official looking person spoke loudly. Trumpets sounded somewhere in the room.

"Her Royal Highness, Princess Jessica!" shouted the official. Her royalness, did not look pleased to be in the room. She was eighteen years old, according to Pearl. She had long dark hair, swept up roughly behind her head with a mother of pearl comb. The curls fell down and framed her pretty face. Her eyes were defiant and her mouth was in a right royal pout. She almost stomped into the room. Immediately she crossed some invisible barrier, the official announced again,

"His Royal Highness, Prince David Andrew and his fiancé, her Royal Highness, Tiallana of Espire" they entered the room.

Andrew! Andrew?

Her rescuer was the Prince David Andrew!

Addy could hardly breathe. By sheer force of will she focused on Tiallana.

She was breathtaking. Her gown was light green, like a new fern. She glided into the room and shone from inside. She was pale with golden hair. Her hair fell to her shoulders, a single strand of white flowers sat on her head elegantly. She was at once radiant and natural.

"The Crown Prince, Thomas" Addy stared transfixed as Dane appeared dressed formally, medals and ribbons adorned his chest where moments before she had rested her head.

He caught her eye, imploring her to understand. The guard continued, unaware of the chaos in her mind, the thickening of her throat, the thumping against her rib cage.

"Her Majesty, the Queen of Llastraul" announced the Official, nearly popping with exertion. Addy gasped for air. The noise of the room seemed distant, it wafered at her ears. She focused elsewhere to restore her sanity.

She turned her attention to the Queen. She had merry eyes and a quick smile. Her hair was short and looked chic-messy. Stylish, it was sun-bleached golden and framed her beautiful face on the sides. Her gown was a shimmery off-gold and the bodice flowed into the skirt. The Queen was staring at Addy intently.

Addy could not wait to escape.

The betrayal sat bitterly on her. She paced the floor at the entrance to the ball room. Why did he lie? The agitation rose in her. She had to get away. She heard the noise of the gathering on the other side of the doors, as she turned she caught a glimpse of Glock outside.

Addy moved down the steps and towards Glock. She heard the guard's horses clomping on the grey cobblestones. The sun was hanging low, the cold had already started to settle. Guards moved about silently, expectation hung in air.

"He will be here" Glock spoke, calming himself, "I know he will. He said he would" he looked at his pocket watch again, "he is cutting it fine" he paced the bottom of the stairs, patting his pocket absently.

"We're ready" Ferris appeared, squinting into the trees on the right of the drive, "Is that?"

"About bloody time," Glock smiled stretching his arms wide.

"Neb! You old bloody dinosaur! Getting slower and slower! What do you call this?" Glock teased affectionately while he walked towards the trees. Addy watched as the friends embraced the beautiful, emerald green dragon that gracefully stretched out in the clearing.

"Umf," the dragon did not seem overtly pleased, "Did you bring me linens Ferris?" Smoke drifted from his nostrils. Ferris extended a neatly pressed pile of clothes, "I'll drop these behind the tree?" He asked walking back to the tree line.

Addy looked on sullenly, golden eyes with the narrowest black slits rested on her. She stared briefly and then lowered her gaze and turned her back on the dragon.

Moments later, a tall man, dressed in black with an emerald green cape, strode from the trees. He walked up to Addy and the same golden eyes with their slithers of black held her.

"Neb" he extended his hand gallantly.

"Addy" her voice croaked, "Uhm, Addy" she said more clearly.

"Interesting" is all he said in his deep voice.

"Come on" Glock slapped his back, "let's get the others so that we can meet the Earth Walkers" he continued walking around the tower.

Roz was spectacular! Addy knew she was a Mermaid. Roz had donned her human facade so that she could liaise with the Earth Walkers. Her hair, deep pink shimmered down her translucent skin and rested just in front of her breasts. She wore a light pink halter top that skimmed her body perfectly, she had a flowy white skirt that ended in a few points. Her feet were bare but for a pink ribbon that twined around her toes and feet. Her eyes were deep aqua and she was breathtaking.

"Addy" her voice was musical. She approached tentatively and then smiled as she embraced Addy, "we have waited so long" she sighed.

"Beautiful" murmured Celia. Her fiery red hair cupping her face.

"Let's go," she clapped her hands.

***

Addy was shuffled into a line, she held the centre, to her left was Glock and Celia and to her right, Roz and Neb. Behind them the Queen, Prince David and Princess Tiallana along with Jessica. Behind them five of the Guards Horses formed an arc, in its centre was Dane. Addy looked up, the wind caught Henry's mane and ruffled Dane's medals. She quickly looked away, pride swelling in her as she remembered holding onto him. Henry whinnied. She was still angry at him.

Ferris marched into view, stomping his staff as the wind rippled his beard and robes,

"Your Majesties, Lords, Ladies" he looked at each in turn, "we have the honor of hosting the Earth Walkers Association tonight. Tweedy has begun the portal opening, we should proceed."

He turned and lead the party down the driveway, everyone

slowly followed in silence. Addy felt the warmth of her tattoo on her wrist, she glanced down and noticed Roz smile as the same tattoo on her upper arm glowed.

The air turned warmer and the breeze picked up, the party followed Ferris. Addy noticed the body guards in the dark on both sides of them. "Not far now" Ferris called out, moving from the cobbled lane onto the lawn. "Just beyond the first tree line" he pointed out as he strode forward. His hair and beard parted in the breeze.

Addy saw Tweedy, his chipmunk cheeks speckled with freckles and his grey curls sprouting like cauliflower from beside his large hat, which held a snow white pointed hydrangea. He had the same bright green clogs on and three-quarter matching green pants as when Addy first met him. Today, however, he wore a snow-white jacket with pockets that were lined with green.

"Miss Addy!" he shouted in his happy voice, smiling broadly as he waved, seemingly oblivious to the rest of the crowd descending on him.

Addy smiled widely.

Such happiness.

Her heart tweaked.

"Tweedy," she acknowledged waving.

"Look" he gestured proudly. In the clearing, a shimmering galaxy was turning on a tiny black dot. The shimmering cloud moved slowly, steadily on itself, "nearly" he whispered. The crowd stopped, looking on expectantly. Ferris took Tweedy's shoulder and pulled him towards the galaxy. Everyone else waited.

"Do you know them?" Roz leaned over Neb, nodding to the shimmering gateway, "Earthwalkers?" Addy smiled, shaking her head, "no".

Within a few moments, Tweedy was moving around the vortex, pulling it out, measuring it up. He kept chatting to Ferris in a low hum. Finally, the black hole in the centre of the vortex, extended forward and a door could be seen.

Addy felt the guards lean in, ready for action.

The door slid to the right and a warm yellow light shone through. Addy felt everyone hold their breath. Ferris stepped forward.

The first person to step through was a guard, he was dressed in white, a large busby on his head. He was followed by three more guards. They lined the exit of the portal.

The first Earth Walker Association member through the portal was a blonde woman, she looked totally flabbergasted and unsure and appeared to be pushed through the door. Her dress clung to her large frame, she was clearly nervous.

"Welcome!" Ferris boomed, "Welcome, Earth Walkers Association. Please come through" Ferris continued, glancing back to ensure he hadn't been abandoned.

She clutched her pink handbag in front of her and smiled nervously at the crowd. She was followed by a tall man who wore a T-shirt with the words "I am Roger" across it. Next came an old man with a bulbous nose, he was very wrinkled but seemed to radiate happiness. An Asian man in traditional dress with a massive head-dress popped out next, he bowed theatrically, dragons were emblazoned across his robe. Two women followed. One had dark dreadlocks neatly tied back and a large ring in her nose, the other wore a traditional Indian Sari, beads draped across her head and fell over onto her forehead, she was gorgeous. Lastly, a man in red and gold brocaded shirt and pants stepped through the portal.

Seven people representing the Earth.

"Welcome, friends," Ferris stepped forward. The blonde woman's eyes widened, she visibly clutched at her throat.

"Ugh," she gurgled in fear.

The tall man smiled and reassured her, "It's okay" he whispered.

"Come through" Ferris encouraged.

The guards moved forward and made space for the party to step down.

"This way. Let me introduce you" he gestured.

"May I present their Majesties, Queen Olivia of Llastraul. Prince David, Princess Tiallana, Princess Jessica and Crowne Prince Thomas" Ferris stood to the side.

"This is the Quinary" he gestured, "Glock" he pointed, "then Celia" she bowed her head in acknowledgement, "Addy" Addy waved, "Neb" he closed his eyes and bowed forward fractionally, "And Roz" Ferris gestured. The men visibly reacted to Roz as she smiled.

"I am Ferris" he bowed, "At your service".

"Thank-you. Thank-you for your hospitality" the tall man spoke up.

"This is Anne, Roger, Arlo, Bai, Imani and Prenasha. Last but not least, Buana, who have all been chosen to represent the Earth".

"Let us return to the Tower. We can have refreshments and discuss our purpose" Ferris lead the way back to the Tower. The Queen had slipped easily into the role of hostess. Celia and Roz were among the visitors, asking questions and explaining things.

Addy stepped aside to chat to Tweedy.

"Impressive," she nodded.

Tweedy smiled. "I am usually protecting the entry. I don't often get to invite people through. It's rather nice" he beamed. "You'd better join the party. I will close this portal and keep an eye out. I think the plan is that they will be here for twelve hours.... Glock thinks it is safer not to try and keep them over twenty four-hour period, something to do with the speed of time relative to where you're at"

"Interesting" Addy spoke absently, "Tweedy, how long does it take to open it up?"

"Well that depends" he rested his chin in his right hand, "If Grunsdy is aligned to Thear between Earth and Thear, like it is now, then it can take twenty minutes to open and close. I wish Thatcher was on the other side, I haven't spoken to him in years" Tweedy walked around the shimmering vortex admiring his work, "why is it fading here?" He spoke to himself, hunching over a stray thread.

Addy thought for a moment of Ternion's prisoners on Earth.

Addy noted that the party had slowly started walking up the drive.

"See you Tweedy" she absently whispered, a plan forming in her mind.

"Later Addy" Tweedy responded engrossed in fixing the structure of his gateway.

Addy glanced at him quickly, making sure that he was totally occupied and then walked swiftly away from Tweedy, turning left in the galaxy's opening where minutes before the Earth Walkers had come down from. A guard looked out over the retreating party, oblivious to Addy tiptoeing behind him.

Addy's heart pounded

I'll just check in on Grit and the Rescue team. Maybe I can even release someone. My mum? I can do something. Talk fest, pah, what will that help.

The black opening loomed up quickly.

What can go wrong? I just want to help.

She slipped off here shoes and carried them. She stepped through the black hole without looking back.

The blackness pulled and sucked at her, she felt the rippling of the air over her skin and felt her magic respond. Fear gripped her throat, "what have I done" she cried in the vacuum. Before she could think, a green shimmer appeared at the end of her tunnel, she slowly walked towards it. As she descended the swirling vortex, a mirror image of that which she climbed into, she saw a familiar view.

The cave exits through which Addy had escaped so many weeks ago, sat stiffly and silently in the afternoon sun. Addy's anger mounted steadily.

My friends are in there.

She felt her power climb, she walked quicker, her evening dress swirling around her legs.

I can get them.

Addy broke free from the tree line, and stopped.

I can retrace my steps, I am sure of it.

She dropped her shoes at the base of a tree and walked over the pine needles, oblivious to her surrounds, concentrating on the cave entrance. She started running, heart pounding, pressure building in her chest, power moved in her, emotion drove her forward. Her hair fell from its chic knot and cascaded down her back.

"Addy. No," she heard the familiar voice somewhere on the periphery of her thought. The door was sturdy and she pushed hard. Power arced between her fingers where her efforts to move the door were futile. "Ugh! No" she grunted.

Addy stepped back and without a second glance, pulled energy towards her, it came quickly and waited for her command. Addy moved her arms in a wide arc and as they came close towards her chest, she released the energy ball. It shattered against the wall, blowing it aside. Rocks and dust fell forward.

"Addy!"

She looked around quickly.

"Dane?" Relief flooded into Addy.

"Oh gosh! Dane!" she moved towards him. But Dane did not embrace her.

"Come Addy. This way" he pulled her away from the cave entrance that she had destroyed, "Quick" he pulled at her.

"What's wrong?" She asked glancing back at her destruction.

"What's wrong? Grit and Penrose are in there. You have just put the equivalent of a siren up for the evil trio! What are you thinking?" He was angry.

"I didn't know" she started.

"Exactly! Why didn't you stop when I called you? Why are you here Addy?" He rested his hands on his hips, "you should be on Thear. Why did you cross the gateway? That wasn't the plan!"

"What plan? Nobody has told me of any plan," she was angry now, "all they are doing is meeting and planning some massive battle that will take place way after everyone's dead! Nobody has told me anything about my mum, about Grit and the Rescuers or the prisoners. I came to help. I am here now" she crossed her arms over her evening gown.

"No. You have to go back before the portal closes. You have to go now, Addy" he insisted.

"No" she shook her head, "I can help Dane" she whined.

"Addy, I know. You can help by taking your place on the Quinary. It's what you are supposed to do. Leave this to Grit and I. We can manage it" he smiled then, "trust me?" He asked.

"Dane, I thought you would understand. I can help you here. My mum is here. All the prisoners..." she started.

"Addy. You must leave immediately. Go back to Thear. For shit sake! Why are you so stubborn?" He ran his hands through his hair. "Please? Do this for us all? Please?" He implored.

Addy felt the frustration building inside of her.

"Addy, you have to train to deliver your true purpose. Why are you so distracted? Do you think you are the only one that can do this? Save these people?" He gestured to the cave,

"No! Dane, you know that's not true. I didn't know if anyone was here, attempting to rescue them" Addy started explaining,

"We are here Addy, we aren't going to leave them to the mercy of the evil three" he was flat and direct, "we'll do our job. Go back. Do yours".

"I am here now. I didn't realize the Crowne Prince was on a rescue mission tonight" she was being petty and her anger fueled her.

"Addy! You are so single-minded. Do you realize the purpose you are to fulfil? Have you even try to understand the legend, the significance of the role you have to play? Don't interrupt me" he held his hand up when Addy started to speak, "No! If you care, stay on Thear. Learn from the Quinary. Understand what it is you need to do when the time comes. Trust us Addy. Trust me. You will not hurt anyone using power when you learn what you need to do" Dane looked tired.

"Dane?"

Movement from behind the rubble had them scrambling back against the cave. Addy glanced to her left and saw the stream of black creatures pouring out of the cave, squinting in the sunshine.

"Shit! Come this way" Dane whispered pulling her further around the side of the hill. They stayed close to the hillside and then ducked into the line of trees.

"Bloody deja vous" he grumbled.

They crouched between the trees for a moment observing the creatures.

"They must not see the gateway. You must run back, quickly. Before it closes" he indicated for her to follow.

"Dane" her breathing was heavy from running.

"Don't be a fool, Addy" he spoke over his shoulder as he ran.

The tree line curved to right which came close up to the black creatures, looking into the trees and around the landscape.

Dane and Addy moved from tree to tree silently. The gateway was tucked further up on the right. Her breathing heaved her chest up and down. Dane gestured for her to go ahead.

She frowned, "Go" he whispered,"I will distract them".

Addy felt responsible for the situation. She nodded. She yearned for his embrace.

But he's going to be king. Why would he want to be with you?

Addy took a deep breath and sprinted. The gateway arms were getting smaller and smaller. She ran at full tilt, looking back she saw Dane fly from the trees calling on the wind. Black creatures swarmed to the direction he flew. The smell of pine permeated the air and Addy saw the rough bark of the trees marking the metres she ran.

Pine needles spat up behind her and her bare feet slipped on the floor. The screeching noise from the left of the trees distracted her. She saw a creature lift her shoes from where she had dropped them. Addy ran and with a leaping dive fell into the black hole of the gateway as the arms disappeared.

The whooshing and sucking was more intense. The air vibrated and wobbled, turbulence chattered the space beside her. She sat heaving air back into her chest.

Mere moments later, Addy saw the shimmer of castle lights, the space was becoming constrictive she realized that Tweedy was closing the gateway. Addy jumped, rolling to stop at Tweedy's feet.

He looked at her, horror stamped across his face. Addy jumped up, smoothing her dress down.

"Sorry," she smiled and saw the party slow at the steps of the Tower, "must run".

19

The ouroboros picture took pride of place on the wall opposite Addy. She focused on the bottom half of its body, where the indigo from its belly and the green from the back of the snake, merged. In the picture water, clear and gushing swept in and out, keeping the rhythm of the tide. This was a time-piece. Addy wondered if Glock was the only one in the room who could tell the time using the ouroboros clock. She knew the ouroboros represented cyclicality, "the ouroboros, Addy, or tail-devouring snake symbolizes how we can constantly recreate ourselves, like the phoenix," Glock's voice reverberated in her memory, "think of it also, as the representation of primordial unity" he had marched around hands caught behind his back, "primordial" he drew the word out, "unity. Meditate on it, Addy".

She pulled her thoughts back to the room. Seven Earth Walkers, four royal family members including their counsellors and five Quinarians, and at least five advisories sat around the enormous table. At its centre were odd shaped in-lays, roughly in line with each person.

"The problems through the central belt of the planet, continue. War, conflict, unrest" Roger from the Earth Walkers Association was explaining, "and across the globe, cyclones

over India and off the coast of France, cyclones over Tokyo
and all four points of Australia. Tropical storms have formed
from Thailand all through to Korea. Gales have blown from
the Antarctic, carrying ice crystals, damaging countries several
hundred kilometres up the coast, countries" he glanced across
the room, "adjacent to this are having heat waves, bureaus of
meteorology cannot explain these phenomenon".

"But" Arlo from the Earthwalkers stood up, "this is not our
biggest concern" he patted Roger's shoulder and walked slowly
along the length of the room, stopping only when he reached
the back corner and then slowly turned back to everyone, "dark
shadows" he barely spoke up, "everywhere. Energy consuming
entities, devouring electricity, gas, energy in any form" he
looked gravely at everyone, "unstoppable, shadows" he said
softly. "They feed off our energy, our feelings, our movement"
he said with gravity, "at first, just a few reports" his shoulders
sagged, "but now every day" he stopped and looked across the
room, "everyday".

"Your Majesties, Lords" Tyeh bowed to the room in different
directions, "Ladies, Friends, Advisors" he rested his hands on
the chair in front on him, "the same problems exist here on
Thear. Significant storms, causing untold damage in every part
of the planet, shadows lurking in our busiest places. Where we
use magic to power our cities, shadows have consumed it" his
stance was somber, "what is this thing we cannot grab, we cannot
catch, we cannot even see most of the time? We need a plan to
stop it" he nodded sharply, dangling the aglet on his beard and
then sat down.

"So, they have commenced their onslaught," Ferris
summed up.

"They are also holding prisoners" Addy spoke before she
thought and then realized when the entire room looked directly
at her, "in a cave" she felt the soft carpet beneath her bare feet.

"We have a rescue team looking into that as we speak"
Glock advised, "do not fear Addy. We cannot afford to break

the Quinary for this. We have much to do to stop Ternion" he looked at her sternly.

Addy nodded. Frustration poured into every cell in her body, she felt her energy prickle around her.

"Just how powerful and big is this army?" The woman with the blonde bob, called Anne asked, her glasses perched right at the end of her nose, they were the same bright pink as her jacket.

"Yes, what numbers are we talking?" Dane's advisor asked.

"This is a magical war" Ferris started, "there are only three people at its epicenter, called Ternion. Their power is significant. Legends have told that only Kivnon can deliver us all from it. A magical war, where the armies have been enslaved by evil and dark means. A power play for domination" Ferris spoke slowly.

Probably more powerful than all of us and growing each hour thought Addy.

***

They started late the next day. The Earth Walkers left at midnight and planning went way past that. Addy stumbled towards the heavenly smells. She loved Pearl's kitchen. The smell of fresh bread and smokey bacon, found a nostalgia within her. Addy sniffed deeply as she entered.

"We'll do more training today" Ferris advised gruffly, "I'll see you down there in an hour" he nodded and walked out of the kitchen, grabbing an apple as he left.

"And good morning to you" she spoke to his retreating frame.

"Yes, yes" confirmed Glock, "we've been talking Addy, sifting through memories" he sipped his tea noisily, "and we want to try a few things today" he cracked open a bright pink egg, "Celia will join us" he expertly sliced through the large egg.

"Sit, dear" Pearl put a warm hand on her shoulder, "you can't train until you have eaten. House rules" she laughed.

Shortly Addy was on the training field. She glanced up to check the energy field was in place.

"I'm not sure why you insist on it, beautiful child" Celia spoke behind her, "you can probably blow right through it".

"Morning Celia" she smiled, "it's just in case a stray flux goes AWOL" she shrugged.

Celia's hair blazed in the morning sun, red streaks struck out behind her, angular and stepped and unique. A single plait of greenery wound from temple to temple, matching her eyes.

Addy never tired of her, she was spectacular to behold. "Comfortable" in her space, Addy thought, as she watched Celia move around gracefully. Her short skirt, deep berry brown, swished around her smooth thighs. Her cream bikini top fit like a second skin, but she looked spectacular both young and fresh and wise and caring.

"Aah! Here he is" Celia commented as Ferris appeared over the hill,

"Slower than usual" commented Glock cheekily.

"I suspect that he over indulged last night and didn't drink the potion I made him" laughed Celia.

"Go on this in not a show" Ferris responded as he approached.

"Why didn't you drink the potion?" Celia asked directly.

"Remind myself that there are repercussions to all our choices" he looked at Addy.

"Sweet" she grimaced, "training with Sir Grump-a-lot" Ferris scowled even more which made everyone laugh more.

"Addy" Glock indicated to the small table off the side of the field, "this is a micro ethometer" he lifted a cube about twenty centimetres wide, up. It had an inlaid dark screen on two opposite sides, the rest looked like thick, clear, green glass. He handed it to Addy.

"What is it used for?" She turned the cube in her hands and then raised up to eye level,

"It is used to check power for a few things, which we'll get to in a moment" Glock explained.

"Think of it as a mini ether reader" Ferris suggested.

"Oh wow," Addy's tone was wondrous, "have you seen inside of this thing?" She asked absently.

In the foreground hundreds upon hundreds of grains of sea sand had formed column structures which when you peered through showed exploding supernova, space, and swirling masses of stars. In the centre a simple golden bubble hung, clinging in the colours of the cube, in the far distance behind the golden bubble were mountains, red and undulating, brooding above a streaming lake.

"Wow" she hushed, turning the cube onto another side, geographic patterns merged and moved into view. The shapes were familiar to Addy, she'd seen them in darker times, pinned to Zyklon's wheel of torture.

Addy looked at Celia and Glock, "what do we do with it?" She asked, placing it back in its holder.

"When Neb and Roz join us later, we'll test whether a complete Quinary enhances our powers." Glock was clearly excited.

"We are going to test a few theories" Celia smiled.

"One such theory, Addy" Ferris stepped forward, patting his robe, "is to understand which elemental power you have an affinity with" he found his pipe and began puffing, smoke billowed up and out. Addy sniffed deeply, she loved the smell. It reminded her of dark cherries, black forest cakes and warm fires.

"As you know now, Glock affiliates well with air, Celia with Earth, of course, Neb with fire and Roz with water" he walked away from the table looking up into the air, "but we don't know if you have all of those, none or one" he shielded his eyes as he glanced up squinting.

"What are you looking for?" Addy glanced up looking into the same distance.

"Nothing. I'm looking at the power over the village" he indicated in the distance.

"Neb and Roz are there" Glock advised, "they'll call if they need us".

Addy switched her gaze and immediately saw the power lines weaving over the village.

"Oh no," she whispered, "we must go" she grabbed Glock's arm.

"No. Neb and Roz are there. They will call us if they need us" he patted her hand.

Addy was still staring at the power lines, "Addy" Celia pulled her attention back to the cube, "when I shoot a single beam of power through the cube, like this" she placed her finger on the metal stand pointing towards the cube, a single energy strand erupted from her finger, beautiful vibrant green. It hit into the cube. Immediately the cube lit up. Leaves, forests and planes, fruits and wild animals, image after image, flashed on the screen, Addy bent down to look inside the glass panel. Buds sprang forth and eggs hatched, the planets were fertile, abundant. In the centre the golden ball was surrounded by green ether, linking chains wove around the bubble, cradling it.

Addy smiled at Celia, "awesome".

"It is indeed" she exuded warmth.

"And when Glock does it" Celia moved away, "come on old man" Celia teased.

Glock put his finger on the stand and released a vibrant orange power line into the cube. Addy knelt down again, intrigued.

"Wow" she gasped.

Oceans moved majestically and clouds rolled around and then the image changed. Trees changed their leaves and wind whirred across the land. In the golden bubble the seasons changed. Addy watched the birds take flight. Air she thought.

"Now if we both do it" Glock indicated for Celia to join,

"You will notice the two beams pushed together into the cube, an enhanced power." Ferris took over the explanation.

The image was fast and flowing, birds, birth, air, green,

planets, seasons, orange, wind, earth. The images flashed quickly, intermittently.

"And we were wondering Addy" Ferris stared directly into her, "whether this reader would reveal that secret for you". Glock and Celia pulled their energy back.

Addy's throat felt thick, "oh no" she thought, "what if have no affinity. What."

"Don't over think this Addy" Ferris warned, "look. I will show you" he stuck his finger onto the stand. A thin beam of beautiful indigo flew from his finger into the cube.

The magic was different.

"It is not a power that comes from me" Ferris explained, "It's what I have access to outside of me" he explained. The scene in the cube was tranquil, a field, a stream, fishing, storms, mountains, people. The golden bubble turned slowly. Empty. Untouched.

"Keep looking at the bubble" Ferris murmured. With his free hand, he wiggled his fingers and a single feather blew on the wind directly into his hand, the bubble fired with orange liquid, a feather blew in the cube.

"Air power" she understood. He nodded, "keep looking" he wiggled his fingers and water pulled from the air into his hand, the bubble filled with blue liquid.

"Water" she said.

"Do you see Addy. All it will do is represent your power" he smiled. Addy nodded.

She wiped her palms on her jeans and smiled nervously at Celia and then placed her finger on the stand.

She watched as the silver streak of energy ran up the cube and enter it.

"You can start" Glock nodded to the ethometer. Addy frowned.

"I have" she raised her eyebrows.

Glock bent down level to the cube. Celia?" He spoke to the cube.

"I don't see the energy stream either" she confirmed, "hang on. I can see where it should be. Like a little hollow in the air" she whispered.

"Oh wow" Celia murmured, "Ferris? Look" she hushed.

"What is it?" Addy asked

"Supernovas, space, stars" they all spoke at once.

"What's in the bubble" Addy asked, already knowing the answer.

"Nothing" Ferris croaked, "but that cannot be!"

Glock peered closer, "It's not nothing" he whispered, "it is the nothing" he said, "can it be?"

"Glock. What are you talking about?" Addy was shorter than she had anticipated.

"Sorry, love" he patted her arm absently, "I think" he stood up and his eyes caught hers, "I think it's dark energy". Celia's brows shot up and Ferris scowled at him,

"Dark energy?" Ferris repeated.

Addy removed her hand from the ethometer and rubbed them together.

"Yes, yes. I am not one hundred percentages sure yet, but it fits" he commented, "dark energy is the opposite to gravity, it is what causes the universe to expand at an accelerated rate and what's more," he looked at the others and then back at Addy, "it occupies the entire universe" he stretched his arms wide, "and accounts for most of the energy in it" he finished satisfied.

"Well that will explain the enormous amounts of power you have" Celia smiled at her.

"What does it mean? I wonder?" Ferris stared at the cube.

"Hola" Roz laughed from behind. They all swung around to greet her.

"What is so intriguing?" Neb asked in his warm French accent.

"Glock thinks Addy's elemental affinity is for the yet unknown, fifth element, thought to be dark energy" Ferris explained.

Roz's face transformed to intrigue, "wow" she flicked Addy's shoulder, "interesting, newbie"

"How do you know?" Neb set his mouth in a perfect oval, "you cannot see dark energy" he stated.

"Yes! And I can see my energy," Addy added in.

"Can you?" Glock asked. Addy nodded. She leant forward and put her finger back in the ethometer. The silver line appeared. She pointed with her free hand, "can you see that?" She followed the silver line.

"No" they all agreed.

"But look" Roz showed like Celia had, "you can see where it should be".

"Most intriguing" Neb murmured.

"I think" Ferris interrupted, "that we should test the full Quinary now" he rubbed his hands together in glee.

"We have waited for this for so long! Addy, centuries we have waited. Our mothers and fathers, hoped to have this moment. They are all looking in on us" Glock laughed.

"Glock" Ferris interrupted, "you go first. Then Roz, Celia, Neb. Then you Addy" he indicated with a double pointed finger at each. Each in turn, put their fingers on the metal stand. Addy knelt down to look at the cube. Colours; orange, blue, green and red ran parallel power beams up to the cube.

"Come Addy" Ferris nudged her.

"Oh" she breathed.

As her silver power thread ran up the stand, the four power threads disappeared, absorbing the colour.

"Don't take it away" Ferris cautioned, "the power is still there?" He asked.

"Yes" everyone nodded.

The silver line entered the cube, Ferris hunched down to see the images at eye level.

"Oh," he muttered, "Oh my" he stroked his beard.

"So?" Glock's eyebrows were climbing higher and higher, "you going to share?" He dripped in sarcasm.

"The golden bubble" he cleared his throat, "it's turned" he cocked his head to the side.

"A little more precision, Ferris?" Neb prompted.

"Addy's power has removed the colour, absorbed it. So, it is difficult to follow, but it appears that its being pulled into the bubble, the bubble is filling with colour, but wait" he leaned in more "it's changing from a bubble, it's, it's, uh, geometric?" He asked rhetorically.

"Changing geometric shapes" he spoke slowly, "sacred geometry" Ferris smiled.

"Five platonic solids?" Neb asked

"Yes" Ferris glanced up briefly, "it looks like it".

"And outside the bubble" Roz asked.

"Space. The universe" he said distractedly

"A lattice of coral, in front of mountains, rivers, lots of space" he spoke as he saw.

"And if one of us pulls away?" Celia suggested, "keep looking" she pulled her finger away.

"The golden bubble is empty now" Ferris stated, the disappointment evident in his voice.

"We will do more research" Glock stated removing his finger, "so exciting" he patted Neb on the shoulder.

"Aah, but what is this, Addy?" Glock's large gestures prompting her to smile.

"It's just" she sighed

"What is it my dear?" Celia soothing voice sent warmth through her.

"Is my power bad?" Her voice was small.

"Bad?" Neb was clearly surprised at the question, "Bad?" He lowered his chin and scrunched his brows together, "I am not understanding" he gestured with his palms up, "explain these bad" his accent was very pronounced.

"Well" Addy was hesitant, "how is it that some people turn dark?"

"It is like this Addy" Roz started, "the most important

decision you make in your entire life" she glanced at each in turn, "is to decide whether the world is your friend or not".

"But what has that got to do with power?" Addy wasn't following.

"Everything, no?" Neb stated, "Power is simply power, energy. It is not good or bad Addyyyy" Neb pulled her name out.

"So, if you have power and you have decided the world is your friend, you use the power in that space" he gestured with his hands in the air, "but if it is not your friend" he looked at her, "you use it, differently" he pulled his mouth down and shoved his palms upwards.

"You choose" Celia smiled, "we all choose."

20

Gravel crunched beneath their feet and sulphur lingered on the breeze. The trees rustled in the air current. Behind them the thrumming of the up-draft from the cliff edge created white noise. Addy pulled her jacket closer, the cold needled into her.

"What do we know about dark energy Neb?"

"It's a property of space. It expands the universe, repels gravity, permeates all of space, takes up nearly seventy percent of the universe" he stopped at the cliff edge, burying his hands into his jacket, "it's an ocean Addy, a large cosmic ocean" he glanced at her and then looked out to the horizon.

"What does it mean for you?" He pulled his mouth down in the u-shape she associated with grumpy Frenchmen, "I don't know" he shrugged and turned his dragon eyes fully onto Addy, "but I think, given it's a property of space, something we cannot see but still connect with, no?" His first two fingers pressed his thumb, "and given its everywhere" he made big gestures, "I think, it means that you are unbelievably powerful."

The slits of his eyes elongated and a translucent eyelid swept across his green iris. "I also think that until you can master that power, your gift is dangerous. Very dangerous." His voice whispered against the updraft.

Addy stepped towards the cliff edge. The Sulphur filled her nose, "Why can't I remember?" The toes of her boots hung over the edge, her jacket chafed in the wind. Her voice was barely audible, with her chin tucked into her scarf and her eyes smarting in the whipping current, "Perhaps I am not a Quinary member after all. Some mistake? I should remember."

Neb lifted his palm, the draft quietened.

"When my dad moved back into his energy form" he glanced to see if Addy was listening, "it's how my DNA got activated. My genetic memory, or Grimoire as Celia and Roz call it, didn't activate for some time"

"Really? What happened? How long did it take? How did you get it? What did you do?"

"Slow down" Neb laughed, "I'll tell you. Everyone's story is different. For me. Eight years!"

"No way!" Addy's jaw dropped, "No!"

"Let me explain" his French accent came to the fore. He squeezed her shoulder smiling.

"I wanted the power but I wasn't ready to take on the responsibility. Some secret universal force knows this" he winked conspirationally, "In the year leading to my dad's departure, he kept trying to explain the obligations and the ethics and the boring bits of the role. Boring for me at the time." He rolled his eyes exaggeratedly. "Ah. The ego, Addy. My ego was big. Very big" he held his palms open wide. "I wanted to roar through the skies changing the weather, the trees, anything at my will. I wanted to go into battles and be feared and I wanted to be the affection of all the girls" he smiled sheepishly. "I couldn't do a damn thing! Oh, I had power, it belted out of me sporadically without my will. I would burn things and destruct without control. The humiliation of fixing my messes every time helped me pack my ego away. The universe also has a sense of humour"

"And, how did you get it?"

"When I used power, not for my purposes. It worked. Something just triggered here" he lay his palm across his heart,

"I released a large amount of energy like this and just like that" click of his fingers, "my Grimoire connected. And then Addy. Only then"

Addy leant in.

"The Quinary all said, 'oh yes, we thought you knew about that trick!' But how are you supposed to know if you don't have the Grimoire" he laughed shaking his head at the memory.

"So, all I have to do is release enormous amounts of energy, not for my own purpose, and it will activate my Grimoire?"

"Oui" he nodded with u-shaped lips again.

"But Addy" Neb swept the yellow gravel with his foot enacting a shy school boy, "your Grimoire brings information about your power. The genetic memory of your DNA. With this comes how to transform that special energy to another at the end of your time. So, if you have reproduced and say, you are ready to physically depart this world. Then your parting will activate the DNA in your oldest child."

'And if I die or depart as you say, before I have children?"

"Your Grimoire will have in it a spell. This is designed so that you can impart your DNA power onto another who has no Quinary power. But, it is dangerous"

"Oh?"

"When you say the words, you might die. The energy you send to your intended recipient, might make them mad"

Silence layered the vacuous noise of the draft in the cliff.

"It's ancient magic" Neb hushed.

"Will Ternion know?"

"Probably" he shrugged. Then dispelling the hush, "Let's not get the head off ourselves"

"Do you mean, ahead of ourselves?" Addy enquired

"Both" laughter rung out brightening the pale sun.

"Come. Let us release that energy".

They walked along the cliff top moving south and then ventured in a little way.

"This is a good spot. Think of something good. Just play

with the energy. Let it move through you, charge it and release it. Nobody can be hurt here".

Addy closed her eyes a moment. Centred on her core; who needs help? How can I help?

"Heyho" Neb's enthusiasm boomed through his voice, "use your energy, layer by layer now, release it. Use the cliff drop or the skies. If you use the earth, feel her geometry first," he smiled.

Addy removed her shoes. The gravel was cold and hard. The earth connected through her souls, she sent a strand of energy down, feeling where it moved the layers, where the cracks were. Where the fissures were, down the carboniferous layers. Addy's senses were fed by her power line. She found a water source, pressured and warm. She traced it back up through its connecting paths, through a weak spot. Then she sent in her power, masses of it. She pulled it from the earth, and pushed it down back into the weak zone.

The buzz started in her feet and slowly moved up her legs. She felt the electric currents move through her, alive. Limestone layers near the top surged with power. Addy pulled power from above, it came to her. She formed the vision in her mind and then felt the earth rumble. Rocks slid over one another. She sensed the water running into the fracture. The power flowed freely. Beautiful. Vibrant.

"Addy?" she heard Neb in the periphery of her mind.

Addy felt love, warmth, joy. So alive. The breeze on her face and the sun on her skin. The power moved from her, into her, around her. One with her energy, she pushed her palms outwards, the earth trembled.

Neb sat on his haunches, speechless.

Joy poured in, energy flowed all around. The earth nudged itself open, plates moving, grinding, rearranging. A rhythm as old as itself. A smooth beautiful crater opened up in the space. And then silence.

Small stones tumbled into the crater; otherwise not a stirring.

Addy watched as the power sizzled across her body, lighting her up. The tension mounted, her heart expanded; she felt the sun warm her face as she noticed the tree tops glistening in the distance.

This was a good place. This was a place for people to come and heal.

Addy pulled her arms down beside her. The movement sent shocks into the fractures below. Water burst up; beautiful big fat silver drops, arching across one another in the crater. The release of the energy brought euphoria.

Addy clapped and danced.

"Fantastic!" Neb whooped and danced over to her.

The water filled the crater, bubbling and steaming in the cold air. Warm beautiful water that would heal weary travelers and soothe pain.

"It's beautiful! People will come for miles to soak here"

Addy beamed, "Looks like a storm is coming over, just in time"

Neb glanced back, "Addy shield," he ran towards the growing mass, "Shield!"

"It's smoke?"

"No! That's what you're supposed to think" Neb glanced over his shoulder at Addy, his arms extended behind him, trying to herd her by will into his shield.

The cloud moved quickly, Addy felt the power all around her. It came from Neb's shield and from the cloud. Her shield waned and fluttered. Not enough power feeding it.

"Keep it constant Addy"

"I can't!"

"Yes! You can! You must! Oui?"

The power came to her but she could not construct the shield. Her head started pounding. The tickle at her nose showed blood.

"Addy your power is designed to protect you. It is an automatic response. Don't try so hard. Just let it happen," Neb's voice was hoarse from shouting above the up draught of the cliff.

The shield still fluttered. Panic hollowed her abdomen; stole her breath.

"Come closer into me" Neb barked over his shoulder as he watched the cloud grow ever larger above them, "this is powerful. Old magic! It's not good".

Neb moved slowly trying to keep the cloud in front of them.

No sooner that his words were spoken, a thin spiral broke away from the mass. Dropping its smoky grey thread between Addy and Neb. Neb focused on the other tendrils the mass dropped in front of them.

"Neb?"

"Just stay behind me" he concentrated on the tendrils now burning great big craters in the yellow earth of the cliff.

"But, Neb!"

The smoke tendril wound itself around Addy's torso.

Why can't I bring up my power? Where are you dammit? I can feel you, please, please come now?

"Neb!"

The fire on the ground created more smoke. Slowly surrounding them in a dome. The smoke was hot. Uncomfortable.

Neb pushed energy at the cloud. The explosion was loud, reverberating across the cliffs and echoing down the gorge. The mass absorbed the energy and began to churn; darker and darker. Lightning rolled in its depths and it spread quicker and quicker above them.

The sound began as a hiss, hardly noticeable in the rumble of the up draught. When Addy became aware of it, the smoke tendril had nearly enveloped her.

Neb's energy both kept the mass from descending but also fed the cloud which crackled with static, throwing power bolts down around them.

"Addy, I need to change" She heard his voice in the distance, barely there in the up draught and the background hiss.

The smoke tightened around her, pulling energy from her, the more Addy called for power the stronger the bonds of smoke became.

The hissing became clear now.

"More power. More power. More power" over and over again Verity's voice hissed vehemently in chant, "More power, more power".

The moment Neb changed, the power released and fed the cloud; Addy felt the surge.

"Neb!" The screech caught his attention as he turned to retrieve her. Addy saw the dragon gracefully swoop towards her. Verity's voice hissed, "Stupid girl! Stupid stupid bitch! Expel your power! Fight back! Get the Grimoire!" Her anger was palpable in the smoke.

She was overcome. She felt Neb's claw on her arm and her body leave the ground.

***

"Glock! Just listen for a minute," Addy moved the stray strand of hair from her face, irritation stiffened the sinew in her neck and collarbones.

"Addy what you ask is dangerous" Glock stood tall and straight, his fists clenched beside him, "I don't think you appreciate the power of your living memory. Connecting with Verity, on purpose, is a dark practice. We stay a-"

"But Glock! It's for our greater good," Addy interrupted.

"No!" anger caught his eye, "it's a moment in that time that will be forever captured in our memory. Forever!" His voice boomed across the library, "do you understand that concept? Passing on the dark practice, forever?" The fire shot and shifted enunciating the silence.

"There may be no tomorrow to pass any memory to, if Ternion win. Do you understand that Glock?" Addy was tired.

"Addy. Glock" Ferris had been quiet, staring at the flames as they argued; his concern weighted his voice.

"You are both right! They stood down from their battle stance, sitting on the edge of the leather sofa.

"Our imminent threat is Ternion; and we may obtain an upper hand if we used your blood to connect to Verity." Ferris explained, "No sit and listen" he shot when Addy stood. She sank back down, annoyed.

"But we risk embedding dark practices in your Grimoires for generations" Glock nodded vigorously, agreeing.

"But Glock mate," he caught his friend's eye, "these are dark times. Not what we're accustomed to. And," he kept their attention, "there are ways to ensure your Grimoire does not have that memory to pass on".

Glock stood up, the power emanating from him grew the fire and knocked the lamp over on the side table.

"Ferris?"

"Calm, my friend"

"You know it's more than that?" Glock held his head, willing his thoughts not to escape, "what if?" He took a deep breath, "what if it's part of their plan? Ternion's? To entice Addy to the dark?" Fear deepened his eyes and took his breath.

"That is not a possibility" Ferris shouted, "not a chance that could happen." Ferris shook his head crossly, "what even lead you to think that?" He grabbed his chest as he looked at Addy.

"Ferris?" Addy's own breath was hard to find, her chest crushing the empty spaces.

"I don't think she wants to" Glock explained softly, 'but her power is new; we don't know it. We don't know Ternion, Ferris? I am only proposing a possibility" but Glock was pained to say it.

"It is not a possibility. I know Addy. Not a possibility" Ferris dismissed.

"Ferris? What if he's right?" Addy knew how that power could feel. When it ran and fed your ego, bliss. It was heady and amazing and like a potent drug.

What if I am already dark? The thought pulled in her core.

"I know it is not a possibility. I feel it. I know it. I know Marj. I know Addy. I know." Ferris was insistent.

Addy's heart swelled. So much faith.

"But if you want answers, we can always ask, we'll, ask MOS" Ferris suggested.

"What?" Glock paled, "You're crazy old man!"

"Whose MOS?" Addy was confused. The men exchanged a heavy look.

"Who is MOS? Can someone please talk to me?" Addy was getting more and more irritated. Power flickered across her skin in tune to her annoyance.

"M-O-S" Ferris spelled, "For Mad Old Seer. She has no name. She has no age. She has no permanent form. She lives in the dark forest at the back of the Room of Reveal"

"Of course, she does" Addy rolled her eyes. "And what do we want to ask her? What are you proposing? And how can we trust her?"

Ferris stared at Glock for long seconds; finally, Glock nodded, the movement hardly noticeable.

"We need Glock to accompany us to the door" Ferris started.

"I will stay for it all" Glock was firm.

Ferris shot him a 'we'll see about that' glance.

"Then, if MOS will speak to us or even show up. We'll ask how you can connect to Verity" Glock cracked his knuckles behind his back, Ferris continued,

"and if she will answer, we will ask how we might protect you" he finished, resting his eyes on Addy.

"From Ternion?" She asked.

"From yourself" Glock whispered.

Addy's stomach pooled in leaden fear, thick and uncomfortable.

An hour later at her insistence they stood at the Room of Reveal's entrance.

Three tall arches guarded the entrance, their interiors lined with cream and maroon stripes. The support column's diamond shape lit up in red flashes as gargoyles and serpents moved over them.

In the walls, the sun's image came from behind a cloud and lit the room. It followed Ferris, Glock and Addy as they walked quietly to the back of the room.

The floor changed. Smooth stone turned to marble. They walked on,

"Don't look at the walls, just straight ahead" Glock was stern.

In her periphery Addy saw images bouncing, running, flying to keep her pace. She focused ahead, the arches kept coming. They came and came, all striped, more and more.

The air distorted, a flaw in the clarity of her vision. Addy blinked and it righted itself. She kept walking.

The arches stretched ahead when she looked ahead but stopped short in her periphery.

Just look ahead. Just look ahead. Fear slowly poured into the hollows inside of her.

The floor changed; large black and white squares spread before them as far as Addy could see. No more arches.

In her periphery, a tiny bird flew and peeped, calling to her. She remembered the bird.

Addy stroked its soft body with the back of her index finger. Soft and downy, it's neck bobbled to the side, it's oversized beak out of place in the petiteness of it. Brittle and bony under the silky feathers; Addy's pudgy five-year-old hands, "I'm so sorry" her voice caught in her throat, "I'm so sorry" she felt the lifeless form roll in her palm, her five-year-old self not understanding but knowing deep down that something wasn't right. The bird stiffened in her palm; "Do you see what happens when you use magic without me?" Verity's voice was venomous in her ear, "What's it feel like to be a killer? Magic kills Adera."

Addy had not used her power again until she escaped from Rodic. I can kill. I can kill. Oh no. The tears were thick and fast. She tried to keep her silence in the strange space.

The tears thickened her throat and nose.

I must focus on forward.

"What is this place?"

"Unique hey?" Ferris smiled.

"Remind me again, why are we here?" Addy heard her own nasal whine and grimaced.

Glock slowed so that they all walked abreast.

"old magic lives here; the Keepers of Knowledge. Well, their essence anyway" Glock spoke seriously.

"MOS might have answers. She might not." He shrugged. "The Room of Reveal. Ancient stories say that this place can make you go crazy. Everything you have done in your life is revealed to you. You become your own judge" Glock went quiet.

"Do you think my blood is what the Nimbus's memory is referring to?" Addy's innards clenched.

"We don't know" Ferris whispered. He cupped her shoulder briefly, smiling to calm her nerves.

"We don't know much, do we?" She stated, "how can we even trust this MOS person?"

"She's neutral. Has no side. She might answer, she might not" Ferris shrugged.

"You took us by surprise, young Addy. We have had to rethink all we ever knew about power" Glock stated, "we have to find answers from those who were here long before the Quinary".

The end of the room came up suddenly. Behind them dragons and gargoyles silently took their places on the chess board. Stepping from nowhere.

"They're protecting us" Glock explained.

The door in front of them was at the top of a short stone stairway, out into an overgrown forest. Tree roots bordered the stone path and ferns and moss lined the path. A creeping shrub decorated the walls.

A tiny nerve twitched in Addy's throat. The anxious flutters curled in her belly.

Where are we? My power is not sensing danger. Why am I so nervous?

The ebony door had no handle but a large knocker; a brass ant with its antennae attached to a brass leaf, dominated the centre. Rich earthiness hung on the stillness.

Glock paused and looked at Ferris and then Addy.

"Here we go"

Here we go? What do you mean here we go? What are we getting into? What are you not telling me? Addy blinked heavily as Glock struck the ant's body onto the leaf three times.

Ferris spoke in hushed tones.

"My dad heard a rumour years back" they both looked at him expectantly, "that Mos was one of the Fates"

"That's ridiculous," Glock whispered, "where are the other two if that is true?"

"Killed by their sister," Ferris whispered.

"Oh sheet!" Glock's eyes bulged as he whispered.

Before Addy could give her view, the ant shook its body, stretched each one of its six legs in turn, used its front legs to slide up each antenna, freeing it from the leaf; which it then proceeded to eat in just a few gulps, revealing a big key hole.

The ant squeezed in through the key hole and they heard its brass legs scratch down the inside of the door. Addy stretched up and looked into the key hole.

The door swung open slowly, silently towards them. She backed off a step.

"Follow me?" Glock offered stepping over the threshold.

"Glocky? You sure?" Ferris held his shoulder, "we can learn this without tainting what you pass to your daughter" Glock pressed his friends hand.

"We all have choices" he nodded gravely and stepped through the door.

Addy took a deep breath. The threshold they stepped onto was on top of a winding stairway, about ten metres up in the air.

Thousands and thousands of books, resting in dark wooden

shelves, lined the walls up as far as you could see. Balconies lead in from secret passages and long ladders rested against the shelving.

The stairway had no barrier and the steps floated in midair. Glock lead the way, then Addy and Ferris followed behind. As Ferris stepped from one step onto another, the step behind him disappeared. There was only one way for them to go.

Addy's lungs crushed behind her rib-cage as she tried not to panic.

Just breath. In and out. She silently coached herself. In and out.

Down beneath them, on the floor, a crystal ball, at least five metres in diameter spun slowly on its stand. Dark and mystic and silent it spun around and around.

Dotted through the shelves, Addy saw tiny sparks, 'fairy messengers' she smiled, remembering. A large fire roared a welcome. Books were stacked on tables beside four great big arm chairs. Their olive green and cream leather looked worn and inviting. Lamp stands lit the room, some floated higher up showing the depth of the space. Cushions, mustard and burgundy scattered the floors and the chairs.

As Addy descended she saw to their right, a wall of electronic screens; the fire reflected in their vacant faces. Scrolls lay out on a table next to a tray laden with tea and treats.

A movement caught Addy's eye. She stepped down the last few steps. Beneath the wooden arrangement on her left.

Was it a peacock decoration? Or a table? Maybe a seat. There. The movement again. Just a ripple.

Addy looked to see Ferris step from the last step. No way back now. The wall behind them was covered in portraits. They continuously changed, a large mass of rolling electronic pictures.

Addy looked from Glock to Ferris inquiringly.

"We wait" Glock whispered.

21

The ripple contorted the air.

"Well," Ferris bent down to have a better look. Addy leant in.

Two tiny furry round ears came up. Then two black eyes. The tawny head lifted and a pink nose and whiskers looked up. The field mouse then pushed down with its tiny pink paws and pulled the rest of its plump body out of the air ripple. When its tail came through, it put its paws together. In the space of an eye blink, the tiny field mouse turned into a beautiful tawny haired woman. Ferris and Glock realized she was completely naked and feigned a coughing fit as they turned to the opposite wall.

Addy sensed her own power trickle across her. No threat. Just a comfort.

The woman lay on her stomach under the peacock. She smiled, content.

"Oh. I. We have just arrived. We didn't have an appointment. Sorry" Addy explained.

She smiled secretly at Addy and then nodded.

She pointed to a hook near the fireplace. A dressing gown hung from it.

"Oh. Of course," Addy collected the dressing gown and handed it to the woman.

Perhaps she can't talk.

"Fenghor always puts the fucking peacock over the portal."
She scrambled out from the art work, "I can never seem to
make him understand. I have knocked myself that many times,
I'm surprised I am not black and blue" she tied the belt. She
brushed at the strands of hair falling down the curve of her
jaw and turned back to Glock and Ferris. "I think he does it
on purpose, little shit! Wicked sense of humour, he has". She
sauntered over to Ferris her eyes narrowed in appreciation.

"Wizard" the word was breathy, "and you, Timekeeper."
She held her dressing gown as if to open the cross over. Then
nodded and moved to Addy, a smile toyed at her mouth.

"Ah! So, you seek counsel?" She hesitated for a microsecond
and then moved to the tea and biscuits.

"We have questions for; uh, for Mos?" Glock got straight to
the point.

She poured tea in silence. The time ticked loudly behind
them. Addy could see Glock tuning into the rhythm.

She handed Glock a cup of tea then stilled a moment.
Listening.

She gave Ferris a cup of tea and then she picked up her own
cup and walked towards the fire.

"Your water is on the table" she threw over her shoulder at
Addy.

The water instantly appeared.

She must be reading my thoughts.

Addy tried to guard her mind.

The woman smiled as she sat down in the large green
armchair and folded her legs beneath her. She smiled straight
ahead, occasionally cocking her head as if to hear.

The woman remained silent. An occasional patter could be
heard behind the books but it just added to the rising quiet; in
and amongst the popping of the fire and the whispered stirring
of the tea.

After long minutes, the silence was so loud that Addy had to break it.

"U-uh" she cleared her throat.

"Are you the one they call Mos?" Addy was direct, her heart slamming behind her ribs caused her to swallow the last word.

Glock's cup rattled on his saucer splashing tea all up his green shirt. He jumped up trying to control himself. "Time is not the same here" he blurted out.

"Pardon us, m'Lady" Ferris interrupted, "we aren't used to seeking counsel, more often we're giving it. We are not familiar with your custom" he spoke with apology all the while sending furtive glances at Addy, willing her silence.

The woman continued to smile without word.

Ferris sat back, crossed his ankles and sipped at his tea. Glock settled back but put his tea on the side table.

Addy could not wait. Time was a commodity she did not have.

"So, the situation is" she started,

"Addy" Ferris warned.

Addy looked at Ferris, stiffened her lips and raised her brows.

I have to do this now.

"I'm the fifth Quinary member. And the situation is that I have had a vial of my blood stolen" Addy got up and walked closer to the woman, cocking her head as she stared into her eyes, "and it's been used to pollinate the daisies in the seventh house of Zeus"

Glock and Ferris sat bolt up-right mouths dropped.

"She's not here. Guys? Seriously. She's here in body but completely tuned out." Addy was clicking her fingers in front of the woman who continued to stare straight ahead, smiling.

Addy, Glock and Ferris were all standing in front of the beautiful woman. They waved and clicked their fingers, all checking for themselves that she was indeed completely vacant.

The air changed. It became cooler and thinner. A wind appeared in the far corner of the room. The essence of the woman sitting in front of them danced in another part the room with great abandonment. The air barely outlined her form, hinted at it; but there was no doubt that it was her.

The wind passed Addy, her hair stood up and she felt its coolness.

The light came back to the woman's eyes and she was alive again.

"Oh. Adera Piper," she whispered in a throaty voice.

Addy flinched. Only Verity ever called her Adera.

"You're afraid of a name." She stated.

She got up then and sauntered over to Ferris. Her chin jutted out to one side. Her clothing changed as she moved. The wrap around shirt clung to her slim figure and the matching vibrant purple skirt skimmed her hips and stopped mid-thigh. She moved with natural grace. She sat down on his lap, keeping her limbs at ninety degrees to his legs as she balanced herself. She twined her one hand into his hair and the other she pushed into his shirt.

"I. Ugh," Ferris was uncomfortable and tried to extract himself from beneath her.

"I wonder" Addy started, "if" she pulled her palms over her jeans; things were not going well.

"What do I get?" The woman asked.

"Pardon?"

"You want something from me. I get something from you. Fair no?" She rested her temple on Ferris's chest, and smiled as she sniffed at his shirt. He put his palms flat down on the sofa. Awkward was the only word Addy could conjure up.

"Well"

Addy took a deep breath.

What now?

"Excuse me" Glock climbed out of the squeaky leather chair, dusting himself off.

The woman trailed kisses down Ferris's neck. He stiffened and try to push his chin right up to the ceiling.

"What will you want from us?" Glock clasped his hands behind his back.

"Not you Timekeeper" she dismissed without taking a breath.

Ferris tried to slide out beneath her but she was hanging onto his neck.

"Adera" her eyes darted at Addy.

"What do you want" Addy asked.

"I don't know yet" she smiled, "but when I do, I'll let you know" she straddled Ferris, nipping at his jaw line.

Ferris was desperate to get away. His eyebrows knitted furiously and he gestured frantically to catch their glances. Addy and Glock ignored the pained looks he sent.

"So, you want Addy to be indebted to you?" Glock asked.

"Mm" she had both her hands inside Ferris's shirt. She puckered her lips and followed them to her hands.

"Miss. I must ask you to stop." Ferris's voice was at least an octave higher, "please?" The woman laughed, disbelief evident in her voice.

"No Addy" Glock said, "we can't have that."

Addy gave Glock a sharp look, "Glock?"

What could she possibly ask me to do?

"Addy, no" Ferris had both the woman's wrists in his one hand and pulled her off of him. She twined her long legs around his thigh.

Ferris looked at Addy and then used his free hand to push the woman's beautiful behind so that he could free himself.

"Ooh! You like to play?" she giggled and turned to come at Ferris again. He stood up quickly.

"Addy, you can't agree to that." Ferris was firm.

"This will help us! It may be the difference between overthrowing them or not! This is the fate of the worlds in our hands!"

What's the big issue? So, I need to return a favour sometime in the future. Big deal.

The woman suddenly focused on Addy.

"Deal?" She smiled.

Addy nodded.

Glock dropped his head and rubbed his brow. Ferris paced away from them and stopped to stare into the fire.

"Let me see" the woman stood and walked to the crystal ball.

"You need to connect with Verity, is that your question?" Addy nodded as the woman spoke, "find out what she is up to?" Addy nodded again.

The woman embraced the ball and slowly moved along it. Rubbing her hands and her body up against the ball. Her eyes were closed. The ball turned slightly faster, a grey mist descended in its depths.

Mos went onto her knees and swept from one side to the next trailing her fingers over the crystal ball.

"Do not leave me alone with her" Ferris warned under his breath.

"It's been a while old boy! Perhaps it'll do you good" Glock raised his eyebrow. Ferris scowled at him.

Mos looked up, her eyes had gone completely green, no pupil or iris, just green orbs.

She stared at Addy who suddenly felt afraid.

"You know the answer already" she spoke in an eerie tone, "you can connect. You have already seen things" Addy nodded,

"But only when she makes the connection, when she wants me to see. I want to be able to connect when I need to see" Addy explained. The orbs went from moss green to dark blue and then slowly lightened until they were pale white mists.

Mos stared into the ball for several minutes, her eyes changed colour several times. She gestured with both her arms,

"Come. See in the ball" she invited.

Addy stepped next to her.

"You need to empathise with her to connect" Mos explained.

"Empathize?"

"Yes. Feel what she feels" she whispered.

Addy looked into the ball. The grey mist cleared and a

familiar picture crystalized in the ball's centre. Two little girls in pretty dresses, playing hop scotch on the wharf.

The loneliness ached inside her chest, Addy stood up quickly, "We must go. Thank-you Mos."

Without moving Glock, Ferris and Addy were transported back to the library in Tower Castle. Addy felt a bit woozy.

"I need to process this. I think I'll meditate" she offered. The men just nodded, Addy suspected they needed time to recover too.

The tower top views were beautiful all round. Addy liked to practice her meditation here. She moved slowly around the huge plants and outside furniture. The sun sat low in the sky, soon it would turn indigo and then darkness. She rested a moment and watched the light show. Orange and green and pink hues, splashed across the last sky of the day. She watched as the sun dipped, its last lights blazed around and illuminated everything. Addy patted the dip in the turret and turned to her carpet on the floor.

"Meditation" she whispered, "you must master your meditations" she mimicked Ferris and smiled to herself, "what is it again?" She whispered into the twilight, "Oh yes, primordial unity" she settled in and closed her eyes.

"Breathe in" she spoke loudly "and then all the way out" she rushed the words as she breathed out. "Breathe in" she whispered this time, "release".

Breathe in.

Breathe out.

She felt the relaxation going through her.

Count your breath.

The silent instruction grounded her. Addy breathed in, the air was cool. Grey shadows danced across her eyelids.

Breathe.

Her hair strands tickled her cheek.

Breathe.

She inhaled. Addy imagined a glowing white light inside of

her. Slowly it turned upon itself and reached through her body. Her magic prickled across her back. She breathed again. The light was behind her eyes now. She saw it fragment and then distort.

What?

Addy saw Grindal and Zyklon sitting on the dais behind Rachel's home. Lethal weaponry adorned the walls behind them. Others were there. A large man without a neck and red eyes, two no, three women, identical.

What is that? A skeleton?

A band played, *Demonic Bucket* the words splashed on the base drum. A few people danced but most huddled in groups talking. On the table in front of Zyklon and Grindal was an ice bucket, large enough to bath a baby, which is what it looked like. It held a deep red liquid inside, it swirled and occasionally burped at the surface where it let off beautiful waves of dark purple. The movement was fascinating.

"Well. Here we go. About time" Addy knew that voice.

Verity?

"Here we are"

Rachel?

Both?

The cage squeaked and clattered as it bumped over stones and grass, pushed by the night creatures from the cave. Rachel wore black jeans, black boots, black shirt. Her blonde hair hung down her right shoulder. She turned and looked directly at Addy, dark heavy make-up adorned her face. She smiled but it did not enhance her features. This was not the Rachel Addy knew. She walked ahead of the cage. This was definitely Inap, there was no sign of Rachel.

She seemed to be coming closer.

No. I'm moving closer to her.

"There's a good lass" purred Verity,

I'm seeing from Verity's perspective. It must be my blood connection.

251

The Demonic Bucket thrashed around in the background, the sound thumped in her head.

"Ah," Verity whispered, the view moved from Inap and focused briefly on Zyklon and Grindal and then turned abruptly to the cage.

Oh no! Oh no.

The emotional trauma hit Addy sharply.

Grit was shackled in the corner of the cage. His body showed sign of severe beatings, blood caked his face and lined his nostrils. His face shone with purple swelling.

"No" Addy's throat constricted.

"Come on Ver" Zyklon whined in his creepy tone, "surely we can play with one?"

"Yes! We can save the others for the next Sabbat feast, just one, little one?" Grindal teased.

"Well. Seeing as we're celebrating. I will let you have one, only" she laughed. Everyone clapped.

"The one right at the entrance, yes that one, "Verity instructed the night soldier. The metal clanged loudly as he retrieved the key and opened the cage.

Oh shit.

Addy focused on the connection and willed herself to calm down. Her energy sparked across her body.

Addy saw the woman. She knew her. She had met her twin. This was Molly Lamper, she recalled. Molly stood in her jeans and yellow t-shirt holding her left elbow across her body. Swinging like a kid might. She was probably about thirty-five years old, beautiful. Her skin pale and her hair dark. Eyes glistened innocently as she stared unseeing into the cliff edge.

"Play nice" Verity chuckled. Grindal and Zyklon sauntered over into the picture. Zyklon walked around Molly. She didn't register anything. Addy felt hot tears squeeze from her eyes and trickle down her cold cheeks. She felt the evil power emanating through the channel.

Grindal moved Molly's hair from her neck, he bent in close

to Molly and then looking directly at Addy, he bit hard into Molly's neck. Addy heard his fangs pierce the skin. Still Molly did not flinch, did not react.

Addy's breath caught. She held her neck, trying to control herself.

As Grindal lifted his head, Addy saw Zyklon had bitten into her wrist. Blood ran freely down her arm. Zyklon swallowed and wiped his mouth with his wrist.

They need her blood.

"Music" someone shouted, the crowds moved in surrounding Verity, Grindal, Zyklon and Molly. The Demonic Bucket started drumming. People swayed around them.

"Vigilate" snapped Verity.

No.

Addy's heart sank.

Molly became aware. She held her neck and then saw her arm. She looked wildly around her.

Molly screamed.

Addy silently heaved as tears wracked her body.

"Quiet" Verity commanded.

Molly immediately clamped up. Tears squeezed from her wide eyes.

"Dance" commanded Grindal. And Molly did.

She moved her hips to the music. Addy could see the awareness in her eyes, she knew from experience that when the frozen power commanded your mind, you could not disobey. Molly could not fight back.

The crowd cheered. Flames sprang up on the dais. Someone offered drinks and still Molly danced. Sweat poured from her face, joined by the tears flowing from her eyes.

"Take your clothes off" commanded Zyklon. And Molly did.

Addy felt the emotion in her stomach. It built and curdled in her. She thought of severing the connection but was compelled to see.

Molly danced, swaying her hips, she reached for the sky.

The hollowness in her eyes were heart wrenching. Her breasts bobbed and swayed as she moved. Her eyes glazed in tears as her will lost the battle with Grindal and Zyklon.

Grindal lifted his hand up and twisted his wrist, Molly pirouetted like a ballerina until she stood beside him. Fear widened the whites of her eyes so that she looked crazy, darting them about.

Grindal bowed to her and the crowd laughed and clapped, he took her hand and gestured with his right hand for her to weave through the arch their arms formed. Molly did. Again, and again and again. When her shoulder popped the noise shivered from Addy's neck through her spine. Molly's eyes showed pain, they were red and crying silently. But she moved and danced on command. A puppet. Grindal and Zyklon commanded her from one to the other and then handed her around the crowd. Strangers touched and pinched and slapped at will.

Addy got sick on her meditation mat.

Verity was quiet.

"It's time" Zyklon announced. The music stopped, people stumbled a second and then stopped.

Addy recognized Ritsa. His oily blonde streaks of hair lay limp on his shoulders. He carried a long stake by a large clamp, burning with flames.

"Take it" Zyklon commanded. Molly did.

The flames licked up the stick, but Molly held on. Addy could see the whites of Molly's eyes. Pain etched in deep. She was fully aware that her flesh was burning in front of her eyes but could not stop it.

"Crackling" someone called out and everyone laughed.

Zyklon stepped forward and held his right hand up. He shot three hoops, energy rings into the air. They shimmered brightly and then formed an arc in the sky.

"Leap through the hoops" he commanded.

No.

Addy's breath rushed from her throat.

"No, you bastard," tears poured down her face, emotion constricted her lungs.

Molly ran. She took a perfect dive off the cliff edge and moved through the first ring. A naked woman flew through the air holding onto a burning stake.

"No no no" Addy wailed. Emotion welled up and she felt her power respond. It leapt through her connection. Verity realized.

"You lowly despicable spy," she hissed. She turned around so that Addy could see the cage of prisoners. Verity ran a power whip though the cage.

"See? See what happens when you play with magic Adera?" the power caught three people. The blood droplets spattered in her vision. Pale passive faces sprayed with their own life essence.

Addy severed the connection.

The sobs wrenched at her soul.

Why? Why? Why?

Addy felt Ferris approach. She needed his strength. His comfort. She moved closer into him.

"Oh dear" Ferris put his arm around her. Addy needed his strength. She needed to know there was good. "There, there" he soothed.

It's my fault. I'm going to save them. I don't know how, but I will. Or I'll die trying.

I owe them that.

22

The Archway was beautiful. The place comforted Addy.

It seems like a million years ago that my ether was tested here, she thought.

The horror of Molly jumping off the cliff returned. Addy grabbed her upper arms in comfort.

I need a plan. I must help them. I will not be responsible for more people getting hurt or dying.

Addy's thoughts ran to the Quinary and the upcoming battle. The plans to stop Ternion were being discussed and challenged as she paced. Glock had calculated that in two days' time the battle would be held. Addy knew that in one day, it was the Winter Solstice and also the New Moon, the last chance for the prisoners. She yearned to stand with the Quinary. Her magic moved inside of her.

We are one. She knew she shared their values.

And Dane. Her heart constricted. She smiled.

He makes me feel lighter. Happier. But he's the Crowne Prince, he needs a Queen that can stand with him, guide the people. I can't even think past tomorrow, never mind a future.

And Mum? The word is even a joy. Mum. In a day, Ternion will drain the prisoners of their magic and discard them without thought. She's just a bargaining tool to Ternion... I must take this chance. I need to know my Mum.

Addy paced back and forth, thinking how to play her cards.

If only I had a Dad. He would give me counsel.

Ferris! Yes! Ferris!

Then Addy had a novel thought. I'll give my power to Ferris. Why didn't I think of this before? Ferris will be a perfect Quinarian! He is wise, powerful, smart and kind. He will stand with the Quinary and stop darkness from overcoming the worlds. He'll free Mum.

Having a plan made her feel better.

Yes. This is a good plan! I will forfeit my power. Ferris will release Mum and the other prisoners. Ferris and the Quinary go to battle against Ternion – the Quinary are at full force and they win.

Just one thing. I still don't have a living memory from the past. I have no genetic download yet. Celia will know how to activate it!

Addy didn't need to look far. Celia spent every opportunity she had outside.

"No. There is nothing anyone can do. You have to wait until you are ready" Celia smiled with kindness.

"But Celia, Neb said that if I used lots of power for a good cause that it would work" she pleaded.

"No Addy. He said, that is what worked for him" she was patient. "This isn't what works for everyone".

"I have to have it now. I can't help anyone" Addy started,

"Of course, you can. You can still use your power. Your on-line Grimoire has been a free essence for millions of years. You might not even learn anything from it! Get on with it Addy. Stop sulking now" Celia smiled. Addy recognized the tough love being dealt.

I need the spell to transfer power. She did not share her thought with Celia.

Frustration hung on her. She walked briskly to the lakes. I need to clear my head!

Light glinted sharply from the thousands of little waves

on the lake surface. The waterfall rushed in the background, creating the barrier Addy needed from reality.

Above, a lone Kite circled the area. The cool breeze crisped the afternoon air. She sat on the flat rock, oblivious to the Snow Drops leaning just slightly towards her.

"Ferris is a good man" she wrapped her arms around her knees, "he's had power for ages, lots of it" she continued to reason with herself, "why would he go dark?"

She watched the Kite circle slowly, her magic vision showed her where the wind parted his feathers high in the air, fluffing them against his body.

"How is it that my plans may not work?" She sighed deeply, "Ferris is wise, stable. I can't see him going bad".

A memory flashed in her mind again, "if 't be true thee transf'r pow'r to those yond art not offspring, then the receiv'r may wend nimble-footed 'r w'rse, dark."

This was the second time she remembered.

This is going to work! I am getting the Grimoire! The memory can't be right!

"I will be transparent" she felt better, "yes. I will tell him of the memory and then of my plan. Why would he not take the power?" She threw her hands up.

She moved from the rock, wringing her hands. Addy was oblivious to the roaring and calling taking place in the background. She paced backwards and forwards, the idea now crystal clear in her mind.

"Aah! Addy" Ferris walked slowly along the path skirting the lake, "fine afternoon for a walk. Why are you pacing, my dear?" He laughed as he strode up close to Addy.

"I have a lot on my mind" Addy smiled.

"Yes. That would be true" he nodded, "come sit. Share your thoughts" he gestured to the flat rock, "if you speak them or write them, they seem to lose their power and their trouble" he smiled.

Addy looked at Ferris, imprinting his face into her mind. He had his eye on the Kite. The wind ruffled his hair.

"I can feel that stare, Addy. What is on your mind?" He spoke without looking at her.

"You have as much power as the Quinary" Addy started, "what is the difference between you and the Quinary members?"

Addy watched the breeze tug at his hair, he stood out starkly from the background.

"My power is not contained within my body. I am simply a vessel for power to flow through, elemental power" he spoke absently, "the only difference between myself and for example Glock, is that he also produces a power, from within, the power wound into his DNA by the Celestials. That power has an affinity with the universe, has a deeper knowledge" his voice faded against the roaring waterfall.

"What would you do if you also had that deeper knowledge?" Addy asked softly, looking directly at him.

"Do not talk of such things Addy." Ferris was direct, a frown pulling his brows together.

Addy's heart was thudding against her ribcage, "Ferris! I can give you that power! Listen to me"

"No" Ferris's eyes went pitch black, his voice roared in her ears, "Do not tempt me! Do you intend to ruin my life?" he stamped his staff down on the flat rock pointing at the lake surface. Addy glanced at him, fear restraining her emotions. Ferris looked demonic, hair flowing in the breeze, magic entwining around his body, dark bands settling around him.

In the lake Addy saw masses of power swirling around Ferris. He put his head back and laughed maniacally. He raised his arms and power arced from his fingers reaching the skies above. Thunder answered his call and lightning powered into him. He coaxed the breeze until hurricanes swirled around his feet. He was heady with the drug of ether. Darkness hung over the images. Villages pulled down their shutters, people scattered away from him. On Earth Addy saw seas throw themselves upon the dry, stark land where carcasses lay festering in the sun. She saw Ferris seek out more power, always craving it, always needing the next hit, like an addict. Addy saw into the distant future where Ferris stood alone, powerful in the dark.

Tears drove down her cheeks, she shook her head looking from the lake back to Ferris on the rock, holding his staff.

"It won't be like that Ferris" she whispered, "You are good at heart. You could have gone that way already. But you chose not to" she tugged at his robe to bring him back.

"I am not as powerful as you" his voice cracked, "yet I struggle, still, after so many years to quell the beast inside of me. What you are asking Addy, cannot be done, child. Do not talk of it again" he suddenly looked old and frail. Beaten, thought Addy.

"Ferris. There isn't another way," Addy started

"Hush!" he stamped his staff on the rock, "the gift is yours, bestowed by the Celestials. Do not hand it away. There are reasons the people who are chosen, are. Reasons, we do not know or understand. The power is yours" he jumped off the rock, "don't be a fool" he started walking up the pathway.

Addy was angry now. She jumped up, "Ferris" don't walk away."

Ferris stilled in his stride, his back to Addy, "Leave me now, Addy" he walked away slowly.

Addy doubled over holding her stomach, trying hard to breathe normally. Another plan unfurled from her subconscious. Addy put it on hold for a moment.

I need to be with Dane. Just one night. She wiped at the tears with the back of her wrists.

Just to say goodbye.

***

He looks younger in sleep.

Addy consumed his profile, infused the smell of him into her. She took in the contours of his bicep, the square of his jaw, his lashes fanned against his face. Beard stubble dotted his upper lip and Addy felt compelled to kiss it, feel his bristle against her as she had last night, 'just one last time' she thought. Her mouth was still swollen from his kisses.

Emotion churned through her. She leaned forward and gently kissed him. I love you.

When the realization slammed into her, Addy turned on her back. As she moved, Dane mumbled in his sleep, "Addy", he turned and lay his warm palm across her flat stomach. Desire unfurled inside of her.

This can't be. When he realizes I no longer have power, that I am not a Quinary member anymore. There won't be use for me. What if I am judging him too harshly. Don't be stupid Addy. He's the future king, for god sake! He needs someone right for him. Someone useful. Someone who can defend the kingdom, help the people. He needs someone worthy of the title, Queen.

Tears trickled from the outer corner of her eyes, she felt her nose become heavy, she needed to control herself.

Addy turned slightly towards Dane, tears trickling quickly down her face. She put her palm gently on his chest and closed her eyes.

She heard his heart beat. She felt the sensation in her fingers. Magic trickled across her skin as she pulled the rhythm into her, making her own heart beat synchronize. Addy pulled a thread of power from the air and traced it into his aura. She leant over his chest and placed a light kiss at the base of his throat.

In the grey light of Dane's pre-dawn room, Addy dressed quickly, she paused only a second to take one last mental image of him. The full moon shone through the window infusing his body with light.

Addy felt her chest crumble in pain, she held her fisted hand to her mouth and quickly turned to the door and slid out.

A guard marched away from her, and she ran quickly to the end of the corridor, turning the corner as she heard his boots turn on the floor.

Addy stilled a moment, rigid against the wall. She used her palms to wipe away the tears.

She braced her shoulders and then when she heard the footsteps retreat from her, she crossed the open space and quietly descended the winding stairs.

Addy did not stop. Around and around the stairwell descended, finally coming to the main entrance. She hung back in the shadows watching for movement. A Brownie hummed a tune under her breath as she crossed the entrance and went into the back of the Tower towards the kitchen.

When it was clear, Addy pushed at the heavy entrance doors and slipped out into the cold dawn.

Goosebumps grew on her skin. The gravel crunched under foot and her breath frosted the air. Addy felt her nose and ears sing with the sharp air.

"My Lady?" The voice made her jump.

"Larkin? Is that you?"

"Yes M'Lady"

"Oh," she smiled to hide the shock, "what are you doing out this time of day? And what did I say about calling me M'Lady?" She tried to look natural.

"We have been monitoring the Cramfloor twenty-eight, five" he gestured in the direction of the laboratory, "tonight, as you know, is the calculated night. For the battle, you know?" He smiled as he raised both shoulders up to his ears, his fleshy locks dangled and turned a shade of purple.

"It's ingrained in me, addressing you as such. The Quinary are central to our existence. You are Royalty" he pulled his mouth down and raised his small eyebrows, expecting the reprimand that Addy always gave him.

"Not so much" she said, "after you, M'Lord."

"M'Lord?" he rolled his eyes, "Are you coming to the Laboratory too?" He asked

"Yes. Yes. Of course," she smiled and gestured for them to keep moving,

"Thank-you, Addy" he smiled and then gently squeezed her elbow.

They walked the short distance to the laboratory in silence.

Addy followed Larkin as he walked into a purple tinted cube, the doors sighed closed behind them. Without the sensation of movement, the cube unfolded itself and Larkin stepped into the large tiled room,

"Glock will be expecting you, no doubt. He will be in the laboratory" Larkin waved as he held a sheepish grin. "If I don't see you later on today, just. Well," Larkin stumbled for words, "Just, good luck, Addy. I know you can do it." He turned away and the purple cube folded up again.

Emotion lumped in Addy's throat.

Seconds later, the cube unfolded on the top level of the laboratory, the Pocket watch.

Addy stepped out, and moved slowly along the outer perimeter, looking for the door at one 'o clock that marked Glock's office.

"Addy! Just the person I was thinking of! How are you, Love? How are you holding up?" He moved towards Addy and engulfed her in his big bear hug, "come, come" he pulled her arm, "I have something you should have" he walked over to a chest of drawers near the corner of his office, "mmm, let me think" he rested his chin on his hand as he contemplated the drawers.

"What is it?" Her curiosity was piqued.

"Aah, yes! This is the one." He smiled at her and then leant into the chest and tickled its side, "show me," he smiled.

The drawer slid open gently.

Addy stepped forward to see.

Glock held a black velvet pouch in his hand, "give me your hand, Addy" he nodded encouragingly.

Addy held her hand out palm up. Glock tipped the pouch, a solid black rock rolled out into her hand.

"A stone?" She raised her eyebrows at him.

"Yes! But not any stone. A capture stone." He patted her shoulder.

"What is a capture stone?"

"There is a magic captured in this stone. Ancient, ancient. Powerful," he held his arms wide demonstrating, "but only the right person for that stone can release its power. Some secret comes with it. It was your mum's, Marjory. She asked me to keep it safe for you" he smiled.

"For me?"

"Mm. On your birth. She had a vision that you would need this stone, some day. I think today is a good day. Don't you?"

"Thank-you, Glock. But perhaps you should keep it for my mum?"

"No. She said it was for you. She said, I would know when you needed it. I think you need to have it now," he pushed the drawer closed again.

"We had such good times" Glock leant against a cabinet folding his arms, his eyes drifted to the window, "in the summer we would go down to the beach, we would swim and laugh and, and just be alive" he smiled warmly, "then we would watch the sunset. Spectacular sunsets. We would have magic competitions" Glock's eyes twinkled as he remembered, "Marjory was so inventive. She would challenge us, 'who can make the most spectacular firework display over the ocean?' or "who can make the bonfire dance the crocodile rock'" he laughed out loud, "you are a lot like her" he stared at Addy, "but you have had a hard life" he nodded, "I get that".

Addy felt the rock warm in her hand, she squeezed it tightly and then dropped it back into its pouch.

"Thanks" she waved the pouch, "I hope I know when to use it".

Addy felt her heart constrict, these are my friends, she realized, the friends I dreamt of when I was washing dishes in Rodic's house. Addy smiled at Glock, she needed to go. Would she see him again? Will he understand what she has to do?

Addy inhaled deeply feeling the emotion pool inside of her core. She went towards the door and turned, "well, lots of preparation to still do, I just wanted to say, good luck".

"Luck? Things will turn out exactly the way they are supposed to" he shrugged. "I will see you later" his attention was already on the dials and screens in his office.

The day had brightened by the time Addy stepped outside of the laboratory tower. The urgency of her task pulled her along, "I must get to Earth" she repeated again and again, "must get to Tweedy", she walked with purpose.

23

"Tweedy? Where are you?" Addy weaved through the trees on the outskirts of the flat spacious oval. "Tweedy?" The smell of the forest and earth and leaves permeated from the floor. Addy snapped a few twigs underfoot.

"Tweedy!" Addy felt the panic rise in her core, "Tweedy! Please answer! I need help! Tweedy" she started calling over and over, "Tweedy! Tweedy!"

Addy stopped a moment, sensing a change in the ether. She looked behind her, slowly turning around. Her foot caught something soft and she fell over.

The large form wriggled beneath her.

"Addy? You're a large lump of human!" His face was covered in dirt and clots of rich dark earth caught in his brows, "How can I have decent conversation when you are trotting all over me?" his voice was stern but his eyes and smile were pleased to see her.

"Conversation?" The question squeezed out quickly,

"Well" Tweedy started, Addy held her hand up,

"No. It doesn't matter. I am in a big rush! Please can you open a portal for me?"

Tweedy's eyebrows shot up spraying sand and dirt into his eyes,

"What? No. I can only do that when I have been officially advised. You know? National security and all that?" His lips shut tight as he brushed dirt from his body, "this is a serious job. Imagine if I just kept popping open portals when anyone asked me. Dangerous! You should know Addy" he rambled on stomping his feet and brushing his body.

Addy rolled her eyes, "oh boy" she desperately thought of another approach.

Grabbing his shoulders, she looked over her shoulder conspirationally, Addy felt awful for she was about to do,

"Tweedy. This is an official matter." She looked deep into his eyes using her most serious demeanor, "I am a Quinarian, remember?"

"Of course, my Lady" Tweedy bowed slightly towards her, "I didn't mean to imply-"

"It doesn't matter Tweedy, I am not offended. I am in a big rush, secret Quinary business, you know how it is?"

He nodded, his eyes looking concerned.

"Please Tweedy, I will get the formality done later on, how long will it take to open the portal?" She let go of his shoulders.

"About twenty minutes, I assume you want to be going back to Earth?"

"Yes please" she started walking away, "I am running a quick errand I will be back before twenty minutes" she walked briskly towards the Tower.

"I must find Ferris" she broke into a sprint.

Addy entered the Tower in a rush.

"Addy" Pearl sounded delighted that she was there, "do you want breakfast?"

Addy ran straight past, "Sorry Pearl, big rush! Have you seen Ferris?" She called running down the passage to the library.

"Well" she heard Pearl speak to herself, "if you stop a moment,

I can tell you" she carried on measuring ingredients into her clear glass bowl. Addy rushed back to the kitchen entrance,

"Sorry" she panted.

"He left in as big a rush as you're in" she glanced down at her recipe book, "never said where he was going. Didn't either have a thing to eat" she traced the line with her finger.

"Pearl. Do you know where he was headed?"

"No dear" she stirred the ingredients around and then smiled up warmly at Addy, "seems all the magic folk have to be somewhere special today" there was concern in her eyes,

"Sorry" she smiled, "it's a strange kind of day" Addy shrugged, the panic rising in her chest.

"Go on love. It is a strange day. Tomorrow we can chat over a leisurely breakfast. Go on," she gestured with her chin to the open door.

Addy felt warmth flood her. This woman was the closest she had ever had to a mum; she really hoped all would be fine.

"Thanks Pearl" she whispered and ran for the door.

Ferris wasn't at the laboratory. She ran around all the towers, he wasn't to be found.

"Ugh! Where are you?" She ran back into the Clock Tower, Pearl was spooning batter into baking trays.

Addy ran back down to the library, she knew he liked this room.

"I will leave a message" she moved things around the desk. "Pen! Where is a bloody pen?" She hissed in frustration,

A long white feather leapt from the desk.

"Great, you'll do." she rolled her eyes.

The pen wrote, "Great! You'll do," on the paper.

"No. Not that"

'No. Not that' wrote the feather.

"Start a new page" she spoke in her clipped no nonsense voice.

The feather jumped to another page.

"Ferris…." She started. The feather scribbled the words, in

exactly the same penmanship as Addy's own hand. Her heart ached, 'what do I say?'

"I am sorry" she faltered, "I can't be who you think. But, I know who can. Addy" she whispered. She glanced around the room one last time, then silently closed the door and ran down the passage, past the kitchen and out of the Tower.

"It's not right." Tweedy paced and muttered, "It is just not right".

Addy frowned, approaching the open space, the portal galaxy churned slowly on its axis.

"What's wrong Tweedy?" Addy was cautious.

"Addy. I sense this is wrong. I think we should wait for the Quinary. You shouldn't go through by yourself." He gestured passionately at Addy.

A cold wind weaved around them, Addy shivered, "It's okay. They know I am going through" she crossed her fingers behind her back, asking forgiveness will be better she thought than asking for permission.

"It's dangerous. Tomorrow is the battle. Ferris told me" he revealed when her eyes shot up,

"Tweedy. The Quinary will be in full force tomorrow. Five. Just like the legend says. Do not worry about it. But, I have to go through the portal to enable that" she was getting desperate, time was ticking.

"Addy. I don't feel good about this" Addy saw that he was having serious second thoughts.

A thought popped into Addy's mind with crystal clarity, she spoke the words aloud.

"Forces of time and space,
Freeze this plane, this sphere, this place
Hold Tweedy, secure,
Just five minutes, as time is measured through that door."

Tweedy was enveloped in powerful bubble. His face contorted in disbelief.

"Addy?" He whispered.

"Sorry! I am really sorry. Tweedy. My mum, Marjory will come through the door. Do not wait for me. You need only wait for Marjory and then close the portal down. Please?" she appealed.

"Addy what are you doing?" He was hurt that Addy did not trust him.

"I will make sure she comes through within twenty minutes. I am sorry! You will understand." She tried to appeal to him. He turned away.

Guilt and pain that she was betraying Tweedy sat heavily on her chest. "I better go now. Good luck" she whispered as she climbed the steps to the door.

"You better come back!" Tweedy shouted as she stepped through the portal, "You better! Ferris will never talk to me again." His voice broke up as the door closed behind her.

After the familiar air distortion, her feet hit the hard ground, the jolt sent shock waves through her neck. Back on Earth, the pale dawn filtered through the strip of forest that separated her from the cave entrance. "No sounds" she filed for future contemplation. Then she ran.

The forest floor slowed her down, her feet gouged the earth and sprayed needles at the trees. The cool dappled light zebra-ed across her body, giving her the illusion of speed. Addy ran, the silence began to unsettle her.

Her breath was steady, the smell of the forest followed her into the short open field. The grass was pale, holding its vibrancy back, waiting. As she reached the cave entrance, her feet became louder. The ground harder, less forgiving. She tried to steady her breath, pressed against the outside wall of the entrance. The last time she was here, Dane was sending her back. Oh, she wished she could see him now.

Addy pushed a tendril of magic out on the ether. "Anyone

around?" She whispered to herself. Quiet. She waited another second, watching the steam rise from her arm. Addy shuffled against the smooth wall, her heart thudded against her rib cage. She slipped into the cave entrance, recalling the stairwell from long ago.

"Down" she navigated herself.

She walked slowly, listening. Her footfalls were loud in the empty space. Step after step she spiraled downwards. She paused when the railing on the left disappeared. The darkness beneath her was intense. "This is it" she knew.

Addy lay on her stomach and edged her legs over the ledge, recalling the big drop to the first ledge. Her fingers ached, holding her weight. "Ugh where's the friggin ledge?" Her feet swung about for a second and eventually her toes touched the ledge. She stretched out, then let go, dropping into the alcove in the cave wall.

Addy sat a moment and listened. A water drop, plinked loudly beneath her. She repeated her previous maneuver, shuffled on her stomach, swung her legs down. The next ledge wasn't far down but was just a hole in the wall. She slowly climbed down the steep wall. Her boot filled with water as she stepped into the cave bottom.

"Oh no" she whispered crossly. She waded slowly and tried not to splash. White swimming creatures, fish she presumed, bumped against her shins. Addy moved slowly, the pathway slowly inclining. The water finally behind her. Addy stopped. Listened, her power enhanced her hearing. Nothing. She bent down and held herself steady against the cave wall as she undid each boot, emptying the ice-cold water out on the cave floor.

A winged creature flapped the air overhead, then there was nothing else.

The silence settled in, Addy only heard her own feet. She created a glow ball, it preceded her along the passage. Four exits, she recalled. The vacuous space glowed mere metres in front of her. The first exit from the main passage appeared quickly, Addy was prepared but no worm came to her this time. It was hazy in the glow light but nothing lived in the space.

When the second exit appeared, Addy dropped to her hands and knees. The vacuum pulled and sucked at her but she was steady. Her breath came quickly from the exertion and she stood and ran. The next two came without surprise.

When she reached the furnace room, there was nobody there.

Too quiet. Where is everyone?

The furnace should have reverberated in its hungry consumption. A disquiet settled on Addy. No rushed padding, no shuffles or sputtering. Just the silence.

Addy started running again. She stopped in the chamber that held her so many nights ago, nothing. She ran to the next and the next. Nothing.

Her heart felt heavy. She stopped and cocked her head, listening. Where is everyone?

The torches had mostly gone out, here and there one sputtered. Addy ran down a winding passage, panic took over. The passage widened and ended in a large chamber. She stopped, the realization came quickly.

This is where they were held.

The cage stood empty, blood spattered across its bars. Thick pools of red congealed on the floor.

Addy felt the shock. Addy closed her eyes and steadied her breath. No! No! I'm too late.

She switched her vision and saw the remnants of the power lines. Some felt familiar but she could not grasp where it was from.

Anger struck. So much torture! Addy felt the pain she tasted it. She reached for her link to Verity.

"Clever girl" she heard in the distant periphery and Verity chuckled, she approved.

Addy focused on the battle that had been in this place, her intuit told her, lots of blood, lots of power. It must be Verity.

Addy sat on her knees in the cold chamber, one torch casting shadows on the wall behind her. She let the power come.

In her vision, she saw Grit held tight by Verity, her power more than doubled from before. He stared straight ahead, pain twisted his face. Her mum was pinned to the wall, chains at her wrists and feet, her senses clear and alert but her power numbed by Zyklon. Addy felt the other power lines, her anger climbed.

She slowed her heart and felt her own power surge through her. In her vision, blood spread across the floor. She didn't wait to see its end. They've taken mum. Verity took my mum!

Her body wracked with pain. Addy felt the sob catch in her throat. No! No! No!

Her keening came to her own ears. No! Verity will not get away with this!

The anger escalated quickly. It took root and grew. Hatred and fear collided in Addy. Years of suffering and living without love. The not having poured into her, the emptiness expanded, it's blackness mounted. Addy pulled at her energy, and it flowed. Her hair spread out around her, static from the electric current. She felt the earth feed her. The darkness of the earth. The power poured into her, she felt heady from the energy and it felt good. Addy leaned into it and her anger fed it. Her tears dried on her cheeks.

Never again. She thought.

She remembered then. Every kick, every put-down, every moment of neglect, every abuse - every word, Addy remembered. She let her mind dwell on the cold house in her young years and she let the pain feed her.

It's my time.

She recalled how Rachel had betrayed her and she let the bitterness dwell inside her. She lingered on Dane and felt the defeat of never having him because he was the king. The anger washed through her and fed the source of her power. She gave the energy the anger it searched for and she felt powerful. She felt good.

The power surged through her, she lifted her face to the ceiling and her arms followed. She lowered them quickly and felt the power kick in. The caves above her exploded. Earth and rocks flew up around her. She felt the vacuous hole fill with air, she twisted her wrist and a vortex lifted her from the cave.

When she opened her eyes, three shadow wolves waited for her command. They sneered and bared their teeth. She looked each one in the eye and saw her reflection in their darkness, her red eyes. Powerful and angry. The wolves howled at her feet. Their anger an extension of her energy. Shadows that waited to kill.

"Find her" Addy snapped. Her voice a primal grunt.

I n the time after twilight, Addy trawled through the indigo
town. The wolves howled and yapped at her command
and faded to shadow on instruction so that they could slip
under doors to strike fear in the hearts of those they found. The
fear fed Addy and as her power extended she encompassed the
breadth of the village.

She blew off doors and destroyed homes. Power swayed to
the flick of her wrist and bowed to her command.

Where is Verity?

People ran, children clutched to their chests; their faces
read disbelief and panic. Addy sensed Verity's energy. She had
been here.

Where are you?

The wolves rushed through and Addy's power followed.
Destruction built in her wake and anger churned in her belly.

She pulled up lamp posts and shattered windows. The village
was deserted. Addy strode on in anger. Rodic's house sat cold
and silent on the hill. She knew it was empty. Rodic had never
been brave and Verity had preceded her. She flicked her wrist
and the power rippled through the stone structure.

She marched on, not a flicker of remorse shimmered in her
countenance. The Oswald's house was at the end of the road.

Lights twinkled in the dark. This is where Mrs. H looked after John's boys. Mrs. H…

Addy swiped her arm; the front door flew from its hinges. The power surged through her, she laughed when the hedonism swept across her. The lights flickered. She marched down the passage, her shadow wolves beside her, they yelped in anticipation.

Addy saw movement. She walked further in.

John Oswald, who taught her English at high school and her neighbor of thirteen years, stood in front of his four boys. Little Josh's face was pale, his eyes wide. The others were quiet, their unwavering faith in their dad admirable.

"Just stay together guys" he whispered.

Addy saw them hold hands. The glow around the house brightened. She frowned.

The wolves snarled and whipped, jowls salivated and sneered.

The vortex spun around the house, crockery rattled and tables vibrated. The dresser chattered across the wooden floor.

"Go John, leave now" Addy's voice was foreign to her.

"Addy?"

"Leave! Why are you still here?"

"We have nowhere to go. We're home."

The light got brighter. Did she imagine it?

Tom pulled his brother Josh to his chest.

Addy's heart thudded.

Movement in the hall mirror caught her eye.

"Aren't you afraid?" Her voice echoed from a distance.

"Of course," John said.

He stepped closer. The appeal was in his eyes.

Addy flickered a glance at the boys. Peter, the third son's leg sat at a wrong angle. Sweat beaded his forehead. They would not leave him.

The vortex pulled at the open passage and whistled at the windows. Addy looked into the mirror. The red glow from her eyes shattered the reflection.

That's not me. No!

The gaunt face, the grey aura, the red anger. She breathed quickly, the wolves growled.

What am I doing? No! No!

The wolves leapt at John. Addy froze. They fell back, an invisible wall protected him. The boys huddled together.

"Dad?" Tom asked.

"I'm okay. Stay back"

Addy knew then. The clarity of the realization lightened her dark mind. Love.

Go. She dismissed the anger. "Go!" she shouted loudly.

The wolves disappeared and the pain drained from her. Addy's grief slipped in. She felt the wooden floor hit her knees. Then the tears came.

What have I done? What I have done? My mum! They killed my mum! The pain was endless and deep. Addy's body wracked and heaved as it unburdened itself.

Her body rested on her upper legs and she stilled herself on the wooden floor.

"There, there" Josh's baby voice penetrated her woe, "it's not the end of the world, you know" he offered.

"I've got this big guy" John smiled at his son.

His hand on her shoulder was comforting.

"I'm sorry" she sniffed.

Pete was pale. Addy knew she could help. She approached cautiously, but he wasn't afraid.

"Can I look?"

He nodded.

"What happened?"

She needed to distract him so that she could sense his need.

"I was on the roof, getting the ball when the storm came".

The guilt hit hard.

Addy sensed the break point. She gently pulled his leg back in line. He winced.

"Sorry" she whispered in concentration.

He smiled, his face pinched. John stood by his side.

"You're a brave boy" he murmured.

Addy accessed her on-line Grimoire; the information was instant. She smiled at how it miraculously was there when she needed it for the good of others. The universe sure was smart!

She pulled the power from her heart, and gently pushed it to his leg. She knew the moment it happened. Pete's face lost its pallor. The pinched look was replaced with awe.

His blue eyes twinkled from his young face, he eased off the couch and tested his weight.

"Awesome." He murmured.

"There may be some inflammation. For a day or so" Addy advised, "A little achy" she explained when Pete looked blankly at her.

"Addy" John started.

"John. I'm sorry."

"Thank-you" the relief made him look younger.

"I've done some damage" she stared at her hands. John stood over her a moment and then put his hand on her shoulder. She had a flash of Ferris, her heart constricted.

"Can you fix it?" He asked, "Can you use this *stuff* to fix it?"

"I can try".

"That's good enough".

An idea started forming in Addy's mind. Her heart felt lighter.

"John, guys? Can you help me?"

They glanced at each other and then back at Addy.

"Okay" Pete offered.

"Thanks. Tom? You on social media?"

Tom glanced at his dad. John nodded slightly.

"Yeah?"

"I need you to start a wave or a trend or whatever it's called".

Tom was interested.

"At a specific time, tomorrow" she checked she had their attention. Her heart beat wildly, this had to work.

"In another world" she caught John's eye.

"Hey, I've seen it all tonight, I believe you."

"A great big battle will take place" she continued.

"An epic battle?" James asked.

"Yes. Between good and bad".

"Awesome" Pete pulled his large knees under the coffee table and rested his head on his hands.

"If bad wins" Addy took a deep breath. The vision of what might be swirled in her head, "if bad wins, we lose everything we have ever loved. Everything". The room was dead silent.

"So, we won't let them" Josh offered.

"That's right," she patted his knee.

"But how can we help? What can we do?" John was a practical man.

"When I came here. Bad was consuming me" she swallowed hard. "I didn't use my power for good" tears swam in her eyes, "but your love" she gestured to them, "was greater than your fear, greater than the fear which powered me" they nodded.

"So, we need to capture that love and release it through a portal, tomorrow, to help good win the battle."

"Great! And, I am trying not to be a Debbie Downer here but. How? Just saying." Tom pointed out.

Addy smiled, "I have a plan".

25

A silver line on the Thearian horizon marked dawn as imminent. Addy entered the hall alone. Each step into the ancient structure cleared her mind. Her Grimoire called her here. An ancient concept that guided her. She passed through the marble arches again. Ancient whispers hung on the air. She heard their message, felt their words.

Addy walked through to the centre of the pentacle. Fire and Earth vertices were behind and to her left and right; water and air adjacent to her, either side. Ether. It waited atop the pentacle, never used before. Just waiting for her.

She walked slowly. Let it soak in. This belonging. The marble floor gleamed. Out to her right the arches splayed as far as she could see. Addy approached the vertex. The ether symbol glowed beneath the marble on the floor. She knelt on her left knee and rested her hands on her bent right one. With a click and a whirr, a disc clicked out around her, separating her. She descended slowly.

Addy felt calm. Her memory, her power, knew what to do. It had received instructions thousands and thousands of years before. She would let it guide her. The disc descended into a large cavern. As it slowed, Addy's eyes adjusted. Lanterns floated about. Large torches buried in the soil created a warm glow beneath her. A murmur flowed around. The disc continued the descent. It hovered in place for a moment, Addy stood up. Coming up to join it, was a silver ring. It rotated and gleamed slowly; the disc and the ring clicked into place. As they connected, a fire sprang up in the silver ring. Flames erupted and burnt in celebration.

Addy's heart leapt. This was familiar. Primal. She stretched her arms wide, took a deep breath and began to rotate. The heat surrounded her, she felt the energy of the cavern. It was electric. She undressed. One item of clothing at a time. The fire consumed them.

Addy breathed. Below the circle and disc water churned, cobalt blue. She saw from the edge of the disc that the sea rushed into the cavern; she knew what to do. Addy took two giant steps and leapt across the flames. The heat licked and teased her, cleansed. She arched her body down and felt the air brush her naked skin as she swooped to the cool beautiful water below.

The bubbles bumped against her and tickled her body. She swam to the surface, she felt the joy as though it had been waiting for her. The water washed over her. The cleansing was good. Addy swam towards the spot where the water entered the cave. A large flat rock protruded from the churning mass. Sea-mist draped the rock and poured from its sides. She dove in deep and found the stepped wedges submerged. She climbed the rock and sat cross-legged in its centre. And then she observed.

The sea heaved, a mass of ocean mist with blue swirls in between. She faced the enclosed beach, the cave large and warm above her. The disc had retreated to the surface. Two parrots chipped away at a vine along the cave wall. The water rushed on the shore. A path wound behind the beach at the far end of the cave. The stone steps did not lead anywhere and they did not seem to come from anywhere.

Just here. Now. In the present.

She closed her eyes. Her breathing slowed. Her heart slowed.

The sea's hush faded. Addy pulled in a deep breath and felt it in her first chakra. She breathed energy into the centre and saw the silver line descend into the earth, she was grounded.

She focused on her second chakra. The energy swirled furiously, she breathed and calmed the centre. She felt the tiny energy galaxy churn below her navel, she slowed it. Her emotion was back in balance.

Another breath found her focus on her solar plexus. The yellow triangle exploded in her mind's eye; she knew this was her social self. Addy blessed the centre and raised her focus again. Her heart.

The emotion swelled through her. She pulled energy through heart's centre. She wallowed in the love. Her breath was deep and rhythmical. Her visions exploded in stunning geometries. The energy centre of her throat warmed. Her personal truth. She acknowledged the time it took for her to find this centre, cleansed it with her power and then focused her energy at her third eye.

Visions tumbled into her mind. Past, present, future. Addy calmed the centre and focused in gratitude at her gifts. Then she raised the energy to her crown and above. She opened the portal above her and let the universe in. She just let it pour into her. The wisdom, the connection, the knowing. She let it come. No judgement, just transcendence. Addy let it flow. The ocean sprayed up against the rock and cooled her body. She smiled.

I am ready.

She stood on the first stone. With the wall in front of her, Addy knew she would return here. This was hers. Her place. Sacred. But a battle waited.

The stone wall pixelated and a perfect round hole appeared. Addy stepped through. Cleansed of body, mind and spirit.

Arga waited inside.

Addy had not seen the Celestial since Dane returned and saw her at the pool.

"You have come a long way" she smiled, her body liquid and solid, intermittently.

"Hello Arga" Addy smiled.

"The room of reveal" Arga whispered on the breeze, 'to see yourself".

Addy nodded.

She was five, in the garden with Verity. The tiny bird hopped and fluttered in alarm. It's wing drooped beside it. Addy's heart swelled. She knew what happened next. She remembered.

She tried to look away.

"Too long you've operated this program. Look. Things are not always as they seem" Arga called in her mind.

Addy observed as her five-year-old self-touch it's wing. The energy flowed into the bird. It went limp.

Addy inhaled sharply. Her chest heaved, again. The wobbly bird with it's too big beak, dead in her hands.

Verity yanked her arm. She dropped the bird.

"Leave it! You've killed it! Isn't that enough? You see what using that magic does? Don't do it again, ever!"

Verity pushed young Addy towards the house. Her heart was broken.

Addy watched. Sad. The door slammed behind them. The bird turned, hopped. Waited a moment and flew off, unhurt.

Joy soared in her heart.

"Arga?"

"It was stunned. Energy overload. Goodness, from your heart. How long did you run that program?"

Addy smiled.

How long did I suppress my power? I thought it was evil. Bad.

"Look" the whisper was feint.

Addy stared at the glass once more. Grit ran down towards the oval, rain pelted him. He leapt into the air, shifting as he soared into the sky. A beautiful hawk, snow white. The timing distorted and she saw him later, shackled.

Addy bit her lip.

The guilt swiped through her.

He was helping me. He's gone, because he helped me. He didn't want to. I know it.

The scene changed suddenly. Just days ago. Her and Dane. The tenderness in his touch. His eyes. The love shone through his eyes. Addy's heart thumped.

Surely, he can't love me. He's a king. What are these messages? I don't understand...

Arga led her to an alcove. On a dais inside laid out beautifully was a leather armour tunic. Addy stepped into it. Arga tied her up. It hugged her body perfectly. The leather extended to mid-thigh, panels fell over the top of her legs. Across her body, a strap wrapped across her, open inserts were dotted along the strap. Beneath the tunic was an undergarment, like tight shorts. From it hung three feathers on each side. A sparrow, an eagle and a hawk. The lessons she had learnt.

"To tread where others may not, we have gifted you these" Arga waved and a pair of long leather boots appeared.

Addy pulled them on.

Arga guided her around a corner. The passage opened up and light came into the chamber from outside. She saw the cave entrance slope away down the mountain. A long stone bench ran up the one side. Geometric shaped spheres rotated in midair. Vivid colour sprang from their surface and glittered the walls.

"Gifts" Addy heard the whisper. Arga was nowhere to be seen.

Addy touched the first one. Fire seared into the air and a pendant dropped out. Red as blood and round and smooth. She knew where it went. Addy picked it up and felt the warmth against her skin. She inserted it into the empty studded strap across her body. The next was water. The droplet captured in a blue button. Again, Addy stuck into the strap. Air whirred in a clear glass pendant, Addy added it to her collection. She knew they were from her Quinary family. The last was a seed, Earth.

When four of the five places on her strap were filled, Addy looked around.

On the table, where a minute before nothing rested was the capture stone. The stone her mum had left with Glock for her. Addy held it in her palm. The warmth filled her. The emotion threatened to spill.

There's love in this.

Addy put it in its slot. She breathed in deeply.

I am ready.

She followed the curve of the passage towards the daylight. She stopped in front of the exit, turned back to the cave and bowed her head.

"Thank-you" she whispered.

Addy turned and as she stepped towards the exit, a sword fell from above straight between her boots. It gleamed in the sunlight. She picked it up. Heart racing. It was light and easy. She grabbed the sheath against the wall and stepped towards the exit.

A light breeze blew towards her. She walked down the hill, their army waited in silence.

A ddy looked around. The cold breeze whipped through the ranks, biting at the soldier's noses but they stood strong and focused. The breeze tugged at the deep red coat tails of the guard and clipped the flags stiffly. Everyone remained stoic. Their swords glinted in the weak light, the untrained ones, right at the back armed with kitchen and garden tools, even they were intently honed in on a spot about a kilometer in front of them. Bows for the Elves, axes for the Dwarves, swords for the Soldiers, Farmers had fists and scythes. A few shields bore crests and symbols.

Addy stood with the Quinary, the energy crackled around them. The power called to her. She felt proud. She let it come. Celia rested her cuffed arm on a panther, sleek, magnificent, her tail twitched at the end.

Roz's focus was insular, Neb stood in person, his dragon eyes waiting, watching. Glock leaned towards Addy,

"You have Aife's sword" he gestured smiling. Addy looked down at the sword in her hand.

"It is believed that the sword chooses the wielder. Whomever wields Aife's sword, will be infused with the knowledge of its use and strategy" he said.

Glock turned to Dane, Addy's eyes followed.

He is handsome in his gear.

Her heart thudded.

"We're ready" Dane murmured.

Glock nodded, took out his pocket watch and then kissed it and tucked it back in his pocket.

"Citizens of Thear!" Glock's voice boomed across the mountain side. He expanded in size, towering above everyone. Every man, woman, Dwarf, Elf, Animal and being Addy had not even come across yet, focused on him.

"What we live for; love, freedom, joy, family, friends!

Is being threatened!

Those that have lost their way, who live in darkness,

Wish to make us their slaves.

To bring that darkness to our lives.

We have fought many battles, side by side.

I know you. We have fought in love and we know freedom.

Today! We fight for Thear!"

"For Thear" the crowd responded.

"Today we march on darkness, and today, some may die for our freedom!" Glock looked around the ranks. Addy saw the faces, proud, purposeful.

"But today, we stand as one! We stand for life, for love and for freedom!

For Thear" he shouted.

"For Thear" the crowd roared.

"For life" Glock shouted.

"For life" the crowd stamped.

"For love" shouted Glock.

"For love!" the crowd shouted.

The pride welled in Addy's chest. Tears sprang to her eyes.

I belong here. These are my people. We are one.

Glock pulled a watch from his pocket again. He shrank to his normal size.

"Five, four, three, two, one" he counted.

The gouge in the mountain blurred and distorted a moment

and then the creatures poured into the plains. Like ants marching they came, Orcs and gnomes, cave creatures, animals. They all came. The ground vibrated.

About five hundred metres off, the longbows shot out. Thearians ran towards the portal, war cries filled the air.

Dane rode down the mountain leading the army. Addy's heart contracted.

"Be safe" she whispered, he looked over his shoulder and caught her eye. Henry reared and they galloped away.

Addy's heart filled with love.

I love you.

With the realization in her heart, Addy looked around. The plains were vast and flat. The Plains of Desolation they were called because many wars and much blood had been shed on them. Nothing grew but dull grey Spinifex. Even the earth was grey. They were surrounded by mountains to the north and west. In the east stood the Great Forest and in the south the Ink Black Sea spread beneath the Cliffs of Harrow.

"Your mission" Neb spoke into her head, "is to keep the battle here on the Plains of Desolation. Do not let it break out" Addy saw the Quinarians all nod. They had all received the message. Adrenalin coerced through her veins.

Neb ran towards the cliffs and Roz took up the edge of the forest. Celia created a barrier north of the Great Forest. Glock and Addy guarded the mountains, Addy in the South West, Glock in the North West.

Swords clattered, blade on blade. Bows plunked and arrows whipped through the wind. Addy ran head long into a band of Cave Creatures.

We have score to settle!

Four arms each. They swung weapons, axes, knives, blood spears and maces. She dodged and moved without thought.

Dust hung thick in the air and sweat rode on the breeze. Addy focused on the sword. The magic infused through her body and she knew; how to move, how to parry, how to dance the war dance. The sword was home in her hand. Strategy whispered on the breeze to her. Aife spoke in her ear as she moved.

More of the enemy appeared. She saw in her periphery that she was moving further away from Glock. Her throat was dry. She dealt with the last creature and another took its place.

Sweat poured into her eyes. The Cave Creatures were relentless.

Where is Ternion?

Addy leapt into the air, her body twisted. She held her arm aloft and three fell. Their blood splattered across her chest. She landed and dropped to her knees. Her breath came fast and shallow. Her heart raced.

Neb was in the air. She could not see the others. She looked ahead to the north. And then she sensed it.

Addy turned.

The sizzle sent shivers along her spine. The shadow leapt at her. A ring of fire sprung up around her. The shadow became substance. It twirled and curved on itself. A hissing serpent. It grew larger and larger, hissing from deep inside its body. Its head appeared from the mass of writhing coils. Skeletal, black and three sided. Red eyes glowed from hollow orbs. Flat nostrils closed loudly like inlet valves, cupping and sucking at the air. Fangs extended from its mouth. The smell was acrid.

It coiled and writhed and hissed. Spittle from its fang sizzled where it hit the ground. Addy moved with grace around it. She lunged and extended. No amount of attack would penetrate the thick scales.

Magic.

She pulled power to her. Lots of it. The heat of the flames singed her arm hair, the smell lingered in her nose. She sent a wave of power to it. The serpent shrilled and screamed and swelled before it moved back on its body and snapped at Addy. Her quick movement avoided a bite but her arm scraped along its venomous tooth. Addy felt the burn.

I'll heal.

She turned and lunged again. The serpent writhed and swayed to move behind her. Addy was quick. It double backed on itself. It hissed and pucked for breath. Addy saw her chance. She turned with her full body weight behind her, lunged into its coils. It retreated, green ooze fell to the soil and burnt a hole that smoked. The stench hit Addy. She turned and vomited the content of her stomach up.

She wiped her mouth with the back of her hand. The serpent coiled tighter. Its head moved slowly from side to side. Addy wiped the sweat from her face and brushed her hair away. Verity strode towards her behind the creature. The serpent lunged, missed. Addy swung the sword, she missed too. The momentum caught the sword in the serpent's fold, it dropped down its body and clattered on the floor beside Addy. She grabbed the sword and as the serpent descended its head toward her, Addy leapt up and plunged the sword deep into the bottom of its jaw. The high-pitched screech was deafening. The creature reared up and then, exploded into dust before her. The grit settled on her sweat slicked body. Addy fell to the floor, her chest rattled. Her arms ached. The spittle was poisoning her. Addy felt it pull through her body.

Is that a mirage?

Addy blinked. The image wavered.

Something's not right!

She stood up. Dust waved across the plain. Little fires had erupted and was consuming the sparse Spinifex. Addy put the sword tip into the sand to steady herself.

Verity fresh and beautiful in a black leather cat-suit, long black boots and silver collars on her arms strode over, flicking her blonde hair in the breeze.

"A sword? Barbaric. Tut tut" she goaded.

Verity waved her hand and Addy felt the energy wind her. She flew back and pulled up dust clouds as she skidded in the sand.

"Give it to me Adera" Verity sneered.

"Come on Verity. Let's talk about this. We don't have to fight."

"Talk? Pfft" Verity pulled her arms wide and looked above her. The energy sprang to life. Wind sprang up in a frenzy and twirled faster and faster around them. It pulled dust into its vortex. Verity held her arms up and then flipped both wrists as though flicking a ball through a hoop. The energy hit Addy and she flew through the air again. She landed on her back in the sand, skidding on her elbows.

She stopped on a rocky platform at the base of the hill. Verity strode towards her. Addy's vision dipped. She could taste the poison. Addy steadied herself with her right hand and summoned energy with her left. Verity pointed her finger at the right hand and shouted.

"An pe dica".

The shackle gripped around Addy's wrist and buried deep into the rock. She was pinned.

Addy threw power at Verity. Verity blocked. Addy threw a quick second blast. Verity flew through the air.

Exhaustion set in. Power use drained her energy.

"Verity. Stop. We can talk about this."

"No talk! Give me the power!" Her voice boomed across the plain.

Red chords grabbed Addy's neck. Sweat ran down her temple. The dust burned her eyes. Addy heard the battle roar around her.

"Checking in" she called telepathically.

"Zyklon on my back but we're holding" Glock quipped quickly.

"Forest is safe, we're at flux" Celia responded.

"Grindal pushing around, on the way to you Addy" Roz warned.

"Where are you Addy?" Roz asked.

"I see her!" Neb shouted, "I'm on my way Power Girl," relief flooded Addy.

A moment later, fire streamed from the sky. Verity turned to block Neb.

"Move Addy" Neb roared in her head.

Poison clawed at her. Her power fought to heal her, draining her energy. She closed her eyes and grabbed the shackle with her left hand. She pulled power to her and sent it into the shackle. The effort drained her. A crack and the shackle broke. Verity frowned.

"No!" Verity shouted. She waved her arms. The air dried. The moisture evaporated, pulling Addy's face taught. Her lips cracked, blood dripped down her chin. Her energy ran up and down her spine preserving her.

"How long for the portal?" Addy pushed to the Quinary.

"Sixty-two seconds" Glock responded.

"Pull Ternion into the trajectory of the portal" shouted Celia.

Neb swooped and ducked. He blew flame after flame at Verity. Addy moved towards Glock. The portal would open about thirty metres from the stacked rocks to her right.

Verity came towards her, laughing.

"Waiting for the Earth portal? Ha! So, stupid. No power on Earth, Adera! And, we're still connected," she smiled as she dangled the blood vial in front of Addy.

For a moment, Addy connected to Verity. She saw the world through her eyes. The felt the hunger, the power, the taste of victory. She saw the darkness and felt fear lurking, waiting. Addy pulled herself back.

She used every ounce of energy to move the last few metres to the rock stack. It cost her. She sat on the floor. The dry air still bleeding her face and ears.

The portal bucked and wavered the air. It slowly took form about one hundred metres off.

"Something's not right" Glock stated, "it can't open!"

Verity twisted a power line around Addy's neck.

"Mine!" Verity screeched, madness burnt in her red eyes.

Addy saw the portal's blockage. Verity's magic.

The blockage, a virtual wall rose squarely in front of the portal. Addy felt Verity's power pull around her chest.

Everything went silent. Addy tapped into her power. It was weak. Poison ate at her. She knew. Behind Verity's constructed wall stood Ferris. Addy blinked. Her mum stood beside him, tears in her eyes. Grit and Meg were beside her.

I am delusional. It's got to be the poison.

On the wind Addy heard the words ingrained in her mind,

"A pact was sealed with blood.
But five are not alone.
Ternion will come.
And only Kivnon can deliver us from despair"

Addy knew that the portal would release Kivnon. The Earth project for change. That's what the Oswald boys coordinated. She knew it would work. Verity's wall held it all back. Verity's grip on her throat was tightening.

Addy watched as Glock pulled Zyklon into the portal's trajectory. Celia, Neb and Roz were in. Addy summoned all the power she could.

"Yes!" Verity shouted, "Bring it to me!"

Her magic stirred beneath the earth. It moved into her feet. And then slowly rose up.

Verity chanted. The magic pulled up and responded to Verity's call. Ancient magic. Dark.

Addy focused. She pulled the magic back to her. She felt Verity buckle slightly. Addy pulled the capture stone from the strap on her body. It was warm. It glowed electric blue.

With all the strength she could muster, Addy threw the stone. She pushed it along with her power. It flew straight and true, guided by love. Verity's hold on her throat tightened. Addy saw her mum's face behind the wall.

"Addy?" Glock called. Ferris sent magic to the wall from the other side. In slow motion, Addy saw the capture stone touch the wall. It shattered into a thousand pieces. Verity leaned into her, waiting to pull the last of her power from her body.

The portal released. The Energy flowed. Kivnon. Change. It flowed strong and swiftly and funneled outwards. Verity stepped back. Addy took a deep breath. Addy basked in the power. Verity shriveled away. Love.

Verity's confusion was evident. The vial at her throat shattered. Addy's blood turned to blue dust and stuck on Verity.

"What is this?" Verity screamed.

Grindal fell to his knees clutching his chest. Addy saw Pelanie kick a black creature in the chest and Razzy swung her around and kissed her on the mouth. The love flowed through the lines, boosting spirits. Ferris smiled.

The air puckered and then thousands of creatures, more enemy streamed from the mountains. They came over the cliffs and out of the forest.

"No!"

Verity laughed over the shouting.

"You can't win Adera!" Verity shot a laser power beam out. It caught Grit. He turned quickly and before he came around again, he had shifted – a beautiful hawk flew through the sky.

I must stop this!

A calm stole over Addy. She knew how to stop it.

Quinary. She called on the telepathic path they had created.

Move. Trust me. Glock, stay on the west in front of the rock stack. Neb, you need to be on the ground, in front of the cliffs. Roz move to the east, Celia north.

Addy? Ferris asked. Addy ignored him.

On my count. I need you to send a beam of power, all the energy you have, palm to palm. Glock send to Neb, receive from Celia. Neb, receive

*from Glock, send to Roz. Roz, receive from Neb, send to Celia, Celia
send to Glock, receive from Roz.*

Addy? Glock asked.

There is no time.

*Call everyone to you. Clear the plains. Thear must be behind the
circle. Now, do it!*

Addy! There is another way. Ferris was insistent.

No Ferris. There isn't. This is how it stops. I know.

On my count! Quinary! Call the troops. Abandon the plains. Now.

Addy saw Verity recover. She turned to look for Addy. The
blue dust from Addy's blood had eaten holes in her visage. She
was both old and young in the same face. Black holes gaped
from her.

"You can't recover from this Adera!"

Addy breathed deeply, she felt the calm infuse her, the clarity
of her purpose settled in.

Ten

Glock fought Zyklon, red and blue power burned in combat.
Creatures, Orcs and Rickets thrust and axed in her periphery.
Addy looked for her mum.

Nine

Marj moved gracefully, sword in hand, power shielding her
from blows.

Eight

Addy moved towards the centre of the battle. Verity whipped
a red line at her. She brushed it off. Energy crackled around
her. She let it move from below. Poison pulled at her. The power
collected beneath her. She let it come.

Seven

Addy found Ferris. He attacked fiercely. He pushed to get to
her. She shook her head.

No! Addy! No! His emotion flooded Addy's heart.

Neb pulled him back.

Six

Addy pulled water power back to the plains. Clouds swirled around her. She silently thanked the energy.

Addy blocked Verity's power. She shoved at the air, Verity flew backwards.

"You can't win!" Verity screamed, she looked around, "Zyklon, Grindal!"

Five

Addy looked for Dane. He fought on the periphery. Addy saw him twist and jab. Blood and sweat smeared across his face. He stilled and caught Addy's eye.

Four

"No!" his cry was primal. Dane dodged a tall warrior, fangs dripping with blood, "Addy! Nooo!" He started running.

I love you. She mouthed. Get back!

Three!

Addy ran.

Two!

Celia, Roz, Neb, Glock – engage!

One!

Addy waited until she saw the circle connect. Dane took to the sky. Addy released the energy. Fire, water, air, earth. And hers, ether power. She called it and it came and then she pushed it across the land, laden with love. The power twisted on her fingers and poured from her body. She felt the headiness but knew it for love.

The power ran from the centre out to the Quinary circle. It destroyed everything in its path. Addy saw the wave ripple away. Verity spun on a circle turned to dust and disappeared in front of her. Zyklon and Grindal followed, black streaks of dust in the sky.

Like a wave the power hit the Quinary line and held. Addy knew it would. It came back towards her. She was its epicenter. It was hers. She breathed deeply, felt her heart centre and smiled. I am loved.

Addy waited, the power will consume her. It rushed back,

a sea of energy, the back-jet rose. It came closer and closer, the hairs on her arms reached for power, vibrations within and around her effervesced as they wait to collide. Addy's hair stood straight up, caught in the aura, gold and silver and full of shimmer all around her. She closes her eyes, arms outstretched and waited to be consumed.

The last thing Addy heard was the Eagle's cry. It reverberated across the silent plains and then, nothing more.

27

The dome stood at least three metres above her. A spectacular network of power. It hummed in the open space. Addy felt it circulate around her where she rested on a pristine bed in the middle of a field. Green trees swayed gently in the breeze, waves lapped on a golden shore to her right.

I think I'm in my own big snow globe.

Addy moved slightly.

Ugh! I really have to pick my battles.

"Ah! Best you remain in that bed. Celia will have our hides. How are you feeling?" Ferris stepped forward from between the palms.

"Okay. What happened? Where were you? Is everyone okay?"

"Ssh! Don't get excited or I will be sent away." Ferris sat down next to her on the bed.

"You may not realise it, but every power chord you see here is monitoring something in your body. Which means" he held up his palm to calm her as she started to protest, "that we have only a few minutes"

"But, Ferris"

"Ssh! I will tell you everything I know" he waved his hand and his favourite chair from the library appeared next to the bed.

"Might as well be comfy" he pulled out his pipe.

Addy loved the smell. He puffed for a minute or two and then sat back tapping his thumb against the pipe.

"The Quinary wanted you to focus on your training. On getting ready for the battle. Glock has known of this battle for three hundred years" he looked poignantly at Addy.

"Imagine that? Three hundred years. But without any information on whether you lived or died or we were victorious or we were not. Anyway. I thought I would relieve some of your angst by going to Earth to help release Marj and the prisoners"

"What?" Addy sat up.

The hum turned to a buzz.

"Now you've done it" he gestured to the rotating power galaxies in the dome above her head.

Addy sat back gently.

"Go on" she gestured

Ferris looked over his shoulder.

"Verity wasn't there when we arrived. But Zyklon was."

"We?" Addy asked

"Ah! Yes. Well, Dane and I" he looked sheepish now.

"And you decided not to tell me… because?" Addy looked at Ferris, one eyebrow raised.

"So, Addy. How would that conversation have gone? Like this, Addy Dane and I are going to Earth to save your mother and friends. And, no you can't come with because you are training for a battle you don't even believe in yet."

"But"

"No. That is exactly what would have happened. So, we decided not to tell you. Unfortunately, not everything went to plan" he looked at the floor.

"What happened?" Addy needed to know.

"I arrived in the cave they were held in. Thanks to Dane's prior knowledge of the caves" he smiled at Addy knowingly.

"I managed to release them all from the mental hold Zyklon charmed them with. They didn't have much recovery time before he swept in with a team of Cave Creatures. We fought. There was a lot of blood. The Cave Creatures weren't trained soldiers, just cleaners. So, we were lucky. We won on numbers and managed to get away. Except when we got outside; then we realised that Molly Ringwald was missing. Grit told us what happened. I am just sorry we didn't go sooner" he whispered.

"And? How did. Well, how did it happen?" Addy needed the truth.

"I felt the portal open. It was unscheduled; but I didn't want to miss it. We had intended hiding out in the village until everyone was strong enough to travel but I decided that we shouldn't miss the chance. Verity also felt the opening of the portal" he fell quiet for a moment.

"Oh no! Ferris, that was me" Addy's heart dropped.

Oh no! I was responsible for my mother's death! Tears welled in her eyes, she felt winded.

Ferris patted her hand.

"Verity fights dirty! She came at us with a vengeance. She was intent on killing. It took all our power to fight back. Marj got sliced across the abdomen, Grit had power snap his collar bone, the rest of us got off lightly. We ran for the portal; when we got back here to Thear, Celia put us in quarantine. Marj had poison sliced across her and with the battle imminent we didn't want to infect anyone" he paused.

"I heard what happened" he blew smoke into the air in a long stream.

"Ferris? How did my mum die?" Tears rolled down her cheeks.

"Good grief Addy! Marj isn't dead." He jumped up and grabbed her chin in his hand, "she is alive and well. Didn't you see her in the portal at the battle?"

Addy's heart skipped a beat.

"What? Tell me again? I thought I was having a vision"

"Your mum, beautiful girl, is alive and well and dying to come over and hug you" Addy sobbed in her palms.

"True?" She struggled to breath.

"True." He hugged her to his shoulder. Addy's shoulders shook as the sobs released.

"Can I see her? Is she okay now?"

"Yes! She is well! She will be over soon!"

Addy's hand shook as she moved her hair behind her ear. She smiled with happiness.

"I nearly killed people in the village..."

"Ssh never mind. You didn't. I knew you wouldn't" he patted her.

"Ferris, the battle?"

"Ternion disappeared" He stated.

"And our loss?"

"A few hundred" Ferris held her as Addy inhaled sharply.

"But it would have been a lot more if it weren't for you" he pulled away and looked deeply into her eyes, "you were brave" his eyes swam with unshed tears, "but don't ever do that again" he said with a smile.

"I thought the power would consume me. There was so much of it" she admitted.

"It may have" he said with a choke, "Dane pulled you out with seconds to spare. We will never know. I have my susp-"

"What? Dane pulled me out?" Addy breath caught, "Is he okay?"

"He's fine! Just fine. The head healer here, sent him home a few minutes ago. He hasn't left your side since you were brought here."

Addy looked at Ferris.

"Four days ago, sweet girl."

"It's a fool or someone in love who threatens Mother Earth" he laughed, "and our Dane's nobody's fool I tell you."

Addy was confused.

The trees rustled. She leant forward to see.

"Mum?" She choked, trying to move off the bed.

"No, don't" Marj moved quickly. She wrapped her arms around Addy, pinning her head to her chest as she cried.

"My Addy, my Addy," she laughed and smiled and cried at the same time.

"Mum?" Addy choked on the sobs.

"You're so brave! I thought I lost you again" she cried fresh tears, "Oh Addy! My Addy!" Marj wiped the tears with the back of her hands.

"Mum?" Addy had no words.

"You need to rest," they all looked to the palms where Dane strode through chased by the healer.

Marj stepped towards Ferris and Addy saw them hold hands as they stepped aside.

Dane stared intently at Addy, he did not take his eyes off her.

He stepped up on the dais and without word, he pulled her into his embrace and held her tightly.

Addy closed her eyes. The smell of him, the feel of him, it made her feel the best of herself. Love bubbled in her core. She felt the sheer joy of being alive.

"Dane?"

"I love you," he whispered.